*They could rope, they could ride...
But could they change a diaper?*

Rodeo rider Will Cody was footloose and
fancy-free...and planned to keep it that way.
Loner Dell Jones was hiding from life...
and from love.
Rancher Jack McLintock just wanted to raise
his siblings and get on with his life....

They were three lonesome cowboys...

UNTIL

*they found themselves playing Daddy...
and liking it!*

BOOTS & BOOTIES

*Gorgeous cowboys, adorable babies—
what heroine could resist?*

Relive the romance...

by Request™

Three complete novels
by one of your favorite authors

Dear Reader,

When the folks at Harlequin told me they were reissuing my first three BOOTS & BOOTIES books, I was thrilled. I grew up reading Western novels; Zane Grey was my hero, a favorite author of my father's and grandfather's. I also read every novel about horses and ranches that lined the shelves of the local library. Eventually, when I moved west at the age of twenty-four, I joined the Zane Grey book club so I could reread those books as many times as I wanted.

Rereading a favorite book is like comfort food or spending time with an old friend. I hope these stories become favorites of yours. An injured bronc rider, a lonely hermit and a rancher ready to call it quits come face-to-face with babies—and women— who will change their lives in a matter of minutes. Ranch life will never be the same again.

Thank you for the wonderful letters. It's always nice to hear from you.

Sincerely,

Kristine Rolofson
P.O. Box 323
Peace Dale, RI 02883

KRISTINE ROLOFSON

BOOTS & BOOTIES

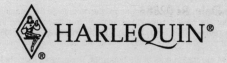

HARLEQUIN®

TORONTO · NEW YORK · LONDON
AMSTERDAM · PARIS · SYDNEY · HAMBURG
STOCKHOLM · ATHENS · TOKYO · MILAN · MADRID
PRAGUE · WARSAW · BUDAPEST · AUCKLAND

HARLEQUIN BOOKS

by Request—BOOTS & BOOTIES

Copyright © 2000 by Harlequin Books S.A.

ISBN 0-373-20171-0

The publisher acknowledges the copyright holder of the individual works as follows:
THE LAST MAN IN MONTANA
Copyright © 1997 by Kristine Rolofson
THE ONLY MAN IN WYOMING
Copyright © 1997 by Kristine Rolofson
THE NEXT MAN IN TEXAS
Copyright © 1997 by Kristine Rolofson

This edition published by arrangement with Harlequin Books S.A.

Visit us at www.romance.net

Printed in U.S.A.

CONTENTS

He'd been called a lot of things...
but never "Daddy"!

The Last Man in Montana

1

WILL CODY PARKED his rig on the west side of the gravel road and turned off the ignition. The dog beside him whined, so Will leaned over and opened the passenger door. The Australian shepherd jumped out and trotted over to the fence line. Lady was smart enough to keep away from traffic, not that there was any. The road was quiet, as empty as he remembered. And when he forced himself to look across the gravel toward the old homestead, a familiar knot tightened in his gut and his hands balled into fists.

It was a familiar reaction, and one that made him take a deep breath as he surveyed the metal sign hanging over the entrance. He planned to drive the two-mile road to the ranch house, but Will hesitated. He could get on the meanest bronco in Montana with less trepidation. But it was his mother's seventy-fourth birthday, his right knee ached like a bastard, and more than anything he wanted to take a couple of those fancy pain pills and sleep for twenty-four hours. He'd been driving all night and he hoped that when he did finally step out of the truck, he could straighten his leg and walk to the house without falling on his face.

His uncle would have rolled over in his grave at the thought of his "no-good nephew" inheriting thirty thousand acres of the best cattle land in the country, but J. W. McLean had left it all to him. It must have been a bitter pill for the old man to swallow, that he had no one else to leave the place to, only an elderly sister and a footloose rodeo rider. Will would have chuckled, if there was anything funny about returning to a place where he hadn't been welcome for sixteen years.

Still, nothing could harm him here. J.W. was dead and buried. One of the most detested men in Montana had died in his sleep, surprising those who'd said that old J.W. was "too mean to die." Well, his uncle had been mean, all right. The devil had better be watching his back.

Will whistled for the dog, shut the door after she hopped back in the cab and started up the truck. William Wyoming Cody was going home, whether he liked it or not. Not that it had ever been much of a home, but he'd learned one thing in sixteen years: a man didn't have to look back if he didn't want to.

"MAMA, THERE'S SOMEONE comin'," Pete announced. He was four years old and he liked to know things first, before anyone else.

Becky shaded her eyes with her hand and looked toward the road. Sure enough, a battered blue pickup hauling a small horse trailer was coming down the drive to the house. She went back to the plants, trying to find a few early tomatoes for the salad. Company at the ranch was nothing new these days. One of Maude's friends arriving early for the party wouldn't be unusual, though it would be anyone's guess why she'd be bringing her own horse. It was a big day here at the Silver Valley ranch, with the Not Dead Yet Club's first party starting in a couple of hours, along with the celebration for Maude's birthday. Maude wouldn't let anyone buy her presents, but had insisted on ordering three different kinds of birthday cake instead.

"Mama?" Pete tugged on her shirttail.

"What, honey?"

"I found another one."

Becky lifted her gaze from the tomato plants, swatted a fly from her arm and looked down at her son. He held a tiny black kitten in his arms. "I told you, Peter, those kittens are too young to be away from their mother. Go put it back where you found it, and be very careful."

"That makes six. I counted."

"Great. Go give it back to its mother."

"Okay." He didn't move. She found one more ripe tomato and put it in the bucket. That would have to do. Maude had told her not to bother making a green salad, but Becky wanted everything to be just right. She opened the gate, Peter following close behind, and stepped into the drive just as the visitor got out of the truck. He was tall, with a wide pair of shoulders, and a big black-and-white dog at his heels. He didn't look at all like someone Maude would hire, though, since he looked about forty years shy of seventy. And they weren't expecting the new horses until tomorrow.

"Hello," she called, walking toward him. "What can I do for you?"

His hat, looking as if it had seen as many miles as his truck, shaded his face. He wore typical work clothes: denim jeans and a plaid cotton shirt. The boots were scuffed, and he limped as he walked toward her. "Hello," he said, not smiling.

That face. She knew that face. She stared at the stranger who might not be a stranger at all.

He gave her an odd look. "I'm Will Cody and I'm looking for my mother. Is Maude around?"

Becky couldn't speak. It was as if the dry Montana wind had taken the words and blown them out of her head. She stood there, in her husband's faded jeans and one of Maude's oldest shirts, perspiration thick on her skin and cow manure stuck to her boots. She contemplated running like a crazy woman into the house, but instead stayed rooted to the dirt and faced the one man who threatened everything she'd worked for in the past year. She opened her mouth to speak, but found she couldn't say a word.

"You work here?" he asked, frowning a little.

She managed to nod, but he had already moved past her on his way to the house, the dog following close behind.

"Good. Have someone take care of my horse," he said.

So Will Cody had returned. Without warning, and out of the clear blue sky. He'd walked in and started giving orders like he owned the place. Which he did. Which could be a very big problem.

"Who was that, Mama?"

"Maude's son. Mr. Cody."

"Why's he here?"

"This is his ranch."

"It's Maude's ranch," Peter insisted.

She smiled down into his blue eyes. He was one smart kid. "Yes, it's her home. Just like it's ours."

Peter thought about that for a moment. "Do I have to put the kitty away?"

"Yes, you do." She glanced toward the house. Maude would be thrilled. It wasn't every day that Will Cody condescended to set foot on the Silver Valley ranch. They should feel honored, blow trumpets, set off fireworks. Feeling especially cowardly, Becky set the bucket of tomatoes by the fence. "I'll help you."

"What kind of dog was that? It had a lot of hair."

"I don't know. You'll have to ask Mr. Cody." Though she hoped he wouldn't be here long enough to answer questions. She'd see that his horse was stabled and fed, and she'd change her clothes and, if Tommy continued to sleep, finish the salad. She'd avoid the houseguest for as long as she could and maybe, with luck, he'd be gone before she'd have to see him again. Maybe he was here to see his mother, then leave. Maybe nothing would change.

Maybe.

Decker was out in front of the sagging bunkhouse, painting the trim white. He grinned when he saw them and waved toward his paint job. "Afternoon, Reb. How's it look?"

"Very nice," she told the old cowboy. His hands were so gnarled she didn't know how he held a paintbrush. "I think you were right to just paint the trim."

He dipped the brush into the bucket and with careful motions spread paint evenly on the board. "You know Maude. She wanted to paint the whole thing, but I like the gray just fine. Easier on the eyes."

"We have company."

He didn't stop painting. "I saw him."

"Is there anyone around who can take care of his horse?"

"A man usually takes care of his horse himself. Least that's the way it was in my day."

Becky chuckled. "You're welcome to tell him that yourself, Deck."

"He has a dog, too," Peter said.

"Nice kitten," the old man said, smiling at the boy. "He'll make a good mouser for the barn."

"Go put it back," Becky told Peter once again. "I'll wait for you here."

"'Kay," the child said, and the kitten woke up and started mewing.

She turned back to the elderly cowhand. "Do you think he's going to stay?"

Miles Decker shrugged. "No tellin' what that boy is up to. He hasn't been back since the day he turned eighteen. From what Maude says, he's not one to stay in one place too long. Which is a goldarn shame, too."

She didn't think it was a shame at all. She wanted him out of here before he could interfere. "He's limping."

That got the man's attention. "He's too old for rodeoin'. A man his age should know better."

Another elderly man stuck his head out the door. "You talkin' about me again?" He winked at Becky and shifted his hat off his forehead. "Decker here is a regular Mickleangelo, ain't he?"

The old cowboy was unperturbed. He moved to the other side of the doorway and kept on painting. "Willie's back," he said.

"Well, I'll be damned!" J. J. Malone's face creased into a wide grin. "It'll be good to have him around."

"He wants someone to take care of his horse," Miles muttered. "In my day—"

"A fellow looks after his own horse," a familiar voice said. The three turned around to see Will Cody standing behind them. A docile chestnut quarter horse stood beside him and tugged gently on the rope anchored to her halter.

"Well, I'll be," Miles said, putting down the brush. He shook Will's hand and, to Becky's surprise, looked as if he was trying to blink back tears. She'd never seen the old cowhand display much emotion, not even last winter when he'd had to put down his favorite horse. J.J. shook hands with him, too, and grinned like a kid at a circus.

"Guess you've come back," Miles said.

"Yeah. For a little while."

"Heard you got hurt."

"Yeah." Will looked embarrassed. "A bronc landed wrong. Messed up my knee."

"Too bad," J.J. said. "We heard you were heading for another championship season."

Will shook his head. "I'm sitting this one out. At least till I get this leg healed."

"Have you seen your mother yet?"

"No. I couldn't find her. I thought she might be out here."

"I'll tell her you're here," Becky offered, anxious to get away from him. She left the cowboys asking questions about the rodeo life as she headed to the barn. Men like Will Cody were all the same, full of themselves and full of stories that were only half-true. She had no patience for bullshit, not unless there was a real bull providing it.

She waved to Peter, who broke into a run when he rounded the corner of the barn, and waited for him to catch up to her.

"Come on, honey. I've got to get changed and check on Tommy. I'll race you back to the house!"

He grinned and took off, with Becky pretending that she couldn't keep up. She let him win, and they cleaned their boots together before entering the house through the back porch. She forgot all about the tomatoes until she entered the kitchen. Too late now. Becky looked at the clock over the stove. She had sixty minutes to get ready for company and tell Maude that her one and only son had finally come home.

"That's a fine woman," Miles Decker said, watching Will turn to look at the woman and her son.

"Yessir," J.J. agreed. "A fine woman."

Will watched her jog beside her son until they disappeared over near the old two-story house. So that was Becky McGregor, the woman his mother had hired to help with the housework. At first he hadn't known who she was. He hadn't been expecting such a young woman or someone so pretty, with yellow hair and big blue eyes. He'd guess she was hiding one hell of a body under those baggy clothes, too. A man could tell those things. "Mom told me she'd hired someone for the house."

"Oh, she don't just work in the house," J.J. said.

"What else does she do?"

The two old men looked at each other, then Miles kicked at a piece of dirt with the toe of his boot. "She earns her keep," he drawled. "She was widowed. Maude asked her to come here. She's been a big help to your ma."

Will looked around the cluster of old buildings. A couple of the sheds looked as if the next good wind would blow them down, and the bunkhouse didn't look much better. The fact that they were getting a new coat of paint seemed almost ridiculous. "So the bunkhouse is still standing after all this time. I thought you and Malone were over at the Circle Bar."

"We're back here now."

"I see that." So the old man didn't want to explain. Well, that was all right, he guessed. His uncle had had a knack for alienating people and everyone knew he'd been the meanest man in the county until the day he died.

"We take care of what we can," the old cowboy said, picking up the paintbrush again. "Your ma's fixing things up real nice."

"I'll be glad to take care of her for you," J.J. said, stepping over to run his hand along the mare's neck. "She's a beauty."

"I'd appreciate that," Will said, giving him the rope. He waited until J.J. left, then moved closer to the cowboy who had treated him like a son. "Is Maude all right?"

"Never better."

"That's a relief. She said her arthritis really bothered her last winter. Where's Hagman?"

"You'll have to ask Maude."

Will frowned. "He's the foreman. Don't you know where he is?"

"Ain't the foreman anymore. Maude fired him."

"Who's in charge now?"

"Well, you should talk to your ma about that. I'm helping."

Will surveyed the man, who must be at least eighty by now. He remembered following him around the ranch when he was old enough to walk. And Miles Decker had taught him how to ride and taught him how to land when he fell. He didn't want to hurt the man's feelings. He cleared his throat and tried a casual tone. "I thought you retired."

Miles met his gaze. "Maybe I would, if there was someone around who could run this place."

Like me. The message was clear. A Cody should be running the ranch. And maybe a Cody would have, if his uncle hadn't disowned him when he'd run off to join the rodeo. He'd just wanted a little freedom, a chance to be wild and show off and see the world. He'd wanted to prove he couldn't be bullied, that he had his pride. He hadn't known it would cost everything he cared about. "I didn't expect to own this place," he said. "I was disowned, remember?"

"Hell, Willie. That don't mean nothing no more, and you and I both know it."

Will wished he'd taken his pain pills when he'd been inside the house. He was tired of fighting the pain. He was tired of fighting a lot of things. "I don't know any such thing, Deck. I just came back to take care of business."

"Your ma will be glad. She said you would come."

"I should have been here before. She keeps telling me she's fine, not to worry. And I didn't, thinking Hagman was still here keeping things running for her."

"He and your uncle were two of a kind. Both ready to skin a neighbor to make a dollar."

Will's eyebrows rose. "I didn't know that."

The old cowboy met his gaze. "Well, I guess there's a lot of things you don't know."

Will nodded, which was the only thing he could do under the circumstances. He'd put every dime he had in the bank for years, waiting for the day when his mother would tell him she was ready to leave the ranch. She never complained, but he knew it was a hard life for a woman her age, and J.W. never spent a dollar on anything that would provide comfort. Chances are the roof still leaked and the pipes froze in the winter if you didn't leave the water running. He had more than enough to buy her a nice little condominium in Billings, in that new retirement community facing the Rockies. "I'm going to find her."

"You go ahead, son. You're one heck of a birthday present."

"MY SON?" Maude swiveled from the mirror. Her white hair was pulled back in a braid, a silver barrette holding it in place. She wore a white peasant dress with lavender embroidery and matching lavender cowboy boots. She didn't look seventy-four, but she was only five feet tall, with small bones, and people tended to underestimate her. "Willie is here?"

"Yep. You look great, by the way."

"Thank you, dear. He said he was coming for my birthday, but I didn't dare hope." She stood up and smoothed her skirt. "He's not going to like any of this," Maude said. "I love him dearly, but he's going to make trouble. I know it."

Becky hoped Maude was wrong. "Maybe not. Maybe he'll want to help."

"Help?" Maude squeaked. "You don't know him very well, do you?"

"I don't know him at all, Maude. I moved to town long after he left."

"Oh, that's right. Sometimes I forget..." She stopped, lost in thought for a few seconds. "It's been so long. I thought he'd never come back."

"Oh, he's back, all right. And he's looking for you."

"I'll be downstairs then." She looked at Rebecca's outfit and sighed. "Will you have time to get ready before the baby wakes?"

"I hope so."

"Where's Pete?"

"Oatey's feeding him, then I'll see if I can get him to rest for a while."

"Then you'd better hurry." She gave Rebecca a push toward the door. "Don't use your precious time worrying about my son."

"But the horses—"

"Are none of his business. He's not the type to put down roots, least of all here. Though I wish he would."

Becky couldn't think of anything to say to that. She wondered how she'd feel when Peter and Tommy Lee moved away from her and started their own lives. She'd be real happy to see them, no matter when they returned. Of course, if she lost this job she wasn't sure how she'd make it from now until they were grown. Becky hurried down the hall toward her room. The ranch house was enormous, built at the beginning of the century by a struggling family from Kentucky. Each generation had added on a wing or a porch, so the house sprawled in several directions. She and the kids had connecting rooms in the east wing, on the second floor, and it had taken Rebecca three weeks to find the shortcut down the kitchen staircase. The place was sparse, though, but she'd brought some of her own furniture to fill in a few empty places.

All things considered, she didn't have time to help Maude hostess her party. She should be at the barn, making sure everything was ready for tomorrow's delivery. There was fence to check in the east range, and Deck said he was worried about one of the cows in the Second Pasture. The cowboys had a name for every chunk of land on the thirty thousand acres.

She hurried into her room and, as quietly as possible so she wouldn't wake the sleeping child next door, undressed and showered. She changed into one of her few dresses, a Western-style blue cotton with a flouncy skirt. She'd bought it years ago for a dance, but it was still in style, at least for what Maude had in mind. The Not Dead Yet members were dressing up this Sunday afternoon, and Maude had insisted she attend. She wanted to help the older woman celebrate her birthday. Maude McLean Cody was someone special, and she owed her a lot. She'd do anything for the woman, including being nice to her son. Even if he didn't deserve to have such a wonderful mother.

THE KNEE WAS killing him. He could've kissed J.J. for offering to take care of the mare for him. And carrying on a conversation with Decker took more wits than he had available to use right now. He set his jaw and made his way to the long kitchen at the back of the house. He told Lady to wait outside, so the dog flopped on some grass underneath one of the trees. He'd hoped it would be empty, but a little kid was there eating a sandwich, and another elderly cowboy sat snoring with his head on the table.

Will looked around the room and half expected someone to kick him out. The room hadn't changed. It was still a farm kitchen, cluttered with cooking equipment, but his mother wasn't here baking bread and asking him how school had been. He took a deep breath, and the feeling of nausea subsided a little.

"Shh," the boy whispered, pointing to the cowboy. "He gets mad if you wake him up."

"Oatey has a temper," Will agreed, remembering the man from years ago. "What kind of sandwich is that?"

"Peanut butter and jelly."

Will moved over to the counter and eyed the contents of the platters spread out over the wooden surface. Covered in plastic wrap, it looked like enough food to feel all of Dry Gulch and then some. He lifted a corner of the plastic and took out a square piece of chocolate cake.

"You're gonna get in trouble," the kid said. "They don't like it if you sneak."

"Who doesn't?"

"Miss Maude and Mom."

"Well, don't tell them." He ate half the piece in one bite, then the other.

The boy glared at him. "They'll think I did it."

Will reached in and took another piece of cake. Chocolate with fudge frosting was his favorite, though he didn't know why women thought they had to put little frosting flowers on perfectly good food. He reached over and tried to hand it to the boy, but the stubborn kid just looked at him. "Don't you want a piece?"

"Well, yeah, but—"

"Take it," Will urged, stepping closer. He set it on the boy's plate. "I'll tell them I took two pieces. They can't do anything to me."

"Your mother will."

"Nope. It doesn't work that way when you're grown-up."

The boy glanced over at the sleeping cowboy before he reached for the cake. "It doesn't?"

"No." Will limped over to the refrigerator and surveyed the food inside. "Looks like they're getting ready for a party."

"Yeah." Pete licked his fingers. "The ladies are coming."

"What ladies?" His mother had never been one for socializing.

"I dunno. Just the ladies."

Will took out a plate full of roast beef and set it on the counter, then found the mustard behind two bowls of Jell-O. "Want some Jell-O?"

"Nope. It dents," the boy answered.

"Yeah. Better to leave the Jell-O alone, all right."

"You'd better be quiet." He pointed to the cowboy whose snoring had stopped. "I'll hafta take a nap when he wakes up."

Will quickly slapped a sandwich together with bread from the loaf he'd found on top of the refrigerator. "A nap? Aren't you a little old for naps?"

The boy nodded glumly. "Ma doesn't think so."

"What's your name?"

"Peter McGregor. I know who you are."

"Yeah?"

"Miss Maude has your pictures in her room."

Will found a container of punch when he put the meat away, so he got a glass and sat down at the table to eat his sandwich. His knee throbbed harder. After he ate he'd take another couple of pills, wish his mother a happy birthday and spend the rest of the day letting Maude fuss over him. He eyed the boy who was watching him pour himself a drink. "What's the matter?"

"You're not supposed to get into the punch."

Will took a long swallow of the fruity drink, popped a couple of pain pills, then drained the rest of the glass. "I told you, grown-ups can do whatever they want." He refilled his glass to prove the point. The kid was starting to get on his nerves, so he tried to ignore him.

Which wasn't going to be easy, especially since the little boy wouldn't stop staring at him. Will tried to pretend he didn't notice and looked at Oatey instead. His uncle had fired Oatey for sleeping through his shift. Of course, he hadn't waited to find out that the cowhand had been up for two nights in a row nursing a couple of sick calves.

He didn't know how his mother had stood living with her brother all those years. He'd bet there weren't three people in town who hadn't been screwed by old J. W. McLean.

Oatey opened his eyes and blinked. Then blinked again as he focused on Will's face. "Well, I'll be," he said, rubbing his eyes. "Haven't seen you in more 'n twenty years, son. How've you been?"

Will hid a smile. He tried to guess what the man's age would be now. Seventy? Eighty? Hard to tell. "Fine, Oatey. How about you?"

The old man shrugged. "Good days and bad days, just like everyone else. Don't know what I would've done if your ma hadn't asked me back."

"She's hired back a lot of cowhands?" What was going on around here? He'd have to talk to his mother about business. Tomorrow.

"I 'spect so. Now that J.W.'s gone, the men came back when Miss Maude asked them to." He nodded toward the boy. "You met my pal Petey?"

"Yeah, sure did."

Oatey stood up and stretched. "He's gotta take a nap now, and I think I'll take one, too."

"You just did," the boy said.

"Yeah, well, I was warmin' up for the real thing."

"Will says I'm too old for naps," the boy announced.

"Yeah?" Oatey didn't look impressed. "Well, we'll ask your ma what she thinks. She's the boss around here, ain't she?"

Peter shot Will a disgusted look. "Yeah, she's the boss."

"Sorry, kid," he said. "Guess you'd better go with Oatey."

"See ya later," the boy said. "Hope you don't get caught."

Will kept a straight face. "Thanks."

"He never gets caught," Maude said. Will looked over to see his mother standing in the doorway. She moved out of the way so Oatey could take the boy upstairs. "See you later, Peter. We'll save you some cake."

The boy turned and looked at Will, who winked at him.

"William," his mother said, and Will started to stand up.

"Don't get up," Maude said. "Finish your lunch. It's good to see you sitting at the table again."

She bent over and gave him a kiss on the cheek. "I knew you wouldn't forget my birthday, but why didn't you tell me you were coming?"

"I wasn't sure myself." He winced as he moved his leg over so she could sit down in the chair near him. "Happy birthday," he said, pulling a small box from his shirt pocket.

"You're hurt again, and you shouldn't be buying me presents. You do too much as it is."

"Open it," he said, and Maude lifted the lid to reveal a pair of intricately carved silver earrings.

"They're beautiful," she said, kissing him on the cheek. "Thank you, dear." She frowned at his leg. "What happened?"

"Just a little problem with the knee."

"When are you going to stop this? You're too old to compete with those youngsters."

He grinned at her and poured some more punch into his glass. "Beats settling down, I guess. And the money is good."

"Can you stay the night?"

"I'll stay a few days, Mother. To sort out things here. We'll need to talk. And why haven't you sent the accounts to me?"

She looked confused. "I didn't send them?"

"No."

"Oh. I *thought* I did." She patted his hand. "Now don't even think about that. You don't have to worry about me or those complicated ledgers, either. Not anymore."

"Why's that?" He was starting to feel pretty relaxed. Maybe coming back to Silver Valley hadn't been such a bad idea after all. That eerie feeling had passed, and now he began to feel ridiculous for stalling for so many months.

"Let's talk about it tomorrow. I'm a little busy right now, dear."

"All right." He could be agreeable when he wanted to be. "When's the party?"

"Any minute. I want you to meet my friends. They've all heard about you and seen my scrapbook."

"You look good, Mother. You feeling okay?"

"Never better." She patted his hand and stood up. "Come help me greet my guests as soon as you're through here."

"Maybe I should clean up first."

"Don't bother." She smiled. "The ladies will love that scruffy cowboy look you have."

He fingered his two-day growth of beard. "You sure?"

"Positive, Willie. Maybe before lunch you could tell us a little bit about the rodeo. The ladies would love that. No one knew we were going to have a guest speaker at our first meeting."

"I'm not much of a speaker," Will protested. "First meeting of what?"

But his mother didn't answer. She was already out the door in a whirl of white ruffles and silver jewelry. Will blinked and leaned back in his chair, then poured himself another glass of that punch. He didn't know what was in it, but it was the tastiest fruit juice he'd had in a long time.

He gingerly propped his foot on an empty chair and began to smile. Thank the Lord for small favors. His knee was finally starting to numb up, and the ghost of J. W. McLean was nowhere to be seen.

2

"MAUDE? IS THERE, uh, something the matter with him?" Becky asked her employer. She didn't want to be rude and suggest that Maude's son might be falling-down drunk, but on the other hand she didn't want anything to spoil Maude's birthday party. The woman had worked too hard to have her special day ruined.

"Well, I don't know," Maude said. She and Becky stood together in a corner of the large living room and watched as Will answered questions from several gray-haired ladies. There was a silly grin on his face, and from what Becky could hear he was slurring some of his words.

"I mean, is he always so...social?" Becky hoped she was being polite. Maybe Maude was used to her son's drinking and didn't think anything of it. That was all they needed now, for a drunk to have inherited the Silver Valley.

"I think he's drunk," his mother declared. "He was hitting the punch pretty hard out in the kitchen."

"The *rum* punch? I didn't think I made it that strong."

"Maybe if you drink enough of it, that's what happens." She looked around at her guests to see if anyone else was getting tipsy. "Do you think it's affecting everyone?"

"No," Becky said. "Just him. But just in case, maybe you'd better start the program so people can eat."

Maude smiled up at her. "Good idea, my dear. You're always so full of good ideas."

Becky wished that were true. "What do you want me to do to help?"

"Nothing for now. Just keep an eye on my boy," Maude said. "If he starts to fall over, try to stop him from crashing into any of the food."

Great. This was her day off, and instead of enjoying Maude's party or working in the barn, she was stuck baby-sitting a has-been rodeo champion who couldn't hold his liquor and was most likely going to throw a fit when he found out who was running the ranch. She edged closer to the group of women around the cowboy and listened to the conversation.

"The worst horse I ever rode?" He rubbed his jaw as if he was thinking real hard. It was a little overdone, Becky figured, but the women didn't seem to mind. "Well, I guess that would be a little bas— 'Scuse me, ladies." He smiled, and one of the women giggled. "I haven't been in the comp'ny of ladies for a long time."

She would just bet he hadn't. She edged closer as he swayed to the left, then regained his balance.

"Now, where was I?" The chin thing again. Now *that* was getting annoying. "That would have to be in Texas, at a rodeo over in Fort Worth. A horse called Texas Tony that no one knew anything about." He chuckled. "I was on him for about three seconds, then—splat—flat on my back and the goddamn horse came back and tried to stomp on me." He widened his eyes. "Took four clowns to get him away. Can you b'lieve that?"

No, Becky thought. She couldn't. "Are you sure it wasn't a bull?" she asked. "I mean, this sounds like a bull story to me."

He shook his head, as serious as he could be while drifting to the left again. She reached out and grabbed his arm before he crashed into Maude's new lamp. "No, ma'am."

He narrowed his eyes and tried to focus on her face. "Honey, have we met?"

"No."

"In Vegas. At the finals."

"No. Maybe you'd better sit down before you fall down, cowboy."

"I'm fine." He gave her another silly grin. "I'd be better if you came a little closer."

"How many bulls do you think you've ridden?" someone asked.

"I dunno. Can't count. About a hundred stock a year, I guess. Broncs and bulls, makes no diff'rence."

"Don't you ever get hurt?"

"All the time, ma'am. I got myself a bad knee now, but it ain't hurtin' me too much right at the moment."

One of the women smiled at her. "You'd better get some coffee in him, Becky. My Chester used to get like that sometimes."

"Thanks, Mrs. Arnold. I'll do my best."

"We'd better get something to eat," Mrs. Arnold told the others. "I think that Maude just set out lunch." The ladies moved toward the buffet table.

"I think I know you," Will muttered. "Bobbie? How the hell have you been?" He put an arm around her shoulder and pulled her against his side.

"I'm not—"

"Colored your hair, too." He sniffed. "I like that perfume, too. You wear that jest fer me, little lady?"

Becky tried to pull away without making a scene, but the cowboy's arm was an iron band holding her close. "I'm not Bobbie," she said, keeping her voice as low as she could. "And don't try to pull that 'little lady' crap on me."

"Ladies!" Maude banged her glass with a spoon and the conversation stopped as all eyes turned to their hostess.

Maude stood in front of the stone fireplace and smiled at her guests. "Thank you all for coming today. We're planning a few special events this summer, so I want you to dust off your saddles and grab your boots, because the Not Dead Yet Club ladies are going to quit knitting and start riding."

"Dead what?" Will said, a little too loud.

"Shh," Becky told him. "Shut up for a minute."

Maude ignored her son. "Is everyone here?"

"'Cept Millie Freeman," someone called out. "Her daughter-in-law took sick, so she's home with the grandchildren."

"I hope it's not serious," Maude said.

"Nah," said Millie's neighbor. "She'll be here next week for the ride."

Will belched, and several women stared at him, including his mother. "What ride?"

"Never mind," Becky told him. She moved to the side, hoping he'd follow. "How about you and me going to find something to drink?" She hoped that would get him out of the living room and away from the women. It wasn't any of his business what his mother chose to do with her spare time, especially since he hadn't set foot on the Silver Valley ranch since the day he turned eighteen. At least, that was the story that Decker told.

"Well, now you're talkin'," he said, an idiot grin plastered on his face. He was incredibly handsome, better-looking than that picture in *American Horseman* magazine that Maude had stuck to the side of her mirror. "What ever happened to that twin sister of yours? She still racing barrels, too?"

"She got married," Becky lied. "Has triplets now and gained two hundred pounds. You want to see her?"

Will gulped. "Triplets?"

"Yep." Becky edged closer to the doorway, and the cowboy tried to go with her, but his legs didn't seem to want to move too well. "Hey, can't you walk?"

He looked down at his booted feet. "I used to know how," he said, and looked at her with a confused expression on his face. "Damn knee."

"I don't think your knee's the problem."

"No?"

"You've had too much to drink, pal."

He shook his head. "Can't drink. Not now."

"You need to lie down," she told him. "Don't you think that's a good idea?"

He stared at her, then he broke into a grin. "Hell, honey, I haven't been to bed in a hell of a long time. If you know what I mean."

"Becky?" Maude called. "Do you need help?"

"I got him," she assured her boss.

Maude turned back to the ladies. "It seems my son has had too much punch and not enough sleep. He drove all night to be home for my birthday," she announced proudly.

The ladies turned toward William and applauded. He tried to bow, but lurched against a leather chair.

"Come on, cowboy. Let's get you bedded down for the night."

"Yes, ma'am."

Maude raised her glass. "I'm going to ask you to drink a toast to my brother." She waited while the ladies refilled their glasses. There was a slight murmur that ran through the group, but Maude waited patiently. "As you all know, my older brother wasn't the most loved man in Montana."

"I'll drink to that!" somebody called, and several ladies giggled.

Will stopped struggling and turned to look at his mother. "What the hell is she talking about?"

"Let's go." Becky tried to leave, tugging on Will's waist without much success. It was like trying to move a tree.

"Nope," he said, then lifted his glass toward his mother. "What're we drinking to, Ma?"

"To a new era on the old SV," she answered, raising her voice and her glass. "My brother did a lot of rotten things in his day. Some people would say 'what's done is done' but, as you all know, I don't believe that."

The audience was mesmerized. Becky once again tried to move the cowboy toward the door, but his arm tightened around her and held her still. "Quit struggling, darlin'."

"So here's to making things right," Maude said. "And here's to a summer full of adventure!"

Becky managed to move Will as the ladies lifted their glasses and drank to an exciting future. She got him as far as the door, then his arms lost their grip around her and he slid slowly to the floor and passed out.

She looked back to see if anyone had noticed, but luckily he'd fallen forward into the empty dining room. His boots were in the living room, but none of the ladies would notice unless they tripped over his feet. She could drag him that far, if she had to, but he was heavier than she thought. And a deadweight.

She checked to make sure he was breathing, then hurried upstairs to find Oatey, but the old cowhand was sound asleep on the floor by the crib. Peter was sitting in bed playing with his action figures.

"Can I get up now?"

She kept her voice low, but the baby stirred. "Not yet." She knelt by Oatey and gently shook his shoulder. "Oatey?"

He opened his eyes and blinked at her. "Yes, ma'am?"

"I need your help for a minute. Sorry to wake you."

"I wasn't sleepin'. Just closin' my eyes for a sec, that's all."

Becky tried not to smile. "Can you come downstairs with me?"

"Yes, ma'am." He sat up slowly, then managed to stand up by hanging on to the crib. The baby sat up and smiled at them.

"Hi, Tommy," Becky said.

"Get up now," he said, raising his hands.

"In a minute. You stay here with Peter. Mommy will be back in a minute."

The toddler looked over at his brother and grinned. "Hi."

"Hi, Tommy."

"I'll be right back," she told the boys. As soon as she and Oatey were out the door, she tried to explain what had happened but Oatey didn't seem to understand what she was talking about. Once they stood in the dining room—a useless room that was too cold in the winter and impractical in the summer—and stared down at Maude's son, Oatey scratched his head.

"Never knew a ladies' fruit punch would do that to a fella," he said.

Peter tugged on his mother's skirt. "Must be those pills he took. They looked kinda big."

"Pills?" She looked down at her son. "You're supposed to be upstairs. Go. Now." Peter sighed and started toward the stairs.

"For his leg, I'll bet," Oatey said. "He looked like it was hurtin' him pretty bad."

So the idiot cowboy had combined pills and alcohol and passed out. She wondered if she should get him to the hospital. "Do you think he could die?"

Oatey bent down and rolled Will onto his back, then he put his ear down to Will's chest. "Heart sounds strong." He reached into Will's shirt pocket and pulled out a plastic vial. "Guess this here's the culprit," he said, handing the bottle to Becky. She read it, but the medication didn't mean anything.

"Let's get him in a bed somewhere until I can call a doctor."

Oatey obligingly picked up Will's arms. "Where do you want him?"

"The den, I guess. There's no way we're going to get him upstairs."

Will groaned when Becky moved his feet.

"He's alive," Oatey announced. "I think we oughta let him sleep it off."

"I don't want him to die," Becky said. "Maude wouldn't like that."

"No, ma'am, but this boy is stronger than an ox. He ain't gonna die. Not now, not when he's finally back home."

They managed to get him through the dining room, around the chairs and out to the hall. Then they rested before heading into the other wing where the offices were. They got him settled on a braided rug, rolled him on his side and tucked a pillow under his head.

"Now what?"

"He shouldn't be alone."

"I'll stay with him," Oatey said, panting as he sat down on the couch. "You go get the little boys and bring 'em back here. No reason why they can't play down here and I'll watch all three."

Becky hurried back to the living room and found Maude. She took her aside and whispered, "Your son passed out. He took some pain pills with his lunch. And then started drinking that rum punch. Do you think we should call a doctor?''

Maude shook her head. "Theresa's here. She's retired, but she might know what we should do." She hurried off and returned with a tall, big-boned woman who looked as if she didn't panic easily.

"Dr. Ames," she said, shaking Becky's hand. "Don't think we've met."

"No, but—"

"Where is he?"

Theresa Ames followed them down the hall and into the den where the cowboy lay sleeping. She looked at the pills, questioned everyone as to the amount of alcohol in the punch and how much they'd seen Will drink, then nodded. "Let him sleep it off. These pills are strong and shouldn't be combined with alcohol, but there wasn't much in that punch. You said he was driving all night?"

"Yes."

"I'd let him sleep. He's not unconscious."

"If you're sure," Maude said, looking concerned.

"I'll call the hospital and double-check," Theresa assured her. "If they think there's a reason to treat him, we'll bring him in."

A look of relief crossed Maude's face. "Thank you, Theresa. I appreciate it."

"No problem." The doctor turned to Oatey. "See if you can get his boots off and find him a bed. Maude said he has an injured knee." Becky and the old cowboy nodded. "Leave his pants on, then. Wouldn't want to make that leg worse."

Since the thought of undressing Will Cody hadn't entered Becky's mind, she agreed right away. "No, of course not."

"Come on, Maude," the elderly doctor said. "Let's go eat

lunch and plan that pack trip. When are the horses coming in?''

"Tomorrow," Maude said, looking at her son. "Did he say how long he was staying, Becky?''

"No."

"I hope he's not going to be difficult," the older woman said.

Oatey guffawed. "Doesn't look 'difficult' right now, does he?''

The three women agreed, and Becky went upstairs to retrieve her children. She had more to worry about than whether or not Will Cody could get his boots off.

MAUDE WISHED HE'D wake up. Oatey and some of the boys had managed to get him into a bed in one of the spare rooms, so he was tucked under the covers and sleeping soundly. That dog of his had cried at the backdoor until Oatey had let her in and showed her where Will slept. She lay down on the rug, her head on her paws, and looked about as sad as a dog could get. Maude sat on the faded corduroy sofa and watched her son.

It was evening before her guests left, with sunset highlighting the sky with a beautiful array of colors. She'd seen everyone off, waved goodbye, promised to show them the horses next week. It was going to be a good summer. Her brother had been gone almost a year now. He hadn't been an easy man to love, but she'd done her best. Even after he'd driven Will off the place, she'd tried in vain to mend the fences. Now he was gone and Will was back for the first time in many years.

Oh, she'd flown to different cities to see her son. He'd bought that little place in Billings and they'd spent some nice holidays together. She'd hoped he would settle down with some nice gal and have kids. She would have liked

Christmases with grandchildren to spoil. But that's what happened when you had your first and only child at forty-one. There was a good chance you wouldn't live long enough to see who your grandchildren took after.

"Maude?"

She looked up to see Miles Decker standing in the doorway. He'd been one of her husband's best friends; Jack used to say there wasn't a better man in all of Montana. "Hi, Miles. Come on in."

He glanced toward the bed. "Well, I don't want to wake him."

"I don't think there's any chance of that." She patted the empty space beside her. "Come sit with me a minute."

Miles stepped carefully over the dog. "That his?"

The dog wagged her tail and looked at the old cowboy. "I guess so. I heard he brought his horse, too."

"Maybe that means he's staying."

"Or he's on his way somewhere else," Maude reminded her old friend. "He hasn't stepped foot on this ranch for sixteen years."

Miles cleared his throat. "About time he came back, then."

"You think he's come back for good?"

"It's hard to tell, Maudie. He's been gone a long time without putting down roots. Maybe he's decided to settle down and run this place for you."

Maude sighed. "I'd like that. I know there's more we could do to make ends meet. Becky does what she can, and does a good job, too, but we're going to be busy with the horses and our guests." She turned to look at her old friend. "I hope Will understands and doesn't change anything."

"You might not have a choice, Maudie. Considering J.W.'s will and all."

"I know. It's just going to be...awkward if he doesn't approve."

"Mebbee he will," Decker said. "Mebbee he'll like the idea of putting down roots and working with a beautiful young woman."

"Do you think Will and Becky will like each other?"

Miles sighed. "I dunno. I'm not much for matchmaking. Hell, Maude, I never even got married, haven't had a date in thirty years."

The two were quiet as they studied the young man in the bed. "He's a handsome devil," his mother said with a sigh. "I don't think Becky would be impressed by a handsome face, though."

"Nope."

"And he's never been around children. But I'll bet he'd make a good father, given half a chance."

Miles looked doubtful, but he nodded. "Anyone with half a heart would like those kids of hers. Don't give no one any trouble, those kids don't."

"True. They're quite lovable. And our Becky's a pretty girl, with a good disposition."

"Hardheaded, though."

Maude sighed. "That's true, but we can always hope."

Miles nodded, and reached down to pet the dog. "Yep. Hopin' don't cost nothin'."

"WHO WAS THAT man, Mama?"

"I told you, Peter. Miss Maude's son, remember?" She fixed him a plate of leftovers from the party. The ladies hadn't eaten as much as she and Maude had figured they would, which meant they wouldn't have to cook tomorrow.

"He took some cake without asking," Peter whispered, leaning closer.

"That's okay. I guess he can take whatever he wants."

"That's what he said. I wanna get big like that, so I can eat cake all the time. With my fingers."

Becky smiled. "Well, that's one of the advantages, I guess." Why had Maude's son decided to come home after all these years? Maude would be thinking he was going to stay and run the ranch now that it was his. Becky didn't think so. Men who liked to rodeo didn't change. Maude would get her hopes up and then he'd head out again, disappointing everyone. They needed help around here. The ranch was just too much to run among the six of them, and it was about time they all faced facts.

But was an injured rodeo king the answer? She wished she knew.

Becky poured herself a glass of the rum punch and leaned against the kitchen counter. The cowboys all did their best, and gave her good advice, too. But there was the haying to do and machinery to repair. The horses were coming and would need to be settled in. Maude had paid top money to buy the best, but it would be Becky's job to make sure they were well taken care of.

She didn't know how many more things she could take care of. And maybe Will would decide she didn't have to take care of any of it. He'd fire her, or send her back to the kitchen. He'd hire someone like Hagman who wouldn't understand that the ranch hands couldn't work twelve-hour shifts anymore.

SHE FELT MORE CHEERFUL the next morning. Becky poured herself a cup of coffee and took it over to the table. The kitchen was dark, the shades pulled against the bright summer sun. She'd been up for four hours, since six, and the heat was starting to get to her. July in Montana could be excruciating. By noon she'd be ready to come indoors and play with the children, but for now she'd have to get back outside and make sure the stalls were ready. Deck had put up a new fence in the horse corral and the three other men had spent last week cleaning the barn. It was slow work, but it had gotten done in time. The trick was to give the men plenty of notice when she wanted something done.

The house was quiet, with the boys "helping" in the barn and Maude gone to town. The rodeo rider was most likely still sleeping it off, thank goodness. The less she had to deal with him the better she'd be.

She didn't know what she was so afraid of. It was Will's ranch now, Will's business to decide how things should be run. His mother would say nothing was going to change, but Becky had a gut feeling that life could be very different from here on if she wasn't careful. She would stay out of the fancy cowboy's way as best she could.

Until he walked into the kitchen. He was showered and shaved and in clean clothes, and he looked very handsome. He ran his hand through damp, dark hair and smiled at her. "'Mornin'."

"'Morning," she said, taking a sip of coffee. She watched as he found the mugs easily enough and poured himself a cup of coffee. He was still limping, but not as badly as yesterday. Maybe sleeping for over eighteen hours had helped him after all.

He leaned against the counter, drank half the coffee then refilled his mug before coming over to the table and sitting across from her. "Did we meet yesterday?"

"Not exactly. You thought I was someone else."

"I did? Who?"

"Never mind. I'm Becky McGregor."

"Will Cody." He held out his hand and she shook it, feeling a bit silly. He looked harmless this morning. She took her hand back and wrapped it around her coffee cup.

"What did I do yesterday? All I remember is being around a lot of women." He gave her a sheepish look. "Then everything went blank."

"You passed out."

"I did?"

"Didn't anyone ever tell you that pills and alcohol are a pretty lethal combination?"

He stared at her for a minute, then realization dawned. "The fruit punch. No wonder it tasted so good."

"You didn't know there was rum in it?"

Will shook his head. "I was thirsty. It was in the fridge. Your kid told me it was for the party, but I drank it anyway."

Becky took another swallow of coffee. "It caught up with you. You were entertaining the ladies for a while, until you fell over. We had a doctor look at you, but she said you weren't going to die."

"*She* said?"

"One of your mother's friends."

"Oh."

They sat in silence for a few awkward minutes. Becky finished her coffee and made a move to leave the kitchen. "Guess I'd better get back to work."

"What do you do here?"

"Anything that Maude wants me to." Becky reached for her hat, but Will stopped her.

"Is she well?"

"Sure."

He didn't look as if he believed her. "I think she's too old for this kind of life. I'm thinking of taking her to Billings with me."

Becky stared at him for a long moment before she could speak. "I think you'd better ask her," she managed to say. "She seems pretty happy."

Will shook his head. "She can't run this place all alone."

"She's not," Becky said. "She has help."

"Not enough. Not the right kind. Besides, she ought to be enjoying her sunset years."

"Her what?"

"Sunset years. I found her a place near me. She won't have to lift a finger to do a thing. Everything's done for her, even her meals."

Becky put her mug in the sink, her hat on her head, and headed for the door. Before she left the kitchen she stopped and looked at the man sitting at the table. "You know what I think?" He frowned, obviously not liking her tone. "*I* think you've fallen on your head too many times." With that she turned around and stomped through the back porch.

He caught up with her at the horse corral, as she was listening to J.J. report on the sick cow, and Cal waited his turn to talk to her about the schedule.

"Better, I reckon," J.J. said, swatting a fly away from his face. "Calf's doin' fine now, too. You decided about hayin' yet?"

"Next week, I think. We'll take turns driving."

The old man nodded, then grinned at Will. "Hey, boy. Heard you slept real good last night."

"Guess there're no secrets around here."

Malone chuckled. "Oh, I reckon there's a few left. You looking for Maude?"

"Where is she?"

Becky answered for him. "In town. She said she had errands to do this morning."

"She goes alone?"

She ignored his disapproving look. "When she wants to."

"What happened to Rob Hagman?"

Becky turned to face the tall cowboy. She hated having to look up, but there was no help for it. "He was let go."

"Why?"

"He was having trouble working for Maude. He acted like it was the other way around. Maude fired him."

"My mother wouldn't—" He stopped and stared down at her. "And who's in charge now?"

There was no getting around it. She put her hands on her hips and glared back at him. "Me."

"You." He shook his head as if he didn't believe her. "Who the hell are you?"

"The foreman of this ranch, Mr. Cody."

His eyes narrowed. "Since when?"

"Since Maude hired me."

J.J. cleared his throat. "Car comin'," he said. "Most likely Maude. You two want to take this somewheres else? I got work to do."

"What the hell is going on around here?" Will Cody folded his arms across his chest and waited for Becky to give him an answer.

"The foreman is gone," Becky said. "Every hand on this place is over seventy. I was hired to cook, but instead I'm trying to run this ranch for your mother because her *son* can't be bothered to come back here and take over."

"My uncle wouldn't let me set foot on this place."

"He's been dead for nine months."

"And I've been working," Will said. "Not that it's any of your business."

"Well, we're all glad you're a big-time rodeo hero, but we've got work to do." With that, Becky jammed her hat on her head and went into the barn. Let Mr. Will Wyoming Big-Belt-Buckle Cody chew on that for a while.

3

LORD, HIS HEAD ACHED. He didn't want to stand there by the corral looking like an idiot, but he didn't seem to have much choice. He was going to look like an idiot no matter where he stood, he guessed. Becky McGregor had that effect on him.

The woman was a yellow-haired hellion. He didn't know what on earth his mother was doing hiring someone with such a nasty temper, but then again, Will thought, looking around at the rest of the ranch staff, Maude had collected the oddest assortment of ranch hands ever to gather in Montana. None of them under seventy, except for the woman.

And a woman, especially so young and inexperienced, had no business running a ranch the size of the Silver Valley. He would tell his mother what he thought as soon as possible. When his head cleared, he was going to have quite a meeting with his mother and plan her future. She was too old for ranch life, and it was about time she realized that. The ranch and she had had their day, and it was time to quit.

He turned to J.J. "Where's Deck this morning?"

"Working another shift." The old man coughed.

"Doing what?"

J.J. spit in the dirt. "I guess you could say we're busy with the little guys," he drawled. "Your ma's waving at you."

Will would have liked to ask about what exactly the calves needed, but he turned to see his mother walking carefully toward him. She looked more fragile than ever, her seventy-four years were starting to show. Still, there was a twinkle in her eyes. It was time, long past time, for her to retire. He couldn't wait to tell her what he had planned.

"Will!" she called. "You're awake!"

When she came closer she hugged him, wrapping her arms around his waist. She felt frail, as if she might break apart at any minute. "I hope I didn't ruin your party. I guess I passed out."

She backed up a step to look up at him. "The ladies thought you were charming, at least most of the time. I'm just glad you're all right. How's the knee?"

"Better. I guess it was good that I got off it for as long as I did."

"Good. I wish you'd quit that kind of life," his mother said. "Have you ever thought about what you'll do when you can't compete anymore?"

She'd given him the perfect opening. "I have a few ideas. In fact," he said, taking her arm, "let's go into the house and talk about it."

Her face lit up. "Really, Will? You know how much I'd always hoped that you'd come home," she said. "I knew it was impossible when J.W. was alive, but I never gave up hope."

"That's not exactly—"

"I know, I know. You liked rodeoing, too. And I can't blame you, not when you were making all that money. Ranching's a hard life, and I didn't expect—"

"Mother," he tried, before she really got going. "That's not what I'm talking about."

"It's not?"

J.J. cleared his throat. "Truck's comin'."

Maude and Will looked toward the road. It was something big, Will saw. Trailing dust and going slowly.

"Where's Becky? Is she ready?"

The cowardly hellion hadn't come out of the barn again. "Ready for what?"

Maude beamed. "Today's the big day. Hasn't anyone told you?"

"Nope. No one around here wants to tell me anything." He really should have taken some aspirin. He pulled his hat down to shade his eyes and waited for his mother to explain.

"The horses are coming."

"What horses?"

"The horses I purchased last month."

"You shouldn't be buying horses," he said, staring down at her. "What kind of horses?"

Becky came out of the barn and Maude waved her over. "Come tell Will about the horses, Becky. I keep forgetting what kind they are."

His eyes narrowed as the young woman came closer, but he ignored her and looked down at his mother. "You bought a special breed? Why on earth would you do that?"

"They're called Peruvian Pasos," Becky explained, standing next to Maude. "Your mother saw them at a stock show last spring."

Will turned to her. "Excuse me, miss, but I'm asking my mother the questions."

"Will!" Maude frowned at him. "Becky can answer any questions she wants to. She's my foreman now."

"I heard." *Temporary* foreman.

"Then don't be rude."

"Don't make me be," he countered. "How in the hell can a ranch this size be run by someone so young?"

Maude looked like she wanted to take him over her knee, the way she used to when he did something wrong. "We're doing just fine, thank you very much."

"We'll see," he said, looking at Becky. "How long have you been here, anyway?"

"About a year and a half."

"And how long have you been acting as foreman?"

"Since Hagman quit, about six months ago."

"And in six months you've started a horse-breeding operation and—" Will stopped before he pointed out that eighty-year-old cowboys shouldn't be solely responsible for all the work. J.J. was still standing there watching him, and he didn't want to insult the old man.

"And what?"

Maude tugged on Becky's arm. "Here they come."

"Later," he said, taking a step back that twisted his knee. "I'll talk to you later." He tried to sound like he was in charge, but neither woman was paying any attention to him. They were staring down the road like it was Christmas morning and Santa was coming. His mother even looked like she wanted to jump up and down, which she couldn't, of course, with the arthritis and all. She sure was excited about the horses. Peruvian Pasos? He'd never heard of them. He hoped like hell they weren't those miniature horses that Easterners seemed so crazy about. He wouldn't let them unload the damn things if that was the case.

He walked over and leaned against the corral next to J.J. "You have any idea what's going on here, Malone?"

"Well, Miss Maude is sure excited about these horses. They're s'posed to really be something."

"Never heard of them."

"Me neither, Willie. But then again, I don't get out much."

Will hid a smile and watched as two horse trailers drove past the house and headed toward them. Maude waved at the driver of the first truck, and when he'd come to a stop near the barn, walked over to greet him. He'd never seen his mother so excited about a horse. As far as he knew she hadn't ridden in years. This had to be Becky McGregor's idea. He'd bet his own mare on it.

He watched while the horses were unloaded, Becky looking each one over carefully and then setting them loose in the paddock. His mother had bought five mares and a stallion, and she and Becky were clucking over them like they were babies. And the horses stood there like babies, too, as if they weren't sure what to do.

"Pretty, ain't they?" Malone said.

All six were a rich chestnut color, with full manes and tails, though set lower than typical quarter horses. They were good-size horses, with a gentle look about them. "I guess," Will said, walking with the cowboy to see the horses.

Maude signed some papers, handed the first driver a white envelope and offered the men something cold to drink. The first man shook his head, and within minutes they were on their way, dust trailing from the tires.

"Well?" Maude said, coming to stand beside her son at the fence. "What do you think of my new babies?"

"What are they again?"

"Peruvian Pasos," she said.

"Supposed to be the smoothest-riding horse in the world." Becky perched on the fence rail. "They're from South America, descended from Spanish war-horses."

"Do either of you want to tell me why we need Spanish war-horses in Montana?"

"For riding, of course," his mother said. "They're for people with arthritis or bad backs or any kind of injury that makes it difficult to ride. I want to ride again," she declared.

"But—"

"No two hooves hit the ground at the same time," Becky interjected. "That's why they're so comfortable to ride. It's a gait called *paso llano*, which means 'fast walk.'"

I'd like to fast walk those fancy horses right off the Silver Valley ranch, Will thought. His mother had no business thinking she was going to start riding again at the age of seventy-four. She was moving to Billings to take it easy. "And do either of you know how to train them?" He couldn't keep the sarcasm from his voice.

"They're already trained," Becky said. "We bought them ready to ride."

"I think we should try them out," Maude said. "Which one do you want, Will?"

He shook his head. "You'd better let them get settled first."

"Really?" Maude's face fell. One of the mares came over and nuzzled Becky's knee. She acted as if she wanted to make friends.

"Oh, yeah," Becky said to Will. "They look real upset to me." The horses walked around the paddock, curious about their new surroundings. They drank water from the trough and ignored the hay.

"They don't have a big butt like a quarter horse," J.J. pointed out. "How about that."

Will turned to him. "Are you going to ride one of them?"

"Beats looking at them," he said.

"The ladies are going to be so pleased," Maude declared.

"What ladies?"

"You met everyone, I think."

"From yesterday? What does that have to do with these Peruvian animals?"

She patted his arm. "We're going to ride them, dear. And now J.J. and Decker and the others will be able to ride more comfortably."

He shot a glance at Malone, who nodded. "We've heard it's just like sitting in a rocking chair," the old man said.

Great. He'd had three offers on the ranch already, and not one buyer had asked for fancy expensive horses to go with it. "What's wrong with sitting in an actual rocking chair, then?"

Everyone ignored him.

BECKY KNEW IT was coming, though she sure didn't look forward to it. But this was Will Cody's ranch now, and he could do as he pleased. Though why he would want to get involved was anybody's guess.

"I'd like to speak with you," the man had said. "In the office. Now."

"Sure," she'd said, trying to act as though she wasn't terrified of being fired. She'd hopped down from the fence and followed him into the west wing of the house. She checked her watch. It was time to check on the kids and relieve Decker of his little charges. She usually spent the afternoon in the house.

He lowered himself gingerly into his uncle's chair, then sighed as if every bone in his body hurt.

"How's your knee?" she asked, almost feeling sorry for him.

"I've had worse injuries," he said, picking up a sheaf of papers from the file marked *June*. "I haven't had a chance to look these over, but do you want to tell me how much my mother spent on those horses?"

Becky sat down in the chair on the other side of the desk. "Five thousand for the mares, six for the stallion."

"Apiece?"

"Yes."

He tossed the folder down, then took off his hat and tossed it on a nearby chair. "My mother has no business setting up a horse-breeding business."

"They're a good investment."

He ignored her words. "She shouldn't be riding at all. It's too dangerous."

"I think you'll have to take that up with her."

"I will."

"Is there anything else? I have work to do." She stood. "You'll find the books in order. Maude keeps track of the accounts."

"Where did thirty-one thousand dollars come from? I thought my uncle plowed every cent he had into buying property."

"You'll have to ask your mother about that."

"I intend to." He shook his head and muttered, "Thirty-one thousand dollars," then looked at Becky again. "Does the roof still leak?"

"Only when it rains," she quipped. He didn't smile.

"And the horse barn is still shored up on the northeast corner?"

She nodded. "And the pipes freeze in the bunkhouse and the plumbing here in the house is temperamental, the floors are cold, the heating system is ancient and the house needs rugs or carpet. Your mother's mattress is so old that it sags in three places and I keep throwing pans out because there are holes in the bottoms. The refrigerator is new, but the stove has been repaired twice, can't take much more, and—"

"Stop." He held up his hand as if to ward off her words. "In other words, thirty-one thousand dollars could have been spent differently."

"It's a business investment," Becky said. "You have to spend money to make money."

"And a fool and his money are soon parted."

Becky hesitated, but decided she'd better find out where she stood. "Are you staying here to run this place?"

"No."

"Do I have a job?"

"What makes you think you can run a ranch, Mrs. McGregor?"

"I've been doing it for the past six months," she replied. "Not that you would have noticed, you being on the road and all."

"That's how I make my living."

"And I make mine here," she reminded him. "Taking care of things for your mother."

"You still have a job. For now." He gave her a level look. "I'm putting the ranch up for sale."

She felt the blood drain from her face. "You can't do that."

"I think I can," he replied coolly.

"But it's been in your family for years."

The argument didn't seem to impress him. "You can stay until the place is sold. Maybe longer, if the new owner decides to keep you on."

"Does Maude know about this?"

"We haven't had a chance to talk."

"She might have something to say about your selling her home out from under her."

"This was my uncle's home. He never let either one of us forget it, either." Then, looking embarrassed that he had said too much, he returned his attention to the papers in front of him.

Becky turned and hurried from the office. She could have wished for a better answer, but she promised herself that no self-centered, irresponsible rodeo rider was going to take her dream away.

TOMMY SANG TO HIMSELF as he played with his bowl of orange gelatin. Becky had fed the boys and set out leftovers for the men in the bunkhouse kitchen. They liked to take the noon meal out there, but she made them come inside for supper. It was just too much work to cook two meals in two kitchens and besides, she and Maude liked the chance to talk over the day's work with the men while they ate.

Maude fixed herself another glass of iced tea and sat at the table reading the Sunday paper, since she hadn't gotten around to it yesterday. She folded it shut and turned to Becky. "That was a good party, wasn't it?"

"Definitely. I think everyone had a good time," Becky assured her.

"Will didn't come out for lunch."

"He's still in the office trying to figure out your bookkeeping system." He'd been in there for over an hour, which was keeping him out of her hair. Will's dog sat politely by Peter's chair and waited for scraps to drop on the floor. Peter pretended to drop them by accident. The animal eagerly gobbled them up.

"She likes potato chips," the boy said. "Weird, huh?"

"Don't give her too many. They might make her sick."

"Okay." He dropped a piece of beef from his sandwich. "Do dogs eat kittens? Do you think she'd hurt the kittens if she saw them?"

"I don't think so." She looked up from mixing meat loaf in a large pottery bowl. "That dog doesn't look mean, but the kittens' mother might have something to say about a dog looking at her babies."

Maude didn't look happy. "I really don't want Will going over the accounts."

Becky's eyebrows rose as she glanced toward her boss. "Why not?" She tried to tease her into a smile. "You haven't been stealing the profits, have you?"

But the woman didn't smile. In fact, she looked guilty. "Not exactly, but William's not going to like it."

"Do you want to tell me why not?" She dumped the meat loaf into two large loaf pans and patted it smooth, then washed her hands. Maude drank her iced tea and waited for her to sit down at the table before she spoke.

"He's been sending me money for years," Maude said, keeping her voice low.

"He has? Well, that's nice," Becky said, looking at the boys. She didn't know how much longer they'd be quiet. The baby concentrated on putting gelatin on his finger and sticking it in his mouth while Peter fed the dog his sandwich.

Maude nodded. "He's been very...generous. He's going to find out I didn't spend it and then he's going to find out that I did and then he's not going to be happy."

It took a moment to follow that one. "Did you spend it or not?"

"I spent it." Maude sighed. "But not on what he wanted me to spend it."

She couldn't imagine Maude gambling or drinking, though she liked to send in the contest entries she got in the mail. "What did you spend it on then?"

"Well, for one thing, the new horses."

"Thirty-one thousand dollars? That was the money your son sent?"

"Oh, there was lots more. He'd always send me money when he won. He kept trying to get me to move off the ranch and get a place in Billings, but I couldn't leave."

"Why not?" From everything she'd heard, Maude's brother had not been the nicest person in the world.

"My brother took me and Will in when we had nothing. I owed him for that. He gave us a home. I couldn't walk out and leave him alone when we both got old, could I? It wouldn't have been right. And what would I do in Billings?"

"Did your son understand that?"

"No."

"But J.W. left him the ranch."

"It was only fair, but Will's not going to understand any of this."

Becky patted her hand. "Sure he will. You're his mother. How can he be angry with you?"

"Well, even if he is, he'll have good reason. But he's like his father, who never had much of a temper either. Takes him a long time to get riled up, then watch out." The older woman finished her iced tea and stood up. "Guess I'd better take my nap. It doesn't look like Will's coming out of that office anytime soon, and if I'm sleeping I can put off talking to him."

"Not so fast, Mother," Will said, entering the kitchen. He had a sheaf of papers in his hand and he looked as if he could chew nails. Becky decided this would be a good time to take the boys upstairs and put Tommy Lee down for his nap, so she stood up and went to the sink. She kept a cloth there for cleaning the baby's face, so she dampened it with warm water and watched Maude sit back down in her chair.

"I really need my nap," the older woman said. "I'm seventy-four now."

"I know how old you are, Mother." He walked past the high chair without seeing the baby, but he nodded toward Peter. "Hey, kid. They give you any cake today?"

"It's for supper," the boy said.

"So this is where Lady went to. I wondered—"

"Daddy!"

Everyone looked at the baby. His eyes were round, his face covered with orange goo, and he was gazing rapturously at Will Cody.

"Who's that?" Will said, stopping to stare at the child.

"My brother."

"Tommy Lee," Becky said.

"Isn't he darling?" Maude asked.

"Daddy, daddy, daddy," the little boy chanted. He lifted his arms as if he expected Will to pick him up. Becky hurried over to him and started cleaning him up. She washed his face, then his pudgy hands. "I'm sorry," she said to Will, as she lifted her son into her arms. He was getting bigger every day, and she didn't know where he'd heard the word *daddy*. It wasn't like he'd ever had one. "He's never done this before. I don't—"

"Daddy," Tommy said, stretching toward the cowboy.

"I'm not your daddy," Will insisted, setting the papers on the table. He turned to Becky. "Tell him I'm not his daddy."

"That's not your daddy, honey. That's Mr. Cody, come to visit Miss Maude." But the child would not be denied. Almost knocking Becky off-balance, Tommy flung his arms out to the tall cowboy who had no choice but to open his arms and take the boy.

Tommy grinned and hugged him.

"I'm sorry," Becky said, trying to pry her son from Will with no success. "He's never done anything like this before."

Peter looked disgusted. "He's a baby."

Maude took the opportunity to quietly push back her chair and tiptoe from the room. Becky saw her go, but Will had his back to his mother as he bent over to set the little boy on the floor.

"No," Tommy said, hanging on. Will looked helplessly at Becky.

"What do I do now?"

"I'm sorry," she said again, reaching for her son. "I don't know what's gotten into him."

"Never mind," Will said, holding the child awkwardly. Tommy grinned and patted his face.

"He's tired," Becky said. "He's been playing all morning and..."

"Who takes care of the children while you're outside working?"

"Decker, J.J. and Oatey take turns."

"They don't mind?"

"No, I think they like it." She reached for Tommy, who suddenly decided that he would go into his mother's arms without a protest. He grinned at Will with a happy smile. "I'd better take him upstairs."

"My daddy died," Peter said, answering the unspoken question. "A long time ago, when I was two."

"I'm sorry." He looked at Becky with an oddly sympathetic look she didn't expect to see.

"Thanks."

Peter bent over and petted Lady's head. "I sure like your dog."

"She likes you, too."

"Think so?"

"Yeah." He looked past Becky to his mother's empty chair. "Where did she sneak off to?"

"To rest."

"Isn't she feeling well?"

"She's fine," Becky assured him, shifting Tommy on her hip. He was growing heavier every day. "She rests every afternoon. She says it gives her enough energy to stay up and see David Letterman after the news."

He sighed. "Go take care of your kids, Becky. I'll talk to my mother later."

"Okay." She hesitated before leaving the kitchen. "You know, she really is happy here."

"I find that hard to believe."

"Maybe you'd better look around. It might not be the same place that you left. And your mother might not be the same woman."

"Nothing's changed," he insisted, his mouth thinning into a straight line. He was still handsome, of course, even when he looked angry. "This place will never change, except to get older and shabbier."

There was no arguing with him. The old house wasn't in the greatest condition, but it had a certain personality. A few coats of paint and some insulated windows could do wonders. "Dinner's at six. If you need anything, talk to Decker or Cal. They're in charge in the afternoon."

He nodded. She left him pulling out a chair and sitting down at the table with the stack of papers he'd brought with him. If he wanted to sell the ranch, he could. The sad part about that was there wouldn't be anything she or Maude could do to stop him.

"I'M NOT LEAVING," Maude told her son. "If you've come to take me to Billings you can just forget that idea."

He looked up from his supper and stared at her. The ranch hands looked at each other and back down at their plates. Becky reached for the saltshaker.

"Maybe this isn't the time to talk about it," the young woman suggested. Will agreed. He didn't want an audience when he and his mother had this particular conversation.

"You can sell it out from under me, of course," Maude added.

"Let's not—"

"You can turn us all out into the street with nothing but our horses and our saddles and—"

"Mother," he tried again. He put down his fork. Everyone at the table looked at him like he was the devil himself. "I never—"

"That's what you came for," she said, a little sigh breaking her voice. "I heard in town today that you put the ranch up for sale and there was some interest in it from that big development east of Bozeman. And I'm not going. This is my home."

"It was my uncle's home."

"And mine." She lifted her chin defiantly, and Becky stood up and started to clear the table. The old cowboys looked as if they wanted to run out the door.

"Excuse me," the young woman said. "I'll put coffee on."

"Sit down, Becky," Maude continued. "I won't have all that dish clatter right now, if you don't mind." Becky sat. Maude looked at the ranch hands. "You'd better stay, too. This concerns our futures, all of us."

Peter turned to Will. "You in trouble?"

"I guess I am, but I sure can't figure out why," he said, looking down the length of the table to his mother. For some reason, he'd ended up with Peter on his left and the little one in the high chair on his right. Becky sat next to the baby and supervised his dinner. It was pretty much a disaster, but the dog would clean up the scraps from the floor. "I thought you wanted to move in with me when you didn't have to take care of J.W. anymore. We've talked about that off and on for years."

"*You've* talked about it," his mother said. "I've decided I don't like the idea."

"And why not?" He pushed his plate away. "What's wrong with the idea?"

"Well, for one thing, Billings is too big."

"You seem to enjoy it when you come to visit."

She looked at him as if he didn't know a steer from a bull. "It's different when you're on vacation, Willie. That doesn't mean I want to live there for the rest of my life."

"You can't stay here."

"Of course I can."

"You can't run a place this big."

"Why not?"

"It's too much work."

"Oh, pooh. I've been working all my life."

"And that's my point," he roared, losing his temper. "It's time for you to take it easy!"

"I don't want to." The look in those dark eyes dared him to argue with her.

Becky tried standing again. "I really think that this is a family discussion," she told Maude.

"I thought we should get it out in the open. We're all wondering what's going to happen, now that Will owns the ranch." She looked at her son. "If you've made any decisions, I hope you intend to reconsider." Her tone was formal, as if she was talking to a banker.

"I'd planned to sell."

There was silence as all eyes turned to him with expressions of surprise, resignation, disappointment and confusion.

"I'd planned to stay," his mother countered.

"You're trying to make me out to be some sort of monster. It won't work."

"Mon-ster!" Tommy called, and banged his fist on the tray of the high chair.

"Shh," Becky said. "Be good."

"You're seventy-four years old," Will continued. "Why would you want to spend the rest of your life on this god-forsaken ranch?"

He was horrified when her eyes filled with tears. "It's my home," she said, her voice quavering. "I thought you'd come home, too."

"I can't," Will said, standing up and tossing his napkin on the table. He shot Becky an apologetic look. "I'll skip dessert," he said. "Thanks for supper."

He grabbed his hat on his way out the back door, and let the screen door bang shut behind him. Once outside, he took a deep breath and headed toward the corral. Lady fell into step beside him.

"Guess you're the only one talking to me, huh, girl?"

She wagged her tail and trotted alongside him as he crossed the wide dirt yard. Damn it, he hadn't come back to the Silver Valley to be yelled at.

4

"I'M TIRED OF BEING bossed around," Maude said, looking around the table. "Someone's been telling me what to do all my life." Becky put a plate of cookies on the table and handed Maude a mug of coffee. "Doesn't anyone understand that?"

"We understand," Becky told her, watching the cowboys look as if they wanted to be anywhere else on earth besides in the kitchen with an angry woman. "Anyone else for coffee?"

Decker stood first, and the other three followed. "Thanks for supper," Decker said, and there was a similar murmur from the others. "We'll just be on our way. Gotta check on the horses."

"Sure," Becky said, trying to keep a straight face as the men hurried out the door. They were tough men who could deal with just about anything on the ranch, but women confused them. "I'll be out later."

"Cowards," Maude muttered, after the screen door banged shut. "All of them, cowards. Except for the one I gave birth to. He turned out to be just plain crazy."

Becky turned to Peter. "You can go play on the porch, honey."

"Okay." He scooped a pile of action figures from the counter and headed for his favorite spot on the ranch. The wide porch that ran along the front of the house was safe from horses and cows. He'd learned the hard way that horses could step on toys and that would be the end of the toy.

"Me, too," Tommy demanded, holding his arms up.

"Pretty soon," his mother said. She started clearing the table. "After I finish here."

"I'll help," Maude said. "Just give me a minute to cool off."

"Well, you sent him running," Becky said. "He didn't look too pleased."

"Imagine, trying to get me to move away from here! Bossing me around. All my life men have told me what to do. Someone else has always known what's best for me." Becky stacked the empty plates into a pile. "And that doesn't mean they were right, either."

"It just means your son cares about you," Becky said. Despite everything, she had to give him credit for that. "Maybe we can't manage this place by ourselves, Maude. We've only been doing it for six months and you know we've been real busy. Some days it's hard to keep up. Some *weeks* it's hard to keep up."

"*You* think I should let him sell this place?"

"Of course not, Maude. I love it here, too, and I'm grateful to you for giving me the chance to work. But you can't blame your son for wanting you to take it easy, buy you a nice house, take care of you."

"Yes, I can."

"All right, have it your way." She set the stack of dishes in the sink and started loading the dishwasher. "I don't want him to sell either. What will we do with the horses?"

"We'll find ourselves another ranch," Maude said. "We'll take the men and the horses and we'll start over."

"We'd never be able to afford it," Becky argued. "We're not even making ends meet in this place, and that's without a mortgage to pay."

"We'll think of something. It's just that nothing's going to have the atmosphere that this place has."

"Maddie, Maddie," Tommy chanted. "I wanna get down!"

Maude moved over to a chair closer to the baby. "Here," she said, giving him a cookie. "Your mama will be all yours in just a minute." She turned to Becky. "I remember when Will was this size. Seems like a hundred years ago, though."

"What kind of baby was he?"

"Smart. Noisy." Maude shook her head. "He wasn't what you'd call a patient child."

And Becky didn't think he'd changed. He looked like a man who was used to getting his own way. No wonder he was a champion rodeo rider. The man was going to do what he wanted to do no matter what anyone or any animal had in mind otherwise. He'd met his match in Maude, though. Like mother, like son.

"He was like his father," Maude continued. "Handsome and stubborn and kind."

Kind? Becky put the dirty loaf pans in the sink and filled them with soapy water. She'd attack them later, after the sun went down. "How long were you married?"

Maude sipped at her coffee and made a face at Tommy, who giggled. "Eleven years. Will was nine when we moved here. We'd had a place east of here, but after Matthew died, well, I just couldn't hang on to it. The bank owned it all anyway, and they weren't about to let a woman have anymore money. So we moved in with my brother. And—" Maude sighed "—he wasn't the easiest person to live with. He did a lot of wrong things, made a lot of mistakes. But he managed to hang on to his ranch, and he took care of us, so I can't complain."

Becky dampened a washcloth and went to the high chair.

Tommy protested the cleaning, but smiled when she was finished. "So handsome!" she told him, and he laughed.

"That's one good baby," the older woman affirmed.

"Yes, I've been lucky." Lucky she didn't miscarry after Jack died, lucky Maude had come to her rescue when she did.

"You do a good job with these children," Maude said. "It's not easy to raise a son alone. I should know."

"TROUBLES, SON?"

"What do you think?" Will sat in a rusted pickup truck parked behind the horse barn and looked at Decker. He motioned toward the passenger side, and the old cowboy accepted the silent invitation to sit inside. The passenger windows had been knocked out long ago, the tires were flat and the seat cracked and sagging, but Will didn't care. It was his truck and he'd sit in it any damn time he wanted.

"Your ma has strong opinions about staying here, I guess."

"Since when?" Will shook his head. "I've been talking about her moving in with me, and she's always said she couldn't leave J.W. Now that he's gone, I expected her to want to leave here as fast as she could."

"Women are strange creatures." He looked around the inside of the '62 Chevy. "They don't make 'em like they used to, do they?"

"You talking about trucks or women?" The men grinned at each other.

"Trucks, I guess," Decker drawled. "You used to come out here when you were a boy."

"This truck belonged to my father."

"Yeah."

"We used to do chores in it. He'd take me to town and I'd feel ten feet tall."

"You put up a fuss when J.W. wanted to sell it. He finally got disgusted and hauled it back here, where he couldn't see it unless he wanted to."

"He didn't have the right to sell it," Will said. "It was mine. Not his."

They sat in silence for a minute while Decker rolled himself a smoke, then patted his pocket for his matches.

"I guess that one hit close to home," Will said, while Decker lit his cigarette and rested his elbow on one bony knee.

"Yep. Guess a man don't have the right to sell what belongs to someone else."

"Trouble is, Deck, this place belongs to me now."

"Your ma doesn't think so."

"She's too old to run this ranch, Deck."

"Ain't we all, son," the old cowboy said, shaking his head. "Ain't we all."

"I couldn't stay past the summer," Will said.

"Wouldn't expect you to."

"And the ranch is still up for sale."

The old cowboy swallowed hard. "Guess nothing stays the same."

The two men sat in the abandoned truck for a while longer, as Decker finished his cigarette and Will tried to figure out just exactly what his mother was thinking. She'd always been tougher than she looked, he had to admit that. But, hell, he didn't want to stay here. The doctor had warned him to let the knee heal, or he'd be in serious trouble soon enough. It might be a good idea to stick around here and wait for Maude to change her mind, whether he wanted to or not.

"Why don't you stick around, son," Decker suggested, echoing his thoughts. "Jest for a while, of course. Till your ma comes to her senses. You should be a little nicer to the women, too. Otherwise you get beans for supper. And none of them chocolate chip cookies.''

He grinned. "What kind of beans?"

"Maude'll get over being mad," the old cowboy promised. "She always does."

"I hope to hell you're right," Will said. "I feel like I'm eight years old and about to be paddled with one her wooden spoons."

"DON'T WORRY," Becky said, when Will approached her at the corral. She had Tommy by the hand, and the child immediately stretched toward Will. "Your mother will get over it."

"That's what Decker said, too," Will replied. He looked dejected, and she almost felt sorry for him.

"Then you'd better take our word for it." She really shouldn't feel sorry for him, she reminded herself. He'd brought it all on himself in the first place.

"Daddy," Tommy pleaded. "Pick me up."

Will frowned and looked at her. "Can you get him to stop calling me that?"

"Have you ever tried to reason with a toddler?" She looked down at the child and said, "This is not your daddy, honey."

Tommy Lee ignored her, and instead tugged at her hand and tried to go to the cowboy. "Pick me up *now*."

"Please," his mother added.

"Please," he said, breaking into a smile. Becky smiled, too. With his blond hair and blue eyes, he was a beautiful child. Peter was darker. His hair had turned slowly to chestnut, but Becky hoped Tommy would stay the way he was now. Will had no choice but to pick up the boy, and swung him easily onto his shoulders.

"Thanks," Becky said. He didn't look quite so intimidating with a child draped around his neck. The contrast was startling, with the man so dark, his face hardened into sharp planes and high cheekbones. Tommy was fair, with smooth pink skin and round cheeks. His chubby hands clutched the collar of Will Cody's denim shirt. "I'm afraid he likes to get his own way."

"Yeah. Well, you've got to give a man credit for trying."

Their eyes met. They both knew he wasn't talking about the child.

"You can't blame your mother for getting angry. Maybe you'd better stop giving orders," Becky suggested. "Otherwise no one on this ranch is going to be talking to you. Especially if the men keep missing out on dessert."

"What about you?"

She would have sworn he was trying to flirt with her. "What about me?"

"You're talking to me."

"Because I feel sorry for you. It must be hard to go through life making people angry."

"I think you have the wrong idea about me," he drawled. He almost looked as if he wanted to smile. "I'm not the jerk you think I am."

"Prove it."

His eyebrows rose. "How?"

"Stay here and help out. See what we're doing here before you decide to sell the ranch right out from under us. Your mother has big plans for the summer. Let her enjoy herself. She's having fun, for the first time in her life. Do you really want to put a stop to it?"

Will frowned. "I don't think you're in any position to give me advice. Not when it's your job at stake."

"I can get a job anywhere, Mr. Cody. I'm a first-rate cook and a first-rate foreman." She put her hands out and took her son down from Will's shoulders. "I happen to like your mother."

"And you don't like me."

She couldn't argue with the truth, so Becky didn't try. "I don't even know you. I *do* know that your mother is a real sweet woman. She's seventy-four years old and she wants to ride horses and go on pack trips and have fun with her friends. We're trying to figure out how to make this place pay for itself. Is that too much to ask of you to give us a chance?"

"I'll think it over," he said, but she had no idea if he really meant it.

"You do that." Becky swung Tommy into her arms and settled him against her hip. "We could sure use the help."

He didn't say anything, but simply looked at her with those dark eyes of his. Becky turned away and headed to the barn to see the new horses. According to Cal, they were settling in just fine. At least something around here was content.

BECKY CHECKED TO SEE how the horses were doing. They were mild-mannered animals, as tame and gentle as had been promised. There weren't many in Montana yet, but in time there could be. She was dying to ride one and see for herself how their gait differed from that of a quarter horse. Maude had gone to the horse show with a couple of her friends this spring, since Becky had been content to stay home with the children. She didn't mind having the men watch the children a few hours at a time, but leaving the kids for a night was too much to ask of the aging cowhands. Maude returned and announced she'd found a horse she could ride. And she'd liked them so much she'd bought six, enough to start a breeding business that was supposed to supplement the ranch income.

"Are these horses supposed to make money or eat it?" Will's voice drawled behind her. Becky kept looking at the mare as Will stepped next to her at the entrance to the stall.

"They're supposed to make money," she answered. "Maude calls it 'diversification.' She says all the ranches are developing other ways to make money besides selling beef cattle."

He nodded. "Sounds like a good idea, but why South American horses? What's wrong with raising quarter horses?"

"Don't knock it till you've tried it."

"Have you?"

He'd caught her on that one. "Not yet, but tomorrow I'm going to put them through their paces and see what all the fuss is about."

"All right," Will said. "That's what we'll do."

"We?"

He smiled at her, and her heart flipped in the most alarming way. Becky told herself it was just because she hadn't been around a man under the age of seventy for months. Except for the vet, who was a nice enough man but didn't have much to say except "Hold her steady now," she didn't often get a chance to talk to anyone her own age.

"I've decided to stick around for a while, at least until my leg heals and I can talk some sense into my mother."

"Good." She stifled an inward sigh of relief. "Maude will be pleased."

"I'm still selling the ranch," he said.

So much for relief. She turned to him, with Tommy's head nestled against her neck. He was tired now, relaxed in her arms. "I guess you'll do what you have to do," she said. "But I hope you'll keep an open mind."

"I'd like to see some of the ranch tomorrow. You want to go over what needs to be done tomorrow?"

"After I put Tommy to bed, sure."

"Good." His gaze flickered to the child. "He's half-asleep."

"He's a creature of habit." She moved toward the door of the barn. "Your mother's probably on the porch, just in case you're looking for her."

He smiled again. "Think she'll talk to me?"

"If you tell her you're staying."

Will followed her out of the barn. "Women are all alike," he drawled. "They're only happy if you tell them what they want to hear."

It was only a short reprieve, Becky reminded herself, ignoring his teasing. She walked beside the tall man down the road toward the house where Peter played with his action figures and Maude read the latest issue of *Country Woman* magazine and planned the next gathering of her friends. It would be the same as it was every evening, except for the man walking beside her. He wanted to change everything, and he had the power to do it. But maybe, just maybe, he'd change his mind.

"COME HERE," Maude said, waving Decker over to the window. "Look at that!" She pointed to Will and Becky walking together toward the house. The baby looked sweet, resting sleepily against the young woman's neck. "They're walking together."

"Who is?" Peter said, looking up from the floor.

"Nothing," Maude said. "Grown-up talk." Peter turned back to his toys. He was used to grown-up talk.

Decker joined her at the window. "Maybe he decided to listen to me."

"About what?"

"About stayin' on for a while."

"He doesn't listen to anyone," Maude said. "Never did."

"They're not talking," Decker pointed out.

"Haven't you ever heard of 'companionable silence'?" Maude studied their expressions. "At least they're not fighting."

"The boy is really trying hard not to limp. That leg must hurt."

"Maybe he's hurt too bad to rodeo."

"Could be. Or could be he'll be right as rain in a couple of weeks. He's made quite a name for himself, that boy has."

"Come away from the window," Maude said, backing up. "They'll see us."

"Yes, ma'am." The cowboy sighed. "Though I don't know what diff'rence that would make."

She sat down in her favorite overstuffed chair and picked up a magazine. "I don't want them to think that I'm—" She stopped. "Little pitchers have big ears."

"Yeah. I know what you're doing. I just think you're crazy, that's all." Decker took another cookie from the plate and sat down on the swing. He rocked himself while he ate. "Things just ain't that simple."

"We'll see," Maude said. "I have a few things up my sleeve, but everyone has to help. These children need a you-know-what and you-know-who needs a husband."

"You-know-who has her work cut out for her," Decker said.

"You're going to help me, aren't you?"

He reached for another cookie. "Yes, ma'am. Don't I always?"

Maude knew he only pretended to protest. None of them wanted to leave the ranch and try to find a new place somewhere else. She didn't intend to be shut up in some little house all by herself, while her son was on the road trying to break his neck. She didn't want to leave her new friends or her new horses or her home. And it was her home, no matter what Will thought. The boy didn't understand, and it was about time he settled down and took over what was rightfully his.

"Where is everyone?" Will hollered.

"Out here." She heard him clomp through the house, but when he stepped out onto the porch he was alone.

"Where's Becky?"

She pretended she was still mad at him. Which she was, sort of. "Putting the baby to bed, I guess. That girl works too hard."

"Good cook, too," Decker said. "You want a cookie?"

Peter looked up. "I do."

"Well, come over here and grab one before they're all gone." Peter took a cookie and, ignoring the adults, went back to the corner to play.

"I wondered where my dog went," Will said, sitting down next to Decker in the swing. He stretched out his legs and winced. "Now I know."

Lady looked up from her position next to Peter, then put her head back down and closed her eyes.

"She's found herself a boy," Decker said.

Will whistled for the dog, who didn't respond. It was as if Lady had suddenly gone deaf.

"She's sleeping," Peter told him. "You shouldn't wake her up."

Now he was being told what to do by a four-year-old. Hell, he should have stayed in Denver and taken his chances with the bulls. He turned to his mother and waited for her to say something. Anything. "I checked on the new horses," he tried. "They look like they're settling in."

She looked at him. "And what about you? Are you settling in?"

"No." Staying for the summer didn't mean settling down.

Maude sniffed. "The horses are smarter than you are."

"I didn't want to inherit this ranch," Will stated. "What ever happened to that cousin over in Great Falls?"

"J.W. fought with him, too. Said he wasn't worth the powder to blow him away."

"No wonder we didn't have any family around."

"I didn't have you until I was forty-one. My folks were gone, and your father's mother lived back East in a nursing home. There was no one left but me and J.W. He'd been living here alone for years, hiring a woman in the summer to cook for the crew." She flipped the page of her magazine and studied the pictures. "I don't want to discuss it anymore, William."

Becky stuck her head in the doorway. "Anyone want anything? I'm fixing myself a drink."

Will nodded. Maybe he could get used to being waited on. "I'll have a beer, if you've got one."

"Sure. What about you, Maude? The usual?"

"Not tonight, thank you. I guess I'm still worn-out from yesterday." She put her magazine on the floor and stood up. "I'll take Peter up with me."

"Thanks. Decker?"

"Uh, no, thanks, Reb." The old man stood up and moved toward the screen door. "The sun's gone down. Guess it's time to get to bed."

"Okay." She disappeared and Will turned to Decker. "Where is everyone?"

"Cal, Oatey and Malone were finishing up a while ago. I guess they're bedding down, too."

Maude went over to the little boy. "Come on, Peter. We'll say good-night to your mama and head up to bed."

The child looked as if he wanted to protest, but thought better of it. Lady started to get up, too, with the boy, but Will told her to stay.

"'Night,'" Peter told the men. "See ya tomorrow."

"Good night," Will said, and Decker waved goodbye as he went out the door and down the steps. Maude bent down and kissed Will on the cheek before she ushered the boy into the living room, so Will figured she couldn't still be upset with him. She wasn't the kind of person to hold a grudge. "I was hoping we could go over some ranch business," he said.

"Not tonight. Besides—" she yawned "—Becky will be able to tell you anything you need to know."

He should have expected that. It was too much to expect that there would be something that the pretty blonde wouldn't know anything about. The sky had grown darker outside, so he switched on a lamp, then went to the office to retrieve the pad of notes he'd made earlier. He might as well start acting like he owned the place. He would have to get the account ledgers in shape, make sure the breeding records were complete and the cattle inventoried. He went back to the porch and sat down, rocking slightly on the wood swing.

Becky returned, handed him a beer and sat down in Maude's chair. They both watched the dog walk past them out of the room.

"Thanks," he said, remembering his manners. "I guess I don't have to ask where she's going," Will said, turning to the woman across from him. She'd set her drink on the wide arm of the chair and crossed her legs. She was slim, he guessed, despite the jeans that looked too large. The belt that held them up was cinched as far as it could go. Her shirt was a faded blue check, the sleeves rolled up to reveal tanned arms. The long yellow braid of hair lay over her shoulder, touching the top of her left breast. She looked every inch the cowgirl, complete with freckles and a sunburned nose. She was pretty, in that outdoorsy way of

Western women. He tried to imagine her wearing lipstick and a short dress and couldn't. It was hard to believe that she was old enough to have two kids.

"Petey likes animals and they tend to like him."

"Yeah, I can see that." He turned to watch his dog slink through the living room toward the main staircase. "I guess he's got himself a dog."

"Sorry."

Will shrugged. "Doesn't matter. She's getting too old to trail after me all the time."

Becky took a sip of her drink and nodded at the notepad. "I see you're not wasting any time."

"I have to know what's here."

"Two hundred twenty-seven cows, one hundred ninety-one calves, fifty heifers, twelve Hereford bulls and nineteen horses, counting the ones that arrived today. We didn't breed the yearling heifers this month."

"Why not? That's a big loss in calf production."

"Yes, but it's labor-intensive. We all just about killed ourselves this spring trying to deal with the problems yearlings have giving birth. I just don't have the manpower for it."

"That's risky," was his only comment.

"Maude and I decided that this way we could handle what we have."

"Have you made any other changes that I should know about? Besides starting a fancy South-American horse-breeding business and cutting down on calves?"

She took another sip of her drink. "No. I've just been trying to keep up with what J.W. had set up, though he'd let things slide over the years."

"What about artificial insemination? I don't see any records."

Becky shook her head. "Your uncle believed in breeding

the old-fashioned way, but that's something you might want to investigate for next year, if you're here. The heifers are separate, in the north section."

"I'd like to see them."

"We can ride out tomorrow. Anything else?"

"Not right now."

"Okay." She leaned her head back against the chair cushion and closed her eyes. He couldn't help looking at her. She looked very young and very tired. A widow, they'd told him. She couldn't have been married very long.

"Do you mind my asking how old you are?"

She answered without opening her eyes. "Twenty-eight going on fifty."

"This is a hard life for a woman," he muttered. "Why don't you want to live in town?"

"I like it here." She didn't look at him. Instead she finished her drink and stood up. "If you'll excuse me, I'm going to bed. Five-thirty comes early."

"Sure. See you in the morning."

"Good night."

She left Will alone on the porch. It hadn't changed much. There was still a stack of magazines in between the chairs and the inexpensive Charles Russell prints on the wall. There were a few tears in the screen, and the wood floor needed a fresh coat of khaki paint, but it was pretty much just like he remembered. His uncle had added it to the front of the house when Will was thirteen. Unlike Peter, he hadn't had time to sit down and play in the corner, that's for sure. He'd been treated like one of the hands from the time he could swing his leg over a horse. He'd been expected to do the work of a man, and he'd done it without complaining.

Until that one night when all hell broke loose. Will drained his beer and put it out of his mind. He had to think of the future now, had to decide what was best for everyone. He'd stay for as long as he had to and no longer.

His knee started to ache, but Will decided against taking any painkillers. He'd stick with the beer and a good night's sleep. Lord, it was quiet out here. The porch swing squeaked a little, but that was the only sound. He was used to crowds and excitement. He was used to competition and honky-tonk bars and eating dirt when a bronc pitched him off its back. He was up for Rodeo Rider of the Year for the second time, and if his knee hadn't wrenched apart, he'd have been sure to win it. He couldn't turn his back on all that and become a man who went to bed at nine and got up at five and worried about rain.

The problem was, he just couldn't imagine living on the Silver V and not going stark raving mad. He'd been forced to live here when he was a skinny nine-year-old kid, but he was almost thirty-four, and no one could make him stay one day longer than he had to.

5

BECKY LOVED her bedroom, with its simple painted iron bed and old yellow starburst quilt. The dresser was oak, the bathroom right across the hall. The upstairs held faded green rugs: its walls were painted ivory. Maude had been right to keep the ranch house simple and uncluttered. Downstairs, in the living room and kitchen, there was enough junk for five families. She missed having a home of her own, but she also knew how lucky she was to have had someplace to live and work, with the children with her.

She loved the nights, loved the few minutes alone at the end of each day when her children were sleeping and the house was quiet. She could soak her tired body in the deep tub and pretend that she could sleep late in the morning. That would be a luxury indeed. When she was done with her bath, she'd put on a light cotton nightgown, check the boys one last time and then patter back to her own room and climb into bed. The alarm would be set for five o'clock; morning always seemed to come too soon. But tonight there was a dog at the foot of Peter's bed and there was a man downstairs; she could hear his footsteps as he walked around the kitchen. He had come to change everything, to sell the ranch and take Maude away. He hadn't thought of what would happen to the men. Didn't anyone wonder what happened to old cowboys who couldn't work anymore? She would have to show him that the ranch was running well, that they could take care of it, that it wasn't too much work for Maude. He could go back to his rodeo life and whatever else he did.

It would be better if he stayed, of course. It would be better to have a strong young man giving orders and making decisions and doing the work that required muscles. She could go back to cooking and playing with her kids and doing what she was hired to do. Will could make the decisions and Maude could have her horses and her friends, with no worry about the day-to-day problems of the cattle business.

Will Cody was nice when he wanted to be. He'd been nice enough to hold Tommy and talk to Peter. He hadn't even seemed to mind too much when his dog abandoned him. He was probably a nice man, Becky decided, snuggling into her pillow. His problem was that he wasn't smart enough to know where he belonged.

THE KITCHEN SECTION of the bunkhouse was the only area Becky ever entered. The bunkhouse itself was old, a leftover from the early 1900s. It was a long narrow building, similar to a motel. Every room had its own front door, and there was a communal bathroom at the back. The kitchen was sparse, but held a large square table, eight scarred wooden chairs, and the usual kitchen equipment lined one wall. The men made their own breakfast and lunch, with Becky seeing that they had enough food on hand. She met the men there most mornings and went over the plans for the day.

"Good morning."

Becky turned around from her conversation with J.J. and Cal and glanced over at Will. "Good morning."

"Are we riding or driving?" Will nodded first to her, then to the two men. "Looks like it's going to be a good day."

"Either way," she said. "It doesn't make any difference to me."

"We'd better take a truck," he declared. "I don't think I can sit a horse yet."

"Okay." Better, in fact. That way she'd get back to eat lunch with the kids. Maude was watching them this morning, and she and Becky planned to ride the Peruvians this afternoon and see what they could do. Becky had gotten up early, done her chores in the horse barn and grabbed a peanut butter sandwich for breakfast. Maude, nearly bursting with excitement, had decided to work in her garden. Tommy liked to make mud pies and Peter liked to water the plants, so it would work out for all three of them. She'd asked Maude if she wanted to go with her son instead, but the woman had looked at her as if she'd lost her mind.

Now she turned back to the men, whose work for the day would include working with the new horses and making sure the machinery was ready for haying season. Somebody was always driving to town for parts these days. Will stood beside her and acted as though he was listening, then they walked past the sheds and corrals to where an assortment of vehicles was parked.

"Where are we going?"

"We can start over at the Second Meadow and check the cows there. Cal said there're a few he's keeping an eye on, and I want to make sure the calves are okay."

"Do you want to drive?" he asked her, hesitating before opening the driver's door.

"Go ahead," she said. "The key's inside."

"That hasn't changed," he said, getting in the truck. "But not much has."

"Your uncle wasn't much for change," Becky said. "He wouldn't even let me experiment with supper. He wanted the same foods, and he wanted them the way he'd always had them."

"Yeah," Will said, bitterness in the word. "I know. He was one hell of a pain in the ass."

"Well," Becky conceded, trying to be tactful. "He wasn't the easiest man in the world to get along with. I don't think he had any friends."

"No," Will said, guiding the truck across the field toward the fence. "I imagine that by the time he died he didn't have a friend left to mourn him."

"Quite a few came to the funeral, actually. Out of respect for Maude, I suppose," Becky said, remembering that cold October day. It had been impossible to stay out of the wind, and back at the house she'd prepared gallons of coffee for the frozen guests. "You were in Europe then, weren't you?"

"Yeah. Germany's crazy about rodeos. I did a couple of exhibitions and some judging. Maude told me not to bother coming back to pay my respects." He glanced over at her. "You probably think I was wrong to listen to her."

"I mind my own business." Becky hopped out when they reached the gate and swung it open. That was one disadvantage to being the passenger. There were always gates to open and close anywhere you went. When she got back in the truck after closing the gate behind them, she was surprised that Will continued the conversation. She'd expected him to be quiet. She hadn't expected him to act like she knew what she was doing.

"I would have been a hypocrite to go to that funeral and mourn that man."

She braced her hand on the dashboard as they went over a rough spot and turned to look at him. "It was that bad?"

"Yeah."

"But he left you the ranch. That must count for something."

"That's the part I can't figure out," the man said slowly. "That's what makes no sense, no matter how much I try to figure it. He should have left it to Maude, but I guess he figured she couldn't run it."

"And you could."

He laughed, but there was no humor in the sound. "I could run it, all right, but I'd just as soon rope an elephant."

"I don't get it," Becky said. "Most people would be turning cartwheels if they ended up owning a ranch this size."

"And up to their ears in debt and hard work," he added.

"I don't—"

"That's a pretty big price tag," Will muttered.

She'd been about to say that she didn't think the ranch was in debt like most operations. It didn't make much money after expenses, of course. And some months were worse than others. She and Maude had spent a long winter trying to figure out how they could get a little extra income.

They traveled north, past groups of Hereford cows and calves. They were pretty cattle, various shades of brown with white markings. The animals looked up from their grazing for a second, but then returned to what they were doing.

"Good-looking animals," Will said.

"You sound surprised."

"I didn't know what to expect," he admitted. "I don't know how you've done this all by yourself for the past six months, that's all."

"We all work hard."

"Did you have much trouble with the calving?"

"Some." It had actually been six weeks of almost nonstop work. Keeping track of more than two hundred mothers and babies had at times seemed close to impossible.

"We lost one calf to cold, two more drowned in the creek before we found them. The usual. We had about ten calves in the sheds at any one time. They took a lot of nursing."

"And you wonder why I want to sell out," he murmured. "This is a hard life, all right."

"It's my job," Becky said, wondering if she could make him understand. "I started out cooking and cleaning for your mother. I sure didn't intend to be managing this operation. I don't know what I would have done without the men. Decker can tell if a cow is going to calf by the look in her eye and J.J. knows everything there is to know about horses. Cal likes tinkering with machinery, and Oatey is good with kids and calves."

"And the summer camp?"

"No one's run cattle up there for years."

He frowned. "Why not? That was good grassland."

She shrugged. "Not enough help, I guess. And we're not running enough stock either."

"I take it my mother hired back the men J.W. fired over the years."

"Yes."

He stopped the truck and turned to her. "Why?"

"She says she's making amends for all the wrong that's been done." She wished Will Cody wasn't quite so handsome, or so close to her. It was unnerving sitting beside him, and she wasn't sure why. She worked with men all day long, and yet she never experienced this self-conscious, run-like-hell feeling that made her want to leap out of the truck and disappear behind the next rise.

He shook his head and smiled to himself. "I should have known she'd do something like that."

"Yes. She's a very loyal person." She needed to get out more. She needed to go to town and be around people, not cattle and kids and old men. The next time the veterinarian was out at the ranch, she'd say yes if he asked her out. He'd done that awhile back, when she was covered with manure and mud, but she'd thought he was kidding. Until he'd asked her again, a few weeks later, and she'd said no because Tommy was sick and she didn't want to leave him.

Will put the truck in gear and continued and the conversation stopped. They found the cow Decker had warned her about and inspected her. She and her calf seemed fine, so Deck would be relieved. To Becky's surprise, Will knew a lot about cows and seemed at ease out in the pasture. They drove for hours, checking fence and looking for trouble, until the sun was high overhead.

"Must be around noon," Will said.

Becky looked at her watch. "Yep. I have to get back to the kids, and I wanted to be around when Maude rode one of the new horses this afternoon."

"Can we keep going and end up at the house?"

"No. I guess there used to be a road, but it washed out years ago. You'll have to go back the way we came." He turned the truck around, and Becky hopped in and out to open and close the gates. "We should have brought Pete with us," she said. "He's just about tall enough to do this job."

"He doesn't need to be out here," Will said. "He's too young to be working."

Becky turned to him in surprise. "I didn't say he was working. He just likes to ride with me and open gates."

"Leave him at home from now on." He shot a glance in her direction. "From the moment I set foot on this place, my uncle had me working. Seven days a week, before school and after school. All I'm saying is, let Peter be a kid for as long as he can. Growing up on a ranch is hard work."

"This is a good place to raise children."

He shrugged. "I guess that depends on who's doing the raising."

They rode back to the house in silence.

IT WAS WONDERFUL to see them together. Maude watched as the truck bounced across the field and parked by the garage. The young people had spent all morning together. She hoped they hadn't fought. She hoped they'd talked. Or kissed. But that was too much to ask. She reined in her horse and figured she'd settle for knowing they'd been in the same place all morning.

She nudged the mare and trotted toward them. It was like riding a couch cushion. None of her bones jarred or ached, nothing hurt. She felt as if she could ride for miles. She felt as if she were twenty again. Well, forty anyway.

"What the hell are you doing?" Will turned off the ignition and got out of the truck as his mother trotted toward them.

"I think you can figure it out," Maude said. She tucked a strand of silver hair under her hat and smiled at her handsome son. She reached over and patted the mare's neck. "Isn't she a beauty?"

"You shouldn't be riding. Not with your arthritis." He walked over and greeted the horse, then took it by its bridle. Becky walked over and rubbed the horse's nose.

"Don't knock it till you've tried it," his mother chided.

"What's this one's name?" her future daughter-in-law asked.

"Duchess of York."

Will looked up. "What?"

Maude chuckled. "The mares are all named after royalty. Seems their sire is King Henry and the dam is Lady Catherine."

Becky chuckled. "Did you know that when you bought them?"

"Yes. We also have Princess Elizabeth, Lady Caroline, Countess Levien and Lady Jane."

Will looked at her as if she was losing her mind, but Maude decided to forgive him. "Let me guess," he drawled. "The stallion you bought is Prince Charles?"

"No. His name is Doug. He's from a different breeder."

"I can't wait to meet him," Will said, walking around the mare. She stood patiently as Will looked her over.

"Let's go then," Maude said. "I couldn't wait for you any longer."

Becky smiled. "I should have known. Where are the boys?"

"I gave them lunch. Oatey is with Tommy. I think they're both having a nap. And Peter's with Malone in the barn. They're saddling up the others."

"Is everything all right?"

Silly question, Rebecca. Everything was fine. Her son was home, her riding plans were going to work out, and she was going to have at least two beautiful grandchildren. "Oh, they were as good as gold. As always."

Her son gave her a questioning look. "What are you up to, Mother?"

"Can't a woman smile without someone thinking she's up to something?"

"No," he replied flatly. He turned to Becky. "Are we going to ride these royal nags or are we going to stand here?"

"We're going to ride, my lord," she quipped, looking especially pretty.

Ah, thought Maude, stifling a satisfied sigh. This was all going to work out after all.

DOUG TURNED OUT to be one hell of a horse. Will didn't think his knee or his back would be able to take more than thirty minutes on a horse, but the Peruvian stallion surprised him. No two hooves landed on the ground at the same time, a motion that gave a smooth ride without bouncing or jarring. Decker, Malone and Becky were on the other mares, who were all as well trained and obedient as the Duchess Something his mother was trotting around.

It was a world away from the rodeo.

"Do you think they've ever seen cows before?" he asked, reining in next to Becky. She was a good rider, with a balanced seat and light hands. She was on the smallest mare, though all the horses were a good size.

Becky motioned for Malone to open the gate. "I guess there's only one way to find out." His mother hadn't stopped smiling, Will noticed, which might mean that she was speaking to him again. The other men wore similar expressions, as though they couldn't believe what they were doing.

"I'll be switched," Decker said, nudging the mare through the gate. "If I didn't know I was on a horse I wouldn't know I was on a horse!"

"Are there any more of these in Montana?" Malone called to Maude.

"Only about sixty," she said, following Decker from the corral and toward the wide grasslands to the east. "But next year there'll be a few more."

"Meaning you still intend to breed them." He wondered if his mother lay awake nights trying to think up foolish things to do.

"Meaning my new business will be a success." She gave her horse a slight kick and trotted off to keep up with Decker, who was clearly enthusiastic.

Becky trotted up beside him. "You don't know when to quit, do you?"

"She has to be made to see reason."

"She's having fun."

"Ranches aren't for fun."

Her eyebrows rose. "Really. You look like you're having a pretty good time. And I don't see you doing any work around here. Why would you have anything to complain about?"

She was right, which ticked him off. There would always be plenty of work. A man could ride in any direction and there would be something to fix or something to feed. There would be a warm wind and the smell of hay and a hot yellow sun hanging in a big blue sky. There would never be enough hours in the day to do everything there was to be done. There would never be enough money or enough time or enough patience to wait until there was a profit at the end of the year.

"What do you do during the off-season of the rodeo?" Becky asked. "There is an off-season, isn't there?"

"Spring and fall."

"Well, where do rodeo riders go?"

"I have a place."

"A condo, ranch, house, trailer, what?"

He didn't know why she was so interested. "Twenty acres, enough to keep a few horses."

Her expression showed that she didn't think that twenty acres could compare to thirty thousand. They passed another broken section of fence. Will sighed. It would take ten men all summer to fix the fences.

"We need help with the haying," Becky said. "I know your knee is bad, but do you know anything about it?"

"Yeah," he said. He'd spent every summer as an unpaid member of the hay crew. He was sure J.W. regretted his sister not having more sons before her husband was killed. "I'll talk to Decker and see what needs to be done."

"Great. That's a load off my mind."

They rode in silence for a few more minutes, through a large meadow and a section of the ranch they hadn't covered this morning. Will looked around, surprised at the sparse number of cows and calves he saw grazing. "You said you're not using the summer pasture?"

"No."

"But you're not running as many cows as you could be. That's one of the reasons you're not making enough money."

"I don't have enough *anything*," she told him. "That's the problem. If you think you can handle things better, you're welcome to try." With that, she urged her horse ahead and trotted up to join the others who by now were far ahead of them. Well, he should have kept his mouth shut, but he couldn't figure out why there wasn't more stock. Had J.W. lost interest in ranching somewhere along the line? The place should have at least managed to break even, but the accounts he'd seen showed that it wasn't even doing that. But that was ranch life for you, Will mused. You could break your back all year and still have nothing to show for it. Unless you loved the life, which he didn't.

Still, it was good to be on a horse, even though his back was starting to ache. And it was good to be out under the vast blue sky and feel like his life was his own.

And there were some advantages, like watching Becky's shapely rear in the saddle. She had a fine figure, but Will wasn't getting anywhere near her. She was a woman with children, a woman who would want commitment and devotion. He hadn't been with a woman in six months, but he wasn't going to mess with Becky.

SHE SHOULDN'T HAVE lost her temper again, Becky fumed, taking the saddle from the chestnut mare. She should smile and be polite and agreeable. When on earth was she ever going to learn to keep her mouth shut? As soon as she finished rubbing down Lady Jane, Becky told herself that she was going to become a model of tact and diplomacy.

It wasn't going to be easy. She looked at her watch. After four already, and the boys would be wondering where she was. There was supper to fix, too. She'd have to use a couple of casseroles she'd put aside for the hay crew. At least she didn't have to clean. Luckily the house still looked good from the cleaning she and Maude had given it Sunday morning, for the party.

She stood apart from the others. Will, his limp more accented than this morning, took care of the Pasos stallion with grim determination written all over his face. He should be off that leg, but he wasn't going to admit it.

"You miss rodeoin'?" Malone asked him.

"Yeah."

Well, that was informative, Becky thought, shamelessly eavesdropping on the conversation a few yards away.

"I did a stint as a clown once," the older cowboy said.

"Yeah? When?"

"Years back. I wasn't any good at it," the old man drawled. "Besides, I didn't think that was a real smart way to make a livin'."

"It's all hard work," the younger man said, "whatever you do."

Malone's reply was muffled, but it sounded agreeable. Then, "This here's the perfect situation," he told Will. "A good-size spread, not too big and not too small. Enough water and enough flatland and plenty of rangeland. A man could settle down and make a fine life for himself and his sons here."

Becky hid her smile behind the horse. In his own way, the old cowboy was doing his part. But talking to Will

Cody was like talking to the wind. You could say all you wanted and your words made no difference.

"WHO'S OSCAR REDDING?"

Maude looked up from her perusal of *Ranch Living* magazine. "Your uncle's lawyer. Why?"

"He called and left a message on the answering machine. Says he wants me to call and arrange an appointment."

"Must be something about the estate," Maude said.

Will shrugged. "I'll call him tomorrow. You and I should go over the records of the business. There are a number of things I don't understand."

Maude tossed her magazine on the sofa cushion beside her and stood up. "I suppose, but I don't know how much good I'll be to you. I'd better get Becky."

"No!" Maude gave him a questioning look, and Will added, "I think she's busy with the kids right now." He didn't want those big blue eyes looking at him and messing up his concentration. That's what happened last time and he'd ended up arguing with her instead of kissing her. He sure as hell wasn't about to do either one.

"Well," Maude sounded reluctant. "I guess."

He let her lead the way to the office, but Peter and Lady intercepted them in the hallway. The dog stayed close to the boy as if she thought Will was going to take her away. "You want to play checkers?"

"Me?"

The boy nodded. "Miss Maude taught me."

Will shook his head. "I don't think—"

"Sure you can," Maude said, pushing him forward. "We can have our meeting anytime. Petey here needs someone to play with and I'll go see if Becky needs help in the kitchen."

"She's cooking," the child said. "We're having something with cheese on top." He turned to Will. "Are you gonna play?"

Will was stuck. "Aren't you a little young for checkers?"

The boy looked surprised. "I don't think so."

"Play with him, Will," Maude said. "Remember how I used to beat you?"

"Don't believe her," he told the boy. "She always lost." Peter grinned and put his hand into Will's.

"Come on," the boy said. "The box is on the porch."

Will had no choice but to follow him. He remembered being small, vaguely remembered a tall dark-haired man with a quiet voice who had patiently played games. He wondered what his life would have been like if his father hadn't been killed. He wondered if Peter would think about that someday. No doubt he would and a small corner of his heart would be sad for what he never had. "All right," he told the boy. "Who gets to be red?"

WILL TRIED TO talk to Maude again after dinner, but the ranch hands needed help with the bunkhouse bathroom. It took most of the evening to fix the plumbing, and someone would have to go for parts in the morning so the shower would work. From the bunkhouse kitchen window he caught glimpses of Becky and the children walking around. She put them in the old station wagon and left. She probably went to town, maybe visited a friend.

"Does Becky have a man?" He turned away from the window and sat down at the battered table with the cowboys.

The four men stared at him. Decker grinned. "Now why would that be any of your business? You interested?"

He was sorry he'd spoken. He should have known better. Cowboys were terrible gossips and loved a good joke. They would tease him to death from now on, given half a chance. "No, of course not. I just wondered."

"Pretty woman," Malone offered, shuffling a deck of cards. "Too bad she doesn't have a husband."

"Why is that?" Will asked, figuring it was too late to stop the conversation anyway, so he might as well find out what the boys knew.

"Mebbee she's picky," Oatey offered.

Decker shrugged. "How's she going to meet anyone around here? She goes to town sometimes, to pick up what we need or get supplies, but it's not like she gets to meet anyone. Except Doc Thomas." He turned to Cal. "Did he ask her out?"

"Yeah. But she turned him down the first time. The second time, too, 'cuz the little one had the scours."

"Who's Thomas?"

"Doc Thomas, the vet. Nice fella," Decker said, looking at Malone. "Are we playing cards or are you just gonna sit there and shuffle 'em all night?"

"I'm talking," he said, slapping the deck on the table. "Will here wants to know about Miss Becky. 'Course it's about time he got his head out of his butt and saw what was right in front of him." He grinned at Will. "No offense, boss."

Will leaned back in his chair. "She's not my type," he declared, making the men howl with laughter. "What's so funny?"

"You are, son," Decker managed to say. "You've been giving her moony looks whenever you think no one's watching. And you frown at her all the time like she's driving you crazy." He chuckled. "I wouldn't know anything about your 'type,' but hell, son, she's a woman and you're a man."

"I figured that part out already." He smiled to show he took the teasing.

"Now, that's a good start," Malone drawled. "I heard figuring it out is the most important part." The men roared with laughter once again, and Will reached over and cut the cards.

"Are you going to play?" he asked. "Or are you just gonna sit here like a bunch of hyenas?"

"Five card stud," Oatey declared, setting a box of matchsticks on the table. "Count 'em out."

Malone began to deal. "Read 'em and weep."

Will picked up his cards as they were dealt. He was glad that the men were occupied with something else besides giving him advice about women. He didn't need to know anything more about women than that women and rodeo didn't mix.

6

"WE'VE GOT TO GET some of the stock up to the summer pasture," Will announced at breakfast. "I drove up there the other day and you're just letting good grass go to waste."

Becky set a platter of fried eggs next to the plate of bacon on the table. "You think it's worth the trouble?"

"Yeah." He helped himself to eggs and bacon, then sprinkled them liberally with salt and pepper. "I do. There are enough of us to do the job, I think, though it might take awhile."

Maude nodded. "I think that's a lovely idea. The ladies are coming out here this morning to see the new horses and take turns riding them."

"Not today," Will said. "I can't baby-sit your club and get any work done."

"You don't have to 'baby-sit' anyone," she said, helping herself to another piece of toast. She spread homemade apple butter on it and took a bite. "We're quite capable of taking care of ourselves, thank you."

Becky sat down with a mug of coffee. "The move to the summer pasture can certainly wait another day."

Will shook his head. "The weather is supposed to be good today, and then we'll have to get busy with the haying. You're not taking advantage of all the grazing land. That's probably one of the reasons why this place isn't making any money." Of course, employing four old men and an inexperienced foreman didn't help either, but he sure wasn't going to voice that opinion. The men worked as hard as they could and Becky did the work of three women, from what he could see.

Becky smiled at him, an unusual occurrence, he realized. "Then we can go to one of the auctions and pick up some more stock," she said.

"Why would *we* want more stock?"

"You just said yourself that we're not taking advantage of the grazing land that we have."

"That didn't mean I wanted to do anything about it. All I'm saying is that there's range that isn't being used."

"Aside from that," Maude interjected, "I think herding cows would be a wonderful thing for the Not Dead Yet Club to do today. I'm sure the ladies will be thrilled to get the chance to be helpful."

"The ladies?" Will said, turning away from the disconcerting blue eyes of Becky McGregor to stare at his mother. "Herding cows? No way."

"Why not?"

"Someone will get hurt."

"We'll all be careful," Maude insisted, turning to Becky for support. "You can drive the truck the back way and meet us there, with the children, for lunch."

"A picnic?" Becky offered. "What a great idea! You'll have to draw me a map. I'm not familiar with a lot of those roads."

The women turned to Will. "What time should we be ready?" Maude asked.

"Never," he muttered.

"They're coming at nine." She stood up and picked up her dirty dishes. "I'd better get my work clothes on." With that she left the table, putting her dishes in the dishwasher before leaving the room. Becky and Will sat in silence at the table for a few minutes longer.

"This won't work," he said finally.

She smiled again. "It *is* a little bizarre. But maybe it's actually a good idea. You need all the hands you can get. You can't deny that."

"But I'd like to." He couldn't resist smiling back at her. For days he'd tried to stay out of her way, which hadn't been easy since they ate two meals a day together.

"It will be fine. Just try to have a little patience."

"Patience?" That got to him. He'd played close to a hundred games of checkers in the past four days alone. The four-year-old kid was starting to beat him once in a while. "I'm the most patient man in Montana. What's so damned funny?"

"You are," she replied, standing up. "I have to go see if the kids are awake yet. It's going to be a busy morning."

"At least you get to stay here," he muttered.

"And you get to ride north with a dozen women."

"We don't have enough horses."

"Sure we do. Cal will stay here and work on the mower. I won't be riding. That leaves more than enough."

"If you say so."

She patted him on the shoulder. It was brief, but he found the touch of her hand disturbing. "You'll survive. And the cows will, too."

"How can you be so sure about that?"

Becky ignored him and disappeared up the back staircase, leaving him alone in the kitchen to brood about the day. What he'd planned as a necessary work day had turned into a dude ranch picnic with a crew of elderly ladies. And he was supposed to be patient?

Every day he had taken the truck and driven for miles over the ranch property, until he was acquainted once again with its ridges and valleys, creeks and hay fields. It was a middle-sized ranch, but one that had everything:

ranges for all seasons, abundant water and level areas for hay. J.W. had run it well in the years that Will had lived there, but things were different now. It had taken him a while to realize that fact. But because J.W. hadn't taken care of the place for a number of years didn't mean that he, Will Cody, had to step in and take over. The best thing for everyone would be if he sold the ranch. He could give the men some kind of pension, he could help Becky find another job, and he could give his mother the life she deserved.

He didn't know why everyone was against a plan that obviously made sense.

"THAT SON OF YOURS is such a dear," one of the women whispered to Maude. "Has he come back to run the place for you?"

"I hope so," Maude replied, reining in her horse. The Pasos were a big hit, though there weren't enough to go around, of course. But the women had been good about sharing them, arranging to switch horses for the long ride back. Will was limping, though not as much as he had last week. He looked healthier, too. Those dark circles had disappeared from under his eyes. "It all belongs to him now."

She watched as he helped Theresa from her horse and led the animal toward the creek. It was a beautiful day up on the high range, and it had been years since she'd been up here. She took a deep breath and exhaled.

"It's a beautiful place. Do you get up here much?" another one of the women asked.

"No," Maude replied. "I haven't been much for riding these past years, and my brother stopped summering cattle up on this range long ago."

"It would be a wonderful place for a camping trip."

"Yes." There were pine trees and fresh water, a spot not

too far from the main house, and not a ride that would be too strenuous for anyone. Food and tents could be brought round by truck, on the back road. She looked around at the others, who appeared to be no worse for wear from the three-hour ride. Of course the cowboys had done most of the work, with the women in the rear making sure no calves wandered off. It had gone surprisingly well, considering the men's shock over the plan originally. "You're right. When shall we do it?"

The other woman smiled. "Why, any time at all, Maude. None of us is going anywhere."

"That's true." She waved Will over, just as Becky appeared with the children.

"Daddy!" Tommy cried.

Theresa turned to Maude. "*Daddy?* What is that all about?"

"Isn't that sweet? The child calls Will that. We don't know why."

"Will's probably the first man the child's seen who hasn't looked like a grandfather," the doctor pointed out. "He may have seen fathers on television."

"He's not even two."

Theresa shrugged. "I've seen stranger things. Your son doesn't seem to mind." The women watched as Will went over and greeted the young woman and her sons. He swung the toddler onto his shoulders and walked over to the cowboys who were taking care of the horses.

"He's grown used to it."

"Well, that's interesting, too," Theresa said. "He and the girl make a nice-looking couple."

"I think so," Maude agreed. "He's going to stay for the summer. I have my fingers crossed that she'll get him to stay permanently. She's a lovely young woman. I couldn't ask for a nicer daughter-in-law."

"A lot can happen in one summer," Theresa assured her friend. "I met and married my Henry in three weeks."

"Really?"

"Oh, yes, indeed. Once you know you've found the right man, why wait?"

"Young people today don't marry like that anymore. They just have sex and maybe live together for a while, then they go their separate ways. I never did understand it myself."

Theresa patted Maude's shoulder. "We're a different generation, Maude. We don't see things the way they do today. Everything's so fast, so busy."

Maude looked around at the rounded foothills at the base of the Rockies. The sun shone brightly in the biggest blue sky she'd ever seen, and a breeze cooled her forehead after she'd removed her hat. "Not here," she said. "Up here everything's the same as it always was."

"And a good thing it is, too," Theresa agreed. They watched as the men followed Will over the ridge. "I guess they've gone to get lunch."

Maude waved at Becky, who had let Peter run after the men. "She works too hard."

"She's young. And she looks happy. Don't worry about her."

"I'll try," Maude said with a sigh. "I want her to stay around for a long, long time."

"YOU'RE RIGHT," Becky said, looking around at the grazing land. "I should have had the cows brought up here early in the summer."

"You can't know everything," Will said, lifting Tommy from his shoulders and setting him down on the blanket spread under a scrub pine. Becky had set up an assortment of simple picnic food for all of the cowhands, and the ladies looked as if they were having a wonderful time. They'd spread out several blankets under nearby trees and were eating the lunch Becky had brought. "You haven't been ranching here long enough."

"Decker suggested it once, but the cattle were doing fine where they were, and I thought it would be too hard to try to herd them up here."

"The lower pastures are getting overgrazed."

"How bad is that?" She didn't want to have done anything wrong, anything that would damage the ranch. She handed the baby a plastic cup of diced fruit and a plastic spoon. He wouldn't use the spoon, but would throw a fit if he didn't have one just like everyone else.

"You have to rest the land once in a while. A lot of ranchers have gone to a four-year rotation program that mimics the way the buffalo used the land."

He sounded more like a professor than a rodeo rider with a killer smile. "How do you know all of this?"

He shrugged. "I read. I have friends around the country who have some pretty big outfits."

"And yet, you never came here."

"I wasn't welcome. I'm sure you've heard the story."

She shook her head. "Just that there was an argument and you left."

He frowned. "That about sums it up. Aren't you going to eat?"

"Sure." She watched as he sat down by Tommy and picked up a thick beef sandwich. So he was going to sit here and eat with her. She could hear Maude's friends now, saying things like, "Look at the young people, don't they look nice together?"

Peter ran over. "Mr. Decker needs another soda pop!"

"Over there." Becky pointed to the red cooler that she'd filled with cold drinks. Peter had managed to escape his

mother and eat his lunch with the cowboys. He grabbed a
can of root beer and hurried back to the older men who,
clustered under the shade of a tree, looked as if they were
deliberately avoiding the group of chatting women.

"Doesn't he ride?"

"Peter?" He nodded. "He's only four."

"He's old enough to start," Will said. "Maude's old
horse would be good for him. As a place to learn, anyway."

"Maybe." She picked up half a ham sandwich and began
to eat. It had been fun to put together the picnic this morning, to have a couple of hours to putter in the kitchen all by
herself. Tommy had played on the floor with the pots and
pans, while Peter had talked to the dog and colored pictures on a thick pad. She wasn't sure her son was old
enough to climb on a horse and take off across the ranch.

"You're frowning," Will said. "Don't you like horses?"

"I'm just thinking that he seems too young to start riding."

"He's not." But Will smiled at her, and the expression
softened the harsh lines on his face. He looked younger
when he smiled. And sexier, too, which of course wasn't at
all the way Becky wanted the man to look. She preferred
him to be distant and cold, bossy and aloof. That way she
could find it easy to ignore him.

"That's easy for you to say," she quipped, and rolled the
wax paper wrapping into a little ball.

"Let me put him up on one of the old mares tomorrow."
He pointed to the group of quarter horses tethered under a
clump of trees. "See the dun-colored mare? She must be
one of the gentlest horses in Montana."

"Yes, she is. Decker always takes her."

"She'd be a good horse to start with."

"I don't have the time to teach Peter to ride."

"I'll do it," he said. "If you let me."

"Why?"

"Every boy should know how to ride."

"Maybe. When they're six." She smiled, knowing she was starting to sound silly and overprotective. Still, she couldn't picture Peter astride a horse all by himself. He'd ridden in front of her for short distances, but she'd had her arms around him and that had given her the feeling that she was still in charge, still capable of preventing injuries.

Tommy stayed close to Will and finished his fruit and pieces of cheese, then Becky handed him a cookie.

"T'anks," he told her, breaking the cookie in half so he could hold a piece in each hand. "See?" He held it up to Will. "Look."

"Looks good," Will agreed, seemingly unaware that there were sticky fingerprints on his short sleeved shirt. He turned back to Becky. "How long were you married?"

The change of subject took her by surprise. "Three years. Just long enough to have Peter and be pregnant with Tommy."

"So you've been a widow a couple of years now."

"That's right."

"What happened? Do you mind my asking?"

"He crashed his truck into a ditch."

"I'm sorry."

"So was I. He was a man who...liked to take chances. Drove too fast, drank too much, partied too hard. I thought he'd settle down when we got married, but I was wrong." She turned away and began to gather up the food and re-package it for the trip home. "I guess we'd better get going. Tommy's going to need a nap soon, and it's a long drive back to the ranch."

"Becky! Will!" Maude called as she hurried toward them. She caught her breath when she came up to the blanket. "Becky, that was lovely. Just the right touch to a wonderful day."

"I'm glad," Becky said, smiling up at her. "Everyone looks like they're having a good time."

"Oh, we all are." She turned to her son. "But I think we'd better start getting back. Decker is going to get the horses ready and lead us down."

He made a move to stand up, but stopped. Tommy was nestled on the blanket next to him, his head on Will's knee, and his eyes were closed. Will looked at Becky. "What do I do now?"

"Don't move," Maude answered. "You don't want to wake the child. Decker will take us back. You can catch up with us."

"I won't be back right away. As long as I'm up here I plan on checking the fence line."

"Then we won't expect you till suppertime." She waved, thanked Becky for lunch again, then rejoined her friends who were gathering by the horses.

Becky looked at her sleeping son. "I can move him."

"Without waking him up?"

"Well," she began, but Peter ran up.

"Mom! Can I go with Mr. Decker?"

"On the horse?"

"I told you," Will said quietly, but Becky ignored him.

"Yeah, Mom. Where else?"

"Don't be fresh," she said, and he immediately looked contrite. "I'm not sure if that's such a good idea."

"Mr. Decker's given me rides before. I know how to sit real still and not bother the horse."

"Oh, you do, huh?"

"Yep." He looked up at her, all earnest blue eyes and golden brown hair. He wasn't a baby anymore, Becky realized. He was growing up and he lived on a ranch and he would want to ride with the men sooner or later, and this was sooner. She looked over toward the men, and Decker caught her eye and gave her the thumbs-up sign. She'd trust the old cowboy with her life, so she turned back to Peter.

"Okay, but be careful and do what Mr. Decker tells you to do."

"I will." He waved at Will then turned around and ran as fast as his little legs would carry him back to the waiting cowboy and dun mare.

"He probably thinks he'd better run away before I change my mind." She sat back on the blanket and continued putting lids on plastic containers of leftover food. She looked over at Tommy. His head on Will's thigh didn't look very comfortable, so she tucked the food into a cardboard box and then scooted over to the sleeping child.

"You don't have to wake him," Will said. "I can sit here for a couple of minutes."

"No, that's okay. You have work to do and so do I." She gently eased her hand under Tommy's head, ignoring the warmth of Will's jean-covered thigh and the embarrassing closeness between the two of them. She cradled the child's head in her hand and moved him so he lay on the blanket. He never opened his eyes, so she covered his shoulders with a dish towel that she'd brought to line a basket of rolls. Will edged away until he was off the blanket, then he stood up.

"I'll be back," he said, before striding off to the group of men, horses and women. Becky packed up the food, dumping the trash into a plastic bag and putting the tin plates into another box she'd brought for dirty dishes. She'd carry everything to the car after Tommy woke up, but for now she'd pack everything up and be prepared to leave. Maybe he would go back to sleep in the car. It was an hour's drive home, a good time for a nap.

When she'd finished that chore, and waved goodbye to Maude, Peter and the rest, Will returned to the shaded blanket and sat down beside her.

"I'll take these to the car for you," he offered, picking up one of the boxes.

"Thanks, but—"

"Stay here with the baby," Will ordered.

Well, that was a good order, Becky thought, smiling to herself. She wouldn't mind sitting under this tree high in the foothills of the Rockies, while a man packed up the station wagon for her. There was a bit of shade and a good breeze, with a view of the ranch valley below that was breathtaking. She should have driven up here more often. If not for moving cattle, then just to sit and enjoy the quiet. But there wasn't time for sitting around, not with all the work there was to do.

Will returned, scooped up the rest of the boxes and plastic bags, and made another trip over the hill to where the car was parked. There were a series of gravel roads that intersected the ranch, but she hadn't driven on all of them, at least not enough to know her way around. That wouldn't matter now, with Will talking about selling. It didn't make sense to sell a place that could be fixed up. That it was old and needed work only made it more of a challenge.

Will returned and, instead of expecting her to stand, sat down on the blanket beside her. He took off his hat, lay back and closed his eyes.

"I thought you were going to fix fence," Becky said, keeping her voice low. She sat between the sleeping baby and the cowboy and fought the urge to take a nap, too. Just looking at the two of them was making her want to yawn.

Will kept his eyes closed. "I've been herding women and cows for hours. The fence can wait a few more minutes."

She knew she should go. If she left now, she could get a head start on dinner before the others came back. If she left now, she would miss sitting in one spot for a while and enjoying the quiet. She leaned back, too, just a little, and rested on her bent arms. That felt so good she pondered stretching out, too. After all, there was plenty of room on the blanket to lie down without touching the man beside her. She shouldn't be the least bit embarrassed, she reminded herself, and scooted down so her head was next to the baby's. Somewhere overhead a bird called, and Becky told herself she was just resting, nothing else. What else could she do, she mused, with Tommy and Will sound asleep? Waking them up would be cruel. She tucked her arms under her head and closed her eyes. The last thing she heard was the sound of the wind.

"Becky?"

The voice was low, near her ear. She turned toward it and opened her eyes, only to find her face inches apart from Will's. His eyes were dark; she'd never noticed the thick eyelashes before. She must have fallen asleep, because she couldn't remember where she was or what she was doing.

"You've been sleeping," he supplied, sensing her confusion. "We all have."

Another face came into view, this time the chubby face of Tommy. He smiled, all pink cheeks and happy expression as he leaned over her legs to peer at her. "Mommy! Wake up!"

"Okay," Becky said, trying to do that. She never took naps, but she rarely sat down in the middle of the day either. She struggled to sit up, and Will gave her his hand and helped pull her to a sitting position.

"How long—"

"About thirty minutes." He grinned. "I guess we all needed the rest."

Tommy found a piece of cookie and picked it up from the blanket and put it in his mouth. "Cookies," he said, smiling at them.

"I'll give you another one later," she promised, and turned back to the man beside her. "He likes..."

He was too close, and his gaze had dropped to her lips. She hadn't realized that he still held her hand, and when she moved to pull it away he didn't release her. Instead he tugged her ever so gently toward him until their lips were almost touching. He hesitated then, as if thinking it over. And Becky was too surprised to move away. He leaned forward enough to touch her lips with his, a brief exploring kiss that deepened into something stronger. He continued to hold her hand, but otherwise their bodies remained apart. Becky tilted her head, he slanted his lips across hers and kissed her as if he meant it. Becky wanted to lean into him, wanted to curl her fingers into his hair and forget that she worked for him now, that they were not alone, that this wasn't simply a temporary lapse in judgment.

When he was done, he lifted his mouth from hers and looked into her eyes. "Sorry," he said, with little sorrow coloring his voice. "I couldn't resist it."

"Daddy! I wanna see horse," Tommy said, saving Becky from having to come up with a response. She didn't know if she was sorry or not that he'd kissed her. But she couldn't think while he looked at her. Tommy tumbled into Will's lap and threw his arms around the man's neck.

"I'll show you the horse," Will said, "but I'm not your daddy." He put his hat on and looked over at Becky. "Can't you get him to stop calling me that?"

"I've tried. He doesn't seem to understand." She held out her arms. "Come here, Tommy."

"No," the boy said. "No, no, no."

Will chuckled. "I guess we're going to go see the horse." He stood up, swinging the child into his arms at the same time.

"I guess you are," Becky said, wishing her voice didn't sound quite so trembly. She stood up and, as Will and Tommy went to pet the chestnut mare, Becky folded the blanket into a neat square and gathered up the few things that still remained. He'd kissed her, but she wouldn't think about that now.

It was meaningless anyway. Just a little temptation in the middle of a quiet afternoon. That kind of thing wouldn't happen again, she knew. She turned and watched the patient way Will lifted Tommy onto the horse and let him pretend to ride the animal. The cowboy, for all of his faults, was kind to the children.

But that didn't mean their mother had to go around kissing the man. He was another one of those men who couldn't stay long in one place, who had to have the excitement of the rodeo and the adventure of traveling from one place to another. He wasn't for her. She needed a man who would come home for supper each night, who would be right there in the bed with her come sunrise.

Becky waited for Will and her son to quit playing with the horse and start toward her. She would take her son home and stop thinking foolish thoughts. And she would certainly try to forget this had ever happened.

THAT WAS DUMB, Will concluded. He had a lot of time to think about what a dumb stunt he'd pulled, kissing Becky like that. It was just that she'd looked so sweet, napping like that. He'd never seen her totally still before. He hadn't slept long, just dozed for a few minutes. And then he'd become intrigued with watching her until the little boy started to stir.

Then he'd known he should wake her, though he hated to do it. She was a pretty woman. He'd like to know what she'd look like with her hair down and all soft and curling around her face.

He should never have taken her hand. He never should have touched her at all. Will grimaced as he came to yet another section of trampled fence wire. He had brought the necessary supplies to fix fence, but it wasn't a job that anyone really liked to do.

But it had to be done, and the others couldn't be expected to work such long hours. He took a hammer from his pack and fixed the wire, muttering an oath when he hit the edge of his thumb on the second stroke of the hammer. He should never have kissed her.

Or he should never have stopped.

BECKY DROVE DOWN the mountain talking nonstop to her son. "You have to stop calling Will 'Daddy.' He's not your daddy."

Tommy just grinned at her. "I ride horse," he said. "Nice horse."

"Yes, it was a nice horse, but you can't go around calling people daddy. It's embarrassing," she muttered under her breath. She'd seen a couple of the women's faces when they'd heard Tommy holler to Will when they arrived. She hoped Maude had explained that the toddler was a little mixed-up and was no one's love child, least of all Will Cody's.

"You had a daddy, but he went to heaven," Becky tried again, but the toddler bounced in his car seat and pointed toward some cattle. "Cows, Mamma, cows!"

"I know." There was no shortage of cows, even if Will

felt they weren't running enough head to make a profit. How on earth was she supposed to know how much stock to run or where to graze them? If Decker or Cal didn't tell her, she wouldn't know. And she couldn't expect the men to know everything about a ranch they hadn't lived on for at least ten years.

From now on, Becky decided, moving slowly along the winding gravel road, she would let Will call the shots around here. It was his ranch; it was time he took care of it. That would leave her time to help Maude with the horses and the entertaining. They would make the most of the SV while they could.

7

"Is the mower going to be ready soon?"

Cal looked up from his cup of coffee and blinked at the morning sun shining through the kitchen window of the bunkhouse. "I reckon I don't know."

"Well, when, then?" Will tried to hide his frustration. They were losing valuable time by not getting the hay cut now. The weather was good, hot and dry, and no rain was forecast for the next few days.

"I need a couple of parts. Waiting for them to arrive."

"In town?"

"Yeah. At Barker's. He said he'd call when they came in."

"I'll give them a call and see what the holdup is." Will turned to Decker. "We'll start with the eastern meadow, then move north."

"Who's going to do the driving?"

"I plan to," Will said, watching expressions of relief cross the men's faces. None of the men wanted to admit their eyesight wasn't what it used to be. "I haven't done it in years, but I guess it's still the same."

"I reckon it is," Decker said. "And the baler?"

Will turned to back to Cal. "That's waiting for parts, too?"

"Yep. The forklift is working okay, though."

Which didn't mean anything right now, if the mower couldn't cut the hay into windrows and the baler, which took the windrows and rolled the hay into round bales, wasn't working either. No wonder his uncle hadn't bothered haying. He'd let the cattle survive as best they could on the winter range without feeding them anything. A hell of a way to run a cattle operation, Will fumed.

He poured himself another cup of coffee and walked over to the window to see if Becky was around yet. He'd taken over the morning meetings with the men during the past days. He thought she'd squawk about that, but she hadn't. She'd just looked at him for a long moment as if she couldn't figure out what he was doing, then she'd gone back to washing dishes.

"I don't understand women," Will muttered, then realized too late that he'd spoken out loud.

"No one does," Cal drawled. "It ain't possible."

Will didn't turn away from the window. A truck was coming up the road, which interested him. It was only eight o'clock on a Saturday morning, not a time to be expecting visitors. "Someone's coming."

"Might be one of Maude's friends again," Decker said, walking over to stand beside Will and peer out the window. Cal got up too and tried to look past Will's shoulder.

"Probably Doc Thomas. I had Becky call him for more vaccine."

Decker went back to his coffee. "He's always happy to get a call from the SV. I think he goes to bed nights prayin' for an excuse to get out here."

Will turned from the window. "Decker, what the hell are you talking about?"

"Doc Thomas. He's a little older than you, never married. He has a little place in town."

"So?"

"So," Decker drawled, looking as if he wanted to smile. "So maybe he likes to visit ranches where there's a pretty blond single lady who smiles real nice and ain't afraid of a little cow manure."

"Becky."

"Well, you have to wonder why no red-blooded man has taken her out of here."

"She's a widow."

"For a couple of years. She's young, and she warn't married long. Plenty of time to have more little ones and set up housekeeping again."

"Does she like this guy?"

Decker shrugged. "Hard to tell. But she might like him more now, with you talking about selling out and her needing a home. She might be looking to the future more than she used to."

Will turned back to the window and frowned. A shiny green truck rolled into the yard by the house and came to a stop. A tall heavy man stepped out, tucked in his shirt and slicked back his hair with the palm of his hand before putting on his hat. He looked for all the world like a man going courting. He looked like an idiot. In fact, he was an idiot if he thought he had a chance with Becky. Will headed toward the door. He intended to find out exactly what was on the veterinarian's mind.

"That was mighty interesting," Decker said to the others after Will hurried out the door. The men crowded around the windows and watched the young man walk past the barns and outbuildings toward the main house.

"You bet," Cal agreed. "This is all gonna get pretty good now."

"Just like Maude said," Decker added.

"Maude?" Oatey glanced his way. "Does that old gal have something to do with this?"

"Well, she didn't call the vet, that's for sure," Decker replied. "But she said the two of them—our Miss Becky and Will—are perfect for each other."

They all nodded their agreement.

Oatey looked doubtful. "Will doesn't think so, I'll bet."

"That boy's got a long way to go," Decker warned. "He'll be a hard one to pin down, I told Maude. She thinks it's only a matter of time. If they spend enough time together, that is."

"Time together," Cal repeated. "I reckon that could be arranged."

Malone scratched his head. "How do we do that?"

"We've got to leave them alone. Things always happen when a young couple spends time alone."

They nodded at Decker's wisdom. They always nodded at Decker's wisdom.

"You want one of us to go out there and cut Doc Thomas out of the herd?"

Decker shook his head. "Nope. The boss needs a kick in the butt, and the vet might be just the one to do it." He turned from the window as Will disappeared from view. "Let's make ourselves another pot of coffee and leave the young people to sort this one out."

Cal nodded. "We'll leave 'em alone then, starting now."

"Damn right," Malone agreed, and Oatey, not to be left out, yawned and nodded his agreement.

BECKY DIDN'T EXPECT to see Mike Thomas at the back door, but she waved him in. "You're around pretty early, especially on a Saturday," she said, automatically pouring him a cup of coffee. He was a nice-looking man, with a square face and light brown hair. His eyes were kind, and he tended to be shy. She'd always felt bad about the twice he'd asked her out. It was hard to be interested in dating when you were so tired you wanted to cry.

"I brought extra vaccine," he explained, stepping carefully into the kitchen. Lady trotted in and growled at him.

"Australian shepherd," the vet said. "Nice breed for herding cattle." He stood still and let the dog sniff his hand before he moved into the kitchen. "When did you get her?"

Becky handed him the coffee. "She's not mine. Maude's son is here for a while and she belongs to him, though lately she's so attached to Peter I think she's forgotten who she belongs to." The dog turned away and left the room, heading toward the den where Peter was watching cartoons on television.

"Thanks." He sat down at the kitchen table and took a sip. "I heard Maude's son came home to sell the ranch."

"That's what he says, though Maude's hoping he'll change his mind."

"Well, if he's anything like his uncle, he won't," the vet declared.

"I'm afraid I don't understand your meaning," Will said, walking into the room. Becky looked up, realizing that Will must have been on the porch long enough to have overheard.

"We were just talking—" she started to say, but Mike had turned toward Will and stood up. The vet stuck out his hand.

"You must be Maude's son. I'm Mike Thomas, local horse doctor."

Will had no choice but to shake the man's hand. "Will Cody. Glad to meet you."

He didn't sound glad, Becky noted. In fact, he sounded like he'd had a rough morning and wanted to take it out on someone. Too bad the shy veterinarian was the first man who got in his way. "Want coffee?"

"Sure."

Lady stuck her head in the kitchen, saw Will and turned

around without greeting him. *Oh, it's only you*, seemed to be her expression, and Becky smiled as she poured the coffee. Maude was still asleep, and Tommy, tolerating his playpen, was watching cartoons in the den with Peter. Becky put the mug on the table in front of Will and turned to the vet.

"I'll bet you've come to see the Pasos."

"Yes, that and to see if you needed any medical supplies. And I also wanted to ask you—"

"Mike," Will interjected, cutting off the man's words. "What do you know about these Spanish horses my mother has bought?"

Mike turned away from Becky. "Well, they're supposed to be fine riding horses, from what I've heard."

"I'd like you to look them over, if you don't mind."

"Well," the vet hesitated, looking at Becky who was leaning against the counter watching the men. She smiled, and he said, "Sure, I'll be glad to have a quick look. I'm due over at the Jeffersons', but it's not an emergency."

"Great," Will said, standing up. "Let's go."

"Uh, fine." He put down his coffee and turned to Becky. "Are you coming?"

"I can't leave the boys alone," she said.

"Then I'll stop in on my way out."

"Come on, Doc," Will urged, slapping his hat on his head. "We're wasting time."

Wasting time? Becky had seen him make a cup of coffee last half an hour while he doodled in his account books or talked about cattle with Decker. He wasn't a morning person by any stretch of the imagination, yet here he was acting like he had as much energy as Tommy.

"See ya," Mike said, casting a wistful look her way. She watched the men leave and heard the screen door shut. Mike Thomas was going to ask her out again. Maybe it would be good to go out with the man. Maybe she needed to get out, date again, see someone other than Will Cody. Perhaps going out with Doc Thomas would dilute the attraction she had to the rodeo rider. Mike was a nice man, even though his conversation tended to be mostly about bovine diseases. He loved cattle and he certainly seemed to enjoy working in this part of Montana. She would say yes. Unless she couldn't find a sitter or one of the boys took sick or Maude needed her for something that no one else could do. She would say yes to Mike and she would put Will Cody and his bone-melting kiss right out of her mind once and for all.

"WELL, I DON'T THINK it's right that you should be baby-sitting, that's all," Will grumbled. He'd had to watch Becky climb into the vet's truck and head for town. She'd mentioned dinner and the early movie at the Ortheum, Dry Gulch's new twin cinema. She'd worn a pretty dress, looped her long hair at the nape of her neck and she'd had lipstick on. Lipstick! For the vet.

"I don't mind." Maude reached over and gave Tommy another cracker. "I can pretend they're my grandchildren."

"That's ridiculous."

"At this rate I'll never have any from you, so why not have fun with Becky's boys?" She tickled Tommy's chin and made him smile.

"You don't know that I won't have children. I've never said that." The little boy broke the cracker in half and stretched his hand toward Will.

"Daddy? 'Racker, okay?"

Will took the soggy piece of cracker and pretended to eat it. "Thanks, kid."

Maude gave Will a withering look. "As if your life-style would be good for raising a family!"

"I've made a lot of money working the rodeo," he said, defending himself.

"Money isn't everything," she sniffed. "Whatever happened to love and family and settling down?"

He sighed and picked up his glass of iced tea. "I will, when I'm older."

"You're old enough now, with a busted knee and a hurt back."

"Don't remind me. It's getting better."

"And you'll get hurt all over again, the minute you start up riding broncs and bulls again. Don't think you're fooling me."

"I don't," he said, but he did. He was fooling himself, too, thinking that he could go back to he rodeo. The doctor had warned him he'd be crippled permanently if he kept working. Trouble was, he didn't know anything else. Ranching didn't count. He sure as hell wasn't going to stay here. Maybe he'd buy a bigger place after the SV was sold. That was a possibility, too. But he didn't want to have employees, he didn't want to have to worry about bank loans and frozen calves born too soon, or horses that got sick for mysterious reasons and fence that always needed fixing.

He wondered what he did want. And he knew.

"Let's go to town," he said, giving his mother what he hoped was a charming, irresistible smile.

"You can. I can't." She pointed to Tommy. "I'm baby-sitting, remember?"

"We'll all go. We'll take the kids and get some ice-cream cones. They still have ice cream at the Dairy Freeze, don't they?"

She gave him an odd look, like he'd lost his mind. "Well, yes, I guess so, but—"

"You like ice cream, Tommy?"

The little boy smiled. "I like Daddy. Ice cream?"

"Good. It's two against one." He stood up. "I'll take a quick shower and clean up, then we'll take the wagon and go to town. Is the car seat still in there?"

"It should be."

"Fine. Ice cream it is, then." He hurried upstairs to clean up before Maude could change her mind. Becky wasn't the only person who could go to town on a Saturday night.

"WE CAN'T SPOIL Becky's evening," Maude said, coming to a halt on the sidewalk.

"We're not spoiling anything," Will lied. He fully intended to interrupt any romantic inclinations that the veterinarian had toward Becky. He looked up at the marquee. "She's seeing one movie, we'll be seeing another."

"Oh, boy!" Peter grinned and hurried to the poster of a three-headed monster.

"That looks scary," Maude protested.

"It's supposed to be funny. It's a Disney picture. Rated PG." And it got out three minutes before the romantic comedy next door, the one he was sure Becky and the horny doctor were seeing.

"Popcorn," Tommy said, pointing to the window where a large machine popped corn. Will tightened his grip on the boy before he could lunge out of his arms. "Does this kid ever stop eating?"

"He's a growing boy."

Will stepped up to the window and bought the tickets. "One adult, one senior citizen and two children," he told the teenager at the cash register.

"I hate being called that," Maude grumbled.

"What?" He lifted Tommy from his shoulders and realized they hadn't brought extra diapers. Then he tucked him under his arm and corralled Pete, who had wandered down the sidewalk in search of pennies.

"Senior citi— Where are you going?"

"Herding calves," he muttered, guiding them all inside the theater. Originally one screen, the folks who owned it had split it into two smaller theaters. The one showing the PG-rated monster movie was packed with kids. Big kids, little kids and noisy kids, all eating candy or popcorn. Most were throwing candy or popcorn at each other.

"I'm not sure this is such a good idea," Maude said, rejecting one seat because it was covered with something sticky.

"Over here," Will said, finding four seats on the side. It was a damn good idea to be in the same place as Becky and her date. The guy was new in town. He could be some kind of sex pervert.

Peter looked around, clearly impressed by the activity. "Can we have popcorn?"

"Popcorn! Popcorn!" Tommy bounced up and down in his seat, then climbed on Will's lap and waited for the popcorn to appear.

"Sure." He gave the baby to Maude and took Peter with him to buy soda pop, a big container of buttered popcorn and a fistful of overpriced candy bars. They would have fun. They would see their mother afterward, and she wouldn't be able to resist going home with them instead of the mysterious doctor. He was doing her a favor.

Will started to doubt himself fifteen minutes into the movie. Cartoon monsters were still monsters, and Tommy started to whimper whenever the purple one with the big teeth appeared on the screen. The child sat on Will's lap, his arms wrapped around the man's neck. Peter was entranced, ate enough popcorn to feed a yearling calf for a year, and belched his way through a container of root beer that was supposed to be a medium and looked like half a gallon.

It took a few minutes to get out of the theater when the movie had ended. Tommy cried for his mother and Peter had to go to the bathroom, so Will took him and left Tommy screaming "Daddy, Daddy!" at the top of his lungs.

When he returned to the lobby with Peter, Becky and her square-faced date were talking to Maude. Tommy was in Becky's arms and the doc had the nerve to smile at the child as if he liked kids.

Tommy screamed. Will hid a smile. The doc looked a little like the nasty big-headed monster that ate all the little boys' licorice sticks. "Not my daddy," the little boy hollered. "Go away!"

The vet backed up a step. "I don't think I've met your younger son," he said to Becky.

"He's overexcited," Maude said.

"He must be tired." Becky patted Tommy's back and said something soothing as Peter and Will joined them.

"Hey," Will said, as Tommy lifted his tearstained face from his mother's shoulders and looked at the cowboy. Will felt his heart drop. He held out his arms and took the boy from Becky. Poor Tommy looked as if he'd had enough excitement for one day. "He had fun at the movie, for most of the time," he tried to explain. Becky looked as if she didn't believe him.

"I didn't know you were coming to the show," she said.

"Hi, Doc," Will said, nodding toward the now confused looking man. Good. Let him see that dating Becky wasn't going to be as easy as he thought. "How was the movie?"

"Fine," the man said, taking Becky's elbow. "We were just going out for a drink. Too bad you can't join us."

"Yeah. Too bad." The doc didn't sound sorry, Will noticed. Relieved was more like it.

"Mom?" Peter looked up at her. "When are you coming home?"

"Soon," she promised, giving Peter a kiss. "You go home and go to bed. I won't be much longer."

"Take your time," Maude insisted. "They'll go right to sleep."

"Mama?" Tommy reached out one hand, while his head rested on Will's shoulder.

"Night-night," Becky said. The vet shifted impatiently. "We really should—"

"Say good-night to Mommy," Will interjected. "She'll be home soon."

"'Night, Mommy." Tommy, his face sticky with dried chocolate, yawned.

Becky looked torn, as if she wanted to go home with the children, yet couldn't get rid of her date. Good, Will thought. She needed to be home anyway.

"Let's go," Will said, taking Peter's hand. "I'll tell you a story about a rodeo clown before you go to sleep."

"Take your time," Maude repeated, saying good-night to the couple.

"I'll be home soon," Becky promised.

Will tried to look as if he didn't care. "No hurry." He led his little family down the sidewalk and around the corner to where he'd parked the station wagon. That had gone well. Nothing romantic was going to happen between Becky and the doc while she had visions of her sons looking as if they needed her at home. He got the kids settled inside the wagon, then began the long ride back to the ranch.

"Are you proud of yourself?" Maude whispered.

"Proud of what?" Will kept his voice carefully casual.

"That little performance," Maude said. "Now I understand why you *had* to go to town tonight—"

"It's Saturday," he interjected. "Going to town on a Saturday night is not exactly an original idea."

"And why you *had* to go to the movies," she finished, ignoring his words. "You wanted to ruin that girl's evening."

Will looked in the rearview mirror and saw that both boys were asleep. "Ruin it? Do you think so?"

"Becky never gets to go out and have a nice time. And there we were, following her around with her children." Maude sighed. "I hope she'll forgive me."

"Forgive you? It was all my idea." And it was a good one, too. "Besides, the kids had fun. And just how much do you know about that vet, anyway?"

"His father's a minister down in Bozeman. He's highly thought of around here. He's done a good job."

"And he's looking for a wife, too, I'll bet."

"Well, not everyone is like you," Maude commented. "Most men want to find a good woman and settle down."

"Yeah, well, I'm not most men." What he wanted to do was take Becky into the barn or the stable or the nearest bedroom and make love to her. Most men would want the same thing, but he didn't point that out to his mother. "And the doctor there might not want to get married either, especially to a woman with two children."

Maude sighed. "That's the trouble. I never got a chance to marry again after your father died, and I always regretted it. I hate to see Becky stuck on the ranch, with only a few old people for company. She needs to be around people her own age."

"She could get a job in town when the ranch is sold. Or she could move to a town like Bozeman." Will realized he didn't like that idea much himself.

"I thought we weren't going to talk about selling out, at least not for a while."

He shrugged. "I still think it's a good idea."

"I don't."

"It's for your own good."

"I should know what's for my own good," Maude declared. "I'm older than you, and wiser. Just because you want something your way doesn't mean you're going to get it, young man."

Will smiled over at her. "Yes, ma'am, I'll keep that in mind."

"And leave Becky alone, unless you're planning to stick around." She closed her eyes and leaned her head back, ending the conversation. Will frowned into the darkness as the miles sped by. They would be home in a little while, and he found himself looking forward to turning down that road. For the first time in his life he felt he had a place to come home to.

A dangerous thought, he realized, gripping the steering wheel. He wasn't the kind of man to stay in one place. He was used to traveling, to being on his own. He was accustomed to living a life that didn't depend on the weather and the price of beef and the opinions of women. It was a good life, but somehow he had the unsettling feeling that it was all going to change. And there wouldn't be a damn thing he could do about it.

SHE SHOULD HAVE expected Will to be awake still when she got home. After all, it wasn't even eleven o'clock. It just felt later, especially since she'd been up since five, but the living-room lights were on. Becky opened the back door quietly as Mike drove away, and walked swiftly through the kitchen and up the back stairs to her room.

She didn't want to see anyone, least of all Will Cody. She didn't know what he'd been doing, taking her kids to the movies and acting as if he were having a good time. Tommy Lee had snuggled into the cowboy's arms and called him Daddy and later her date had asked an awful lot of questions about Maude's son and his plans for the future.

It had been embarrassing. She hurried to the boys' room, peeked to make sure they were all right, then left their room to go to her own.

"So, you're home," Will said. He leaned against the doorjamb, effectively blocking the door to her bedroom. The hall was dark, except for the small glow of a night-light by the stairs. "You're home early."

"I'm tired."

"Or he's as boring as he looks," Will muttered, reaching for her doorknob. He swung her door open. "There you go. All yours."

"Thanks." She waited for him to move away, but he didn't. "That was nice of you to take the kids to town."

He shrugged. "They're good kids."

"Yes."

"I might've fed 'em too much."

"That's okay." She waited once again for him to move out of the way.

"What about you?"

"What about me?"

"Did the vet feed you?"

"Yes."

"Did you have a good time?" Becky made a move to go to her room, but he shifted his body slightly to block her. "You didn't answer my question."

"Yes, I had a good time," she replied. She didn't want to stand there in the dark hallway and banter with Will. She felt sad and vulnerable and very much alone tonight, and she didn't want to stand in the hall and tell Will Cody—especially Will Cody—that Mike Thomas had kissed her and it had been a kiss devoid of any passion. At least on her part.

Which was disappointing, because after kissing Will a few days ago, she would have figured she was desperate for a little passion.

"Did he kiss you?"

Becky looked up at him, wondering if he could now read her mind. "That's none of your business."

"Did he kiss you like this?" He bent down and brushed his lips against hers for a sweet, brief moment. Then Will looked at her, and when she didn't answer, he tried again. "Or was it more like this?"

This time he took longer, applied more pressure, tempted her to open her lips with the teasing touch of his tongue. Becky tried not to react, but she touched his forearms in an instinctive need to hold on.

When he lifted his mouth from hers, he didn't move. "Well?"

"I think you'd better—"

"You don't look like a woman who's been kissed," he murmured, touching her cheek with his palm. "At least, not when you came home."

"It's none of your—"

"So he didn't kiss you like this, either," he said, ignoring her feeble protests and taking possession of her lips again. This time his arms went around her. This time her hands crept up to his shoulders. She parted her lips, he took her mouth with his tongue and kissed for long, heated moments until Becky wondered if her knees would hold her. His body was hot and hard, his cotton shirt soft under her fingertips. She touched a triangle of warm skin above the unbuttoned collar of his shirt and wished, for the briefest second, that she could touch more of him. Her body was warm where it was pressed against his, and his mouth tempted her to lose all reason and forget herself.

He ended the kiss and took a deep breath, looking shaken.

"Are you finished?" she managed to say, lifting her chin and taking a step backward, out of his arms. Out of danger. She wouldn't give him the satisfaction of knowing how he'd affected her.

He smiled, and she knew she hadn't fooled him at all. "Now you've been kissed, Miss Becky."

"Am I supposed to say thank-you?"

Will shook his head. "You're supposed to go into that room and shut your door, before we forget where we are."

"And *who* we are," she reminded him. "I'm not one of your rodeo one-night stands."

"Which makes you much more dangerous," he muttered, and backed away from her door. Becky went inside and shut the door behind her. God help her, she wanted to invite him in. She wanted to be held, and she wanted to be loved. And she didn't want to be alone anymore. But Will Cody was not the man for her, and the sooner she could leave the SV the better. There was no sense fooling herself any longer. This wasn't really her home, and the whims of a cowboy could change everything.

8

"YOU SHOULD'VE seen it," Maude said, handing Decker a mug of coffee. They leaned on the fence and looked at the Pasos cavorting in the small pasture. "He was jealous last night. I know he was."

"Will was jealous of the vet?" Decker grinned. "That's goldarn funny, Maudie."

"When he found out Becky was going on a date, he dragged us all to town and to the movies, too, where he had it all figured to just happen to run into Becky and the doc. Acted real casual, too, like he took kids to the movies every Saturday night of his life."

Decker didn't look as if he believed one word she said. "What did Becky do?"

"Well, she wanted to be with those kids, naturally. Which was what my silly son was counting on. But she couldn't be rude to the doc, either, so they went off to get a drink and we came home." Maude surveyed the horses. They were beautiful. and next year there would be foals. And the year after that, too. Everything was going so well now. It made her smile just to think about it all.

Decker gazed at her as if he still didn't believe what she was describing. "And Will? He came home too?"

"Oh, yes, and was he ever pleased with himself! I gave him a piece of my mind on the way home, just so he wouldn't know how tickled I was."

"A smoke screen."

"Yep. He was *jealous*, Decker. From his hat right down to his boots, pure jealous. It was a sight to see, all right." She adjusted her hat against the glare of the sun. "Going to be another hot one today," she muttered. "I don't know what happened after I went to bed, but I made sure to go right upstairs. I can see the road from up there anyway, and it wasn't an hour and a half before Becky came home."

The cowboy grinned. "Must've been a quick drink."

Maude nodded. "She must have hightailed it back to the ranch pretty quick. I feel kinda bad, like I spoiled her evening."

"I wouldn't worry about that, Maude. You've got what they call the 'big picture' in mind," Decker agreed, eyeing his boss.

"That's right, I do. I want her to stay and Will to stay and I want grandchildren. I want this ranch to stay in the family, like it's supposed to. And if Will falls for Becky, then everything will fall into place."

"You're an optimistic woman, Maude."

She shook her head. "I'm a practical woman, Deck. I know what has to be done, and the next step is for Will and Becky to, um, make love."

The old cowboy scratched his head and replaced his hat. "I don't know how the hell you're going to figure that one out. That stuff is sure tricky. In my day, things were simpler."

Maude smiled. "We just need to keep them together. He's a hot-blooded man, and she's a woman who's been alone a long time. Things will take care of themselves."

Decker nodded. "All right. I'll tell the rest of the men. They're already laughin' about the way Will moons around over that young woman."

"Good." Maude sighed with contentment and watched

her beautiful horses. "I've got too much at stake to let it all disappear now."

"We all do," Decker reminded her. "Every single one of us is out of a home if Will sells this place."

"I know." Maude sighed. "I'm doing my best, but that boy is sure stubborn. He won't see what's good for him, not when it's right under his nose."

"He'll come around," Decker promised. "The boys and I will help."

Maude nodded, hoping she looked more confident than she felt. A jealous cowboy was nothing new, but one who would settle down and marry a widow with a couple of kids? Now *that* was going to take a miracle.

"MAUDE, I'VE DECIDED to start looking for another job," Becky said. She'd waited until after lunch, when Tommy was with Oatey having a rest and she and Maude were alone in the kitchen. Peter was helping Decker with the horses, and she and Maude were trying to cook a few meals ahead. During the haying they would need more food and have less time to cook it.

"For heaven's sake. Why?" Maude, taking a pan of hard-boiled eggs from the stove, stopped and turned around. Her expression made Becky feel terrible.

"Be careful you don't burn yourself," she said, turning on the cold water faucet as Maude placed the pan in the sink and poured off the boiling water.

"I don't know why we're going to all this trouble for dev-iled eggs anyway," Maude grumbled.

"They're Decker's favorite. I promised." She left the eggs in the cold water to cool for peeling and went over to the stove to stir the lasagna noodles.

"You can't leave," Maude said, following her. "Just what exactly brought this on?"

"I just think it's time," Becky said, pretending to be engrossed in the pan of boiling pasta. She couldn't say *I'm trying to avoid your sexy son.*

"I'm not letting Will sell the ranch, if that's what you have on your mind," the old woman declared. "We're still going to raise horses and the Not Dead Yet Club is going to pay to ride them. I was talking to a man from Silver Adventures the other day and he's even—"

"Maude, I can't." Her adventures, silver or any other color, were over. It was time she stopped pinning her hopes on breeding horses and the dreams of a very kind but unrealistic employer. The timer went off, announcing the noodles were cooked, so Becky turned the stove off. "Would you take the eggs out of the sink?"

"You want me to leave them in the pan?"

"Sure. I just need the sink free for the colander." It took a few minutes to drain and rinse the noodles, and by the time the job was done Becky's face was flushed and perspiration dotted her forehead. A hot July afternoon wasn't the best time to be cooking, but she didn't have any other free time today, and the job had to be done. According to Decker, the haying would begin soon.

Maude fussed nearby. "I just don't understand," she muttered, watching Becky run cold water over the lasagna noodles.

"This stops them from cooking."

"Not that. Why you think you have to find another job."

"Because you and I both know that everything around here is going to change, whether you like it or not. You can't stop your son from selling this ranch, and you can't blame him for wanting you to move near him."

"*He* should be moving near me," she sniffed. "Everything would be perfect if he'd show some sense."

"He is," Becky said, turning to her friend. "He's trying to

do what's best for you, no matter how much you don't think he's doing the right thing. We need help with this place and you and I have to admit it."

"At last," Will said, stepping into the kitchen. "Someone is making sense."

Becky didn't turn around to look at him. She wiped her brow with her sleeve and started opening jars of spaghetti sauce.

"Becky's leaving," Maude told him. "I expect you to do something to change her mind. I'm going to take my nap." She gave her son a withering look as she passed him on her way out of the room. "Do something intelligent, like make her understand she has a job here."

Becky winced. She didn't need Will Cody to talk her into staying, especially after last night.

Will shrugged. "I came in to tell you that your son is going to have a riding lesson. Do you want to watch?"

"Yes. No." She finally looked up at him and hoped she wouldn't blush. She was too old to blush because a cowboy had kissed her. "I don't know."

He tilted his hat from his forehead and frowned at her. "You're not leaving because of what happened last night, are you?"

"Of course not."

"Well, good. Because it's going to happen again." His eyes twinkled with mischief.

"No, it's not," Becky said, but she smiled. She could take his teasing; she couldn't take his lovemaking.

"I guess," he drawled, stepping closer, "that's a matter of opinion. You coming outside or not?"

"Okay, but just for a few minutes. Until I see what you and Peter have cooked up." She untied her apron and tossed it on a chair. "I'm getting food ready for the haying."

"Maude's not having another one of her parties, is she?"

"Well..."

He put his hand up. "Don't tell me. I'm sure I'll hear about it soon enough."

Becky grabbed her hat from its hook on the porch and went outside into the bright summer sun. It was hot, with a breeze blowing that did little to cool the air. When they reached the corral, Becky saw her son standing with Decker beside a little mare. He waved when he saw her, and Decker's face broke into a grin.

"Well, well," the old man said. "I see we've got an audience, boy."

Peter didn't leave the horse's side, as if he was afraid that if he did, his mother wouldn't let him return. "Hey, Mom," he called. "I'm gonna be a cowboy!"

"Tell me he's going to be okay." She didn't want to be nervous; she knew better. But he was just a baby, too young to control a huge animal like a horse.

Will gave her a pat on the back. "Look, he'll be fine. He's four, so it's high time he learned about horses."

"No rodeo tricks, okay?"

"Lady, you have one hell of an imagination," he said with a sigh. "We're going to walk that mare around and teach the kid how to behave on a horse." He dropped his hand from her shoulder and walked toward the boy.

"Be careful," Becky urged one last time, but Will turned around and smiled at her.

"Be quiet," he said.

"Okay." She tried to smile, but it wasn't easy. She stayed on the other side of the fence and watched as Will and Peter led the horse into the small riding corral on the east side of the horse barn. With her heart in her throat, she watched Will boost the child onto the back of the horse and walk beside him around the corral. Peter's expression was a combination of excitement and concentration, but he dared to smile at his mother as he passed her.

He looked like his father at that moment, in the days before the marriage had soured and Jack had refused to grow up and take care of his family. Before things had changed, and she'd realized she'd married someone who didn't want anything to do with his family or his responsibilities. He wanted all the good times and none of the hard times that came with raising kids and earning a living.

It had been up to her then and it was up to her now. Which was why she needed to start looking for another job. Will Cody might give his mother another month or two on the ranch, but come fall and the calves gone to market, it would be over.

She waved to Peter again, and her heart burst with pride. He needed a father to do these things, and maybe she ought to think about finding him one of those, too. She looked at the handsome cowboy who rode beside her child. He was a good man, but not her type. He was another wild one, with his eye on the horizon all the time. They might be attracted physically, but she'd be in trouble if she let it go any further than that.

Becky waved once more and returned to her kitchen. Peter was in good hands, and there was lasagna to assemble. She didn't need to stand around and gawk at Will Cody for the rest of the afternoon. She had better things to do, such as tell herself to get a grip and start acting her age.

THEY TOOK TURNS driving the mower, until Will realized that Decker's eyesight wasn't that good, Cal had trouble with gauging distance and Oatey just plain hated the equipment. Malone was the only one, other than Becky, who could cut a straight swath through the field without wrecking something. Oatey had returned to where he was happiest, with the children. It had only taken four days to get the part they needed, and Will had woken each morning glad to see the sun shining. Rain would be the last thing they needed. He wanted to cut as much as possible and show prospective buyers that the ranch could support its cattle with its own winter feed.

Oddly enough, there had been no more contact from the three people interested, but maybe that was typical in the real estate business. Becky hadn't made any more noise about leaving and Maude spent a lot of time on the phone planning things he knew he wouldn't like. Will wiped the sweat from his brow and turned off the engine as Maude drove up with Becky.

"Dinner!" the younger woman called, hopping out of the old truck. He didn't know where she got her energy. He'd taken over planning the day's work with the men, but Becky was still up early, taking care of her kids and cooking breakfast. It seemed as if she was always in the kitchen or with Maude taking care of those fancy horses. Will planned to keep the stallion and maybe a mare or two and take them back to his place. That damn horse was like riding a Cadillac.

"Where's Malone?"

"Gone to get something from town, I think," Maude said. "Here, Becky," she said, turning to the woman. "Take this to Will while I go back for some more ice. I plumb forgot the lemonade."

"That's okay," Will said. "I can drink water."

"I only brought one jug. I'll have to go back and get the big cooler." Maude fanned herself. "The heat must be making me forgetful."

"Then let someone else come out here from now on." He walked over to the tree where the women had set up lunch. "That's what we have help for."

"I like the drive," his mother insisted. "And the men are busy."

"With what?" It seemed like he and Becky were the only ones putting in a full day's work lately.

"I'm planning a camping trip."

"Not during haying season you're not."

"When you're finished, then. Next week."

He shook his head. "I'm not taking your club of old ladies camping. Someone will get hurt and sue the pants off us."

"I talked to a lawyer. There are ways around that," Maude insisted. He didn't look at his mother, though, because Becky had taken off her hat and was fanning herself as she sat on the picnic blanket. The outline of her breasts was obvious underneath the faded man's shirt.

"The same lawyer who's been calling me?"

"Yes. You really should make an appointment with him, Will. There are things you should—"

"Later," he said, watching Becky pick up a handful of grapes. She was oblivious to him as she popped one after another into her mouth and chewed delicately. "I don't have time to go to town."

Maude sighed. "Well, have it your way, then." She went over to the truck and got in behind the steering wheel. "I'll be back with water and lemonade in a few minutes."

"Yeah," he said, not paying her the least bit of attention. He turned back to Becky and sat down across from her on the blanket.

"Want a sandwich?" she asked. The top two buttons on her shirt were unfastened, giving him a glimpse of collarbone and soft skin. Will eyed that intriguing V, then noticed that Becky was holding out a sandwich.

"Thanks." He took it, realizing that the two of them were alone for the first time since Saturday night. Four days, and he hadn't forgotten how it felt to kiss her. He planned to do it again, but she had a knack for avoiding him. Either that, or there were too damn many people running around the ranch.

"Nice day," she said, looking past him to where the hay he had cut lay piled in thick rows, and in the distance were the foothills of the Rockies, the mountains rising far in the distance. Will took a deep breath and leaned against the tree. There was some satisfaction in putting up hay. More than he remembered. The thick rows would be formed into rolls, then lined up together like long cinnamon rolls. In the winter, one of the men would put the forklift attachment onto a tractor and move each roll where it was needed. The cows, their breath frosty on dark winter mornings, would gather round to feed.

"You're not still thinking about leaving, are you?"

"If you're thinking about selling," was her reply.

"I don't have much choice," he said, hoping he could make her understand. "This place doesn't make any money. It's a losing proposition."

"You couldn't figure out how to make it work?"

"I doubt it."

"Have you even tried?" She poured them cups of water and handed him one. "You've said yourself that your uncle wasn't running enough cattle. And he hadn't bothered with the haying much, either. Maude wants to charge people for riding around the ranch, which might bring in some cash in the summer until the fall sale of the calves. If you were here, we could breed the two-year-old heifers and get through calving season. And some of the neighbors have gone from cow-calf operations to fattening yearlings, which has—"

"Whoa." He put up his hand. "You're forgetting something, honey."

"Honey?" She frowned at him.

He wondered once again what it would be like to unbraid that hair and let it fall over her shoulders. It was a shade lighter than the golden color of the distant hay. "Just a figure of speech." He tore his gaze from her hair to look into those blue eyes. "And I have no interest in making this ranch work, except for those things that will get a better price for it."

"Because you hated your uncle?" She didn't wait for a reply. "When are you going to get over that? You own a piece of one of the most beautiful places in the world, and you act like it's a *problem*. What on earth is the matter with you?"

Well, for one thing, he had a tightening in his groin that had nothing to do with owning part of Montana. Will didn't think Becky would appreciate knowing that fact, though. "There's nothing the matter with me," he said, sounding as if he was lying. Which he was, of course.

"Sure there is," Becky insisted. "I can see why you'd want your mother to move to some nice little apartment in Billings, *if* she was unhappy here. But she's not unhappy—just the opposite, in fact—and yet you keep wanting to move her away."

"And I'm supposed to stay," he said. "I'm supposed to give up a career that makes a lot of money—"

"That knee of yours isn't going to hold up much longer, is it? And you've hurt your back, too. Sometimes you hold yourself like you can barely move and—"

"Be quiet, Becky."

"Why? Because you don't want to hear the truth? You have a *home* here, which is something most people would give their right arm to have. And all you want to do is get rid of it."

"What about you, Becky? Is that what you want, a home

like this?'' He didn't mean to sound harsh, and he was surprised and a little ashamed when her eyes suddenly filled with tears.

"Of course," she whispered. "Homes aren't easy to come by, you know."

"Tell me about your husband."

She dropped her gaze and started to pick up the lunch leftovers and pack them into little plastic containers. "What do you want to know?"

"Why didn't he give you a home?"

"Things didn't work out that way. We never stayed in one place long enough." She glanced up at him, tried to smile, but failed. "He was always promising that he would find a place of our own, though, but he never did."

"What was his name?"

"Jack."

"And you were happy?"

"For a while. Until Peter came and I wanted to settle down and not live in a trailer anymore. Jack didn't like to stay put. He took cowboy jobs here and there, drifting where the mood took him. He loved to have a good time, which is what killed him." She looked up at Will then. "He'd been drinking and crashed the truck on the way home from the Big Sky Saloon. Luckily no one else was hurt, but he died a couple of days later from head injuries."

"I'm sorry."

"I'd been working part-time for Maude, doing some cooking and cleaning. After the accident, she took me in. I didn't—don't—have any family left, and Jack's folks were gone, too. Maude said she understood what it was like to be alone, with a child. She paid the hospital bills and the funeral expenses. But I've paid her back," she told him. "Every dime."

"That couldn't have been very long ago," he said. "Tommy—"

"Wasn't even born yet. I didn't know I was pregnant until a few months after the accident." She let him take her hand. He looked at her and wondered if she even realized she was holding on to him.

"No wonder you care so much about my mother."

Becky nodded. "She's been a good friend."

"Look," he said, choosing his words carefully. "If I promise to do my best to not hurt her in any way, can we declare a truce?"

"You never answered my question," she said, pulling her hand away with a gentle tug. "What's so bad about staying here?"

"I love rodeo. It's that simple."

"I don't believe you. What happened here that makes you hate it so?"

Now it was his turn to look away. He gazed toward the ranch, hoping to see the truck returning with water. "I worked like a dog here," he said. "My uncle was a harsh man. There aren't any good memories here."

"Well, *make* some," Becky demanded. "You can't ride the rodeo circuit forever."

"Make some memories," he repeated, studying her serious expression. "Just like that. You think it's that easy?"

"Why not?"

"Why not," he echoed, leaning closer to her to close the gap between them. He took her by the shoulders and kissed her long and hard. He sensed her surprise, and then her response, and her lips parted to allow him entrance. He pushed her gently onto her back and followed her down, in the shade of the tree with the smell of fresh cut hay surrounding them. The birds were quiet, but the breeze made the leaves shiver and rustle, and Becky's lips were warm and sweet. He kissed her for long moments, while he was slanted over her, his weight on his elbows. Those lovely breasts were against his chest, her arms had come round his neck, and the tree protected them from the hot afternoon sun. He kissed her again, then moved lower, to that intriguing cleft of skin between her collar, shifting his weight to allow him to touch her breast and down lower, to her waist. She kissed him back, moaning a little into his mouth as he found her lips again and tugged her shirt free of her waistband. It was easy work to release the snaps that held the shirt closed, and he slid his palm over bare skin to touch first one lace-coated breast and then the other. He cupped it gently, thumbing the sensitive nub with his thumb until Becky broke off the kiss.

"Are you telling me to stop?" he asked, wanting her more than he could remember wanting a woman before.

"This isn't what I meant by making memories," she said, her voice soft. Her lips were swollen from his kisses and her cheeks were flushed.

He dipped his head and brushed his lips against the mound of her breast above her brassiere. "You're as beautiful as I thought you'd be," he said. "It's a pretty damn good memory to me."

"I don't need any more memories," she said, lifting one hand to touch his hair and brush a lock from his forehead. "A widow has too many. I need a man who isn't going to leave. And we both know that's not you."

His smile was wry as he began to fasten the snaps he'd so easily opened. "You're too smart, Miss Becky."

"Yep." She sat up and scooted back against the tree. "I'm a real genius, all right." She looked past him toward the hill. "Here comes someone. I guess we're lucky."

Lucky? He didn't feel the least bit lucky. He felt unsettled and hot, so he reached for the last of the water and drained the bottle. Becky was right. He wasn't a man to make promises he couldn't keep, just to get a woman to go to bed with him. A woman like Becky didn't need a man like him making love to her. But, damn, he wanted to.

SHE THOUGHT about him for the rest of the afternoon. She thought about how good his fingers had felt on her skin, how his lips on her breast made her want to strip off her clothes and make love to him right there under that scraggly old tree. To hell with the hay, to hell with the future, to hell with everything. She would have made love to him and damned the consequences.

If she was a different kind of woman. Becky rolled the piecrust and wished she *was* a different kind of woman. She'd be satisfied and smiling now. She'd be soaking in the tub, reveling in the memory of having a man inside her. She would smile all through supper, a woman with a delicious secret.

There were no secrets and no bubble baths. There was piecrust, and the case of peaches that Cal had brought back from town. And there was Tommy, cranky from having a nap that was too short, and Peter, hiding on the porch so his little brother wouldn't break another one of his X-men action figures. Maude had been on the phone all afternoon, planning a camping trip that would make Will crazy and most likely entertain the cowboys. She'd learned they liked to show off a little, especially for the ladies.

She was going to have to make some decisions soon, such as where to live. And what to do when Mike asked her out again, though she wondered if he would. He'd been a little stunned by the children, a little suspicious of Will. That had been quite a date, uneventful until she'd rounded the corner of the lobby and seen Maude and Tommy. For a second she'd been afraid that something was wrong, but Maude had smiled and Becky's heart started beating again.

And then beat faster when she'd seen Will.

She had to face it, Becky decided, lifting the circle of piecrust into the pan and tucking it gently into the shape of the dish. She was attracted to the man. It was perfectly natural, after all. He was young and handsome, two assets in short supply around here. And he looked at her sometimes as if he'd like to take off her clothes and make love to her right then and there.

And now he was trying to do exactly that, but she was too smart for that. Too smart for a broken heart or hurt feelings or the kind of embarrassment that results from a man making love to you once and afterward pretending you don't exist. She would look out, she promised herself. She divided the sliced peaches between the pie plates, then covered them with circles of dough.

"Mommy! Want to get down," Tommy hollered, banging his toy.

"In a minute." She pinched the dough together, fluted the edges and carefully set the pies in the oven to bake.

"Mommy!" he cried again, obviously losing patience with his mother. Becky wiped her hands and went over to lift him from the high chair. He was a good baby, but he needed a father. Peter could con Will into playing checkers and teaching him to ride, but what did Tommy need? A strong pair of arms to lift him and a man's voice telling him it was all right when he fell down and scraped the palms of his hands on the gravel road.

Well, Becky thought, setting Tommy on the floor, there was no sense dreaming of things they weren't going to have. At least not right now. She led the boy onto the porch and sat down on the swing. Tommy went over to his favorite toy, a pile of brown wooden logs that Maude had brought from the attic. He liked to build log cabins and corrals for his collection of plastic horses. Tommy was a quiet builder, while Peter liked to be moving and doing, full of conversation and being around people. Both boys had taken to Will too easily, as if they were starved for attention.

Which wasn't true. Maude and the cowboys spoiled the children, and there was always someone to play with or talk to. That was another reason she'd hate to leave this place, Becky knew. She sat down in the swing and watched her children play. They'd found a family here, which made it even harder to walk away. But she'd learned a few years ago that nothing was guaranteed to stay the same. She was stronger now, and wiser. She had skills and references and a way to make a living.

Becky rocked herself in the swing and looked out the screened windows to the front yard. She would miss this old house, but it was time to start thinking about moving on before she made a mistake, like falling in love with the wrong man once again.

9

"HOW MANY?"

"Eight," Maude said, looking at her list. "Each one is paying one hundred and fifty dollars for the privilege, too. Including lunch and dinner on Saturday and breakfast Sunday, plus the use of the horse."

"Twelve hundred dollars?" Becky was impressed. "That's a lot of money for one camping trip."

"They voted on what they thought was a fair price, even though I told them that I would do it for free, just for the practice. No one thought that was fair, though. And they're bringing their own sleeping bags," Maude announced. "But I think we'll have to buy them from now on. We can't expect everyone to bring their own gear. How much do you think you'll need for the food?"

Becky looked down at her own list. "Eight plus the two of us. How many cowboys?"

"Decker, Malone and Will. Cal and Oatey will stay here and take care of the ranch."

"I can't go, Maude. I can't leave the kids overnight. Oatey is wonderful for short periods of time, but I don't think—"

"It's all settled. I've hired Millie Freeman's daughter-in-law. She's a mother of three, so she should be able to handle your two little ones. And she could use the money, too."

"I can't do that, Maude. It's another expense."

"It's worth it," the older woman insisted. "I need you to

cook. Just driving the food up there isn't going to work, though I think that's a good plan. All right? I promise the children will be fine, and you could use a break yourself, you know."

Becky couldn't resist. After all, an overnight camping trip in the hills overlooking the summer range was something she'd never done before. "Maybe Millie's daughter-in-law, I think her name is Lisa, could come over this week and meet the children."

"Fine. I'll give you her number and you can talk to her. I think her youngest boy is the same age as Peter."

"Maybe she'd bring him with her. Peter would love company."

"There," Maude said, smiling. "Didn't I tell you it was a good idea? I'll need you to have the lunch ready, plus breakfast. You know, eggs, bacon, coffee in a metal pot over the campfire. Real ranch food."

"How about steaks for dinner? There are still plenty in the large freezer."

"Excellent." She crossed that off her list. "Now, all I have to do is talk to Will and tell him he's going to be busy next Saturday night."

"I don't know if he's going to like this," Becky cautioned. When Will wasn't haying, he spent a lot of evenings in the office, going over the accounts and questioning his mother about the way his uncle had run things around here. Apparently the books had to be in good shape for prospective buyers to examine.

"He'll be fine. Especially when I tell him that we're making money."

Becky had her doubts. "He's been working awfully hard this past week. I don't think he's taken any time off."

"Then he'll be glad of the vacation."

Becky didn't think that Will would consider escorting

nine women on a camping trip much of a vacation, but she had to admire Maude's optimism. "What about dessert? Cookies are a safe bet and will travel well, though I suppose I could do an angel food cake and berries, too."

"Whatever you think, dear." Maude looked back at her list and crossed off something else. "I know this is going to be the start of something wonderful."

Becky had her doubts, but she kept them to herself.

WILL REINED UP beside Decker. "If there was a list of crazy people in Montana, I figure my name would be at the top of the list." The two men rode behind the group of gray-haired cowgirls, making sure that none of them fell off their horses. This was the same group who had herded cows a few weeks ago, but the fact that nothing had happened last time didn't reassure either man.

"Yep," Decker agreed. "You and your ma are two of a kind."

"Don't lump me in with Maude. I can't believe I let her talk me into this crazy scheme. Camping with her Dead Club," he muttered, pulling his hat low against the late-afternoon sun.

"*Not* Dead Yet," the older cowboy corrected. "That's the point. Just because we're old doesn't mean we're getting ready to take our last breath on this earth. I'm close to eighty-two now, and I'm doing okay." He patted his horse's neck. "These here foreign horses sure help my old bones, though."

"Maude's crazy about those horses." Will rode his chestnut mare, only this time without pain. His knee had healed just fine, though it twinged some when he worked eighteen-hour days. The ache in his back had been replaced by a different ache, the kind brought on by a yellow-haired woman with big blue eyes.

"Could be a real money-maker."

"The horses?"

"Yeah, and givin' trail rides. Maude might have a good idea in this, Will. Kinda helps the cash flow along until the calves are sold."

Will glanced over toward him. "Yeah? And when did you get interested in cash flow?"

"We all chipped in to buy these horses. Kind of a retirement program." He grinned. "Though you chipped in the most, according to Maude."

"Yeah, without knowing it." He had to smile. All along he'd thought his mother was buying new dresses or furniture or anything to make her life more comfortable. Instead, she'd squirreled it away and started her own business.

"You selling the place puts a new wrinkle in our plans," Decker stated.

"I'm sorry about that." Will hated that part, and didn't know what to do about the fate of the old men, though he'd lain awake nights worrying about it. "I've got a little place outside of Billings. You're all welcome. I could add a bunkhouse."

"How big?"

He was embarrassed to tell him. "Twenty acres."

Decker chuckled. "Why, what would we do in the city?"

"Relax."

"Don't want to relax," Decker said. "We want to raise horses and look at the mountains and do a little work now and then to make sure we're still alive. Don't want to sit in your house with nothing to do except play cards."

"But where else will you go?"

"Not your concern, son," the old man replied. "You take your ma and you go back to Billings. Don't know what she'll do with herself there, though." He pointed to the crowd of women up ahead. "She's made some friends and she's bought horses and all she wants to do is stay here."

"But she's no spring chicken, Deck. She's not young enough for this kind of life anymore."

"She's doing okay. She's where she wants to be." The older man gave him a long, steady look. "Let her be."

"She'll work herself to death."

Decker shook his head. "Let her be," he repeated. "Don't be so quick to rush in here and change things." He nudged his horse and trotted off, away from Will and toward Malone. Will was left by himself, eating dust. He wasn't trying to hurt anyone, but none of them understood. There was nothing for him or Maude on this ranch now, and she'd promised to leave. Nothing ever stayed the same. This remote ranch was no place for any of them, not for old cowboys or old women or a young woman with small children. And especially not for a man who'd spent his adult life trying not to come home.

"OH, AND HE was a *huge* bear," Malone announced. "Darker than night, bigger than one of them football players you see on TV. He came up and whacked my hat off with his paw." He made a motion and his hat went flying, to land in Dr. Theresa's lap. The ladies tittered, but their attention remained on the old cowboy. Becky, standing in the background beyond the reach of the firelight, chuckled watching him. She'd heard this story before, and every time she heard it the bear got bigger and blacker, with better aim.

Malone leaned toward the light of the fire and pointed to a long scar on his temple. "Bear claw," he said. "Son of a, uh, gun caught me right there."

"What did you do next?" one woman asked, clearly awestruck.

"Well," Malone drawled, coming to his favorite part of the story. "I whacked him back. Just took my rifle and whacked him on the nose as hard as I could, and he backed up and hollered at me, then went down on all fours and took off into the brush."

"My goodness!" one woman cried. "You were so lucky."

"Yes, ma'am," Malone said, retrieving his hat and sticking it back on his bald head. "And that bear was, too, because I couldn't get my rifle in position in time and had to settle for hitting him on the nose."

Becky turned as Will came up to stand beside her. He was smiling.

"Those stories get better and better," he whispered.

"Decker is getting ready to outdo him." She nodded toward the older cowboy, who had edged closer to the fire. He leaned forward, looking impatient as the ladies started asking Malone questions about bears.

"And Deck's going to have a hard time, too." Will chuckled. "I didn't think this evening would go this well. I have to give you and Maude credit."

"Thank you." She looked over at Maude, who looked up and winked at her. Becky gave her a thumbs-up sign. "She figures if we can do this once a week we can make enough money to put a new roof on the house."

"Once a week?"

"Sure. There are plenty of people in Billings and Great Falls and even Bozeman who would like to ride around a real ranch. And *we* have special horses for those who can't be jarred. That gives us an edge."

"An edge," he repeated, shaking his head. "Do you know how many trail rides you'd have to give to pay for those fancy animals?"

She wished he wouldn't stand quite so close. "We're not

including the cost of the horses, Maude said, because they were a gift."

"And, according to the records, a gift from me," he reminded her.

"Maude likes to think of it as an investment, but she doesn't like counting it into the profit and loss figures. At least," Becky added, "not until the mares foal and we can start a breeding program."

He tugged on her braid, which hung down her back between her shoulder blades, and sent little shivers down her spine. "Do you ever wear your hair loose?"

She wished he wouldn't touch her. She wished he would. "At night," she whispered.

Will lifted the braid and draped it over her shoulder. His fingers brushed the top of her breast. "Your hair must be long."

"Um, yes." She stood still when she knew she should move away. She should make sure there was enough hot water in case their guests wanted another round of whiskey-spiked hot chocolate. The tents were set up under the pine trees, the weather had cooperated with a clear sky filled with stars and the sliver of a moon. It was the kind of night meant for campfires and stories and stolen kisses in the pine-scented darkness. And she didn't need kisses, Becky told herself as she turned to Will. He wouldn't dare kiss her now, not with all these people.

Will smiled at her as if he knew what she was thinking. "If we were alone..." he said, letting his voice trail off.

"We wouldn't be alone. Not up here at night or any other time," she reminded him. "There is no reason for us to be alone."

"I can think of one," he said, giving the braid a little tug before releasing her. Becky didn't reply. She turned back to the campfire and pretended to be listening to Decker's story. She couldn't admit she was attracted to him, not in a physical way or any other way. They'd almost made love last week on the picnic blanket, and she'd been damn lucky she'd come to her senses in time. She didn't need a man in her life, and she didn't need this particular man.

But it was tempting, Becky thought, hiding a sigh. Sleep couldn't come soon enough. She would hide in her tent and pretend she liked being alone at night.

She would avoid him from now on.

BECKY ROSE AT DAWN to fix the coffee and get a fire going. She dressed quickly in the tent, then once outside splashed her face with cold water from a basin, brushed her teeth and rebraided her hair. She wasn't the only one up. Will came out of the brush with an armful of firewood. He hadn't shaved, but that didn't lessen his attractiveness. He wished her a good-morning and helped her build the fire. She fetched water from the nearby stream and made coffee on the propane stove as quietly as she could, then poured them each a cup.

It seemed natural to sit on the log and look at the fire while they drank their coffee and everyone else slept in tents scattered among the pine trees. Becky had shared a tent with Maude, who had confessed her exhaustion and gone immediately to sleep. Becky had lain awake worrying about the future and wondering how the boys were doing with Lisa Freeman. She'd tossed and turned within the confines of her sleeping bag before drifting into a dreamless sleep. Now it was barely dawn, and there was no telling how long the others would sleep. One of the cowboys could be heard snoring from a distant tent.

"Couldn't you sleep either?" Will asked.

"Oh, I slept fine," she lied.

"Really."

"Must be the fresh air. I wanted to get up early and get the food going. I thought if I started the bacon and got it cooked ahead, it would be easier to feed everyone."

"You're always thinking," he murmured. "Always so organized and prepared."

"I have to be. That's my job."

"Maude was lucky to have found you."

"She said she knew how I felt, what I was going through, being widowed and raising a child by herself." She stood up and started going through the large cooler for the bacon. It didn't take long to fix a couple of cast-iron skillets on the grate over the fire and start frying bacon. She didn't let Will help, which seemed to annoy him. "Did you camp much when you were a boy?"

"Some," he said, pouring himself a fresh cup of coffee. "In the summers, when the herd was up here I'd come up and ride fence and check the cattle. Then I'd stay, if it got late. I liked it. It was always peaceful, just like it is now." He stood and looked down at the valley below them. In the distance a tiny ribbon of road was all that could be seen in the pale light of early morning.

Becky set up the food on the folding metal table she'd brought from the ranch. She'd covered it with a red gingham cloth to give it a Western look and last night's buffet and steaks fresh from the campfire had met with no complaints. Today she would serve blueberry muffins, with bowls of fresh strawberries and chunks of melon. The ladies would have their eggs cooked to order, their bacon hot and crispy. There were leftover cookies for those who wanted to take a snack for the ride back to the ranch, and jugs of lemonade the cowboys would pack for a rest stop on the way down the mountain later.

They kept bumping into each other, something that was

both pleasant and embarrassing. "How do you want your eggs?"

"Fried." He reached for the carton of eggs. "I can do it myself."

"Are you trying to make me look bad?" she teased, reaching for the carton and taking it away from him. "I'm the camp cook here."

"We were always taught that the cook was the boss." Will smiled, giving her a look that made her knees wobble alarmingly. "So I guess I'll have to do what you say."

"It's about time you realized that." She put the bacon into one pan and cracked the eggs into the empty one.

He followed her over to the campfire and sat down to watch her cook. "I'm a slow learner."

She turned to face him. "We can do this, you know. We can make this ranch work with trail rides and camp outs, plus the income from the calves and from selling a Paso or two."

"I'm not arguing that someone could do that," Will insisted. "All I'm saying is that my mother isn't young enough to do it and you can't do it alone or with a handful of old cowboys who can't see past their horses' ears."

"But—"

"'Morning!" Maude called, coming up behind them. "I swear the smell of coffee woke me up." She peered past Becky's shoulder. "Looks like my son has the first breakfast."

Becky flipped the eggs over before turning to Maude. "How did you sleep?"

"Just fine. I'm a little stiff," she admitted, stretching her arms above her head, "but the fresh air does wonders for a good night's sleep." She clapped her hand on Will's shoulder as he began to stand. "Stay where you are. I'm going to get some coffee."

"Take the log," he said. "I'll get your coffee."

She winked at Becky and did as she was told. "How long have you two been up?"

"Not long."

"Long enough to have a difference of opinion, I see."

"Just a discussion," Becky said, reaching for Will's tin plate.

"Is he flirting with you?"

Becky blushed. "No, of course not. Maude, for heaven's sake!"

Will returned with the coffee and handed it to his mother. "Why is Becky blushing?" Becky gave him his breakfast and he sat down on another log and looked at both women.

"She's too close to the fire, that's all," his mother explained. "It's chilly up here this morning."

"It won't be in a couple of hours," he said, digging into his eggs.

The talk turned to the weather, and Becky gratefully slipped away from the fire. Spending too much time with Will was dangerous, and she'd be better off remembering that fact from now on.

HE WATCHED HER work, watched the kind way she treated their guests and the way people responded. The cowboys loved her, and she took care of them in a way that didn't make them feel old. Maude depended on her, that was obvious. They all did. He wondered what she would do when she left the SV, where she would go and if her employers would appreciate her the way they should.

He wanted her, with a fierce protective lust he'd never experienced before. He watched her move around the campfire and pour coffee and serve food to the gray-haired ladies and he wanted nothing more than to take her into the nearest tent and make love to her.

After he unbraided that yellow hair, of course.

She was aware of him, too. They were the two youngest people on that side of the mountain, both single and healthy. Some of the women had looked at both of them with knowing looks and smiles, something he could do without. He wasn't going to grab Becky by the hair and drag her off into the woods in front of everyone, but damn it, he was going to kiss her before the morning was out because she was driving him crazy.

Ever since that afternoon in the hay meadow, he'd thought about making love to her. He'd thought about taking it slow or doing it fast and hard. He'd thought about that hair falling across his chest and he'd thought about how he'd feel inside her. And he'd resolved to stay away from her, because she wasn't the kind of woman a man like him should make love to.

He hadn't slept much.

"Will," Maude said, sounding impatient.

"What?"

"Don't snap at me. I've been trying to get your attention for three minutes now, and you're glaring at the campfire."

He looked down at her and forced himself to concentrate. "Sorry. I was thinking."

"Well, forget that for a while. I need to ask you a favor."

"Sure. What?"

"Becky's going to need help packing all this stuff back to the truck. Can you stay and help her? You can catch up with us afterward."

"Can't Malone or Decker do it?" He frowned. He didn't want to be alone with her, not really. Fantasizing was fine, but he wasn't made of steel either.

"No. I need Decker with the horses and J.J.'s arthritis is bothering him this morning."

"Which leaves me," he stated flatly. "If you're thinking you're going to get me to fall for Becky and stay here on the ranch, you're wrong."

"Will!" Maude's eyes widened. "You're all wrong for Becky. You're not at all her type." She patted him on the arm before she returned to her friends. "Just carry the boxes, dear. And catch up with us when you can."

Not Becky's type? What the hell was that supposed to mean? He frowned once again and headed toward the horses. If the men were so damn sick, he guessed they'd need help saddling up the animals.

Decker grinned when he saw him. "Mighty fine mornin'."

"Yeah?"

"Well, I thought so," the old man said. "You get clean-up duty?"

"Yeah."

"Thought so. Miss Becky's going to need some help packing this stuff out."

"So I heard."

"You mind your manners, now," Decker said. "You'll scare the ladies with that look on your face, like you wish you could shoot somethin'."

Will ignored him and reached for a bridle. There were a lot of things he'd like to do, but none of them involved shooting. And all of them involved Becky McGregor.

THREE HOURS AFTER the women had awakened, they rode off down the mountain toward home. Well-fed and feeling like they had had an adventure, they were on their way back to the ranch house, where they would climb off their horses and, according to Maude, rush to the telephone to tell their friends, who would also want to book trips up the mountain, of course. Theresa took photographs to send to a nephew who worked for a travel magazine.

"From rags to riches," Maude said, kissing her son goodbye before she got on her horse. "We're on our way now."

It was no time to argue, Will decided, not when Maude was smiling at him and looking so pleased with herself. "I'm glad you had a good time."

"You did, too, my boy," Maude said. "I could tell."

"Yes." He couldn't argue that fact. "I always liked camping up here, and it was good to hear the stories again and sleep under the stars."

She leaned over and kissed him on the cheek. "This is your home," she said, straightening once again.

"Yes, ma'am," Will said, stepping away so she could follow the others. He stood on the ridge and watched them ride for a few minutes. Decker was in the lead this time, the others following at their own pace. Maude rode beside one of the taller women, the doctor maybe, and Malone brought up the rear. They were in no hurry and were even going to stop for a snack along the way. Will returned to the campsite and started toward Becky. He promised himself he would be all business, would pack her up, carry the stuff the mile or so to the car, then leave.

He would not touch her, even though they were alone on a mountain with only the summer wind for company. He would stay far away and carry what she told him to carry. He was hers to command.

"You don't have to do anything," she said. "I can manage. Really."

Will looked at the table and boxes and the two coolers, then back at one of the most maddening women in Montana. "You're going to get all this stuff to the car by yourself? You're parked a mile away, easy."

"I have plenty of time." She folded the tablecloth and set it in one of the boxes.

"Why, Miss Becky, if I didn't know better I'd think you were trying to get rid of me."

She looked up then and saw his smile. "And you'd be right. Really, I can do this myself. Go on with the others."

"But what about the bears?" He stepped closer and gazed down into those blue eyes. "And mountain lions, too. Didn't you listen to Deck's story?"

Becky smiled, and Will felt his heart flip over inside his chest. "I listened, all right. I happen to be used to hearing cowboys tell tall tales."

He touched her cheek, ran his finger along her jaw and wondered at the softness of her skin. "If I told you I didn't sleep last night for wanting you, would you think it was another tall tale?"

"I'd be sure of it," she whispered, but she didn't move away from his touch. He lifted her chin with his index finger and bent down to kiss her. Before he touched his lips to hers, he paused.

"It's true," he said, brushing his lips against hers in a teasing motion. He waited for a reaction from her. Would she pull away or kiss him back?

"I have work to do," she said, but her hands touched his arms and crept upward.

"Like what?" His lips moved to her cheek, to her ear, to the long column of her neck. She smelled like coffee and sunshine and her skin was soft against his tongue.

"Oh, lots of things," she said, closing her eyes as his lips returned to hers.

He kissed her for a long moment, until her arms went around his neck and her body was against his.

"Over here," he said, breaking the embrace and taking

her hand. He led her to his bedroll, still open underneath the pine tree.

"We're crazy," she said, looking at the bed and then at him. "I don't do things like this."

"I won't make love to you if you don't want me to." He meant it. He'd never forced a woman, never seduced someone to do what she didn't want to do. His fingers touched her shirt, unsnapped the first snap, then the second.

"I want you to," she admitted. "That's what's so crazy. I keep telling myself that it's wrong."

He opened two more snaps, pulled the shirttails from her waistband, slid his hands around her bare waist. "Why?"

"I've never made love on a mountain before."

Will smiled down at her. "Haven't you ever done anything completely wild, something that made no sense but just felt right?"

"Is that how you describe what we're doing right now?"

He slipped the shirt off her shoulders to reveal a white lace bra and tantalizing breasts. "Yes. Tell me this isn't what you want. What we both want."

Becky felt the warmth of the sun on her skin and suddenly felt free. And young and sexy and desirable. She was alone on a mountain with a man who clearly desired her. A man she desired, too. She reached for him then, unbuttoning his shirt the way he had undone hers, slipping the sleeves from his arms and sliding them off his hands. She smoothed her palms over his furred chest, tracing the scars she found there.

He moaned when she touched his skin, when she kissed the jagged scar above his belt buckle. Within minutes they had managed to take each other's clothes off, though Becky didn't know how they did it, not with belt buckles and jeans and boots to contend with. But he was naked above her, her skin was on fire, and she pulled him closer because she couldn't touch him enough. She felt him hot and hard against her thigh, ready to make love to her, when he pulled away and looked down into her eyes.

"I didn't bring anything," he gasped. "This is going to be a problem."

"Yes," Becky said, staring into those dark eyes. She tried to hide her disappointment and how much of an idiot she felt. Now was not the time to tell him that she was a woman who got pregnant as easily as a brood mare.

"Damn," he said, touching his lips to one breast, then the other. "I should have thought about this."

This exquisite torture, she decided, was not for the faint-hearted. "The first aid kit," Becky said. "There's one with the kitchen gear."

"You think there's a condom in the kitchen?" He smiled down at her.

"It's worth a try."

"Don't move," he ordered, lifting himself off her. "And cross your fingers."

She closed her eyes instead, wondering if fate was playing some kind of cruel joke. Wondering if she should be crossing her legs instead, or pulling on her clothes and running like hell down the other side of the ridge to the truck. She was a sensible woman, a mother, a widow, and she lay naked on a bedroll in the middle of nowhere hoping her handsome cowboy-about-to-be-lover could find a condom.

She should be ashamed of herself.

"Hey," Will whispered, lying next to her. "You can open your eyes now."

"No. I don't think I'd better. I think I've come to my senses," she muttered. "I think I should get dressed, but I'm too embarrassed to move." She felt his lips brush her bare shoulder and she shivered.

"You're beautiful."

She couldn't speak, because he'd lowered his mouth to her breasts, first one and then the other, sending sparks of need through her body. He took her hands away from her abdomen and kissed the skin there, and then lower. When she would have protested, he captured her wrists in one hand and held her still while he sought what she would have kept from him. He urged her thighs apart with a gentle hand, then touched her with his lips and tongue until she could no longer protest. Until she was weak with longing and desire, slick with readiness for him. His fingers touched her, sending a lance of intense pleasure through her, making her moan.

He rose above her then. "You were right," he said. "There were some condoms in there, though God knows why." And Becky opened her eyes.

"Thank goodness," she answered, looking into his dark eyes, seeing the passion that echoed her own. He took her then, sliding slowly into her with a breathtaking ease that made her gasp.

He hesitated, frowning. "Am I hurting you?"

"No." She reached for his hips to draw him closer. "It's just...been a long time. I was surprised, that's all."

Will touched her lips with his. "You feel so good. Just the way I imagined." He moved within her again, deeper this time, until he filled her completely. He moved again, slowly, waiting for her response.

Her fingers tightened on his skin as he made long, slow love to her. She lifted her hips to meet him, answered his need with her own, until the world came to a dizzying peak and tossed them both over the edge into someplace familiar and strange and dazzling, all at once.

10

IT WAS WITHOUT a doubt the best morning she'd had in a very long time, Becky mused. Though it most likely wasn't morning any longer, from the sun shining high in the sky. She lay snuggled beside Will on the bedroll, the gingham tablecloth tossed over their naked bodies. She wondered when the others would make it back to the ranch, and if anyone would miss the cook or the boss. It was a two-hour ride, but they were stopping for snacks and getting their pictures taken at Silver Creek. Surely it hadn't been an hour since they'd ridden off, though Becky thought her world had certainly shifted in a short period of time.

She turned toward Will, who opened his eyes and smiled at her. "Come here," he said, shifting so her head rested on his shoulder.

"I wonder what time it is," she said, relishing the feel of her skin against his.

"Does it matter?"

"I guess not." Did she dare be irresponsible and decadent just a little while longer? "I don't have to fix lunch."

He chuckled. "Are you always thinking about food?" His fingers began to stroke her breasts. Becky closed her eyes and felt a swift longing to have him inside of her again.

"No," she managed to say, as his hand trailed lower, across her abdomen. "I can't believe we did...what we just did."

"What we're still doing," he corrected, touching her where she was still moist from their lovemaking. "What we're going to do again."

"But—"

He cut off her protests with a quick kiss. "As soon as we go down that mountain you'll go back to being a mother and a cook and a foreman—"

"You're the foreman now," she reminded him.

"And I'll go back to being a son and a boss and—"

"A pain in the rear," she finished for him. "You're *especially* good at that."

His brown eyes twinkled as he looked down at her, his face only inches from hers. "That's not what I was going to say." She shrugged her bare shoulders and he placed a kiss on one of them. "We're not finished here, lady."

"So the first aid kit was well-stocked?"

Will nodded. "Yes. I'd like to know which one of the men thought he would need them."

"You'll have to replace them so no one knows," she said, realizing that they could be caught after all. She didn't want the men to know that she and Will had made love. The men's clumsy attempts at matchmaking hadn't been aimed at sexual activity. She knew they hoped that something wonderful would happen, like Will staying forever. The cowboys were romantics; Becky wasn't.

"I'll bet my championship belt buckle that no one around here is going to miss them." He nudged her hips closer until their bodies were touching from chest to toe. Becky sighed with pure contentment, and Will Cody made love to her once again.

SHE MANAGED TO sneak upstairs and shower while Maude and her friends held an impromptu meeting of the club. Of course, she'd greeted Peter and thanked Lisa Freeman and checked to see that Tommy was still taking a nap before she'd hurried to her room to clean up. Peter had been invited to go home with the Freemans for the rest of the day, which Becky gave him permission to do. It seemed that Josh and Peter had become instant friends who couldn't bear to be separated. She had kissed him goodbye and promised Lisa she'd pick him up before six. It was Sunday, after all, and a trip to town could fit into the schedule with little trouble.

She hadn't been missed, she realized with no small feeling of relief. No one had said, "What were you doing on that mountain all that time?"

No one had mentioned that she and Will had been together. Alone. For several hours. No one noticed that her cheeks were flushed and her eyes sparkled with a secret. She looked at herself in the mirror and felt positively ridiculous.

She wasn't in love with him, of course. Now *that* would be foolish, falling for a footloose rodeo rider. She certainly didn't need another man who couldn't stay in one place for more than a couple of months. Will Cody would be driving off in his truck, his horse trailer behind him, heading back to his own world very soon.

Becky unbraided her hair, stepped in the shower and rinsed off the itchy bits of leaves and dirt stuck to her skin. What they had done was a crazy fluke, something that would never happen again. In fact, Becky resolved, she would have to have more willpower from now on.

"WELL?" MAUDE LEANED closer to Theresa, who perched on the sofa beside her. "What do you think?"

"They had sex, all right," the doctor pronounced. "Written all over her face."

Maude nodded. Becky thought she'd sneaked upstairs with no one the wiser, but she'd had to talk to that nice Freeman woman, of course. She'd had to let Maude know she was back. And she'd looked a little flushed and rumpled, too, which was another good sign. "That's what I thought, too. She was in a big hurry to get out of here and get in the shower."

"There were leaves in her hair."

Which was a very good sign. At least her son and Becky had been up to something there in those woods. "I'd give a lot to see what my son looks like."

"I'll bet," Theresa drawled, "that he's a tired young man who is most likely quite pleased with himself. But men are better at hiding these things."

Maude looked doubtful. She'd always thought it was the other way around. "You think so?"

"We could take a walk out back and go see for ourselves."

"Maybe when the others leave," Maude said. Several of her guests were still drinking lemonade and discussing how they would organize looking at each other's photographs. There was also the matter of the old-fashioned barn dance to consider. Things were definitely looking up.

HE WASN'T IN LOVE with her, of course. He respected the way she worked so hard, and he damned well enjoyed her cooking. She was a good-looking woman with a way with animals and people, and the sex, well, he'd never experienced anything quite like that before. Of course, he hadn't been with a woman in many long months. And there was something about making love outdoors that could have had that effect. Next time he would untie that braid, he promised himself.

"'Bout time you got back," Decker said, standing in the door. "We've been entertaining the ladies with one man short."

"I'm not much for entertaining," Will said, dismounting. He unpacked his gear, unsaddled the mare and, as Decker opened the corral gate, set her free to run in the pasture. He turned toward his friend. "I thought the ladies had left."

"Nope. They're still in the house, chatterin' away about their big adventure."

"Maude's happy, then?"

"Yep. She's just about over the moon."

Will put his hands on his hips and surveyed the ranch buildings. Half were coated with fresh white paint, the others were a dusty gray. "I guess if you didn't know any better, you'd be impressed."

Decker didn't smile. "There's someone here waiting for you."

"Becky got back? Good."

The old cowboy shook his head. "Not Becky. She came home a while ago and is in the house with the women. There's a man here to see you, says a real estate agency in Billings sent him out here. Said you had an appointment."

Will winced. He'd forgotten about that. "Hell," he swore. "That was set up weeks ago. Must have slipped my mind."

"Yeah, well, he's been walking around, looking things over. I kept him out of Maude's sight. Didn't want to upset her."

"Thanks."

Decker continued to frown at him. "Didn't do it for you," he said. "Did it for Maude. Don't want her day ruined."

"Yeah." Will should have felt relief that a prospective buyer had finally shown up. He couldn't remember the man's name, but he wished him to hell right now. "I'll take care of it."

"Last time I saw him he was over by the bunkhouse. Drove up in one of them shiny new Jeeps, wears shiny new boots."

Will sighed. Of course, anything shiny was suspicious to an eighty-year-old cowhand. "I'll go find him."

He wondered why he felt a little sick to his stomach. He'd eaten too many eggs, that's all. He'd had the kind of morning most men could only dream of and now it was time to come back to earth and face what he had to do. Trouble was, he'd had too much time to think on the ride home. And he didn't like the ideas that had occurred to him, either. It was best, Will decided, striding toward the bunkhouse, to keep his mind on his original plan and not get sidetracked by women, but he'd told himself that before and it hadn't helped a bit. He was damned if he did and damned if he didn't and damned if he stayed on this ranch a minute longer.

And he was damned if he knew what to do with the real estate agent.

BECKY PUT ON a dress. She told herself it was Sunday and she was tired of blue jeans and clothes that smelled like horse. She would do laundry, she would sit on the porch and play with Tommy. She braided her damp hair and wondered if it would ever rain. Maybe she would take Tommy with her when she went to town; they would have ice cream and she would try to forget that she had made love to Will Cody this morning. Twice. And it had been incredibly satisfying and, all in all, surprising in many ways.

She lifted Tommy from his crib, changed his diaper, and took him downstairs. There was a breeze on the porch, and the house was dark and silent. Maude must have drawn the shades against the afternoon sun after her guests had gone home. Becky sat in the swing while Tommy found the box of miniature logs and plastic horses that were kept in the corner. Lady, stretched out in front of the door, lifted her head to see who was coming. When Peter didn't appear, she put her head down between her paws, sighed and closed her eyes.

"Daddy's horse," Tommy said, lifting a horse to show his mother.

Becky shook her head. "Mr. Cody's horse, Tommy. Not daddy."

The toddler ignored her. "Daddy's horse," he repeated, making the horse move across the wooden floor. He stood up and, stepping over the dog, went to the screen door, the horse clutched in his chubby fist. "Daddy!" he called. "Come here!"

There was no arguing with the child, Becky decided. He was convinced that Will was his father and, with a toddler's stubborn defiance, continued to call the man "Daddy" every time he saw him. Becky looked outside and watched as Will walked a short, stocky man to his car. She didn't recognize the man who shook Will's hand so seriously and handed him what looked like a business card before getting in his Jeep, but that didn't mean anything. He could be the contractor giving a bid on the new roof, or that lawyer who had been trying to contact Will with no luck. Maybe he'd given up trying to get him on the phone and had decided to come out to the ranch.

Tommy let out a bone-chilling scream of great joy. "Daddy!"

Lady whimpered and tried to move away from the child without knocking him over. Becky watched as Will looked toward the porch, then started in their direction. Tommy would have screamed himself blue if Will had turned in the opposite direction.

Maude stepped out on the porch, and Becky turned to greet her. The older woman sat down in the big leather chair and looked very upset. "Something wrong?"

"Yes," Maude said, sighing.

"I thought your camp out was a big success."

"It was, but I've just about had it with that boy," she said, as Will drew closer to the porch and started up the steps.

"With Will?" Did Maude know about this morning? Becky took a deep breath and tried to look casual as the cowboy carefully opened the door without knocking over his littlest fan. Lady took advantage of the chance to flee to a deserted corner. Will picked up Tommy and admired the plastic horse before turning to the women.

"I guess the ladies all left?" he asked. Tommy took off his hat and placed it on his own head.

Becky nodded, suddenly unable to put two words together. He wore the same shirt she'd taken off him this morning and the sight of those buttons did something to her heartbeat.

"I guess *your* company left, too?" Maude echoed, glaring at him. Will winced and set Tommy on the floor.

"Go find some more horses, kid," he said gently. Tommy kept the hat and grinned, content to have his hero in the same room. Then Will sat beside Becky in the swing, keeping a careful, polite distance between them. "Yes."

"Who was that man?"

"A real estate agent from Billings. He'd been sent here to look over the property. There are several people interested in it already."

"How convenient for you," Maude said, looking as if she'd like nothing better than to take him over her knee and spank the living daylights out of him. "And what about us? Where do we all fit into this?"

Will leaned forward, making the swing rock in a gentle motion. He planted his boots on the floor and stopped the movement. "I give up," he said, running one hand through his hair. "I'm done, finished, through."

Maude raised her eyebrows. "What exactly does that mean?"

Which is what Becky would have asked, if her tongue could move and form words.

"You can keep this place, if you want to live here so badly. I'll spend the next few weeks fixing it up the best I can before I leave. I'll get my deposit back on your condo and use it for the new roof. You and the others can stay here as long as you want to." He shrugged. "I can't fight you anymore on this, though I still think running this place is too big a job." He glanced toward Becky and added, "For all of you."

She should have felt relief. She and the boys still had a home; she still had a job. Nothing would change. But the words *before I leave* beat a painful rhythm in her heart. *Before I leave.* In a few weeks. "A new roof," was what she said, her voice sounding hollow even to her own ears. "That would be wonderful."

Every wrinkle in Maude's face headed upward as she smiled at her son. "Nothing's going to change?" she asked, as if having to hear the words again.

"No. I'll keep sending you money. You can do what you need to with it," he said, rubbing his palms on his thighs as if he was nervous. "But I'd hold off on the expensive horses for a while. And the minute your doctor tells me you shouldn't be living out here, then it's off to Billings with me, understand?"

Becky wanted to reach over and put her hand over his

and tell him he had done the right thing, but she clasped her hands together in her lap.

"I understand perfectly," Maude said. She rose and kissed her son, who stood up and hugged his mother and patiently listened to her tell him she was relieved and happy and could now go forward and have an old-fashioned barn dance to celebrate.

"This calls for a drink," Maude announced, smiling at the two of them. "I'll be right back," she called, hurrying into the house.

Will sat down again in the swing, this time a few inches closer. She wondered if he did that on purpose. He reached over and took her hand and looked down at her fingers.

Becky waited for him to say something, but he remained silent. "Why did you change your mind?" she asked finally.

"I'm not sure."

Which was not the answer she'd hoped to hear.

"I guess it's because I've never seen her so happy," Will said. "I had a lot of time to think on the way down the mountain today." He smiled his very handsome smile. "I was in the mood to think about things." He released her hand, placing it back on her thigh. "Are you okay?"

"Sure." He was leaving, he was smiling, he was acting as if this morning was nothing more than a pleasant sexual encounter between consenting adults. Which, of course, it was. And nothing more.

"I wondered—"

"Here we go," Maude said, carrying a tray of glasses, a pitcher of iced tea and a bottle of whiskey through the door. She set it down on the battered table beside the chair. "What would you like?"

"Tea is fine," Becky said, wishing she could have something stronger, but she had to go to town in a while. It would be good to get away from here, she decided, taking the glass Maude handed to her. She could use the time with her children. She could start acting like someone with a brain again.

"Will?"

"Just a swallow for me," he said. "I'm taking Becky out to dinner tonight."

She turned back toward him. "You are?"

"If Maude will baby-sit, that is. You're wearing a dress. Shame to waste it."

The older woman handed her son a glass. "Of course I will. How lovely for the two of you to go out."

"I can't," Becky said. "I have to pick up Peter in a few hours and—"

"I have to shave and shower, so we're not in any hurry. We'll go out after we get Pete," Will stated. "Unless you're too tired."

She met his gaze and saw the teasing light in his dark eyes. He was daring her to refuse him, knowing she wouldn't admit she was tired—from either last night's camping trip or this morning's lovemaking. "I'm not that tired," she said, wondering what he was up to. Surely this couldn't be a real date. Maybe he thought that after this morning he owed her a meal.

A reverse date.

"Don't look so suspicious." He laughed. "My mother will think I'm up to no good."

Maude lifted her glass. "To the success of the ranch."

Will sighed, but touched his glass to Maude's, then Becky's. "To your continued good health," he added.

"And to a new roof," Becky said.

"Daddy," Tommy said, hurrying over to Will and standing in between the man's knees. "Can I have drink too?"

"Here," Becky said, holding her glass to his lips.

Will sighed and took his hat from the child's head. "Can't you get him to stop calling me that?"

"I've tried and tried, but he won't stop."

He lifted the child onto his lap. "Tommy, I'm not your daddy."

Tommy grinned and took the hat back. "Daddy's hat," he said, grinning at the women.

Maude chuckled. "Maybe you'd better give up on that little problem, too. As long as you're in the mood to mellow."

"Mellow?" He gently pried the brim of his hat from Tommy's grip and set it on his head. "I'm not mellowing. I'm just backing up a little."

"Whatever," his mother said, taking a healthy sip of her drink. "It's a distinct improvement."

Sex will do that, Becky mused. It must take the edges off a man who figures he has too much on his mind. Or else it made him in a hurry to leave.

"I DIDN'T EXPECT this," Becky said, setting her menu aside. "Do you always feed the women you make love to?"

Will met her gaze. Those blue eyes held an expression that looked vulnerable, despite her calm manner. They sat at a corner table of the Coach House, the only decent restaurant in town, and half-empty because it was a Sunday night. "That's one of those trick questions," he drawled. "If I say yes it means I make love to a lot of women. If I say no it means I'm a cheap bastard who lets his women starve." He smiled to show he was teasing, but Becky didn't smile back.

"I apologize," she said instead, taking a sip of water from the tall stemmed glass. "I'm feeling awkward."

He wasn't. In fact, he was feeling that he definitely wanted to make love to her again, but he was smart enough to keep that thought to himself. "Don't," he said. "I thought you'd enjoy eating someone else's cooking." *I thought it was time I had you all to myself again.* Her hair was tied with one of those colored cloth things in a low ponytail, and her dress was a shade darker than her eyes. With the rose lipstick and those gold earrings, she almost looked like a stranger.

"I would, but I didn't want you to feel that you owed me anything because of what happened this—"

"Becky," he said, stopping her from finishing. "You're a beautiful woman and I'm glad you let me take you out. Can we leave it at that?"

Her cheeks flushed a becoming shade of pink as the waitress hurried over to take their order.

"Will Cody?" She peered at him from behind thick glasses. Her hair was red and curly, her face round and familiar.

"Uh, Lynn?"

She grinned. "Lynn Kelly, that's right." She looked over at Becky. "We went to high school together. A long time ago!"

"Yeah," Will answered, wishing he'd picked a different restaurant. He'd managed to avoid seeing anyone he knew these past weeks and he'd hoped to keep it that way. "How've you been?"

"Fine, fine. Married. With three children, two girls and a boy."

"Congratulations."

"Thank you. You know him. Jeff Carson? His twin sister was Lily Carson. Didn't we double date to one of the proms?"

Oh, hell. Of all the restaurants, he had to get Lily Carson's sister-in-law for a waitress. "Yeah, I think so."

She lowered her voice. "That was a shame about you and

Lily. She left town right after graduation and went to live with her aunt and uncle in Seattle. Has just the one child. Never married." Lynn looked over at Becky. "Hi there. Don't you work out at Silver Valley?"

"Yes. I'm Becky McGregor."

"I *thought* you looked familiar. Glad you came in for dinner tonight."

"Thank you."

Will had had enough socializing. "Tell Jeff I said hello."

She grinned again. "I'll do that, Will." She picked up her pad, took their orders and hurried back to the kitchen. "Help yourself to the salad bar," she called over her shoulder, and Will stood up.

"I'm starving," he lied in a hearty voice. "Want your salad now?"

Becky gave him an odd look. "All right."

He didn't know what he piled on his plate, but it looked edible. Becky took her time, seeming to enjoy the array of food laid out for her to choose. He waited patiently, glad to see that she was having a good time. When they had taken their seats again, he attempted to steer the conversation toward the new horses. Becky didn't go along with him.

"So, you have a past," she teased. "I'm finding it hard to picture you as a teenager."

"Then don't." He knew he sounded rude, and cleared his throat. "Tell me about the horses. Where did you hear about Pasos?"

Becky ignored his question. "Who was Lily? Your first girlfriend?"

"Yes." He speared a forkful of salad and began to eat.

Her eyebrows rose. "A touchy subject, I see."

He shrugged. "Why should it be?"

"I don't know. You tell me."

Will considered her request, then figured he'd have no

peace until he answered a question or two. Women were too curious by half. "Lily—" he paused, not pleased with having to speak her name "—was my high school girl-friend. We broke up before I left town."

"Did she break your heart or did you break hers?"

"Let's say it was a mutual decision." There. That should just about do it. He looked down at his plate and eyed the spoonful of cottage cheese he'd somehow chosen. There was no way in hell he was going to eat it, so he pushed his plate away and reached for his water.

"Did you leave town because of her?"

"Not exactly. My uncle was the problem there." Will frowned, remembering, and wished he hadn't. "I never thought of leaving," he admitted. "At least, I thought of go-ing for a while and then coming back. I was cocky and full of adventure and I wanted to get out and see the world. I never thought that leaving meant never being able to re-turn." He'd never thought his uncle would have been so willing to believe the worst.

Becky gave him a sympathetic look. "Your uncle must have been a very difficult man."

"Yeah. He was always looking for the bad, no matter what."

"Here's some nice hot rolls," Lynn chirped, dropping the basket in the middle of the table. "Anything else I can get for you?"

"I think we're all set," Will said, trying to smile. He hoped like hell she wouldn't start talking about high school again. That's what had gotten him into this mess in the first place. "Thanks."

"Oh, you're welcome." She patted him on the shoulder. "It's just so *good* to see you again. I can't wait to tell Jeff." With that, she moved on to another table of diners.

"She seems nice," Becky commented.

"Yeah." He didn't want to talk about Lynn and he didn't want to talk about Lily and he sure as hell didn't want to talk about himself. He'd brought Becky here to find out more about her, to be able to talk to her without distractions. Without Maude and the children, Decker and the rest of the men. He didn't know what he wanted to say to her, but he wanted to be able to look at her in peace. "You said you weren't married long."

She looked surprised at the shift in conversation. "No, not really."

"Is that hard for you?"

"Is what hard for me?"

"Not having a husband."

Becky put down her fork and considered the question. "We had our...difficulties," she admitted. "The marriage was in trouble and we were trying to work our way through it. The sad thing is that we never got a chance to find out if we could have made it work." She studied him from across the table. "Now it's my turn to ask a question." He nodded. "What made you decide to keep the ranch?"

"Guess I was tired of being the villain."

"No," she said. "There's more to it than that. You're happy here."

He laughed. "No, ma'am, I don't think that's the reason."

"Why not?"

"It's just not, that's all." Lame, even to his ears. "Maude's the one who's happy, for now. I expect she'll tire of this dude ranch business within a year or two."

"Maybe. Or maybe you'll get tired of rodeo." He watched her tuck a strand of golden hair behind her ear and wished he could touch her.

"I'm not a family man, Becky," he whispered.

Her smile was sad. "I know. When are you leaving?"

"After I arrange for the new roof and fix a few other things that could give you trouble this winter. Then I'll be on my way." He paused, then plunged in with what he wanted to tell her. "You told me last week that I should make some good memories, to replace the bad ones. You were right, and this morning was something I'll always remember."

She took a deep breath, and smiled. "Me, too."

His heart tumbled over and settled in his throat. He wished he was anywhere else but in a restaurant so he could lean over and kiss her. He couldn't be in love with her—he never fell in love, avoided it by sheer willpower—but lust was a powerful substitute. And lust was all it could be.

11

BECKY DIDN'T WANT to be in love with Will Cody. In fact, she just plain refused to be. She ignored the way Peter followed him around, begging for either a riding lesson or a checkers game. She pretended she didn't see Tommy Lee's excitement each morning when he spotted his "daddy" drinking coffee at the kitchen table. She tried very hard to forget about that morning under the pine tree and, lying alone in her bed at night, she'd had time to regret those hours.

Better not to have known passion again, if she could only have it for such a short time, she decided, after two weeks of pretending Will was nothing more to her than the owner of the SV and the man who had seen that the old ranch house sported a new roof. He'd done other things too, such as insulating water pipes to prevent the water freezing this winter, and buying Maude a new mattress. He'd replaced the old gas stove with a new model, much to Becky's surprise, and cleaned up the back porch. Decker was going to paint it white come fall.

Oh, they all agreed the summer was a good one after all. The horses were healthy and the calves were growing and the hay lay in neat round rolls, ready for winter. The bunkhouse was painted, the wooden floor covered with a new braided rug ordered from the Sears catalog. The men's bathroom had had new plumbing installed. It seemed there was nothing Will Cody couldn't do.

Except stay in one place.

Becky wiped the perspiration from her forehead with her shirtsleeve and continued to can tomatoes. She'd bought several flats of tomatoes in town the other day, and it wasn't hard to process them. Just messy, with blanching them to remove the skins, and making sure the canning jars were ready. She liked lining them up on the counter after they were finished and waiting for the satisfying *pop* that announced the lid had sealed properly.

"How pretty," Maude said, entering the kitchen and surveying the tomato-filled jars lined up on the counter. "My goodness, you did all this while I slept. I should feel very guilty."

"I'm not done yet," Becky told her. "I think I can get another dozen quarts done this afternoon."

"It's awfully hot in here."

"And hotter outside," Becky assured her. "I think everyone is taking it easy this afternoon. Which is good."

"Where are the children?"

"Peter took a ride to the creek with Will, and Tommy is still upstairs asleep. I put the fan in his room, which seemed to help."

Maude went over to the refrigerator and took out a pitcher of iced tea and a tray of ice cubes. "Come sit for a minute, Becky. Can you take a break?"

Becky turned her back on the sink full of tomatoes. "Sure," she said, grabbing two glasses from the cupboard. "Why not?" She sat down across from Maude and watched the older woman pour tea into the glasses.

"Is anything wrong?"

"No," Becky replied, taking a sip of the drink. "Why?"

"You've been quiet lately. And truthfully, dear, you look a bit pale."

"I'm fine. Just a headache."

Maude nodded. "I see. So my son hasn't done anything to...upset you?"

"Of course not. How could he?"

"Well." The older woman hesitated. "I suppose he could have done *something*. I thought it was so nice that you two went out to dinner."

"Maude." Becky sighed. "Please tell me you're not matchmaking. If you are, you have to know it wouldn't work."

"Why not?"

"We're too different."

"Didn't you have a good time?"

"Sure." To get her off the subject, Becky said, "We met an old high school friend of his. Lynn Kelly. She was our waitress, said she went to school with Will, that they had double-dated to a prom. Will didn't look too happy talking about it."

Maude shook her head. "I never knew what happened, but I always figured it had to do with some girl."

"Someone named Lily?"

"How did you know that?"

"That's the person Lynn mentioned." Becky had to ask. "Was she the reason Will left town?"

"I don't know," Maude answered, looking sad. "He never said, and my brother refused to talk about it. I wondered, though, if, well, never mind."

"What?"

Maude shook her head. "For a while I thought she might have been pregnant—I heard rumors, and she left town shortly after graduation, too—but I never wanted to believe that my son would run out on a girl if he'd gotten her pregnant."

"I can't believe Will would do that either." Meaning she didn't *want* to believe he was capable of that, but she didn't know him when he was eighteen. She didn't know why he'd left town and never returned, or why he and his uncle had quarreled to the point that Will had been disinherited. Or at least thought he'd been.

"It's a mystery." Maude sighed.

"Have you ever asked him?" Becky finished the drink and stood up. She would go back to her tomatoes and stop talking about Maude's son. She didn't want to know about Lily, she realized, feeling a little sick to her stomach.

"And let him think I believed the worst of him? No." Maude stood, too, and carried her glass to the counter. "Can I do something to help?"

"No. It's not going to take long to finish this next batch now that I have everything set up. You should go out on the porch, Maude, where it's cooler." Once again her stomach flipped, making her realize she shouldn't have eaten such a large lunch in this heat. "I'll join you as soon as Tommy wakes up."

"You work too hard," the older woman grumbled, but she refilled her glass and headed toward the porch, leaving Becky alone once again in the kitchen.

She wasn't in love with him, she thought. And even if she was, just a little bit, she would get over it. She didn't have any other choice.

"It's AWFUL HOT," Peter said, as they approached the creek. They were on their way home from what had become a very short ride. Will had realized pretty quick that it was just too damn hot to be out looking at cows and teaching a five-year-old kid how to stay on a horse.

"Yeah," he agreed, stopping by the water. "You want a drink?"

"Sure." The boy hopped off the horse like an experienced wrangler and led the horse to the water for a drink.

"We'll tie the horses in the shade," he told the boy. "We'll cool off for a minute before we head home."

"Neat!"

Will had no idea that that meant Pete would remove his boots and socks and stick his bare feet in the water up to his knees in a matter of three seconds. "Whoa, there, boy," he called. "That water is deeper than it—"

"I'm okay," the boy called, stepping farther into the muddy creek.

"Wait for me," Will hollered, stepping closer to the creek. He wouldn't mind taking off his clothes and jumping in that water.

"It's not cold," Peter said, moving forward.

"You've gone far enough." Will sat down and had one boot off when Peter slipped, fell over backward into the water and disappeared. Will was beside him in seconds, lifting the choking child into his arms with a silent plea that the boy was all right. He was choking, he was breathing, Will repeated to himself, depositing the boy on to the creek bank.

Peter coughed and turned wide eyes on Will. "That," he managed to spit out, "was pretty scary." Tears welled in his eyes.

"I'll bet." Will took a deep breath and willed his heart to stay in his chest. He'd thought he'd lost the boy there for a minute, and it had been scarier than riding any bull or half-loco bronc. He hugged the boy to his chest for a few minutes, and Pete rested his head on Will's shoulder.

"I don't know how to swim," the child confessed.

"The bottom of the creek is kind of uneven," Will explained. "You hit a low spot, that's all. But you should learn how to swim, even if you're just in a little creek."

"You gonna teach me?"

"Maybe." He set the boy on his feet and looked at him,

soaking wet and muddy, too. "Your mother's going to have a fit."

"We have to tell her?"

"Yep. She's going to wonder why we're all wet." Becky was going to be upset when she learned he nearly let her son drown. He didn't relish explaining it to her, either. When the water had closed over Peter's head, Will had felt a panic like he'd never felt before. So this was what it was like, being a father. Trying like hell to keep the little rascals safe, swallowing the lump of fear after you knew that you couldn't do the job.

Peter wrapped his arms around Will's neck and gave him a hug. "I love you," the child said.

Will sighed and patted the boy's fragile back. "Yeah," he said, unable to say the words in return. He didn't love the child. He couldn't. He wasn't that kind of man. "Don't cry," he said, tucking the sobbing boy against his chest once again. "Everything's going to be fine. You're okay now."

"MY SON ALMOST drowned? How did this happen?"

Becky stood in the door to Will's bedroom as he stepped out of the bathroom. Fortunately for both of them, he thought, he was still wearing his jeans. He rubbed his wet hair with a towel and looked at her. "He fell in the creek," he replied. "I fished him out right away."

"You were supposed to be watching him."

"I was. He was a little too anxious to go in the water and didn't realize that the bottom dropped off. Those creek beds are—"

"I *know* how they are," she said, entering his bedroom. He backed up a few steps, hoping she'd come in even farther.

"Shut the door if you're going to yell," he said, wondering what those orange spots were on her shirt. She looked like she could use a shower, too. "I think Maude has company."

She shut the door, and Will tried to hide his smile. She was in his bedroom and she was marching toward him. She was talking to him, which she hadn't done in two weeks except to say things like, "Please pass the butter" and "Are you done with dinner?"

Becky looked upset, though, which was too bad. "Look," he tried, tossing the towel on the bed. "It was an accident. Nothing bad happened."

"It *could* have."

"But it didn't." He smiled down into those worried blue eyes. "It scared the living daylights out of me, too. I thought I'd never stop shaking." He put his hands on her shoulders. "He's fine, and I think he's learned to stop when someone tells him to stop. I'm sorry."

She tilted her head. "Really?"

"Really." He bent to kiss her lips. Just one of those reassuring kinds of kisses, of course. He didn't mean to slant his lips across hers. He certainly didn't mean for the kiss to lead to an overwhelming desire to make love to her.

"You're muddy," she whispered.

"You smell like...tomatoes." He nuzzled her neck. "Makes me think of making love to a pizza."

Becky pulled back. "Thanks a lot." She laughed in spite of herself. "I shouldn't yell at you. I'm sorry. You saved him, and that's all that matters."

He held on to her shoulders and spoke clearly, so that she wouldn't continue to worry over what might have happened. "The water wasn't deep. He lost his balance, that's all, though he gave me a scare there for a few seconds. Where is he now?"

"Oatey's giving him a bath. Suddenly he's too big for his mother to be in the bathroom with him."

He kissed her again. "I think you're just right," he said, taking her hand and leading her toward his bathroom. "And you could use a shower, too."

She looked down at her tomato-splattered shirt. "Thank you so much for pointing that out."

Will chuckled, leading her through the door. "I'll do anything, say anything, to get you to take a shower with me." He turned and started unbuttoning her blouse.

"You're limping again. You hurt yourself jumping into the creek, didn't you?"

He shrugged, opening her shirt and running his palms along her bare shoulders. "Nothing an ice pack won't cure."

She placed her hands on his bare chest. "Someone could find us in here."

"Not if we're quiet," he said, lowering his voice. "Oatey is taking care of the boys, Maude has company, and you and I are taking a shower."

"Together?"

He slipped the sleeves from her arms and tossed the shirt to the tiled floor. "Why not?"

"It seems so—" she hesitated, still touching his chest "—intimate."

Will resolved to be a hell of a lot more intimate than just standing under a shower head, but he kept his mouth shut and concentrated on unsnapping the waistband and opening the zipper of Becky's jeans. She wore cute little light blue bikini underwear, which he pushed down past her hips along with the jeans, and Becky wriggled out of them in quick fashion.

"Your turn," she said, standing naked before him. The snap had been undone earlier, since she'd interrupted him.

She surprised him by reaching for him, sliding the zipper down with some difficulty. The denim was still damp and stuck to his skin. She eased soft fingers between his skin and his cotton briefs, and Will had to force himself not to take her right there on the bathroom floor.

She pushed his jeans lower, then lowered his wet briefs past his hips. He helped her then, knowing he couldn't take much more of her hands against his body. He kicked his clothes aside, then held her against him while he kissed her and took her mouth with his tongue. Her breasts were against him, a tantalizing feeling that threatened to take his breath away. They kissed for long moments, until he regained his senses. They wouldn't have much time, so he reached over and turned on the water.

"Wait," he said, reaching for her hair. He carefully drew the elastic from the end of the braid, then separated the thick strands of golden hair, running his fingers through the ripples made by the braid and draping the strands over her shoulders. It was as beautiful as he imagined, and he wanted to feel it on his skin when he made love to her.

He didn't know how they managed to shower without making love right then and there, in the cocoon of tile and steam. They washed each other with soap-slicked hands and watery kisses as the warm water rained down over their bodies. He turned off the water, grabbed at the towels stacked on a shelf, and led Becky toward his bed.

"We're soaking wet," she whispered, hesitating before the bed.

He wrapped her in a towel. "Better?"

She stood on tiptoe and kissed him. "Almost."

He lifted her by the waist and sat her on his bed, then proceeded to lick drops of water from her knees. She laughed, and he went higher, to the sweetness between her thighs. Sweet and ready and all his, Will discovered. He fished a condom from his nightstand, joined her on the bed, and entered her with slow, deep strokes.

Becky lay on her back beneath him, her legs drawn up to tangle with his, her eyes smiling as he moved within her. "I wish we had hours," he whispered. *Or a lifetime.* The thought surprised him, and he pushed it aside as he withdrew slightly, then moved into her again. He felt her climax almost immediately. She sighed and contracted around him, and he moved faster, deeper, until he'd come inside her with an almost alarming intensity. He rested his forehead on her shoulder until he could regain his senses, until his shuddering body could function enough to move from Becky's.

He rolled to his side and fell back on the pillow. His bare leg still touched hers, and he liked knowing all that wonderful female softness was beside him. At least for a few minutes. Becky turned to face him, so he tucked her into his arms and against his chest. The long hair was tangled between them, as erotic a feeling as he'd imagined.

"I should go," she said. "They'll be looking for me."

"I need you here."

She smiled as if he'd said something funny and attempted to move away. He lifted himself to release the yellow hair caught under his shoulder. He watched as she quickly found her clothes and dressed. She gathered her wet hair at the base of her neck, made a quick ponytail and looked back at him before she touched the doorknob. "I hope I can get back to the other end of the house without being seen."

"You look perfectly normal," he lied. She looked like a woman who had just been made love to. Her cheeks were flushed and her lips swollen from his kisses. She was barefoot, carrying her sneakers in one hand as she opened the door enough to peek out to the corridor. She didn't say goodbye, just slipped out of the room and shut the door behind her with a quiet click.

Will lay alone, naked and satisfied. He realized his knee ached, but the pain didn't register above the intense pleasure that still pulsed through his blood. He didn't know how he hadn't made love to her in two weeks, didn't know how they had managed to stay apart when it was obvious that any time they were alone, sparks flew and the temperature in their small part of Montana rose several degrees.

He had to leave, of course, though he'd missed most of the rodeo season and wouldn't be able to compete again, not seriously, until winter. If he didn't go soon, he wouldn't be able to. Becky would start expecting him to stay and be a respectable rancher. A father. A husband, even. He closed his eyes and wondered what the hell he was going to do. He'd enjoyed himself here. He hadn't expected to find a ready-made family in a place he hated.

Will sighed, willing himself not to think about the little blonde with the tempting body. He should have known better than to make love to Becky again, that's all.

BECKY WAITED four more days. Four agonizing days, waiting for relief from the worry that twisted her stomach and made her want to hide in her room with her head under the pillows. On Monday she could no longer stand the suspense and took the boys to town with her. They needed supplies, she told Maude. They would need more canning jars and lids, more sugar for canned fruit, more white vinegar for pickles. The pickling cukes had been hard to stay ahead of.

The smell of vinegar made her queasy, as did brewing coffee and cow manure. It was fortunate that Will spent his days acting like the foreman of this place, while she spent her time being busy in the kitchen. She'd begun to find the heat unbearable and the warm wind suffocating.

She'd found it hard to breathe normally, especially as the days crept slowly on. The trip to town didn't help. The boys were cranky, not pleased with the long ride in the station wagon. Tommy objected to riding in the shopping cart and Peter begged for expensive boxes of brand name cereal. She promised them ice-cream cones if they would behave for just a few more minutes. She paused for a long moment in the feminine products aisle, said a brief prayer and tossed a blue box into the cart.

"What's that?" Peter asked.

She wished he wasn't so darn smart. "Girl stuff," she said, covering the box with a large package of toilet paper.

"But it's blue."

"So?" Becky cleared her throat. "What kind of ice-cream cones are we going to get?"

That distracted them, thank goodness. She made it through dripping chocolate ice-cream cones, the hot trip home, Tommy messing his pants twenty miles from the ranch, and Peter's incessant questions about swimming lessons, having a friend spend the night, and when he could go riding again. She stopped on the side of the road and threw up. She told herself it was nerves. She wasn't used to this kind of heat—everyone said it was a record-breaking summer—or having an affair or canning this much fruit. She told herself it was too soon to feel sick, that it could be a touch of the flu. Or food poisoning.

Becky told herself a lot of things, until she locked herself in her bathroom later that afternoon, when the kids were resting and Maude had gone to visit yet another new friend, and the men were somewhere staying out of the sun. She followed the directions precisely, though her hands shook as she read them.

And when all was said and done, the results were positive. She had made love to Will Cody under the pine tree twenty-three days ago. She was ten days late and, according to the little plastic indicator, she was pregnant with Will Cody's child.

"LOOK ON THE bright side," Decker drawled. "He's still here."

Maude poured her old friend another finger of whiskey. "He's starting to talk about leaving again. Couldn't you come up with something else for him to fix?"

"Hell, Maudie, I broke that damn toilet twice. He'd start gettin' suspicious if something happened again." He took a sip of the drink and watched the sky darken from the kitchen window.

She sighed. "I'll make him promise to stay for the dance."

"Damn dance," Decker grumbled. "I suppose you expect us to get all spiffed up and lead them ladies around."

"Yes, I do. There will be other men there. I've sent invitations to all the ranches within seventy miles. You won't be alone."

He still didn't look happy. "Least it's a square dance."

"That was Theresa's idea. She said as long as we were going to have a barn dance, we might as well be authentic. She's such a smart woman."

"Authentic, huh? I think you've lost your mind. Camping trips are one thing, dances are something else."

"I've got three more trips lined up," Maude confided. "I put an ad in the Bozeman newspaper and got all sorts of phone calls."

He frowned. "Who's gonna do all the work?"

"We are. If my son is foolish enough to leave I suppose I might have to look around for a nice teenager to help us with the heavy things." She took another sip of her drink. "Maybe I should get someone to help Becky, too. She's looking a little tired lately."

"Peaked," Decker agreed. "Like she's got something on her mind."

"She's not happy. And you're right. She's not eating."

"Maybe she's sick. Oughta see a doctor."

Maude nodded. She didn't like the way the young woman picked at her food every meal. She seemed edgy, too, and never sat down and had a second cup of coffee in the mornings anymore. Maude missed those morning chats. "I'll suggest it. Do you think she's working too hard?"

Decker shrugged. "I thought Will was doin' most of the work around here, but what does an old cowboy know about women?" He answered his own question. "Not much."

Maude ignored him. She should have known better than to expect Decker to have any worthwhile insights. Something was wrong, although Will still looked at Becky with that certain expression, like he wished they were all alone. It was very romantic, and Maude was finding it harder and harder to ignore. Yet Becky was the problem. She acted cheerful, but not the kind of cheerful that a person could believe. It was forced, as if she was putting on a show for everyone. As if she didn't want anyone to know what was going on in her head.

Becky could be in love with Will, of course. And hurt that he was still talking about leaving. He'd put a few things in the bed of that old pickup truck, and he had made some phone calls and talked to some of his rodeo friends. He was still fixing things and teaching her how to keep track of expenses and keep up with the bookkeeping. So there was still hope. As long as that young man was on this property, there was still hope. If ever two people were meant for each other, it was those two.

Maude hauled herself out of the kitchen chair and put her empty glass in the sink. "Well, I'd like to sit here and drink with you, but I've got to keep up with the books. Will's orders," she muttered. "Part of his new plan."

"Least you're fortified," Decker said, grinning.

"Take the bottle out to the bunkhouse," Maude said. "*Then* tell the men they're expected to dance with the ladies on Saturday night."

"Yes, ma'am," he said, standing up and taking the whiskey bottle by the neck. "That's one order I'd be happy to carry out."

"Thanks." Maude went into the office and sat down to survey this week's pile of receipts. Thirty minutes later, her pencil paused in midair and she squinted at the narrow piece of paper in her hand. She dropped her pencil, folded the piece of paper and carefully tucked it in the pocket of her jeans. Now it was time to get serious. It was time to come up with a plan, something that would make everything come out just right. Maude smiled, and patted her pocket. She'd been waiting for years for such a lovely, lovely gift.

"I THINK THIS is my dance," Will drawled, sweeping Becky in his arms as the band began playing "The Tennessee Waltz." She didn't have time to refuse, though she'd been staying away from him all week. There was no sense being around him, she'd decided. Not until she figured out what she was going to do about the baby.

The baby. She closed her eyes. Suddenly the inside of the barn was spinning around.

"Are you all right?" His arms tightened around her and she wanted to lean her head against his shoulder and scream, *"No, I'm not all right!"* Then he would demand to know what was wrong, and she would tell him that old condoms from first aid kits weren't reliable and she was going to have his child. And he would hold her very gently and tell her they would get married and live happily ever after. And pigs would fly and cows would milk themselves and the price of beef would triple.

"I'm fine," she said, and smiled. "Just a little dizzy."

"It's hot in here. I wouldn't have thought so many people would come to this shindig."

"Everyone brought food, and the band is playing for free."

"They should," Will said, trying to keep step with a band that wasn't quite on tempo.

Becky chuckled. "That's not nice."

He looked down into her face. "Where have you been all evening? I thought this would end without my getting to dance with you."

"I was, uh, busy. With the food."

"Too busy. Did the boys go to bed?"

"Yes. I hired one of the Carter girls to stay with them." The Carters were Dr. Theresa's nieces. There were three of them, all in high school and all sturdy, reliable girls who were happy to earn the money, Theresa had assured her. The middle one, Debbie, had come with her aunt and would stay until the party ended.

"My mother is in her glory," Will said.

"It was...nice of you to stay for her party. I know you must be anxious to be on your way."

"I couldn't refuse her." His arm tightened around her back again. "Becky, about this summer, I wanted you to know—"

"Don't," she said, stopping him from saying anything that would make her cry. "Let's not talk."

"But—"

"No. We had some wonderful moments together. You don't have to say anything. We're both adults who knew what we were doing." She looked up into his wonderful dark eyes and wondered if their baby would have those eyes. Those eyelashes. That mouth.

"If you keep looking at me like that, I'll have to scandalize the crowd and kiss you," he warned. "Maude would swoon with joy."

"And get her hopes up."

"Yeah." He stopped smiling and looked past her shoulder.

"What's the matter?" she asked, and turned around to see what he was looking at. A small group of people was gathered around someone on the dance floor. "Oh, no. It looks like someone fell."

Will dropped her hand as the music stopped and the two of them hurried to the edge of the straw-covered dance floor. Maude looked up at them and made a face.

"I slipped," she said. "I feel ridiculous."

Theresa was by her side, examining her friend's ankle. "Looks like a pretty bad sprain. Let's get some ice on it."

Becky tried to get closer to Maude, and Will was right behind her.

"I knew something like this was going to happen sooner or later," he muttered. He knelt beside his mother as Decker quickly produced a dish towel filled with ice from one of the washtubs that held cans of beer and soda pop.

"Let's get her to the hospital," Will said.

Theresa and Maude exchanged looks, then the doctor patted Will on the arm to reassure him. "Nothing's broken. I'm positive. But sometimes sprains are more painful and take longer to heal than breaks. She's going to need to stay off her feet for a while."

Maude shook her head. "Oh, dear," she said, sounding pitiful. Several people offered advice, Theresa kept the ice covering Maude's ankle and foot, and Maude insisted the band keep playing.

"How did you fall? Is there something slippery we should have cleaned up?" Will asked.

"I don't know," his mother said. "It just...happened."

He picked her up in his arms. "Let's get you to bed."

"I don't want to make a scene," she protested, but she put her arms around his neck and moaned a little.

Becky looked back at Theresa, who hurried after her patient. "Keep the ice on it," she said. "It will keep the swelling down."

Becky didn't know if she should follow them or act as hostess in Maude's place. She felt a little sick to her stomach again. Maude lying there hurt had been a frightening sight. Will looked furious, as if he wanted to burn down the barn.

Decker came up and stood beside her. "Don't worry, honey. Maude's fine. She's a tough old bird."

"He'll never let her stay now. Not if she's hurt."

Decker patted her on the shoulder. "I hate to think you're right, honey, but I'm afraid you jest might have a point."

12

"THAT'S IT," Will declared. He was clearly worried, and Becky didn't blame him for being upset. It had been a shock to see Maude helpless on the barn floor. Still, Maude hadn't looked as if she was in a lot of pain. Her cheeks had been flushed, and her eyes bright. Becky had decided her place was with the family.

"That's it," Will repeated, setting Maude on her bed. "You're coming with me. We're moving you to Billings, to a ground floor apartment within walking distance of—"

"I'm not going anywhere," his mother grumbled, arranging her skirts to protect her modesty. "Not with a hurt ankle. Right, Theresa?"

"Right," the doctor declared. She moved closer to the bed and made sure the ice pack covered Maude's ankle. "You're staying put, at least for a few more weeks."

"Weeks?" Will looked horrified.

The doctor nodded. "Weeks. At least. You'll have to leave now." She turned to Becky. "Would you help me get her into a nightgown and into bed, please?"

"Sure." The women waited for Will to leave the room, then Maude began unbuttoning her frilly white blouse. She smiled at Becky.

"I'm fine, dear. Don't worry about a thing."

"But—"

"Theresa and I can manage," Maude insisted. "Go out

there and calm Will down. Tell him I'm not going anywhere."

"All right." Becky hesitated before turning the doorknob. "He's awfully upset, Maude. I think you should start thinking about what he's saying, moving to Billings and all. You can't run the ranch with broken bones."

The old lady winked. "Worry about nothing."

Becky smiled as if she believed her, but once she left the room and shut the door behind her, she leaned against the wall and closed her eyes for a long moment.

"I knew something like this would happen."

She opened her eyes to see Will standing in front of her, his hands crammed into his pockets, his dark eyes filled with worry. "It was an accident," she said. "And she's going to be fine."

"And what about next time? A fall from a horse? Tripping on the stairs?" He shook his head. "I can't leave her here. She's too damned independent. She thinks she's invincible."

Becky didn't try to argue with him. It was obvious she and the men couldn't keep Maude from harm. Their little balloon had burst: there would be no more pack trips or barn dances; there would be no Paso-breeding business or day tours from the travel company Maude had written to. It was over.

And that would save Becky from staying here and growing bigger every week. It would save explanations and her pride. Especially her pride. How could she tell him she was expecting his child? Yet how could she not?

Theresa opened the door. "You can come in now." She eyed Will. "Stop looking like she's dying. It's only a sprained ankle, for heaven's sake."

He didn't smile, but let Becky step into the room ahead of him.

"I'm calling that real estate agent first thing Monday morning," he said. "I'll make all the arrangements for the move to Billings."

"I'm not leaving," Maude said. "I can't go anywhere for at least a few weeks, right, Theresa?"

"Right."

Becky watched both women and wondered what on earth was going on. Maude looked remarkably cheerful for a woman who had just suffered a painful sprain and a scare, too. She looked almost happy to be in the bed giving orders. And Theresa, busy adjusting that enormous ice pack, was having trouble meeting Will's gaze. The two women were up to something, and Becky leaned against the far wall of the bedroom, folded her arms across her chest and watched to see what would happen next.

"Of course," Maude said, her voice suddenly weak. "You can go back to the rodeo, dear. We'll be fine here, just like we've always been."

"I can't leave now," he said.

"We'll talk on the phone, just like we always have," she assured him. Decker poked his head through the door.

"Just wanted to see how you was doing," he said, removing his hat. "Told the band I'd find out so they could make an announcement."

"It's a sprain," Theresa explained. "Nothing more serious." She looked at her watch. "I think the band stops playing at eleven. Will, why don't you go say good-night to the guests?"

"Good idea," Maude said, nodding. "It's only polite."

He scowled, but left the room. "I'll be right back," he said, and Decker followed him down the hall.

"There." Maude grinned at her friend. "I think that went very well, don't you?"

"Beautifully," Theresa said. "Though it's a good thing

I've retired. I think I've stretched the Hippocratic oath far enough for one night, thank you very much."

Becky stepped forward, lifted the ice pack from Maude's ankle and saw a very normal-looking foot. Red from the cold, it wasn't swollen or bruised. She looked back at Maude. "You're not really hurt?"

"Nope."

"Maude! What are you doing?"

She shook her head. "I'm not telling you, not yet. We both have our secrets, don't we?"

Becky swallowed. Maude couldn't know. It was impossible. She'd carefully hidden the pregnancy-test box in the bottom of her closet until she could decide how to throw it away without anyone seeing it. Still, there was a light in the old woman's eyes that made Becky flush and back up a couple of steps. "You can't do this to him."

"He's going to stay," Maude declared. "All's fair in love and war."

"Not necessarily," Becky said.

"Oh, yes, it is." Maude smiled once again. "Don't worry, dear. Everything is going to be just fine. I have a plan."

"I should be terrified of your plans by now."

"Haven't they always worked out?"

Theresa hurried to adjust the ice pack as they heard footsteps in the hall. Several members of the Not Dead Yet Club stuck their heads in the door and wished Maude a speedy recovery. One offered to postpone Thursday's meeting until Maude was up and around.

"I'll keep you posted!" Maude waved cheerfully at the ladies in the doorway. Becky offered to make a pot of decaffeinated coffee and hurried to the kitchen. She didn't know exactly what Maude was up to, but she didn't want Will to think that she was part of his mother's scheme. Theresa and Maude would have to handle things by them-selves.

And she would have to figure out what she was going to do with her own secrets.

THERESA DECLARED THAT SHE was going to take her niece and head home, Will paid the teenager before Becky could protest, and soon the house was quiet. Except for the sound of Maude arguing with him. Becky brought them coffee and tried to leave.

Will blocked her way. "Not so fast. Tell her you can't run this place by yourself."

Becky turned to Maude. "You know it's true, Maude. I'd be happy to try, but I think I'd better move on. I've been thinking about it for a while and, now that Peter is going to start school in a couple of years, maybe I should move back to Des Moines. I have an aunt there, and she'd be—"

"*You* are not going anywhere," Maude said, pointing to Becky before turning to her son. "And *you* are not selling this ranch. You can't now."

"Of course I can." He softened his voice. He knew she was going to have to make some big adjustments, and he was prepared to be patient. But he was also prepared to take care of her, even if she didn't want him to. "I know you love it here, but maybe we could lease it out, so we could visit once in—"

"No, you idiot, it's not your ranch anymore." She grinned. "You never met with that lawyer, did you?"

"Well, no, but—"

"And you never read your uncle's will, either."

Will frowned. "Why would I want to do that? It was over thirty pages long."

"You should have read it."

"Excuse me," Becky said, backing out of the room. "I'll leave you two alone to discuss—"

"This concerns you, Becky," Maude said. She nodded toward the pine chair by her bed. "Sit down, please."

Becky sat, but Will noticed that she didn't look too happy about it.

"Did Theresa give you any pain pills?" Will asked. "Are you feeling dizzy or a little woozy?"

"No. The will you didn't bother to read, son, states that the minute you have a child, the ranch belongs to him. Or her. Oh, you control running it and all that, but it's held in trust for your child. Or children. You can't sell it."

"So? I don't have any children. Never did."

Becky turned white when Maude looked at her, leaving Will wondering where all the air in the room had gone. Suddenly he found it hard to breathe. "What...are you talking about?"

His mother turned to Becky. "I'm right, aren't I?"

Becky opened her mouth but no sound came out, and she turned to Will with a helpless expression in those blue eyes.

"Becky?" Will stared at her, unwilling to believe that she could actually be...pregnant. The word gave him chills and, on a deeper, insane level, a feeling of pride. "Are you..."

She nodded and grew very pale. So pale, in fact, he was afraid she'd topple off the chair and crash to the floor.

"You can't sell now," Maude repeated, sounding quite pleased with herself. "It's out of your hands."

"That's quite a plan," he managed to say. He turned to Becky and steadied her with one hand on her shoulder. He looked down into those gorgeous eyes, but they didn't affect him. Not this time. "Were you going to tell me?"

She shook her head.

"I see," he said. "You were going to make a little visit to the lawyer first, I'll bet."

"No. I didn't know anything about the will," she said, turning to Maude. "You shouldn't have done this, Maude."

Will didn't let his mother respond. "Of course she should. She and her brother are more alike than I ever dreamed." He turned around and went to the door, then stopped. He was angry, his eyes cold as he looked at the women. "You've both got what you wanted now, what you wanted all along. The ranch is all yours to do with whatever you want." He looked at Becky again. "You took some pretty big chances, lady. Guess you thought it was worth it."

He slammed the door on the way out, and they heard his angry footsteps disappear down the stairs.

Becky pressed her palms together and willed herself not to tremble. "Maude, how could you?"

"No choice." Maude sat up and kicked the ice pack off her ankle. "I thought he'd stay if I was hurt. I didn't think the damn fool would start rattling on about selling out first thing Monday morning. I wanted him here, so you'd have time to tell him about the baby."

The baby. There was going to be another fatherless child on the Silver Valley ranch. The thought made her feel like crying, but she promised herself that she wouldn't cry in front of either Cody. "How did you know?"

"The receipt from the store. I record all the expenses now, the way Will taught me. Those new computer scanners tell what you bought, right there on the slip. I wasn't sure, so when I was in town yesterday I checked at the store and sure enough, that's what it was. One of those early pregnancy tests."

"You didn't know it was positive."

"Sure I did. You've been acting strange lately, my dear."

Maude swung her legs over the bed and tried to take Becky's hand, but Becky pulled away. "Not drinking coffee, looking terribly pale and worried. I put two and two together and—"

"Came up with a disaster." Becky stood. "It was none of your business, Maude. You shouldn't have meddled."

"My future grandchild is none of my business? How can you say such a thing?"

Becky turned away and left the room without answering. She didn't follow Will downstairs. Instead, she walked toward the other wing, to her own room. She checked to see that the children were sleeping, then went into her room and locked the door behind her. She was going to cry for about a hundred hours and she didn't want to be interrupted.

"HE'S LEAVING." Maude hurried out of the kitchen and stood on the back porch to look out the window. "He's been packing up his truck since dawn."

"Well, Maude, what did you expect?" Becky fixed herself a cup of tea and wished the hot shower she'd taken had made her feel better. She'd finally drifted into sleep around two, then woke at six feeling queasy and weepy. But she'd be damned if she'd let either of them know it. "I'm going to be leaving, too."

"You can't," Maude said, still looking out the window. "Your child is going to own this place."

"I won't have Will thinking I tricked him into getting me pregnant just so I would get my hands on this ranch."

"He doesn't think that."

"Of course he does." Becky sighed. "Why wouldn't he?" She took another sip of tea and added more sugar. Tommy finished his cereal and patted his head with milk-soaked hands. "Don't do that, Tommy. Be a good boy."

"Okay," the child agreed, and dropped the empty cereal bowl on the floor and watched the plastic dish bounce twice and scare the dog. Lady, sensing that something was wrong, hid under the table while she waited for Peter to wake up. She whined as Becky retrieved the bowl and put it in the sink.

"Very nice, Tommy," Becky said, hoping this next child would be a girl. And then she felt like crying again, so she stuck her hands in the soapy water and started washing dishes.

Maude returned to the kitchen. "Your pregnancy was a lovely accident. I have to admit, it couldn't have worked out better."

"For you, maybe. I could have done it a little differently." She should have put that ad in the paper and found herself another job.

Maude patted her back. "It will all work out. My son won't turn his back on his child. He's just upset, but he'll come around soon enough."

"I don't know, Maude," Becky said, reaching for the frying pan. She breathed through her mouth so she wouldn't smell the bacon grease. "I'm not real happy about raising another child alone, but I don't want to hook up with a man who doesn't want me, either. I had one bad marriage, I don't want another one."

Maude looked as if she wanted to argue, but Peter came down the back stairs and yawned. "Hi," he said to everyone, then disappeared under the kitchen table to greet the dog.

Decker walked in, his face solemn. "That boy's in a real bad mood this morning. He's loading up his truck right now. What the hell's going on around here?"

"Hell!" Tommy grinned at the cowboy. "Hell!"

"Now you be quiet," the old man told him. "No sense

sitting in that high chair cussing like an old wrangler." He looked at Becky. "You don't look too good either. You and Will have a fight?"

"I guess you could say that."

"Well, go make up. This place is crazy enough as it is." Decker poured himself a cup of coffee. "That boy said he's figuring to enter the rodeo in Casper tonight and ride tomorrow. What kind of talk is that?" the man grumbled.

Becky knew she should talk to Will privately. She'd considered that last night, in the quiet of her room, after she'd used thirty or forty tissues and her eyes were swollen almost shut. She'd realized then, through buckets of tears, that she loved Will Cody and wanted to have his child. But she didn't want him to marry her out of pity or for a chunk of Montana real estate or for some noble reason about giving the child a father.

She wanted him to love her, and stay because he loved her. She wasn't going to settle for less. She didn't need him. She could manage quite well on her own, which she had spent the last two and a half years proving to herself and anyone else who happened to notice. If Will Cody wanted to leave, he should leave. She wasn't going to do a damn thing to stop him, either.

NO ONE STOPPED him. Will packed his few belongings in the meager light of dawn and loaded the truck bed with the few things he'd brought with him last month. He didn't pause to question why he was so angry, but it seemed to well out of him as if it had been there for a long time waiting to boil over.

The cowboys stayed out of his way. Men had a hell of a lot more sense than women, that was certain.

He was going to be a father. The words hummed along with him as he worked to clean out the horse trailer and get the little mare ready for a trip. *He was going to be a father.* How crazy was that? He wasn't a father, though. He was a god-damn sperm bank, and those energetic sperm had handed the deed to the SV into the hands of Becky's waiting egg.

An accident of nature or the result of brilliant planning? Maude had seen that they were alone on the mountain, Becky had been warm and willing, there were condoms in the first aid kit. Condoms that were old, that could have had pinholes put in them and been resealed. He'd heard of those things happening. He just never thought it could hap-pen to him.

But a child meant keeping the ranch. And Becky and Maude had been hell-bent on keeping the ranch. He looked back toward the house. If only Becky would come out and talk to him, tell him it wasn't true, look up at him with those soft blue eyes and tell him it had all been an accident, that she had never pretended to love him....

He shook his head. She wasn't going to come out and say that, because none of it was true. The only truth was that he loved her, loved her as he had never loved any woman be-fore, and she was content to let him go.

She had what she wanted, and what she wanted wasn't Will Cody.

LADY STUCK HER HEAD through the narrow window that separated the cab of the truck from the covered back. Once again she whined, a high piercing sound that went right through his head.

"All right," he told her, and pulled off to the side of the road. "You're the one who wanted to ride in the back." He shut off the ignition and got out of the truck. They'd been on the road for almost an hour, heading south on a back road toward Wyoming, and there wasn't another car or truck in sight. He hopped out of the truck and lifted the back window. And froze.

"Hi, Will," the child said. Peter was curled up on Will's sleeping bag, his head using the saddle as a pillow.

"What the hell," Will began, then took a deep breath. He didn't want to scare the child, but the temptation to holler at him was irresistible. He took a deep breath as Lady came over and licked his face. "What in God's name are you doing in the back of my truck?"

"Going with you and Lady," the child replied, as if it was a sensible explanation.

"Going with me and Lady," Will repeated, pushing the dog from his face. "What do you think your mother's going to say about this?"

The child shrugged. "She won't be mad. 'Cuz I'm with you."

"I think you're a little wrong there, kid." There had been no goodbyes. Of course, he waited for Maude to come out and scold him. He wondered if Becky would follow him to the truck and tell him he was going to be a father, the way a man should hear it. She hadn't. He'd said goodbye to the men, then returned to his truck. "How did you get in here?"

"I just did, that's all."

Which was why the dog had uncharacteristically insisted on riding in the back, of course. Will held out his hand. "Well, come on. It's not safe for you to ride back here. Come on up front."

Peter untangled himself from the sleeping bag and crawled over to Will. "Okay. Are we going to a rodeo? Decker said you were gonna ride in one again."

"No." He lifted the boy from the truck and set him on the gravel road. Lady hopped out, too, did her business in the grass, then trotted back to them with her tail wagging.

"We're going to head back to the ranch, before your mother has a fit."

Will settled the boy in a seat belt, shoved Lady between them, and turned the truck in the opposite direction. So much for leaving. He couldn't get away from the goddamn place no matter how hard he tried.

He turned the radio on and began to whistle.

"DON'T SEE HIM nowhere around the barns," Malone declared. "I think he's with Decker. Must be."

"No." Becky shook her head. "Decker thought he was with you."

"Then mebbee he's with Oatey."

"Oatey's asleep in his bunk. Last night wore him out."

"Ain't surprised," the man muttered. "He danced with all those women, every dance." He patted Becky's arm. "Now, don't you worry. Pete's probably taken them action figures and is building a fort somewhere under a tree where we can't see him. I'll keep lookin'."

"All right. Thanks." Becky held Tommy in her arms and made another search of the house. She called Peter's name until Tommy held his chubby hands over his ears and cried for her to stop.

"Pete go for ride," the child whimpered.

"A ride? I don't think so, honey." She set Tommy down and got on her hands and knees to peer under Peter's bed. "Peter McGregor, you had better not be playing a trick on me!"

Silence. And the knot in her stomach tripled in size.

"Daddy's 'ruck." Tommy sat down and started to sob. "Me, too. I want go Daddy's 'ruck, too."

"Daddy's truck?" She turned to him. "Did Peter go in Daddy's truck?"

Tommy cried harder, so Becky scooped him up into her

arms and went to find Maude. Peter had been upset that Lady was leaving, furious that Will was packing up to go away. Becky had thought he'd gone off to cry, so she'd given him time to be alone. But when she'd looked for him she hadn't found him in any of the usual places around the outbuildings, and the cowboys hadn't seen him either. That was almost two hours ago, which meant that Will, unaware he had an extra passenger, could be close to Wyoming by now.

Becky, with Tommy in hand, caught up to the woman in the garden. "I think he's gone with Will."

The older woman turned pale. "Will wouldn't take the child, I know—"

"No, of course not," Becky hurried to reassure her. "But Peter was so upset. He could have climbed into the truck with the dog. Do you think I should call the state police? Will could be in Casper before he discovers him."

Maude looked past her and smiled. "I think he already has. Look."

HE DIDN'T HESITATE this time when he approached the long road to the ranch. In fact, his foot bore down on the accelerator as much as he dared. There was no knot in the pit of his stomach, no feeling that he'd rather be anywhere else on the earth except here, heading toward the Silver Valley ranch.

No, this time he felt like he was coming home. There was a kid beside him, and a woman waiting for him. There was a baby who called him Daddy and one on the way, a boy or girl who should know who his or her father was. He'd had a lot of time to think, this long hour back to his home. There was no fooling himself any longer. He was glad to be turning around, relieved to have a reason.

Will sped as fast as he could, letting the dust fly behind

him in thick gray clouds. He didn't have a chance to park the truck in his usual spot. The women met him partway down the road, and he stopped right there and rolled down his window. "I've got him," he said, unnecessarily, because Peter sat in the front seat waving to everyone like he was in a damn parade. Becky opened the passenger side and was hugging and scolding the child at the same time. She looked at Will.

"Thank you," she said, her eyes suspiciously bright.

"I would have come back anyway," he replied, wishing he could take her in his arms and tell her exactly what was in his heart. But she had her arms full, and Tommy peeked around her knees and grinned at him. Will opened the door and stepped out in time to see his mother hurrying to greet him.

She wasn't limping. "You've recovered," he said, trying not to laugh.

"And so have you, I think," was her reply. She gathered up the boys and took them by the hand. "I'll keep these two out of mischief while you figure out what's right in front of your face," she told her son. Lady barked, so Will opened the back gate and let her out.

Then he and Becky were alone, standing in front of the dusty truck. Several of the men, pretending to be fixing something, stood by the fence and sneaked peeks at them from underneath the brims of their hats.

"Maude will be watching from the porch," Becky said.

He didn't want to talk about Maude. "Marry me."

"Because I'm having a baby? No, thank you." She lifted her chin. "I'm raising two kids alone now. I can raise one more."

Will stepped closer and took her by the shoulders. "I came back to do the right thing."

She raised her eyebrows and didn't look impressed.

"You've never wanted this ranch. You made that clear. So why did you come back? Because of the will?"

For you, he wanted to say. "My uncle had the last laugh. Or so he thought. He kicked me out of here sixteen years ago because he thought I'd gotten my girlfriend pregnant. He wanted me to pay her off. He didn't want to share one acre of the ranch with a stranger."

Becky went pale. "Lily?"

He nodded. "Yep. Trouble was, I was still a virgin and Lily had been two-timing me with an older guy. When he left town, she decided to tell people the baby was mine. She had her eye on this ranch and my uncle's money."

"And your uncle didn't believe you."

"He was more than happy to think the worst. We had a fight, I left. He told me not to come back, that I was a spineless, irresponsible coward." He smiled down at Becky. "And, from the way I acted this morning, he was right. It was just when I heard that part about the will, I knew that old bastard was still trying to run my life, and I resented the hell out of it."

"I didn't mean to get pregnant," she whispered.

"And I didn't mean to fall in love with you, either," he said, gathering her closer into his arms. "So tell me you'll give me another chance and you'll make an honest man out of a broken-down rodeo rider."

She pulled back to gaze into his face. "Are you sure? You're the last man in Montana I thought would be ready to settle down and become a father."

"And a husband," he added, touching her lips with his. "Don't forget the most important part."

Becky, wanting to believe, kissed him back. But when they drew apart, she still hesitated. "I don't want you marrying me because you think you have to. For the baby."

"Sweetheart," he said, gazing down at her with a tenderness that made her knees go weak. "There is no other place I'd rather be."

"Really?" She wanted to believe, wanted to hold him close to her forever, wanted to have his children and sleep in his bed each night and know that when she woke in the morning he would be there. Forever.

"Really." He tucked her hand in his and headed toward the house. "Do you think you have time in your busy schedule to arrange a wedding?"

Becky smiled. "I'll bet Maude and the Not Dead Yet Club will be happy to help. Any objections to getting married on the ranch?"

"Honey," he drawled, smiling from ear to ear. "If you want this cowboy, you can have me anywhere, anytime."

"I like the way you think," she said, stopping to let him kiss her one more time before they entered the house. From somewhere in the distance she heard Maude and the cowboys cheer.

And cowboy makes four...

The Only Man in Wyoming

1

RIVER OF NO RETURN. Lost River Valley. The signs, few and far between on the isolated road, were just a little too symbolic of Allison Reynolds' predicament. Now she'd made yet another wrong turn and found herself on a gravel road, somewhere in Wyoming, with no idea where to go next. She studied the road map while the babies, tucked in identical car seats, began to fuss. She could go straight and hope to run into a town eventually.

Unless, of course, she was heading west by mistake, in which case she would bump into a mountain range and never be heard from again.

Sylvie, never patient, began to cry. And Sophie, willing to go along with her twin's complaints, added her own pitiful sobs to the noise inside the car. Allison closed her eyes and prayed for patience. And quiet. And for a four-star hotel to appear in front of the Ford Probe, which had been making a terrible racket since Allison had guided it across a pothole the size of a moon crater a few miles back.

All in all, it was not a good day. It was not an especially good month or even a good year, Allison decided. She opened her eyes and turned around to comfort the children.

"Sweethearts," she crooned, hoping her voice sounded calmer than she felt. "It's okay. We're going to be out of this nasty car soon." They looked at her with tear-filled blue eyes and continued to scream. "Auntie Allison will fix everything and we'll be on our way."

Auntie Allison wanted to run screaming back to Kansas City. She got out of the car and checked the tires on the driver's side of the little white hatchback. It wasn't exactly a family car, but she'd had it for six years and it had served her well. White and sporty, with a small back seat, it had held up for four years and seventy-three thousand miles. Until they'd crossed into Wyoming, that is. Allison avoided stepping in the muddier ruts in the road and walked around to the other side. The front left wheel looked a little crooked, as if it was about to fall right off its axle. Allison's heart sank.

What had ever made her think she could do this alone?

DELL JONES hated to go to town, especially near the end of calving season, but there'd been no choice. He'd had to go to the bank, get the week's mail and pick up the supplies for Calvin. Running out of coffee when all of them were working half the night constituted a real emergency as far as Dell was concerned. He shoved the pickup into low gear and rounded the crest of the hill, and that's when he saw her. Her golden hair hung in fluffy waves past her shoulders and the body encased in jeans and a bright blue sweater was everything delicate and fragile. Dell didn't recognize her, and he figured he knew everyone in the county.

He wondered for a brief moment if she were real, and he took his foot off the gas pedal and watched her walk around the front of the car and kneel on the driver seat. That long hair hung down to a particularly shapely rear, and Dell gulped. She was real, all right, and she was in trouble. There was no other reason for a woman to be parked on the side of this road, not at the end of April. It was too early for tourists and too late for hunters.

Dell parked the truck in the middle of the road, kept the engine running, and rolled down his window. He didn't want to scare her. Women were jumpy these days, and he didn't blame them. Damn, he wished he'd shaved. Not that it would do any good. An ugly mug was an ugly mug, with or without whiskers.

She'd turned around and looked at him. Blue eyes. Oh, Lord, of course she'd have blue eyes and look like an angel, heart-shaped face and all.

"Ma'am? Can I help you?"

The woman looked uncertain, and didn't move, so Dell tried again. "I live near here," he said. "On the Lazy J ranch. Do you need help?"

The angel nodded, then sighed. "I'm lost and I think my car is damaged. I was just going to call a gas station and see if I could get towed to town. Then I realized I didn't know what town I'm close to."

"You're thirty miles from the nearest town, ma'am, and Wells City is a real small town at that. You want me to take a look at your car?"

She studied him with a pair of big blue eyes, then said, "Please" with a touch of reluctance, so Dell moved his truck out of the middle of the road and shut off the ignition. He thought he heard babies crying, and as he approached the car he tipped his hat from his forehead and peered through the car windows. Sure enough, two little babies were screaming at the top of their lungs.

"Lady," he drawled, turning to look down at her. "What in hell are you doing out here?"

"I'm lost," she confessed. "And I hit a pothole and now the right front wheel is crooked."

"Where were you going?"

"Seattle."

He turned and stared at her. "He'd expected her to say "Cheyenne" or "Salt Lake," not a city that was still hundreds of miles and a couple of states away. She followed him around to the other side of the car, where Dell hunkered down and examined the wheel.

"Can I drive on it?" she asked.

He shook his head. "I'm guessing you have a cracked or broken axle. When that goes, it'll make a flat tire seem like a picnic in comparison." Raindrops started falling, and the sky darkened into a charcoal gray. It would be dark soon, and though the Lazy J was in no shape for guests, and no matter how much he wanted to get home, there was no way Dell could leave the woman here with her car phone and her hopes for a tow truck.

"Did you say the nearest town is thirty miles away?"

"Yes, ma'am, but I'd be glad to take you to my ranch. It's five miles, as the crow flies, from here."

"Thank you," she said, very politely. She backed up a step. "I can't. The babies—"

"Are hungry," he finished for her. "I can take you into town in the morning. You're welcome to stay at the ranch tonight and I'll have one of my men tow your car to town tomorrow."

"I couldn't possible. I mean," she said, her cheeks flushing. "I mean, it's very nice of you, but—"

"You don't know me." He didn't smile, but he wanted to. "Tell you what," he said, pulling his battered wallet from his back pocket and handing it to her. "Give the county sheriff's office a call and see what they say about Wendell Jones."

She took the wallet and opened it, glanced at his picture and back at him. "You must think I'm being pretty paranoid."

"Nope. You're being smart. There should be a card in there listing telephone numbers."

"Thank you."

He waited by her car while she made the call. The babies had stopped screaming, though they sighed and hiccuped as if they had given up trying to make themselves understood. They looked at Dell and their bottom lips quivered. Twins, of course. The back of the car was packed with duffel bags, boxes of disposable diapers and a small cooler. There were pink blankets and bright rubber toys crammed between the car seats, plastic pacifiers everywhere. The babies stared at him, and Dell smiled. He waggled his fingers and wondered if they liked cowboys waving at them. They didn't seem to mind.

He heard the woman's quite voice on the phone and knew it was only a matter of a few minutes more before he would be bundling all her belongings into his truck and heading home before the rain started in earnest.

It was supposed to be a hell of a night, with another storm coming. Already the wind was blowing colder air, the kind that got in a man's bones and wouldn't let go. Dell shivered and one of the babies smiled.

"All set," the woman said, stepping out of the car to move toward him. "They were very nice."

"And?"

She smiled, and he noticed there was a tiny dimple in her left cheek. "Someone named Officer Baker told me I should thank my lucky stars that you came along. He said there was a storm coming, so go home with you and worry about finding a mechanic tomorrow."

Dell nodded. "Good advice. You going to take it before we both get wet?"

She stuck out her hand. "Yes, Mr. Jones. I'm Allison Reynolds."

He hesitated before touching her, but then took her small hand into his large one for a brief second. She wore no wedding ring, which made his heart soar. He wondered what that meant; he wondered if Fate was playing a cruel joke. "Call me Dell," he said.

HE WAS THE LARGEST man she'd ever seen. At least six foot six and an easy two hundred pounds, though he looked like he was made of pure muscle under that suede barn coat. His clothes were spattered with mud and his dark hair was too long. The beard gave him a slightly sinister look, but Allison had seen kindness in his brown eyes. He had a large nose in a large, square face that matched the rest of him actually, and he'd just about scared her to death when he'd stopped his truck in the road. She'd realized just how helpless she was at that point, but he'd looked so sorry for her that her fear had disappeared.

Now she was riding in the cab of a pickup truck, her belongings and those of the twins' packed around boxes of groceries under a blue tarp in the bed of the truck.

"I'm really sorry to put you through this much trouble," she said as the rain pelted the windshield. She held the babies awkwardly, and they squirmed a little but otherwise behaved themselves. She hoped it would last.

"Couldn't leave you out there," he said, his voice gruff. He turned the wipers on.

Well, she supposed he couldn't. "Your wife won't mind company?"

"Never been married," he said.

Which was not exactly a surprise. A wife would never let him go to town looking like he'd slept in the barn. And she would have made him shave days ago, too.

He glanced toward her. "Where's your husband?"

"I'm not married, either."

Those dark eyebrows rose, but he looked back at the road, then slowed the truck to make a left-hand turn.

Allison didn't feel like explaining the babies to a stranger. Let him think anything he wanted to think. She didn't want to talk about it. She didn't want to get weepy in front of a stranger, and she didn't want to be reminded that the little children in her arms would someday ask questions. She could answer the ones about their mother, but how could she say, "Your father already had a family"?

"Welcome to the Lazy J," the man stated as they bumped along the road toward a group of buildings clustered together at the base of the foothills. Everything was gray or brown, though some of the fences looked as if they had once been painted white.

"This is really very nice of you."

"No problem." He didn't look at her again. He concentrated on avoiding some of the worse ruts and yet he didn't jerk the truck hard enough to make it difficult to hang on to the children.

"I'm sure it is." She wondered if he ever smiled. He wouldn't look quite so fierce, she was sure. He parked the truck by the front porch of a grayish one-story house, then came around to Allison's side of the truck and opened her door. He took one of the babies out of Allison's arms and tucked her under the flap of his coat. It was raining harder now, so Allison covered the baby's face with the blanket and made a dash for the front porch. Once there, she flipped open the blanket just as Sophie opened her mouth, ready to scream again.

"It's okay," she assured her little niece. "You're going to be out of those wet pants and have a nice warm bottle and won't have to go in the car seat again, okay?"

Wide blue eyes stared up at her as if she didn't believe a word being said.

"Ma'am?"

She looked up to see Mr. Jones holding open the front door for her. Another giant stood inside the doorway and backed up a step when Allison walked through. This man was dressed in jeans and a plaid work shirt, and he stared at her and past her, to Mr. Jones.

"Hello," she said.

But he still wasn't looking at her.

"Car trouble," Mr. Jones explained to the man. "Found them out on Sourdough Road." The man nodded, and looked down at the baby. "Calvin is my uncle. He's a little hard of hearing, but he reads lips. Just make sure he's looking at you when you talk to him, and speak right up."

"Oh." She smiled at the man, whose gaze dropped to her lips. "Hi. I'm Allison and this is Sophie."

"Hello," Calvin said in a loud voice. He nodded, but he looked disapproving.

"Who am I holding?" Mr. Jones asked.

"Sylvie."

"How can you tell?"

"Sylvie's chin is a little bit pointed, and she has more hair."

Mr. Jones set the baby on a wide brown sofa and went back outside again. Allison turned to Calvin. "Would you hold her for a minute please?"

He nodded, and she handed him the baby and shrugged off her wet jacket. She was glad she'd taken the giant's advice earlier and put it on over her sweater. She'd bet the temperature had dropped ten degrees. She took Sophie back and walked over to the couch. The large living room was warm, though no fire crackled in the fieldstone fireplace. Besides the couch, the room held two dark green recliners, a scarred coffee table, an enormous dark dining table on the far wall, and one large television set. She bet one of those enormous satellite dishes was in the backyard somewhere, too. She felt as if she and the girls had entered a land of giants. Was the ranch filled with oversize cows, too? The thought almost made her laugh out loud, then she wondered if she was simply overtired.

Mr. Jones returned with an armful of their belongings, including the flowered diaper bag, which he had slung over his shoulder.

"It's not fancy," Mr. Jones was saying, looking around his living room. He looked embarrassed, as if he had just realized how bare the room must look. "But at least you're out of the storm."

"It's wonderful, really," she assured him, bending over the babies to unwrap them from their blankets and remove their pink jackets and knit caps. "Is there a place where I can change their diapers?"

"Ah, you can use the spare room."

She tucked one in the crook of each arm and followed Mr. Jones down a dark hallway and past a bedroom, bathroom and office. Calvin followed them as they turned right into a large room that looked as if it hadn't been used in years. A wide double bed, covered with a faded starburst quilt, was centered against the far wall. Two tall dressers matched the golden oak headboard, and the yellowed lace curtains at the windows had seen better days.

"Used to be my mother's room," the giant explained. "There's a bathroom across the hall." He scratched his head. "I don't have any, uh, baby things."

'I had a folding playpen in the trunk of my car. I'll use that." She set the children in the middle of the bed and began to unbutton Sophie's terry-cloth sleeper.

"I'll go get it. I put it in the back of the truck." He put her suitcases on the floor, then set the diaper bag on the bed. He didn't look as if he wanted to be around to witness a double diaper changing.

"Thank you. Again."

"No problem."

And that was the interesting thing, Allison mused. Rescuing a woman and a couple of babies on the side of the road didn't seem to be any kind of a problem at all for Wendell Jones. The man had taken them in without a second thought, though he clearly wasn't accustomed to company. The naked living room and unused bedroom certainly testified to that. Calvin no longer stood in the doorway, having escaped with his nephew the minute he saw that she was going to start changing diapers.

Allison smiled down at Sophie. "I'm not very good at this either, am I?"

Still, she'd had to learn. They were hers to care for now, and she would do anything in the world to do a good job. "Through rain and mud and broken cars," she told the giggling baby. "I will never let you guys down."

"ARE YOU CRAZY?" Calvin's loud voice boomed when Dell entered the kitchen carrying the cooler.

"No." He turned away from his uncle and best friend and set it down on the small table in the corner. He lifted the lid and took out six baby bottles filled with milk.

Calvin waited for him to turn around. "There hasn't been a woman up here for ten years, unless you count the vet's wife, but she didn't come inside the house."

"It's just for the night," Dell assured him, studying the bottles. Who'd have thought that there'd be babies on the Lazy J?

"I'll bet my bag of silver dollars that it's not just for one night. Women are unlucky," the man muttered, wiping his hands on the dish towel. "Where the hell is her husband? A woman shouldn't be traipsing around Wyoming with a pair of babies and no husband."

"I don't think she has one. She said she wasn't married."

Calvin frowned again. "Which is even worse in my book. Did you remember to get coffee or did having a woman in your truck make you stupid?"

"I found her on my way home," Dell explained, unruffled by the old man's grouching. "I'll bring in the mail and the supplies next."

"I'll get them myself," the other man said, heading toward the door to the storage room. He went past the freezer and shelves of canned goods, through the mudroom, and grabbed his coat. "You'd rather go play patty cake or something, and I need the air. Babies and women," he muttered. "What the hell are we gonna do with babies and women?"

He didn't wait for an answer, but slammed the door behind him as he went out into the rainy night. Dell almost smiled. Cal was more scared of females than he was. Cal had come close to getting married once, until the girl changed her mind and broke his heart. Since then he'd been happy to live in the middle of nowhere, cooking for all of the men. It was a position of power, with the built-in right to grumble.

Dell put the bottles in the refrigerator. He'd guess those little girls would be getting hungry, and Allison—Miss Reynolds, that is—would be looking for the kitchen. She wouldn't have any trouble finding it. Calvin had a pot of beef stew on the stove that you could smell for three miles. Fresh loaves of bread lined the counter, and there would be pie for dessert, only Cal would have hidden it somewhere in the pantry. He always hid dessert, though no one on the ranch would have dared touch anything Cal baked without permission.

"Mr. Jones?"

He spun around to see the woman hesitate before entering the kitchen. "Come on in, and call me Dell, ma'am."

"If I do, will you call me Allison instead of ma'am?"

Dell nodded. He could try, but he couldn't promise. He heard Cal banging things in the pantry. "I put the bottles in the fridge."

"Thanks. If I could have a pan of hot water, I'll heat them up."

Cal came through the door in time to see Dell rummaging in the cabinet for a pan deep enough to hold two bottles. "What are you doing in my kitchen?"

Dell ignored him, which he knew would drive the old crank crazy. "Here," he said, handing a copper-bottomed pot to the woman. "Will this work?"

"Yes, it's perfect." She walked past him to the refrigerator, selected two bottles, and put them in the pan. Then the pan went into the sink and was filled with hot tap water. So far it was pretty much the way they heated up bottles for motherless calves.

Dell caught Cal's eye. "The stew smells good."

"Help yourself. I'm gonna eat with the men."

"You sure?"

"Real sure. And you're on duty. I think it's gonna be busy. Have Rob fill you in." With that, he slammed his hat back on his head and went out the door.

Dell wasn't surprised that he was working tonight. Birthing calves in mud and rain was inevitable. It was the season for calves and mud, after all, and nothing came as a surprise. Except for maybe eight hours of sleep and a day without some kind of emergency.

"I don't think your uncle approves of having company." Allison lifted one of the bottles from the water and tested the temperature on her wrist. Then she took the other one out and dried them both with the dish towel Cal had dropped on the counter. "I didn't mean to chase him out of the house."

"He'll live. Did you get the babies settled?"

"I sure did. Thank you." She smiled again, and his heart flipped over. "It seems like I'm always thanking you."

He felt his face flush, and hoped the red was hidden by a three-day growth of beard. "You can stop anytime."

"Okay. I'm going to go feed them."

"Supper's ready whenever you're hungry."

"Great. Give me at least half an hour, okay?"

"Take as long as you need to. I've got some work outside." He looked at his watch. "It's already five o'clock. How about you just help yourself whenever you want to? It's calving season." He wondered if she knew what that meant, then decided, she wouldn't know. "Dinner isn't anything fancy," he warned her. "Just stew and bread."

"I like stew and bread." With that, she left the kitchen and disappeared around the corner. He knew if he stuck his head into the hall, he would see her hurrying down the hall back to her babies. Those babies were little. When had Allison's boyfriend left her? When he found out he was going to be a father? Or had he died? There'd been a touch of sadness in those eyes, come to think about it. And the babies were young. He hadn't had much experience with kids, but it seemed like when he'd seen Mrs. Petersen's baby, it hadn't been much bigger and the little rascal had been three months old then, because Lucille Palmer had leaned across the counter at Roy's Diner and chucked him under the chin and said, "How old is that little sweetheart?" And Mrs. Petersen had said, "Three months, but he's big for his age."

Then Lucille had winked at him and said, "Just like you, Dell. Big for your age."

And he'd turned red and asked for a refill on his coffee.

Dell thought about those babies and wondered how long Allison had been on her own. She didn't look like she was very good at it. And from the size of their mother, he'd guess Sophie and Sylvie were small for their age. They looked like her, as much as a baby could look like anyone. Fair skinned, wisps of golden hair and big blue eyes meant they'd probably grow up looking like Allison. Lucky girls.

Dell picked up his hat and prepared to go back out into the storm. He should have offered to eat dinner with his guest, but for the life of him he couldn't imagine sitting across the table from her and trying to make conversation for twenty minutes. He didn't know how to entertain a lady, for heaven's sake, and he was too old to learn now. Besides, he told himself, heading through the pantry to the mudroom, then out the door, if Allison didn't have to look at his ugly mug during supper, she'd eat better. He was doing her a favor.

SHE HATED to eat alone. It always felt like she was being punished, which had been her mother's way of teaching her to eat peas. She'd sit at that table, long after Sandy had been excused, and push cold peas around the plate with her fork. Eventually her mother would relent and let her go to her room, but those minutes alone at the dining room table, staring at a small pile of cold peas, had seemed like hours.

But she couldn't expect Mr. Jones—Dell—to entertain her. He was still a little frightening, though he'd gone out of his way to be kind. She figured he wasn't used to having company; it made him uncomfortable, which was something she didn't want to do to someone kind enough to rescue her and her little family from a spring storm and a broken wheel.

The kitchen was empty when she peeked in. The children, their tummies full and their diapers hopefully dry, were sound asleep in the bedroom, leaving Allison with the house to herself. It was the kind of place that she would have been leery of decorating, and yet it would be a challenge. There were stacks of books in corners, and the furniture was old and dark. The place needed brightening without changing its masculine, Western feel. Even the front porch had been filled with stacks of magazines and dust-covered boxes.

She opened cupboards until she found the one that held a stack of white bowls, then she opened drawers until she located the silverware. The room was clean and utilitarian, with almond Formica countertops and vinyl flooring the practical color of dried mud. Allison was ladling stew into a bowl when she heard someone come inside. In a few minutes Dell came into the kitchen. His hair was wet, his face covered with splatters of mud and he was in his stocking feet.

"Bad night," was all he said, attempting to slick his hair from his forehead.

The rain slashed against the window above the sink. "Do you have to go back out?"

"Not for a while. We just got a couple of calves in out of the storm, and Rob's going to ride out again one more time."

She got another bowl down from the shelf. "Do you want to eat now or later?"

"Later?" His bushy eyebrows came together in confusion.

Allison wondered if she'd said something wrong. "After you clean up," she stammered, hoping she wasn't hurting his feelings. "I didn't want to fix your dinner if it was just going to get cold. I didn't mean you *had* to clean up, or that I expected you to. You're fine just the way you are, being a rancher and all." She took a deep breath and forced herself to stop babbling.

"Oh." he looked down at his mud-spattered clothes. "Guess I don't look too presentable."

"You're fine, really." She started filling the empty bowl. "Sit down and eat with me."

"I'll go wash up."

He left the room and Allison wished she'd kept her big mouth shut. If she wasn't careful, she'd be telling him to shave, cutting his hair and rearranging the living room furniture. The couch would look better facing the fireplace. Allison winced as she carried the bowls of stew to the round table in the corner of the kitchen. She'd never been a person who minded her own business, but now would be an excellent time to begin.

2

HE MADE SURE he used a lot of soap, because he'd almost scared *himself* just by looking in the mirror. His bedroom was the first room off the hall, a bathroom right beside it. Everything needed painting, he realized. The whole damn house looked like nobody cared.

Which wasn't true. He cared. He just didn't know what to do after the caring part. His parents had been gone for years, and neither one of them had been real interested in what the house looked like. To her dying day, his mother had enjoyed her horses and let the rest take care of itself. He wouldn't be thinking about these things if there wasn't a woman in the house.

He cursed the mirror, scrubbed and dried his face and hands, made an energetic attempt to tame his hair, then returned to the kitchen and his houseguest. Allison had started a pot of coffee and set the table for two people.

"What would you like to drink? Water or milk?" She took two tall glasses from the cupboard beside the sink. She had to stand on her tiptoes to reach.

A shot of whiskey. Then another one. "Water's fine, thanks."

"Okay." She filled the glasses from the faucet, then put them on the table. "I sliced the bread and found the butter. Is there anything else?"

Flowers and wine, he thought. The sound of violins. "No. Looks fine."

"Okay."

Dell waited for her to sit down. He didn't want her to think he didn't have any manners. She sat, tucked a paper napkin in her lap and Dell sat down beside her. The round table was tucked into the corner, so there were only two chairs. He and Cal usually ate standing up, or at different times.

She picked up her spoon, and so did Dell. He tasted Cal's stew and prayed he hadn't gone overboard with the chili peppers this time. Sometimes the man had a mean streak.

"It's very good," Allison Reynolds said. She looked at him as if he was supposed to say something back.

"Cal makes a he-heck of a stew."

"Does he do all the cooking?"

"Yep. He was a cook in the navy before he came back to town, and it just seemed natural for him to keep on doing it here."

"He hasn't always been deaf?"

"No, ma'am. Allison," he corrected himself before she could protest. "An explosion on a ship took most of his hearing."

"Have you lived on the ranch all your life?"

He took a drink of his water. "You sure ask a lot of questions."

"I'm sorry." She held his gaze with her own. "I've been in a car with two babies for three days. It's hard to have a conversation with the radio," she confessed with a little smile that tugged at his heart. "I get tired of talking to myself."

Dell realized he hadn't answered her question about the ranch. "My grandparents homesteaded this ranch. My parents had been dead for quite a few years now, and I was an only child. I grew up here and I expect I'll grow old here, too."

They ate in silence for another minute or two. It was sure strange to talk to a beautiful woman instead of watching the news or reading the latest edition of *Time* magazine.

"Go ahead," he said, breaking the silence as he buttered a thick slice of Cal's wheat bread. "Ask something else."

"Is this a real cattle ranch?"

"Real?" he echoed, looking at her. The expression in those blue eyes were sincere and interested. "What do you mean by 'real'?"

"I've been driving past ranches and roads to ranches for days. Do you make your living from selling cattle?"

"That and hay."

"Do you like it?"

"Yes." He couldn't imagine doing anything else. His father had made him go to college, but he'd only lasted three semesters. He'd majored in agriculture; he'd wanted to be home.

Allison smiled at him again. "It seems to fit you."

He nodded. Of course it did. He was tall and strong, comfortable in trucks and on horseback. He wouldn't be like any of the other men she'd ever met. He was big and ugly and usually covered in mud that he had to be reminded to wash off.

Dell finished his stew. It wasn't easy having company. Tomorrow he would make sure her car was towed into town, he would urge the mechanic to work overtime to fix it as soon as possible and he'd spend the rest of his day outdoors.

When she left, he would be relieved. He could go back to eating alone, without having to answer questions or chew with his mouth closed and keep his elbows off the table. Women were different creatures, all right.

"ARE YOU OUT of your mind?"

"No, Mayme. I'm safe, and so are the girls. We could still

be on the side of that gravel road, watching the rain hit the windshield," she reminded her friend and lawyer. "And all three of us would be drinking cold formula and crying our heads off."

The older woman's voice was filled with doubt. "The world is full of crazies, Allison. Be careful."

Allison smiled into the telephone receiver. If Mayme ever knew that she was in the Land of the Giants, she'd *really* worry. "He gave me his driver's license and I called the sheriff's office to check on him before the girls and I got in his truck."

She heard the sound of papers being shuffled. "Give me your address and phone number, just so I know where you are."

"We're on the Lazy J ranch, somewhere in the eastern part of Wyoming, off Highway 211." She gave her the phone number. "The man's name is Wendell Jones."

"Wendell?"

"Dell for short. Only he's not."

'Not what?"

"'Short.' Allison chuckled.

There was a pause. "Have you been drinking?"

"I'm just tired." She fought the urge to giggle. "Riding in a car with twin babies for three days will do that to you."

"You should have taken my advice in the first place and hired someone to go with you."

"I tried. Now I know why no one leapt at the opportunity. Besides, I couldn't fit a box of tissues in that car, never mind another person." And she'd wanted to prove she didn't need Ryan's help. That she didn't need anyone's help. Of course, by taking the wrong turn—not once, but three times—she'd proved she couldn't navigate Wyoming without having to be rescued. "Has Ryan returned the contracts?"

"Yes, but he's been dragging his feet. Maybe he's having second thoughts about letting you go." Allison didn't say anything, so Mayme continued. "I'll transfer the money as soon as you set up an account in Seattle." She sighed. "I'll sleep a lot easier when you're safe and sound and where you're supposed to be."

"I'm fine," Allison reassured her once again. "I couldn't be in a better place."

"Is there a *Mrs*. Rancher?"

'No."

Another silence. "Is Mr., uh, Jones young or old?"

"Middle age, I'd guess. Mid-thirties."

"Hmm... He's one of those bachelor cowboys?" Mayme was fond of reading romance novels, especially the ones set west of the Mississippi. "That could be interesting."

"Not exactly." Allison lowered her voice. "He's kind of shy."

"Ah, the strong, silent type," Mayme declared in a knowing voice.

"I don't know if you'd describe him that way," Allison said. "We had a nice conversation during dinner."

"Let me guess. You asked a million questions and the poor man had no choice but to answer them."

"Well, sort of."

"You should have been a newscaster, Allison, not an interior decorator. You ask more questions than any person I've ever met."

"How else am I going to find out what people want? The more questions I ask, the more I learn about the person. And *then* I can decorate their home. You should see this place, Mayme. I could spend six weeks here fixing it up."

"If your car stays stuck, you might have to."

"Mr. Jones is taking me to town tomorrow," Allison said. "Hopefully the car can be fixed and I'll be on my way." She looked over at the playpen as Sylvie began to fuss. "I have to go. The girls are starting to wake up."

"Give them a kiss for me, and take care of yourself. If your Wyoming cowboy is as tame as you say, maybe a day or two of rest will be good for you."

"Sure," Allison hurried to agree. "I'll call you in a few days."

"Keep me posted," her friend demanded. "And get some sleep."

Allison agreed, and replaced the receiver on the old black phone. Mayme, divorced and childless, had no idea how useless it was to tell the mother of twins to "get some sleep." Allison crossed the room and looked down at the babies. Legally she was their mother, their guardian. She was all they had, and now they were all she had. Somehow the three of them would have to muddle along together. Sylvie lifted her head and started to cry, so Allison lifted her from the makeshift bed and cradled her in her arms.

"Hey, sweetheart, are you going to say hi to me?"

The baby's lips turned down as she stared up at her aunt.

"Haven't decided, have you?" She walked her around the room and gently rocked the child in her arms. The oldest of the twins was the light sleeper; Sophie slept through almost everything unless Sylvie bawled directly in her ear. Allison picked up the phone and decided she'd better return it to the hall. Mr. Jones had gone outside again after dinner, and there had been no one in the house when she'd made the collect call to Mayme. She'd taken advantage of the long cord and taken the phone into the bedroom so she could hear the babies if they woke.

She'd debated earlier about taking a bath and getting ready for bed. It was after eight, and the children usually woke around ten for another feeding. No one had ever told her that motherhood meant waiting all day for a good time to take a shower. She left the bedroom door open so she could hear Sophie if she woke and walked down the empty hallway toward the living room. She wondered if her host was back yet. He'd left after dinner, saying he had a couple of cows missing. She wondered if he counted them every day.

Calvin and Dell were in the kitchen eating pie. They both stood at the counter, their forks raised in midair, as she entered the room.

"Hi," she said, stepping through the doorway. "Sylvie and I are taking a walk."

Calvin's gaze dropped to the tiny baby, then back to Allison's lips. "Want some pie?"

"Thank you. I would love some." She turned to Dell. "Did you find your lost cows?"

He nodded. "They were in a hollow. We got them—and their calves—out of the rain and warmed up." At her questioning look, he added, "A little heat works wonders on the calves."

"Do you always work this late?"

"During calving season, yes."

Calvin carried a plate filled with apple pie over to the table. "Is this where you want your pie?"

"That's fine, thank you." She sat down in a chair off to the side so she wouldn't have her back to the two men, then adjusted Sylvie in her left arm so she could pick up her fork with her right hand. "I'm not used to being waited on."

"How old are they?" Calvin asked, nodding toward the baby.

"Three months," she said. She could see the unspoken questions in the men's eyes. They were wondering what a woman with three-month-old babies was doing driving across Wyoming. "I'm their aunt," she explained.

"Their aunt?" Mr. Jones repeated. He set his empty plate in the sink and refilled his coffee cup. She wondered if he ever slept.

'My sister—" She took a deep breath. "My sister died when they were born. There was no one else to take the children."

"But why are you going all the way to Seattle?"

"That's a long story," Allison hedged. She wasn't going to explain that her boyfriend had refused to help her with the babies, or that she'd sold him her half of the business and, determined to start over with "her" children, accepted her college roommate's offer of a part-time job in Seattle. "Mr. Jones, do you think anyone in town will be able to fix my car tomorrow?"

"Dell," the big man corrected. "Call me Dell."

"Dell," she said, and he smiled just a little bit.

"I don't know about your car. The rain's still coming down real hard, so I don't even know if we'll be able to get to town in the morning. There's not a lot you can do about mud."

"But I can't stay here," she said, taking a bite of pie. "Is there a hotel or motel in town?"

Calvin, reading her lips, shook his head. "Nope. Not this time of year."

"You're welcome to stay here for as long as you need to," Dell said. "Once the rain stops, we'll figure out how to get that car of yours fixed up."

"I hate to put you through all of this trouble.

"No trouble," Dell said, then took a sip of his coffee. "Make yourself at home. Let me know if there's anything you need that you can't find."

Sylvie chose that moment to complain and wave her fists

around. "I don't know why she always gets mad when I eat," Allison laughed, shifting the child in her arm. "When she's old enough to pick up a fork she'll think she's in heaven."

"Give her to me," Dell said, crossing the room.

"You're too dirty," the older cowboy said. "I'll take her." With that, he elbowed Dell out of the way and took the child out of Allison's arms.

"Just make sure you support her neck," Allison said when he looked down at her.

"Yes, ma'am." The little girl looked up at him and smiled, which was all Calvin needed to make him smile for the first time since Allison had arrived. "What's this one's name?"

"Sylvie," Dell supplied, surprising Allison with his ability to tell the girls apart. "I have hundreds of cows to remember," he explained. "A couple of little girls isn't so hard."

"Sylvie," Calvin repeated loud enough to make the baby widen her eyes and open her mouth to let out a squeak of protest. "What's the matter with her?"

"You're yelling," Dell told him. "Say something quiet."

"Like what?"

"I don't know. Sing a lullaby or something."

"Don't know any songs like that," Calvin shouted, rocking the baby awkwardly. "I can't carry a tune anymore. Can't tell what I'm singin' half the time."

"Just walk her around a little bit," Allison suggested. "She likes that."

"All right." He carried the baby out of the kitchen and disappeared into the living room. Allison heard him singing "Don't Fence Me In."

Dell didn't waste any time taking up the thread of the conversation. "Why are you travelling alone?"

"I didn't have a choice."

"It's not right," he said, crossing those big arms across his chest.

She wanted to tell him it was none of his business, but that would have been rude. And not necessarily true, since he had rescued her and taken her to his house. She was sleeping in his mother's bed and eating his uncle's apple pie. "Like I said, I didn't have a choice."

"Are you running from someone?" He frowned. "Are you in some kind of trouble?"

"No, nothing like that." She turned away from him and took another bite of pie. She didn't want to explain that grief made a person do strange things, things you'd never dream of doing unless you were desperate to leave pain and sorrow behind. "My life is not that exciting, believe me."

He sat down beside her at the table, and carefully adjusted the chair so his knees wouldn't bump hers. "Guess it was my turn to ask all the questions," he said. Then, "I'm sorry about your sister."

Allison glanced toward him. "Thank you."

"I hope everything works out in Seattle."

"It will," she assured him. *It has to.*

He leaned back in his chair and craned his neck toward the hallway. "I think I hear the other one."

Allison looked at her watch and jumped up. "I didn't realize it was this late," she said. "They're ready for their bottles."

"You have enough food?"

"There's formula in one of the boxes you carried in. I brought enough for the whole trip, though the process has taken a lot longer than I thought it would."

He shook his head as she hurried past him. "Lady, you have no business being on a 'trip' with two little babies."

Allison ignored him. She knew he was partly right. Leaving Kansas City had been an act of a desperate woman. She had a job waiting for her, the motel reservations had been made. The Probe had had a tune-up and the car had been packed, the apartment empty and the furniture in storage. And the more everyone said, "Allison, you can't take care of the babies," the more she was determined to do exactly that. It was better for all of them if they started over someplace new.

HE HELPED Allison heat up the bottles and then left the house, leaving Allison holding the quietly whimpering Sophie and Calvin feeding Sylvie. He didn't return for several hours, until he saw the light go off in the bedroom. There were calves to check, of course. And one of the men said there was a black heifer down by the creek, but she'd come up empty. He'd searched through the darkness and the rain until he'd found the calf drowned in the creek, then he'd brought the cow in and gotten her to accept the motherless calf that had arrived at daybreak.

All in all, it had been one hell of a day. The temperature had dropped, but held at thirty-nine. The wind and rain hadn't let up, though, which meant the roads would be thick with mud and he would have his houseguests for another day.

Dell kicked off his boots and stripped off his clothes in the mudroom, then threw them in the pile in front of the washing machine. He wrapped himself in the flannel robe he kept on a hook behind the door and headed into the kitchen. He didn't think he'd run into Allison. The lights were off and the house was quiet, so he walked softly through the kitchen and across the hall to his room. He hoped they would all get a decent night's sleep. Allison had dark circles under her eyes and she'd yawned three times while heating up the baby bottles. She could use some rest. She could use some help. And a husband.

Too bad she wasn't going to stick around. Not that she'd give him a second glance, Dell thought, looking at his ugly mug in the mirror. He would shower now, and shave in the morning so he would look halfway decent. No sense letting the woman think he was some kind of Wyoming wildman.

"MY, DON'T YOU LOOK pretty."

"Shut up." He poured himself a cup of coffee and ignored his uncle's grin.

"You cut yourself, right there under your chin."

Dell faced Calvin and made sure he spoke clearly. "I was tired of looking at myself," he explained. "And it's not such a big cut. Just a nick."

"You coulda bled to death trying to impress the lady."

Dell gave up and went into the living room. He found the remote control, switched on the television and turned it to the weather channel. He kept the volume soft, just to annoy Calvin. And to let Allison and the babies sleep, of course. He went over to the window and looked out into the gray dawn.

"Looks like your new friends won't be goin' nowhere this morning," Calvin stated flatly. Dell turned around as Calvin stepped closer to the television.

"Leave or not, it doesn't matter," he said, then realized Calvin couldn't hear him. He watched as the local weatherman pointed out a nasty front heading south from Canada. The rain wasn't due to let up soon, that was certain.

"Got us another storm coming. Where are you riding today?"

Anything that could happen during calving season usually did. Dell sipped his coffee. "I'll go out through the east meadow, see what's up. Then I have to figure out how to get Allison's Probe into town."

Calvin scoffed. "You looked out the window? The rain hasn't stopped. No way are you going to haul a car down to town today. Or tomorrow, either."

"She's anxious to get that car fixed."

"Yeah, well, women always think they have to have everything they want," Calvin declared. "Doesn't mean they get it."

"I guess," he drawled, not wanting to discuss the whims of women with a man who had no more experience with the creatures than he did. "You don't know a hell of a lot yourself." He felt obliged to point that out.

"Never brought one *home*," Calvin said. "Now that takes bigger balls than those on Marty Kiefer's Hereford bull."

"Didn't have a choice."

Cal shrugged. "Guess not, but it looks like she's not going anywhere for a while. You can't put her in a motel, not with those little babies." Calvin sighed as if he had the weight of the world on his shoulders. "Wouldn't be right."

"I could drive her into Cheyenne."

"Yeah, you could. And what would you do with her car?"

"I see what you mean." The car would be a hundred miles away, in Wells City. He'd have to figure out how to get it to her, or she'd have to figure out how to get it. And she'd have to cart two babies around with her.

"But it's not your problem," Calvin reminded him.

Dell sighed. "I'm the one that brought her home. Which means I'm the one who has to figure out how to get rid of her."

"Women are dangerous."

Dell thought of sitting down at the table with her last night. He had tried to ignore her blue eyes and her neat little body and the way she smiled when she asked him questions. And like a fool he'd shaved this morning.

"Damn right they are."

IT HAD BEEN a good night, Allison realized. The girls had slept from eleven until four, a total of five hours. She'd retrieved the bottles from the refrigerator and heated them in the bathroom sink without making any noise that would wake a sleeping cowboy, and the children had gone back to sleep after having clean diapers and full tummies.

They'd all woken at nine to find the ranch house empty, half a pot of coffee and a dozen cinnamon rolls waiting on the kitchen counter. Allison strapped the babies in their car seats and set them on the table where they could see her while she fixed the day's supply of bottles, drank a cup of coffee and heated two bottles.

She fed them one at a time, in the peaceful kitchen. The rain continued to pound on the roof and against the windows and the wind continued to howl. It was not a day to be outside, but she imagined Dell Jones wouldn't let a little rain bother him. He was the way she'd always pictured cowboys would be in Wyoming: tough and strong, wearing boots and jeans and driving a truck.

"We'd better get used to rain," she told Sylvie, who burped obligingly. "Seattle has lots of rain, I hear. We'll ride the ferry, and go up in the Space Needle, and find a nice little apartment with plenty of room for two cribs." She put Sylvie back in the car seat, then picked up her younger sister and another bottle. "I'll have to get you matching umbrellas," she crooned. "Bright yellow, with pink flowers. How about that?"

Sophie ignored her, latched onto the bottle's nipple and drank as if she hadn't eaten in three weeks. Allison heard the back door open and the sound of boots being stomped against the floor. She turned as Dell hesitated in the doorway of the kitchen. He was clean shaven this morning, which made him look different. He wasn't quite so scary, but his size alone would make any smart person think twice about taking him on. "Good morning."

"Ah, good morning." He took off his hat, and droplets of rain spattered to the floor as he hung it up on a hook. Then, pouring himself a cup of coffee, he leaned against the counter and frowned.

"I'll bet you've been up since dawn," she said, looking at her watch. "I slept late, but so did the girls. It won't take me five minutes to pack, so I'm ready when you are."

"Ready?"

"To go to town."

"Uh, ma'am—Allison, we're not going anywhere today. I can't get your car down to town, not with the storm last night. But I'll try again tomorrow. You're welcome to stay here as long as you need to," the cowboy added.

"Can I take a bus to Cheyenne and stay there until my car is fixed?" She'd looked at the map last night to see how far away from civilization she'd landed.

He shook his head. "Aren't any, least not from here. I'm not sure how often one goes through Wells to Cheyenne, though. Someone at the café might know, but I can't get to town. The storm took out part of the ranch road last night, and it's going to take a few hours to fix it after the rain stops."

Allison considered her options. She had packed their belongings this morning. Before falling asleep, she had worried about the Probe's wheel, then decided that it was a minor problem and could be fixed within hours. How much damage would a pothole do, after all? She'd comforted herself with her options. She'd never considered that a road would be washed out. "I'm really sorry about all of this," she said to her host. "I'm sure you never thought you'd get stuck with all of us for more than a day."

"We'll try again tomorrow. I called Pete at the garage and told him I was bringing a car in for him."

"Do you think it will take long to fix?"

"I don't know. It depends."

"On what?"

"Whether it's the wheel or the axle. And whether he can get the parts he needs."

"Oh." Her heart sank. She hadn't thought about replacement parts. It was a Ford. She'd assumed parts could be found everywhere for a Ford. Sophie finished the bottle and spit it out of her mouth, so Allison tucked her against her shoulder and patted her back. "I know we've been a lot of trouble," she said to the cowboy. He didn't bother to deny it.

"You can't help the rain."

Allison shook her head. "I could have stayed on the right road in the first place, and none of this would have happened."

She noticed he didn't try to make her feel better. Instead he held the plate toward her. "Want a cinnamon roll?"

"Sure." At this rate she'd weigh twenty pounds more by the time she rolled into Seattle because, no matter what Ryan said, she was going to make it on her own. Allison looked past Dell's shoulder toward the kitchen window. Rain streaked down the glass and coated her view of the outside world. She and the children were safe and warm, protected from the harsh Wyoming spring, thanks to one Good Samaritan cowboy named Wendell.

3

"I'D REALLY LIKE to help," Allison insisted, standing by the counter as Calvin assembled the ingredients for bread dough. He ignored her, which meant he couldn't hear her or chose not to. She tapped him on the shoulder, forcing the man to look at her. "Can I do something? The girls are asleep."

"No." He turned away to open a can of yeast.

"I've never baked bread before," she shouted. He turned and nodded.

"Lotta work," was all he said. She watched as he sprinkled yeast into a bowl with water in the bottom and then stirred it gently.

"Can I watch?"

"Guess there's no harm in that."

So she watched the dough-making process. The man's huge hands held a scarred wooden spoon, which he used to mix the flour into the yeast mixture. He turned the mass of sticky dough onto a floured board and proceeded to knead it with gusto.

"Gotta get the air out," he told her.

She was surprised the dough wasn't screaming for mercy, but she leaned against the counter and stayed quiet for as long as she could. Finally, when he set the rounded dough into a clean, greased bowl and covered it with a cloth, she had to ask, "Do you do this every day?"

"What?" He cupped his ear.

She raised her voice to cheerleading decibels. "Do-you-do-this-every-day!"

He nodded. "Just about."

"Lost art!"

"Yes, ma'am." He put the dishes in the sink, washed and dried his hands. Then he gave her a vague smile, went through the pantry to the room where she could see coats hanging, and put on a jacket, hat and gloves. She heard the door slam and watched out the window as he headed toward the barn. Or at least, she assumed it was the barn. There were a lot of buildings behind the ranch house, and it was still raining so hard that she couldn't see much.

Well, so much for conversation. She filled up the sink with soapy water and washed the few dishes Calvin had left. She took her time rinsing and drying, too, and stacked the clean dishes on the other end of the counter. That felt good, so she scrubbed the counters and the table, then wiped them dry.

She checked on the sleeping girls, gathered up the dirty laundry she'd collected in a plastic bag and took it to the kitchen. She'd seen a washer and dryer in the storeroom off the kitchen, and she didn't think the men would mind if she washed baby clothes. The room was lined with shelves laden with large quantities of food, but in the midst of one wall the washer and dryer sat waiting. It didn't take long to find the soap and start a load of wash, and then there was nothing else to do in the quiet house.

Allison left the kitchen and went into the living area. The dining table was a sturdy oak rectangle, but the chairs were missing. Books, lots of them, were stacked against the wall behind the table, between the fireplace and the wall. She went over and examined their bright covers. Mysteries, suspense, techno-thrillers and some Montana history books leaned against the wall. She sat down and flipped through them until she found a medical mystery written by a woman. She didn't really care for serial killer books, but she couldn't afford to be fussy.

She wished Dell would come back inside. He was a quiet man, but at least he answered her questions and didn't seem to mind talking to her. Calvin preferred to ignore the fact that she was there. Allison took the book to the back bedroom and checked on the children again. It was almost lunchtime, but they'd had a busy morning. They'd sat in their little chairs and watched everything that went on in the kitchen. They didn't seem to mind Calvin's loud songs or Dell's awkward manner while he held them. They didn't seem to mind anything except riding in a car for more than thirty minutes at a time. It was going to be a long trip to the west coast, Allison realized, but once they were there everything would be fine. One of her college roommates had promised to help find the "perfect apartment" and the "perfect baby-sitter," too, for when Allison began her new job. Which Carla had insisted would be the "perfect situation."

The perfect situation would have been for Sandy to have survived the car accident, married her lover and lived happily ever after. *I could have been the perfect aunt instead of a definitely less-than-perfect substitute mother.* Allison curled up on the bed, opened the book and was asleep in two minutes.

"HOW LONG?" The two men stopped in the shelter of the calf barn's door and looked out at the rain pelting the mud.

Dell shrugged. "Don't know. After the rain stops I'll have the men work on the road."

"This business of having a woman around is making me crazy."

"Well," Dell drawled, "it's not doing my nerves any good, either."

'Your nerves," Calvin scoffed. "You don't have a nervous bone in your body, son. Never did, not as long as I've known you."

Dell shoved his hands into his pockets. If his uncle only knew that just looking at Allison made his insides tense to the point of pain, he'd laugh until he fell face first into the mud. "Yeah, well, it's not like either one of us is used to having company."

They stood in silence and watched the rain for a few minutes. Behind them, young calves bawled for their mamas and rustled through the hay.

"That's what you need. A woman. You should get to town more."

"I'm not too good at being around women," Dell confessed.

"No reason you should be. You don't have any practice."

"No one to practice on." It wasn't easy to talk to women when you had a face that could scare a grizzly to the other side of the mountain.

"'Cept your houseguest."

"She's the kind of woman you practice *for*."

Cal shrugged. "She'll be gone soon. If you're not gonna get rid of her, you might as well practice talking to her. If you make mistakes, it won't make any difference. By next week, she won't even remember your name."

Dell's heart sank. "Well, that's true, I guess."

"Don't seem right that a man your age doesn't have a lady friend," Calvin commented. "Not that I want you dragging some wife up here." Here the man shook his head. "No, sirree. We don't need any women on the Lazy J, messing with my kitchen and wanting lace tablecloths and pink napkins and making us take off our boots at the back porch and—"

"We take off our boots sometimes," Dell pointed out. "Unless we're just getting coffee and going back out again."

"Mark my words," the older man said. "You get a woman up here and you'll be saying 'please' and 'thank you very much' and keeping your elbows off the table like some Boston greenhorn."

Dell sighed. "There's nothing wrong with having manners."

Calvin turned his collar up against his ears and prepared to cross the yard. "Watch your step, son. And get someone to fix the road. I'm getting a bad feeling in my gut about all of this. It's okay to go to town once in a while for a little female companionship, but it's something else when a woman is walking around my kitchen watching me make bread."

Dell stayed in the shelter of the door and watched Calvin slop through the mud. The sun had to come out eventually, and when it did the roads would be passable, flowers would bloom and the warm Wyoming wind would blow the ruts dry. And Allison and her children would leave and the world would settle back to normal.

He hated "normal."

DELL ATE DINNER with her again. There wasn't any choice and besides, he'd given some thought to that "practice" idea. He'd always thought he'd be one of those men who didn't need or want a steady woman in his life. Of course, his body had protested over celibacy, but a man could get used to a lot of things if he had to. He worked hard and he took a lot of cold showers and he sure as hell didn't watch any of the x-rated channels that came in over the satellite dish.

"So," he tried, "what are you going to do in Seattle?"

"I'm an interior decorator." Allison buttered a cinnamon roll. "I would love to know how to make these."

"Don't you cook?"

"No." Allison smiled at his look of surprise. "Well," she amended. "I'm pretty good at stir fry. But that's just chopping and frying, and following the directions on a seasoning packet."

"Oh." He searched his mind for something else to ask her. Like how she ended up with the two babies who lay on a blanket by the couch. And why she wasn't married. "Do you have a job waiting for you?"

"Yep." She took a bite of the roll and chewed slowly. "A friend of mine offered me a job with her company. Do you think Calvin would give me the recipe, or is that against the rules?"

"The rules?"

"You know. Cook Rules. Never give out your recipes."

"You'd better ask him yourself."

"Why doesn't he eat dinner with you?"

"He likes to eat with the men and he says that I don't have the sense to come inside and eat dinner at six o'clock. He leaves me something to heat up whenever I feel like it."

"It's nice of you to take the time to keep me company," Allison said. "It's been a long day."

"It's a lonely place for a woman," Dell agreed.

She shook her head. "It's the rain. I don't mind the quiet, and the girls are sleeping like little logs. I think they're tired from traveling."

"You still have a long way to go."

"Two days. Maybe three, if we stop early each day. It just depends on how much sleep I can get the night before."

"Going to Seattle must be important."

"Well, we sure couldn't stay in Kansas City."

Dell didn't ask why not. The lovely light vanished from her blue eyes and she looked a little sad. Which meant someone had broken her heart. There was another man, of course. Why wouldn't there be? He finished his last bite of roast beef, pushed his plate aside and wiped his face with his napkin. "I hear that's not a bad town," he said, remembering that he was supposed to keep the conversation going. "I've been to a couple of cattlemen's conferences there."

"I'm looking forward to a change," Allison said. "It will be good for the girls, too."

Dell searched his brain for a safe subject. Life in Kansas City wasn't something to bring up again, and mentioning her sister would just make her feel sad. Those happy little babies were orphans and Allison was alone. They'd already covered the weather and he knew she didn't like the rain. "Calvin might have some cookbooks around here, if you're curious about his recipes."

"Really? You don't think he'd mind?"

Dell decided not to answer that question. His uncle was as cranky as an old bear about his kitchen. "What he doesn't know won't hurt him."

She smiled. "Maybe I could copy some of them while he's outside."

"Yeah, that's what I was thinking, too." He got up and went over to the cabinet to the right of the stove and opened the door. Inside was a stack of battered cookbooks and an assortment of papers. "I'll bet you can find anything you want in here." He shut the door and poured himself a cup of coffee. "Do you want any?"

"No, thanks. I think that serial killer mystery I'm reading

will keep me awake. I borrowed one of your books. You have quite a lot of them."

"I read in the winter. At night."

"You could use some bookcases." She finished her cinnamon roll and wiped her lips. Then she winced. "Sorry. I should mind my own business."

He sat back down at the table. "No, you're right. I had some old ones, but I gave them to the boys in the bunkhouse and never got around to replacing them. I don't spend too much time in the house, so I've kind of let things go."

"The rain stopped," Allison said. "Do you think we'll be able to get the car to town tomorrow? I mean, if you're not busy with something else."

"If it doesn't rain in the night, we should be all right. Most of the calving is over, so I can take the afternoon to go to town. You don't have to go."

'I'd like to, though, if you don't mind."

Mind? He would drive along Main Street with a beautiful woman beside him in the truck. People would talk about it for months. "What about the babies? There's not a lot of room in the cab of the truck for car seats."

"Oh, that's right. I'm not used to thinking about trucks," she said. "I'm not sure what to do about formula and diapers. If the car can be fixed soon, then there isn't a problem. But if it's going to take a few more days, I'm going to need things for the babies.'

"You can give me a list."

'Thanks. You don't mind?"

"No."

"Thank you." She looked at him and leaned her chin in her hand. "How come you're not married?"

He cleared his throat. "Well, I'm not sure," he lied. He

wasn't married because he hadn't found a woman who would look at him twice.

"Don't you even have a girlfriend?"

"No."

She frowned. "I guess there aren't a lot of single women in Wells City."

"No."

"You should get into Cheyenne once in a while. If you learned to line dance, you could—"

"Line dance?"

"Sure. Everyone's doing it in those country-western clubs. You could meet women that way."

He took a gulp of his coffee. He couldn't imagine his size fourteen feet moving across a dance floor. "I don't—"

"I could teach you," she said. "It's easy."

Which holding a conversation with this woman wasn't. "Easy," he repeated, feeling like an idiot. "I don't think so."

"Have you ever tried?"

"Well, no, but—"

"No buts," Allison declared. "I'll teach you to dance in return for towing my car to town."

"You don't owe me anything," Dell tried, starting to feel panic rising within him.

"I have some tapes in my bag. Do you have a cassette player?"

He nodded.

"Good. Maybe later, after I get the girls to bed and you're done with your chores."

"We could play cards," Dell said. "Instead."

"Or do both," Allison declared, standing to clear the table. "Do you think Calvin would mind if I washed up these dishes?"

"No." He would throw a fit, but it didn't matter. If scrub-

bing plates kept Allison from dancing, she could scrub all
night long.

"Good." She left to check on the babies, adjusted their
blankets, and talked to them for a minute before she returned to the kitchen. "Did you have more calves today?"

"Yep."

"How many?"

"About sixty today, far as we can tell. All healthy, too."
He couldn't keep the satisfaction from his voice.

She smiled. "So we both took care of our babies today."

"I guess you could say that." He helped clear the table,
then watched as she filled the sink with soapy water and
began to wash the supper dishes. "I could help," he said.

"No way. I'm sure you have lots of other things to do,
and I'm happy to be doing something besides fix bottles
and change diapers."

"All right." He moved away from the counter and
headed toward the coatroom.

"Don't forget," she called after him. "We have a date
later on!"

A date. He didn't turn around, for fear she would see the
terrified expression in his eyes. "Yes, ma'am,' was about all
he could manage to say. Within seconds he stepped outside
into the darkness to take great gulps of the damp night air.

"Okay," Allison said. "Here we go." She adjusted the volume on the cassette player and stepped into the center of
the room. She'd pushed the couch against the far wall and
rolled up the rug, which was a definite improvement, she
decided. Sylvie and Sophie, wide awake before their ten
o'clock feeding, sat in their seats on the couch and watched
their aunt walk across the living room toward the tall
rancher.

Dell reluctantly stood beside her.

"Here's how it goes. Step, step, forward, kick. See?" She moved two steps to the right, took a step forward, then kicked. "It's in time to the music, one, two, three four. You do it."

"Step, step, front, kick," he repeated without moving and inch.

"Stand beside me and do what I do." She tapped her foot to the music, then started to move. Dell did the "step, step" part, then stopped. Allison turned to look up at him. "What's wrong?"

"I'm not much of a dancer," he said. He looked down at his feet as if they were alien beings.

"You'll be fine. Step, step, front, kick. Remember those four words."

He sighed. "Why am I doing this?"

"So you'll know how, in case you ever want to go dancing."

"Never have before," he muttered, but he smiled down at her when he said it.

"There's a first time for everything. Come on." She moved to the right, and he followed her, then forward and they both kicked in unison. "Very good," Allison told him. "Are you ready for a few more steps?"

"No."

"Sure you are." She explained the next part to him, then rewound the tape to the beginning of the song. "Watch my feet."

"I'm trying to watch yours and mine at the same time."

"Do whatever works," she told him, and had him do it over and over again until he seemed comfortable. When the song ended, she stopped the tape. "There. That wasn't so bad, was it?"

He stared down at her. "What's the name of that dance?"

"I think it's called the Honky Tonk Stomp."

Dell nodded. "Okay. I got it."

"Let's do it again, this time all the way through." She pushed the play button, waited for the count to begin, then started. "Step, step, front and kick."

"Yes, ma'am," Dell said, keeping up with her. He stumbled a couple of times, but made it through to the end of the song without complaining.

"That was great!"

Dell shook his head. "My big feet aren't used to moving this fast."

"Want to try again?"

He sighed. "You're going to make sure I know how to dance, aren't you?"

"Yep." She put her hands on her hips and smiled at his sad expression. "Don't look so pathetic. You'll have women crawling all over you."

He raised his eyebrows. "What makes you think I don't have women crawling all over me *now?*"

She laughed. "I haven't seen any, Mr. Jones," she teased.

"There could be hundreds of women hiding in the barn, just waiting for me to check on the horses."

Allison started the song again. "They'll all have to wait until I'm finished with you."

He chuckled, and Sylvie started fussing. Allison picked her up, tucked her in her arm and started dancing. "Come on," she urged Dell, who wasn't moving. "We'll run through it again, then add the next steps."

"There's more? How long can the damn dance be?"

Sylvie smiled, and Allison kept moving with the beat of the music to keep the baby content. "Just keep doing the steps until you feel comfortable with them."

He muttered something she didn't hear, because Sophie let out a scream of protest about being left alone on the couch. "Here," she said to Dell. "You dance with Sylvie for a few minutes."

"I can't—" And then Sylvie was in his arms and smiling. "She won't mind?"

"She loves it." Allison scooped up Sophie and returned to the center of the room. "Let's keep going." She led him through the steps, then showed him how to turn to the side and start all over again. When they turned the third time, Calvin was standing in the doorway watching them. His arms were folded on his chest and he looked as if he was witness to insanity. Allison waved to him and kept dancing, but Dell stopped. Then the song did, too. Allison, out of breath, stopped the tape and adjusted her grip on Sophie.

"Do you want to join us?" she asked the older man in a loud voice.

"No, thank you, miss," Calvin replied, nodding politely to her before turning to his nephew. "Never figured you to be doing the Honky Tonk Stomp.'

Dell couldn't hide his surprise. "How'd you know that's what we were doing?"

"I watch the Nashville channel sometimes when I'm cooking. Never tried it, though. Leave that to the younger people." His eyes twinkled and he cleared his throat as he stared at his nephew and the tiny baby in his arms. "And the girlies, too, I reckon."

The "girlies" must be Sophie and Sylvie, Allison decided. "We're all having a good time."

"I just came in for a piece of pie. Don't let me bother you none." He turned and went back into the kitchen as Sylvie squirmed in Dell's arms and started to fuss.

"We have to feed them or dance with them," Allison said. "Which is it going to be?"

"Dance, I guess." He glanced toward the kitchen. "I am never going to hear the end of this."

"Just one more time," she suggested. "Then I'll feed the girls and put them to bed for a while."

"Do they sleep all night?"

"No. Not yet. But they might last till four or five, if I'm lucky." She pushed the button and the music started again. "Remember the steps?"

"Yep. Step, step, front, kick."

"You're going to be a real ladykiller the next time you go to town."

He scowled, which made him look much fiercer than he was, and he missed the kick. "Damnation!"

"But you're going to have to start smiling and look like you're having a good time."

"I'm not."

"Sure you are. Just think, you're dancing with a beautiful girl named Sophie and you're doing fine." Allison watched him out of the corner of her eye. He really was being a good sport, and she felt better than she had in months. Maybe it was the exercise. Or maybe it was because it was the end of a long winter and life was beginning to look a little more cheerful.

WELLS CITY was no city. Population 8,243 said the battered sign at the outskirts of town. Allison sat beside Dell in the truck as they drove down Main Street. They passed a supermarket, then continued on down the street past a bank, hair salon, boot repair shop, drugstore and restaurant on the right, and what looked like some clothing stores and a newspaper office on the left. Allison craned her neck to see. Dell drove through the main part of town to the gas station on the corner of intersecting streets and stopped by the sign that said Automotive Repairs.

"Looks like the men got her down here all right," Dell said, pointing out the car.

Allison saw her Probe parked off to the left of the building. The back tires and the hind bumper were coated in mud, but at least the car was in the care of a mechanic and would be fixed soon. "I hope it wasn't too much trouble for them."

"They didn't mind. I gave them the afternoon off, so they were right pleased to do it. Come on, let's go tell Pete your story." He got out of the truck, and Allison hurried to open her door and follow him across the parking lot. The wind almost took her breath away, but the air wasn't as cold as a couple of days ago.

Pete turned out to be a stocky man a little younger than Dell, wearing greasy overalls and a dark blue baseball cap. "I haven't had a chance to look at your car yet," he said, wiping his hand on a rag. He gave Allison a quick once-over, then glanced at Dell before turning back to Allison. "You got any errands in town?"

"Well..." Allison hesitated. "A few groceries." She didn't want to be away from the babies longer than she absolutely had to. They would probably sleep the entire time, but she didn't like letting them out of her sight. "I really need to get the car fixed as soon as possible, though."

"Okeydoke. Give me half an hour or so. Grab a cup of coffee or somethin' and let me check out that wheel. Front right, right?"

"Right."

'Thanks, Pete," Dell said.

"Yep." He gave Dell a wink, then grinned. "My pleasure."

Allison wondered what the wink was all about, but once again hurried to match Dell's long strides past the gas pumps, past the truck, and across the empty street. "Where are we going?"

"We'll get some coffee," he said, heading toward a place on the opposite corner called Roy's Diner.

"I could get the baby formula while you're having coffee," she offered. What if Calvin had a problem with the girls? They'd already been gone close to an hour, and now another thirty minutes would be added to the time spent away from the ranch. And it was almost forty-five minutes from the ranch to town.

"We can do that on the way out. It's on the way." He opened the heavy glass door and ushered her inside. The restaurant was small and cozy, with dark blue booths lining the walls and a counter with red-topped stools facing the kitchen. A tall redheaded waitress stared at them when they walked in. She was about thirty, with hair the color of copper swept up in a French twist and secured with bobby pins. Her white waitress uniform revealed a little bit of cleavage and as she looked at Dell, she patted her hair in place with red-painted fingernails.

"Hi, Lucille," Dell said.

"Hey, Dell." She tucked her order pad into her pocket and followed them over to a booth.

Now this was interesting, Allison thought. Maybe the redheaded waitress had a thing for the shy rancher. Allison looked at her and didn't like the amused expression in those green eyes. You'd think Dell had never been in here with a woman before from the way the woman acted. Like she'd seen a ghost.

"What can I get you, Dell?" Lucille ignored Allison.

"Allison?" Dell slid her a plastic menu. 'You want coffee and pie?"

"Sure. What kind do you have?" she asked, forcing the waitress to look in her direction.

Apple, blueberry and Boston Cream. We're out of cherry and peach. The menu's wrong."

"Apple, then. And a cup of coffee." No. Lucille wasn't the woman for Dell. She'd eat him alive in about three days and the poor man wouldn't know what hit him. The ranch house would smell like fingernail polish and hair spray.

"I'll have the same," Dell said, oblivious to Lucille's curious expression.

"I see you have company," Lucille hinted, desperate for information.

Dell frowned. "Allison isn't company. She—"

Allison hurried to finish for him. "Is an old friend." Let the woman think that Dell had a secret life with a mysterious woman. She lowered her voice and gave Lucille a woman-to-woman look. "We're...old friends." She tried to make *old friends* sound sexy and mysterious, and from the way the waitress raided her eyebrows, Allison guessed she'd succeeded.

"For heaven's sake." Lucille turned to Dell. "I'll be right back with your coffee."

Allison ignored Dell's surprised expression and shrugged off her jacket. She looked at her watch. "Do you really think Calvin will hear the girls if they cry?"

"He volunteered to wear his hearing aid. That's a miracle in itself. He says he hates the damn—darn thing."

"I can't believe he offered to take care of them." She couldn't believe she *let* him, but if the mechanic could fix her car she would need to drive it back to the ranch herself. The older man had seemed sincere in his offer to listen for the sleeping babies and to feed them if they woke up hungry. Changing diapers wasn't mentioned.

"Allison, you can't go around letting people think we're living together."

"Do you have a thing for Lucille?"

He looked shocked. "Hell, no. I just don't want people to get the wrong idea."

"I didn't like the way she was acting. As if it was funny that you had a date."

"It's not funny," Dell said. "It's downright hilarious."

"Why?"

"*Why?*" he echoed. "Look at me. I'm not exactly..." He frowned, searching for the words.

"Not exactly what?" she prompted.

"Not what. Who. I was trying to think of the name of the actor who starred in those Lethal Weapon movies."

"Mel Gibson," Allison said. "You're right, you don't look anything at all like Mel Gibson."

Lucille set the mugs on the table and filled them with coffee. "Mel Gibson? Who says Dell doesn't look like Mel Gibson?" She guffawed, and Allison hoped her red hair would turn green the next time she took a shower.

"Dell is more like Robert DeNiro. Only bigger," Allison announced, her teeth gritted. "Don't you agree?"

Lucille acted like Allison had said something funny again. "Robert DeNiro! That's a good one!" She went back to the counter and grabbed two plates of apple pie.

"Enjoy." She slapped them on the table. "When you need a refill on the coffee, just wave."

"Thanks." Dell picked up his fork and looked at Allison. "Aren't you going to eat?"

"I was serious," she insisted. "You do look a little like DeNiro, especially since you shaved."

"Sure," he said, but he didn't sound the least bit convinced. "More like Frankenstein, I think. I'm always asked to be the monster in the junior high's haunted house at Halloween time. They give me a chain saw, with the chain taken out, of course. I make a bunch of little kids scream their heads off."

"That's awful."

He gave her an apologetic look. "I won't do it again, but it raises a lot of money for—"

"No, I mean it's awful that they ask you to be the monster. Just because you're tall."

"And ugly," he reminded her, taking a sip of his coffee. He didn't seem the least bit perturbed.

"You're not ugly."

He ignored her comment. "It's going to be all over town by tomorrow that ol' Dell Jones was in the café eating pie with the most beautiful woman in Wyoming. Folks will be trying to figure that out for a long time to come."

"Good. Let them think what they want." Allison saw Lucille coming toward them and she raised her voice. "You're going to spoil me for other men, Dell," she purred. "Especially after last night. I didn't get much sleep."

Dell choked, prompting Lucille to whack him on the back a few times until he caught his breath.

"Darn," she said, looking at her hand. "I broke a nail."

"I'll take some more coffee," Allison said, giving the woman a polite smile. "I can barely stay awake this afternoon."

"Sure, honey." Lucille gave Dell a sideways glance. "Whatever you say."

"Thanks. Everyone in Wyoming is so nice. Dell always told me I'd love it here."

The waitress hesitated. "You've known Dell long?"

"Long enough."

"You staying for a while?"

Allison shrugged. "Maybe. I just don't know what I'm going to do from one day to the next."

4

"I DON'T KNOW what you're going to do next," Dell muttered once the silent waitress had left their booth and returned to her conversation with Jessie McDougal. Those two women would talk till the sun turned purple. "But I'm going to drink my coffee now."

"I'm sorry." Allison frowned. "She annoyed me. I didn't mean to embarrass you, really."

He sighed. "It'll be all over town."

"I'm sorry," she repeated. "I honestly don't know what came over me."

She looked so sorrowful that he had to smile a little. "I don't mind. Everyone will wonder how old Dell Jones found himself a woman."

"You're not old."

"Thirty-five."

"You're in the prime of your life," she insisted.

"And you?"

"Twenty-seven."

"You look younger."

"I feel older." She smiled. "I guess motherhood will do that to a person."

He cleared his throat. "There wasn't anyone else besides you to, uh, take the children?"

"No. Their father is already married, with two kids and a wife who didn't know her husband had been having an office affair with my sister."

Dell didn't know what to say, so he ate another forkful of pie. He didn't know much about office affairs.

"That shocks you," she said. "It shocked me, too."

"Well, I guess people do all sorts of things that surprise me." He managed a smile again. "I should be used to being surprised." Allison had only been in his life for two days, but she'd managed to silence gabby Lucille and fill his quiet house with the sounds of children and music. She'd made him *dance*, for Lord's sake.

Allison set her coffee cup on the table. "Why are you shaking your head?"

"Just thinking," he said.

"About how long you'll have to put up with me, I imagine."

"Well—"

"I guess that depends on what the mechanic says about the car," she said. "I'm trying not to worry, but did you see the way he frowned when I described the sound it made after I hit the pothole? Do you think it's going to take a long time to fix?"

He shrugged, torn between wanting Allison to be happy and yet hoping she'd have to stay a few more days. Or weeks. Or months. He was insane to wish for such torture. "Pete's a real good mechanic. He'll find out what's wrong."

She looked at her watch. "I hope so. Do you think we've given him enough time?"

Dell pushed his half-eaten pie away. He'd had enough, and it sure wasn't as good as Calvin's. He picked up his hat and put it on his head. "Yeah. Let's go."

"I want to get back before the girls wake up."

"Cal's been nursing calves for years," Dell assured her. "A couple of babies needing bottles isn't going to bother him any."

She didn't look convinced. She shrugged her coat on before he could help her, opened her purse and took out her wallet.

"What are you doing?"

"Paying."

"Not in my town, you're not." Dell grabbed his wallet, tossed down a ten dollar bill and glared at his houseguest. "There. Put your money away."

'You're not scaring me with that look," she said. "I think it should be my treat."

"You're not going to pay," he said. "Not when you're with me."

She shoved her wallet into her purse and slung the strap over her shoulder. "I need to do something to repay your hospitality, Dell."

"Why?"

"Because I want to. It's the right thing to do."

He could think of a few "right things to do," but none of them included walking across the street to the gas station and talking about tires.

"HOLD HER real gentlelike," Calvin ordered. He hoped he wasn't talking too loud for the little things. He put the babies in the young cowboy's arms and watched to make sure that Jed had a good grip before he let go.

"How do you tell them apart?"

"Sylvie has a pointy chin." He set the oven timer for five minutes and kept a careful watch on his charges.

"I ain't never held twins before," Jed said, staring down at the babies. "They're real cute."

"Yeah, well, treat 'em gently cuz I'm in charge of 'em," Calvin said. "Dell and the lady went to town to see about her car and left me to watch the girlies."

Jed grinned from ear to ear, and held his arms perfectly still. "How long do I get?"

"Dollar a minute." He squinted at the oven clock. "You paid for five, you have two minutes to go."

"Hello, little girlies," Jed said. "How are y'all doin' today?" He gave Cal a worried look. "It's not extra if you talk to them, is it?"

"Hell, no. They like it." In fact, they were smiling a little bit at the skinny cowboy. Calvin tilted his head to see if they were really looking at Jed or at something past his shoulder. They were such tiny things. He couldn't really believe that they were here on the ranch. Women and babies were pretty scarce at the Lazy J, all right. They were definitely an event, though having babies around all the time would sure get old real fast.

The buzzer made an ugly sound, and the girls' eyes widened. Calvin hurried to shut it off. "Time's up." He turned to the men waiting in the store room. "Who's next?"

Cussy Martin elbowed his way through the crowd. "I am, goddammit."

"Watch your language," Cal cautioned, taking the ten dollar bill from the man. "I don't want the girlies listenin' to that kind of talk."

Cussy flushed bright red. He took off his hat and muttered, "Sorry."

"Sit over there, and try to keep a civil tongue in yer head." He supervised the handing over of the babies from Jed to Cussy, then set the timer for ten minutes.

This was going well. If Dell and the lady stayed away another hour, there'd be a nice chunk of money in the bean pot. He kept a careful eye on the clock, ordered Jed to keep an eye on the road. There was no way he'd hear the truck drive in; Dell had surprised him more than once, and he didn't think his nephew would take kindly to his selling baby-holding time. Not that there was anything wrong with that, Cal figured, but Dell had some strange notions.

And he'd been on the sensitive side lately.

It was all the woman's fault, of course. He hoped that car of hers was fixed up soon. He wasn't sure how much more of this Dell could take. No matter what his nephew said, Calvin had eyes. And he could see that Dell was on his way to falling in love with the little gal with the sweet smile and yellow hair. Hell, Dell had been alone too long, but the boy had no business pining after a city girl with more problems than a three-legged steer.

"PEOPLE ARE SO friendly here." Allison manuevered the shopping cart down the aisle lined with baby food. "Everyone knows you."

"Yeah."

"I'm glad we called Calvin. I feel so much better." She selected twelve cans of concentrated baby formula and put them in the cart. Calvin had assured her that the babies weren't crying, that the bottles were ready to be warmed whenever the girls fussed for their meal, and that nothing whatsoever had gone wrong. The man had sounded almost cheerful, especially after he'd turned the volume up on the telephone receiver and understood who was on the other end of the line. "I've left them with a sitter before," she explained as Dell followed her down the aisle toward the cases of disposable diapers "And I'll have to hire someone when I get to Seattle, of course. But I really don't like leaving them."

"Cal sounded fine."

Allison looked back to see two thirtish women greet Dell with smiles and friendly hello's. He was certainly a popular man. Everywhere they'd gone this afternoon, from the grocery store to the post office, men and women had gone out of their way to greet him and be introduced to her. It was true what they said about Westerners. She looked at her watch. Pete had asked for more time to call around to see if he could find a part, but he hadn't sounded too optimistic about finding one right away. He'd muttered something about foreign parts on a 1990 Probe, something about a cracked ball bearing, and problems with the axle, but Allison hadn't been able to understand what he was talking about. She'd heard the part where he'd said he could fix it, if he could find the part. That was all that mattered. Maybe she'd have to stay in Wyoming another day, but she'd accepted that already. Staying at the Lazy J couldn't be called a hardship, although she was anxious to get to Seattle and get settled once and for all. All three of them needed a home.

So here she was, in the grocery store in Wells City, while Dell chatted with the local ladies and she filled the cart with baby supplies. She'd buy enough for at least a week, and hope she'd be in Seattle before having to replenish the supply of diapers, formula and baby powder. She would stay at a hotel for a few days, find an apartment, check out the new job, hire a nanny, unpack and—

"Kelly Beatrice," Dell said.

Allison looked up to realize she was being introduced to more of the population of Wyoming. A pretty woman with straight brown hair and green eyes smiled at her. She looked like the kind of woman who rode horses all day.

"Hi," Allison said. "Nice to meet you."

"And I'm June Beck," the other young woman said, shaking her hand. She had lighter hair pulled back into a braid. Both women wore jeans and heavy winter jackets. "I hear you're visiting Dell for a few days."

Allison nodded. Neither woman looked as amused or intensely curious as the waitress, so she answered the question honestly. "Yes. While my car is being fixed."

"That's what Dell said," Kelly replied. "That you had some tough luck on our Wyoming roads."

"I was lucky Dell came along and rescued us."

"Us?" The woman's gaze dropped to the contents of Allison's grocery cart. "You have children?"

"Twins."

"How old?"

"Three months."

June smiled. "I have a six-month-old and a three-year-old, both boys."

"And I have three-year-old twin boys," Kelly said. "So I know what you're going through."

Allison wished she could take Kelly back to the ranch with her. "And you survived it?"

"Yes." The woman chuckled. "But I'm waiting for them to be old enough to go to school. Each phase is something different, and by the time I get used to it, they're on to something else. But it's fun," she added. "And I'm expecting another child in the fall."

"Congratulations," Allison told her. "Another set of twins?"

"Not that I know of."

Dell cleared his throat. "We'd better be getting along."

"It was nice meeting both of you."

"Same here," June said.

"Good luck with the twins," Kelly added.

"Thanks." The women pushed their carts past them and turned at the bottom of the aisle. Allison looked up at Dell. "You must know everyone."

"I grew up here."

"Those women seemed very nice." Allison surveyed the disposable diapers. The selection never ceased to amaze her. Though she'd found it was cheaper to use cloth diapers, she'd opted for the disposable kind during the trip.

"I went to school with both of them."

"Ah," she teased. "Old girlfriends?"

He shook his head and helped her rearrange the shopping cart to fit four boxes of diapers inside. "We'd better get going. You need anything else for the girls?"

"No. That should do it. I won't have to shop again until I reach Seattle." Allison noticed Dell didn't look too happy. Maybe she shouldn't have flirted with him to make that waitress's mouth fall open. Maybe she shouldn't have disrupted his life in the first place. She would try to fade into the background from now on, she promised herself. Dell was such a nice man, after all. He didn't need her teasing or her questions or her interruptions. "Are you *sure* you don't have a girlfriend?"

"You sure ask a lot of questions about my private life," he muttered.

"Well, everyone keeps looking at us and whispering. Even in the post office. I can't figure it out, unless they're surprised to see you with another woman."

He sighed, and took the cart from her and headed toward the register at the front of the store. She had trouble keeping up with his long stride. "It's not you," he said once they were in line behind a woman whose toddler screamed for a candy bar. "It's me. No one can believe that I'm here in town with a woman. Not just any woman, either. With a *beautiful* woman."

"I'm not beautiful," she said. "I'm *okay*," she added. "Maybe a six and a half. Or maybe a seven when I'm dressed up and I fix my hair." She smiled to show she was teasing. She expected him to smile back, but he didn't. Dell Jones was way too serious.

"You're a ten" he said with a sigh. "A 'Baywatch' ten. A beauty queen. And you're with the homeliest guy in Wells City. Or even in Wyoming. It's making people laugh."

"No, it's not," she insisted. "I think you're exaggerating. About a lot of things." She looked around and noticed no one looking at them now, except the man bagging the groceries.

The toddler, sniffing back his tears, looked at her and whined, "Can-dee."

"No candy," Allison told him, and he smiled at her.

"See?" Dell observed. "Even the child knows beauty when he sees it."

"Stop it." Allison looked up into his face. He was certainly not a handsome man, or even an attractive one. His nose was too big, his eyebrows too bushy and dark. But the expression in those eyes was sincere. Somehow she knew she could trust him, the way she'd known she could trust him when she'd first seen him. But then, she hadn't been a very good judge of men lately. And trust wasn't high on her list of traits to acquire at this time in her life. Patience, yes. And strong maternal instincts, of course. But trust in one's fellow man—emphasis on the *man?* No way.

"Your turn," he said, gesturing toward the empty conveyor belt. "I'll bring the truck around and meet you out front."

"Okay. Thanks." Allison watched him slip through an empty aisle and leave the store. He was the largest man she'd ever seen, and yet he had such a gentle way about him. She turned back to her groceries. Dell Jones was too nice a man to live alone. She hoped he'd leave his ranch once in a while to go dancing.

"Look," Dell said, not taking his gaze from the road ahead of him. He was afraid that she was crying, and he knew that he couldn't bear to see her tears. "It's not that bad. You're welcome to stay for as long as it takes to find the part." Pete had scratched his head and said he didn't know where the hell he was gonna get an axle to match the Probe's, that it was gonna take a while and no, he didn't have one goldarm guess how long it would take, but he'd do his best.

Dell had felt his heart sink. He was half in love with her already. A few more days and he'd be downright pathetic. A man had his pride and he wanted to hang on to whatever he had left.

"I don't know what else to do," she answered, her voice soft. "If it was just me—"

"But it's not," he said, daring a glance in her direction. She looked upset, but there was no trace of tears. "You have the babies to consider. You can't haul them on a bus to Cheyenne and stay in a motel."

"I know." Her voice still sounded sad. "I shouldn't have left Kansas City."

He wanted to ask why she'd left. He opened his mouth, then closed it. If she wanted to tell him, then she'd tell him.

She did. "I figured I—we—needed a fresh start. I didn't want the girls running into their birthfather as they grew older, and neither did he."

A sharp pain pierced Dell's heart. How was a child to grow up without a father? It didn't seem right. "A child should have a father."

"Yes," Allison agreed. "In a perfect world."

"In any kind of world."

"And if the father doesn't want her? Or them?"

Dell looked over to the woman beside him and shifted the truck into a lower gear as they approached the hill to the ranch. "Then he's not much of a man."

"I'll agree with you there." She looked out the window as rain started dotting the windshield. "When is it spring around here?"

He let her change the subject.

"YOU'R SURE CHEERFUL," Dell told his uncle after Allison had thanked Calvin for taking care of the babies and bundled them off to her room for a diaper change. "Babysitting must agree with you." He expected Cal to deny it, but to his surprise the gruff cowboy just smiled and turned back to slicing bread. Dell raised his voice. "You didn't have any trouble?"

"Now why would I have any trouble?"

Dell shrugged, and filled a glass of water from the faucet. "Taking care of two babies for four hours couldn't have been easy."

It was Cal's turn to shrug as he turned to his nephew. "They slept most of the time. Till you all decided to come home."

"I told you, we got stuck while Pete tried to find out where he could buy a part for Allison's car."

"Yep, I heard. She's gonna be here for a while longer, is she?"

"Yeah. She's pretty upset about her car." He watched Cal for signs of disapproval and expected the older man to have a complaint. Calvin turned back to his loaf of bread and continued to slice. "Well, see if you can keep her out of my kitchen."

"I'll try."

"I'll take the girlies, though," Cal added. "Next time you hafta go to town."

"That's real nice of you."

"Nothing nice about it," he stated. "Taking care of babies is easier than taking care of calves. Cleaner, too."

"Maybe it wouldn't be so bad to have kids on the ranch someday."

"Someday?" Cal snorted. "You've gone from learning some silly dance to having babies pretty fast, haven't you?

First, you've gotta get a date." He shook his head. "I'm telling you, son. Women are trouble."

"Maybe some women," Dell conceded. But then he thought of Allison's smile and the way she looked in her jeans. He almost smiled when he remembered the look on Lucille's face as Allison spoke of being *tired from last night*. "Not all."

"Yeah?" Cal shot him a sympathetic look. "Guess you'll have to find out the hard way. With any luck, Pete will find what he needs to get that girl on her way before you make a fool of yourself."

"I'm not going to make a fool of myself," Del insisted. "I'm thirty-five years old."

"Women'll fool you at any age." He stacked the bread on a platter. "I made a pot of chicken tortilla soup. You and the lady can eat anytime you want."

Dell looked at the clock. It was almost five. If he ate now, he could spend the rest of the evening in the barn. "Anything going on outside that I should know about?"

"The calving's winding down, all right. Looks like a pretty good year, considering the weather."

"Good."

"You can spend some time with the ranch accounts," Calvin suggested. "If you're looking for something to do."

"Don't worry," Dell said, taking a long swallow of cold water. "I'm not forgetting I have work to do."

Cal pointed to the pot on the stove. "There's your supper. I'm eating with the boys and we're going to play a little cards."

"Poker?" Dell brightened. Nothing like a good poker game to get his mind off women.

"Gin rummy."

Dell peered into the soup kettle. "How hot did you make it?"

"Not much. You can add your own hot sauce."

"Good."

"Wouldn't want the lady to burn her mouth now, would we?" Calvin winked, but before he headed out the door to the mudroom, he turned to his nephew. "You be careful. I don't want to be picking up the pieces all summer."

"You don't have to worry," Dell replied. And he meant it, of course. He stood alone in the kitchen and decided he would not fall in love with Allison. He was too smart a man to fall in love, especially with a woman who was obviously so beautiful. A woman with babies. A woman heading for Seattle to start a new job. He would avoid her from now on, he promised himself. And he would start right after dinner.

ALLISON DIDN'T KNOW what was the matter with the girls. They'd slept like little angels until two o'clock. First one and then the other woke up and began to fuss. Allison didn't feed them right away, since they'd had their bottles around midnight. It wasn't time for another feeding, but the two girls were complaining about something, but Allison couldn't figure out why they were so upset. They'd been sleeping longer this past week or so, letting Allison sleep from midnight until five or six in the morning. But tonight Sophie and Sylvie wanted to be held, and they wanted to be walked. They wanted to look around the room from the vantage point of their aunt's arms. They made it clear that they didn't want to be put down.

So Allison, afraid their cries would wake Dell, walked the babies around the bedroom until she thought her arms would drop from her shoulders. Whenever she tried to put them back to bed in their little playpen, they would lift their heads and begin to cry. Their pitiful cries sounded as loud as fire alarms in the darkness, so Allison would pick them up again and, with a child tucked in each arm, walk around the room for a while longer.

"Are you hungry?" she asked Sophie, whose left side of her mouth lifted into a tentative smile. Sylvie matched her sister's expression, making the two of them look identical in the dim light. Neither child looked sleepy or in pain. "Okay," she told the girls. "We'll try having a middle-of-the-night snack and see what happens. You two wait here while I get your bottles, all right?"

It wasn't all right, which the girls made perfectly clear the minute Allison set them down in their bed. They screamed once again, and Allison knew that within minutes she would be guilty of waking their host. It wasn't right to wake a man who worked eighteen hours a day. He'd gone outside after dinner and hadn't returned before she'd gone to bed. The house had been quiet at midnight, so she'd assumed he was either asleep or working in the barn. Through the kitchen windows, she'd seen lights in some of the distant outbuildings.

She would have to tiptoe to the kitchen and warm up the bottles without waking Dell, which wasn't going to be easy with an armload of babies. Allison opened her bedroom door and saw a faint glow of light from the other end of the house, which meant that someone had left a light on in the kitchen. She made her way along the dim hall, past Dell's closed bedroom door, and into the kitchen where the light over the sink illuminated the room.

Allison settled the girls in their car seats, then lifted them onto the kitchen table. "Please," she told them. "Be good girls. You don't want to wake up Mr. Jones, do you?"

Sylvie glared at her and let out a howl of complaint, which Sophie immediately copied. Allison hurried to the refrigerator, grabbed the bottles, stuck them in a pan of hot water and returned to the girls. "You have to stop," she told them, trying to make her voice sound as soothing as possible. "You're making too much noise. Hush, now."

They didn't want to hush. They wanted to cry, which they continued to do, until Allison retrieved the bottles, tested the temperature, and attempted to give the babies their unscheduled feeding.

"What the hel—heck is going on out here?" Dell stood in the entrance of the kitchen and stared at the three of them. The babies twisted their necks to see who had arrived and let the formula drip from the corners of their mouths before they began to scream again. Allison set the bottles on the table and tried to explain. Which wasn't easy, considering that Dell was only half dressed. He wore no shirt, so his wide chest was bare and covered with dark hair. He'd zipped his jeans but forgotten to fasten the snap, and his large feet were bare. The poor man looked half-asleep. And totally sexy, which surprised her.

"They're not happy tonight," Allison explained, conscious of her thin flannel nightgown. It came to her ankles and covered her arms, but the neckline was scooped low and edged with lace. She would be all right if she didn't bend over.

"I can hear that." He stepped into the room and spoke to the girls. "Are you two giving your momma a bad time?"

"They know I'm not their mother."

"You're their mother now," he pointed out. He unfastened the safety belt across Sophie and scooped her into his arms. She promptly stopped crying, but her sister continued to complain. Allison soon had the baby in her arms, which seemed to make her happy.

"It's like they just want to be held."

Allison looked at him with surprise. "Do you think so?"

"Well, sure seems that way. Try putting her down and see what happens." Sure enough, Allison made a motion to tuck Sophie in her seat and the little girl immediately screwed her mouth to howl.

"I don't understand. They've never acted this way before. And they'd just started sleeping longer in the night." Allison sank into one of the wooden chairs and cradled the baby in her arms. "I thought we were all going to start getting some rest."

"You are," Dell said, his voice soft. "Starting now. Give me Sophie and go to bed."

She stared up at him. "I can't do that."

"Why not?"

"You've taken us in, which doesn't mean you have to take care of us twenty-four hours a day."

"I didn't say I *had* to. I'm offering. How long has it been since you've slept through the night?"

Allison couldn't remember. She'd taken the children when Sandy had died and the hospital had pronounced them well enough to leave the nursery. Ryan had complained about the noise, the interrupted nights, the mess in the apartment, until Allison had moved into the babies' room to sleep. "More than three months."

"It shows."

"Which wasn't polite of him to point out. "I'm getting used to it. They say it can't last forever."

"Go to bed, Allison." His voice was low and quiet. "I'll sit up with them for a while, and when they go to sleep I'll bring them in to you. That is, if you don't mind."

Mind? She wished he'd put a shirt on. That enormous chest was disconcerting, especially when he walked toward her and held his empty arm out for the second baby. Allison stood and put Sophie in the crook of his arm. Her fingertips brushed Dell's skin and a small part of the crispy mat of dark hair that covered a chest the size of a king-size bed.

She shouldn't be thinking about beds, she reminded herself as she withdrew her hand from further contact with Dell's warm skin. She folded her arms across her chest and surveyed the two babies who gurgled their contentment.

"I'll see if they want to eat," Dell said. "They can't stay awake forever."

"And neither should you."

He shrugged. "I'm used to being up half the night. You don't have to worry."

"I worry about everything," she confessed. "I can't seem to stop."

"Get some rest." Dell backed up a few steps so she could walk toward the doorway. "The girlies and I will be fine."

She believed him, though she wondered why she took his word so easily. "Thank you. I'm always thanking you for something."

"You don't have to. It's not as if I didn't offer."

"You've offered too much."

He shook his head. "Shut up and go to bed."

Allison smiled and left the room. She walked slowly down the hall, giving Dell time to change his mind about taking care of the children. She wanted to hear if they screamed when she left the room, in which case she'd hurry back to the kitchen. But they were quiet, and Allison left her bedroom door open to hear them cry, to hear Dell call if he needed her.

She was asleep in minutes. Almost before she could wonder at the strange sensation touching Dell's skin had caused.

5

HE COULD STILL FEEL the touch of Allison's fingers against his skin, even after an hour of carrying the babies around the living room. His plan to avoid her hadn't lasted long. Here he was, half-dizzy with desire, walking around the house in the middle of night with an armload of babies. Allison had touched him. Unintentionally, of course. She had put the babies in his arms and couldn't avoid touching him. He understood that, but knowing it was accidental hadn't lessened the impact of having those gentle fingers sweep over his heart.

His little charges had finally closed their eyes, but Dell didn't stop walking until he was certain they were really asleep and not just relaxing? When he put them to bed, he wanted them to stay asleep so Allison could rest. Dell stopped walking, but the babies didn't open their eyes, so he walked slowly down the hall toward Allison's room.

Allison's room. He thought of it as that already. Long after she'd driven away, he would most likely think of it as Allison's room. The door was open, but he hesitated before stepping inside. He could hear her slight, rhythmic breathing and smelled baby powder and the faintest floral perfume as he passed the dresser and headed to the playpen. He steeled his heart against the intriguing scent of a sleeping woman only three feet away. There was enough light from the kitchen to see that Allison lay curled on her side facing the playpen. He would give a million dollars if she was his, if he had the right to join her in the double bed. She would be warm and sweet. She would be welcoming to a beat-up cowboy. He probably didn't look too bad in the dark, and his body was big, but all muscle. He wondered if she would think he was too big, too hairy.

There was no reason to wonder, of course. She wasn't staying. She wasn't his. She was his guest, and she would never know that he harbored a secret longing to take her in his arms. He took a deep breath and turned away, toward the playpen.

Now here, dammit, was an unexpectedly tricky part. How was he supposed to put one baby down without letting go of the other one? It was a long way down to the bottom of the playpen. He considered bending over and releasing one child, then the other, but rejected that idea as too risky. What if they woke up? Or worse, hurt themselves? He turned toward the bed and swallowed hard. He could leave one baby on the bed with Allison while he positioned her sister on the playpen's mattress, but that would risk Allison waking up and thinking, well, thinking there was a cowboy touching her bed.

Hell and damnation. He had no choice but to bend over and ease Sophie onto the mattress, near the little ridge made by Allison's feet and not too close to the edge of the bed. Then he turned and carefully set Sylvie on her back in the playpen before hurrying back to the bed for Sophie.

"Dell?" His name was a whisper in the darkness that sent warmth surrounding his heart. He froze, and Allison smiled sleepily. "Is everything okay?"

"Yeah. It's fine," he assured her, resisting the urge to kiss her forehead and tuck the yellow quilt over her shoulder. While he grappled with how to explain why he was standing by her bed, she closed her eyes and went back to sleep. Dell wasted no time getting out of there. The baby's eyelids fluttered as he scooped her into his arms, but she didn't wake when he bent over and lay her beside her sister. He covered them both with a pink blanket and watched them for a few moments until he was certain they weren't going to wake up and holler again. Then he left, shutting the door soundlessly behind him before hurrying down the hall to the kitchen and a shot of some rare kind of Scotch he'd won at last year's May Day dance.

He sat in the semidarkness, in the battered recliner, and thought about his home and his life while he drank the kind of whiskey a man saved for special occasions. It was an occasion, he decided, thinking hard about how he wanted the rest of his life to be. He didn't want to be alone anymore. He liked the smell of baby powder. He thought the sound of a sleeping woman's gentle breathing was music, and the touch of her fingers against his chest had made him almost choke with surprise and longing. He would keep her if he could, though there wasn't much to offer her in the way of luxury and excitement. The Lazy J was a good ranch, one hell of a good ranch, he amended. The land had served his family and himself well; they'd preserved their share of heaven, all right. But the house was plain and stark, the furnishings old, the fancy things that would appeal to a woman nonexistent. Stacks of books and magazines weren't exactly decorations, though he and Cal sure hadn't minded living with reading material within easy reach. Dell sat and thought some more. If he were a woman, what would he want? He reached down and set his empty glass on the floor, then reached for the JCPenney catalog, the big one that was underneath the stack of *Outdoor Life* and *Sports Illustrated*. He ought to be able to find something in those pages that would give him some answers.

SHE STUDIED *All About Babies* the next morning, while she drank coffee in the kitchen, but she couldn't find anything that explained why babies would fuss and cry at night if they weren't teething, didn't have colic pains, or hadn't been asleep all day.

Calvin, his hearing aid in place, cut up meat for a stew and fussed over dough in a thick pottery bowl before turning to look at Allison's reading material. "You studying?"

Allison nodded and flipped to the section called "Setting Schedules." "I don't know why the girls were awake most of last night. It was as if they just wanted to be held."

"Maybe they were lonesome."

She looked up at him and, hoping the hearing aid worked, raised her voice a little. "Exactly. They wanted to be held and talked to and played with, as if it was the middle of the afternoon." She yawned. "It was very strange."

Cal shrugged. "Guess they like company."

"In the middle of the night?" She shook her head and scanned the paragraphs describing a typical baby's routine. None of this was new to her. "At this rate, they'll be two years old before any of us sleep eight hours in a row." She glanced out the window, where blue sky and spring sun waited. "I'll take them for a walk today. The fresh air will be good for them."

"How?"

"Good question. I don't suppose I can get the stroller to work on dirt."

"Not dirt," Calvin said. "Mud."

"Maybe we'll sit on the front porch, then."

He nodded. "I'll show you a better place. More sun. After I get this stew fixed."

Calvin was as good as his word, for an hour later found them heading out of the back door toward a set of buildings on the other side of a muddy yard where several roads crisscrossed. The girls had been fed, washed and dressed, then tucked into identical infant sleeping bags for their outdoors adventure. Allison, with Sylvie in her arms, followed Cal and Sophie across a wide field of mud toward a neat gathering of outbuildings. One housed a screened porch that faced southeast, judging from the way the sun's rays touched the windows. Allison carried a thick blanket she'd found in the closet and, once on the porch, laid it like a mattress pad on the floor and let the girls lie on their backs and kick.

"What're they lookin' at?" Calvin cracked open one of the windows and let in a breath of spring air.

Allison followed Sophie's gaze as she tried to reach for a sunbeam that crossed her chest. "The sunshine, I think. They're at the age now where they're noticing things and want to try to touch them."

"Huh," the older man said, sitting down in a well-worn wooden rocker. He gestured toward its mate. "You'd better sit down. You're looking a little peaked."

"Actually, I feel fine. Dell helped—" Allison stopped, not wanting Calvin to know that she'd kept his overworked nephew awake last night. She glanced at the old cowboy, but he paid no attention to her, so she assumed he didn't hear what she'd said. His attention was fixed on the way the girls flailed about on their blanket.

He turned to Allison and frowned. "They warm enough?"

"I think so. We're out of the wind, and the sun is shining." She looked around the porch. The wooden floor had been swept clean, and the windows that lined the upper half of the walls gleamed. "What building is this?"

"Number two bunkhouse. Holds four men."

"How many bunkhouses are there?"

"Used to be four. Now we just use number two and

three. Number one has the tack, and number four is for summer, for the hay crew."

"You all work so hard."

"Dell most of all," Cal added. "Can't get that boy to slow down."

"Maybe he should take a vacation."

Calvin chuckled. "That'll be the day. He loves this place, it's in his blood, and there ain't nothin' that's gonna keep him from it for very long."

Allison wished she had that feeling about where she lived. "He sure works hard."

"Yep. He got that from his father. Never saw such a hard-workin' man in my entire life. My brother could do a day's work in a morning and keep goin'. Guess that's why the old place is still doin' okay after all these years."

Allison wondered what "doin' okay" meant. She'd assumed the sparse interior of the ranch house meant that Dell didn't have the extra money for furniture and the luxuries that would make the place look, well, homey. He must have put all his profits, if there were any, back into buying cattle and land.

"Well, speak of the devil," the old man muttered. Allison looked up to see Dell riding toward the bunkhouse. He wore an unzipped green down vest over his flannel shirt and his dark hat was tugged low on his forehead and gave him a sinister look. The horse was a massive black animal that looked like a replica of the black stallion in the books she used to read when she was nine. She watched as Dell, unsmiling, dismounted, tied his horse to the railing and pushed the door open to the porch.

"Ma'am," he said, tipping his hat.

"Hi." She smiled, glad to see he didn't look tired after taking care of the babies last night. His gaze dropped to the floor.

"They okay down there?"

"Right as rain," Calvin answered. "It's good for them to have a change of scenery and some fresh Wyoming air."

"How would you know that?" his nephew asked.

Cal jumped. "You don't have to yell. I've got the hearing aid on this mornin'."

"Sorry." He glanced at Allison and his expression lightened, which made her smile once again. He didn't look like an outlaw when he wore that almost-smiling look.

"It's a beautiful morning," she said.

He nodded.

Calvin leaned forward. "You should take Miss Allison for a ride." He turned to Allison. "You ride, don't you?"

"Not exactly. I mean, not since I was twelve."

The old man nodded and turned to Dell. "Good enough. I'll stay here with the girlies and we'll enjoy the sunshine."

She wasn't sure about interrupting Dell's work and searched for an excuse. "They're going to need to have bottles in about two hours."

"Yep. I'll get one of the boys to help me carry 'em back to the house."

"Cussy is in the main barn," Dell said. "I'll tell him to listen for you."

"I can ring the old dinner bell."

"Yeah. Good idea." He turned to Allison. "You up for a ride?"

"If it's not any trouble. And if you give me a horse about half the size of yours." She wasn't kidding, either. She didn't want to be sitting six feet off the ground if she fell off.

"Done."

Allison stood and looked down at her leather boots. They weren't cowboy boots, but they had a little bit of a heel. She wore jeans and a pale blue sweatshirt. "Will I be warm enough?"

"I'll get you a jacket," he said, disappearing into the bunkhouse for a minute. He returned with a thick brown barn jacket, which he handed to her. "It gets cold out there in the wind."

"Thank you." She shrugged it on and folded the sleeves back. She smiled down at the babies and told them to behave. They looked at her with identical curious expressions and both smiled at the same time. "I'll be back soon," she promised everyone.

"Take your time," the older man said, leaning back in the rocking chair. "We're just gonna sit out here and enjoy the sun."

Dell held the door open for her, and she walked out into the sunshine.

"Never known Cal to be so domestic," the cowboy muttered behind her. "Come on," he said, untying the big horse. "Let's go find you a mount."

"This is a lot of trouble, isn't it?"

He stopped and looked down at her, surprise lighting his dark eyes. "Why would it be any trouble?"

"But your work—"

"Can wait," he finished. "I should have realized you'd like to see some of the Lazy J while you're here."

"I've never been on a cattle ranch before," she admitted, falling into step beside him. She had to hurry to keep up with his long strides as they headed toward a big red barn. Several cowboys were grouped around the big double doors in the center of the building. When they saw them approach, they straightened and stared.

"You can meet some of the men," Dell said. "And we'll find you a horse." He led her over to four men who definitely looked as if they made their living outdoors. Dell introduced them as Cussy, Jed, Sam and Rob; the men tipped their hats and looked curiously at her.

"You get that car fixed, ma'am?" the tallest one asked.

"Not yet. I guess it's going to take a few days to find a part."

"You want to saddle up Gertrude for the lady?"

The balding man called Jed shook his head. "That old mare is half dead, boss. Like riding a tree stump."

"Do it," Dell said. "The lady wants a quiet mount." The cowboy shrugged and disappeared into the barn. Dell turned to the others. "Cussy, when you get through out here, listen for Cal. He's got the babies on the porch on Bunk Two. He might need a hand."

"Cal's got the girlies again?" The thick-set man grinned. "How'd you manage that?"

Dell shrugged. "He just seems to like 'em."

Cussy chuckled. "Damned right, he does. Why, he's—"

Another cowhand elbowed him in the ribs. "Watch your mouth, Cuss. You wouldn't want to say anything to offend the lady, would you?"

Cussy paled. "No, course not."

Dell ignored them, instead turning to Allison and surveying her outfit. "You look close enough to a cowgirl."

She brightened. "You think so?"

"Sure." The horse was brought out for her, and Allison eyed the animal with some relief. She was a medium shade of brown, with a black mane and tail, and Allison figured if horses could yawn, this sleepy-looking horse would certainly do so. "Climb on," Dell said, "and I'll fix the stirrups."

She remembered this part, left foot in the stirrup, then grab the saddle horn and swing the right leg over. At least, that was the way it was supposed to work. Luckily the brown mare was small, and Allison mounted on the second try. Dell held the mare's reins while his own horse waited patiently behind him. She grasped the reins and looked down at Dell. "Okay, so far, so good. Now what?"

"Just stay in the saddle and keep up." He adjusted the stirrups, checked the cinch, patted the little mare's neck and then mounted his own horse. "You know how to ride Western, don't you?"

"Yes. Right rein on the neck to go left, left rein to go right."

He nodded and swung his horse around. "Come on," he called, giving his horse a nudge with his heels. "It's time you saw the Lazy J."

"Why do you call it the Lazy J?" She noticed the remaining cowboys got out of her way fast enough.

Dell shrugged. "The brand is a leaning J in a box. I guess my grandfather thought that was as good a reason as any to name the place the Lazy J." He led her toward the bunkhouse. "We'd better check on the babies before we get going."

Allison followed him to the porch, where he dismounted, talked to Calvin, and returned to Allison, who didn't want to try to get down from the horse and get up on her again. "Is everything okay?"

"Yep. Sylvie's asleep and Sophie's not far behind. Cal's reading a magazine and acting like he's retired." Dell chuckled. "Lord only knows what we'll eat for dinner tonight."

"Stew. I watched him make it this morning." Allison urged her horse to keep up with Dell's, but the mare was clearly interested in walking slowly. Which was fine, too, Allison conceded, feeling safe and comfortable as they rode west toward the foothills of the Rocky Mountains. "Where are we going?"

"To check on the new calves. Thought you'd like to see some of 'em."

"I'd like that." She realized she'd like just about anything right now, whether it was looking at calves or breathing in fresh spring air or gazing at the distant dark mountains. She loved those babies, but for the moment it was wonderful to take a break from their care. Yesterday she'd worried about the car, buying supplies, getting back to the ranch before Calvin had problems with the children, but today she was outdoors. The babies were content; their baby-sitter wore a hearing aid. Sandy would have loved to have seen this, Allison thought. A familiar stab of pain lanced through her heart. Thinking of Sandy always hurt. She wondered if it always would, and hoped that somehow, as everyone promised, time would lessen the pain. Ryan had urged her to "get a grip on herself," while well-meaning friends gently questioned the wisdom of keeping the children to raise.

"Allison?"

She looked over at her host. "Yes?"

"I was just asking if you were doing all right with Gertrude."

She wondered if all cowboys were gentle giants like the one who had rescued her. "I'm fine."

Dell nodded, looking as if he believed her, and pointed to a mountain range off to the west. "The ranch runs halfway up those foothills," he told her. "We summer a herd of cattle up there."

"This must be a very large ranch."

"One of the biggest in the county."

"Calvin says you work too hard." She urged Gertrude to fall in beside Dell's black horse.

He gave her a curious look. "What else is there to do?" Then he cleared his throat. "I like the work. It's all I know."

Allison looked around as they rounded a hill. Cows and calves dotted the brown landscape under a pale blue sky, a view that took her breath away. She'd driven past a few places like this and seen them from the interstate, but riding horseback through this country was a much different experience. They rode together for more than an hour before Dell turned his horse in the direction of the ranch buildings. Allison, relaxed and comfortable on Gertrude, surveyed the cows and calves that dotted the pastures. "You're a lucky man," she told him.

He nodded slightly. "In some ways."

In many ways, Allison wanted to say. He knew who he was and where he belonged. There was a lot to be said for having a home. As soon as she reached Seattle, she was going to make sure that she and the girls had one of their own.

"I COULD DRIVE out there and get you," Mayme suggested, and Allison tilted the telephone receiver away from her ear a little. "I could bring you back here, where you belong, and you could forget all this nonsense."

"I appreciate that," Allison replied. "But everything is fine, really. I'm sure it won't take long to fix—"

"How long exactly? Do you know?"

"No. The mechanic is going to call when he knows where he can get a part."

"Let me bring you home," Mayme pleaded. "You and the babies have no business staying with strangers. I could be out there in a couple of days. I'll rent one of those horribly domestic minivans."

"That's quite an offer." Allison laughed. She stood at the kitchen counter and looked down at her dusty jeans and mud-covered boots. Mayme wouldn't recognize her; she'd always prided herself on wearing unusual, colorful clothes. People expected a decorator to be dressed in fashionable and "artsy" clothing. Now she needed a shower and clean clothes, and those clothes would be another pair of jeans and a sweatshirt that would soon have formula dribbled on the shoulders.

"I'd do it. For you." Mayme's tone turned pleading. "Please, Allison. Reconsider this whole idea. Ryan was never happy about your leaving the business, or leaving him, for that matter. I'm sure you two could work something out."

The smile faded from Allison's face. Dell passed her as he stepped into the kitchen and gave her a concerned look. "He made his feelings clear."

"People change."

"Not that much, they don't," Allison said, not wanting to prolong the conversation. Dell might need to use the phone, or the babies could be fussing and she wouldn't be able to hear them. "Look, I have to go."

"I called your friend in Seattle and told her you'd been delayed."

"Thanks. She wasn't too worried, was she?"

"We're *all* worried." Mayme sighed. "I hope your cowboy is taking good care of you and the girls."

"We're fine. Spoiled, even." She smiled across the room when Dell looked at her, and he looked surprised.

"Call me if you need me," her friend urged.

"I will. Bye." Allison hung up the phone and turned to Dell. "I called my friend back home again. She's worried about me."

He nodded. "I can understand that."

"You can?"

"Yeah. You don't get enough rest."

"That part's getting a little better. Thanks again for the help last night."

"It was nothing." But he didn't sound convincing.

"It was," she insisted. "Let's hope they sleep a little better tonight."

"Yeah," Dell said, smiling at little. "Let's hope we all do."

Allison smiled in return. "Thanks again for the ride this morning. The girls have been sleeping all afternoon. I might even have time to clean up before supper."

He looked at his watch. "Take your time. I just came in for a cup of coffee and then I'm heading back out until six or seven."

"I'll just go ahead and eat by myself then?" She tried hard to hide her disappointment. She'd enjoyed their meals together, and she had a lot of questions about the ranch now that she'd seen some of it.

"Uh, yeah. I mean, no." He turned away from her and poured coffee into a stained white mug. "I'll make sure to come in by, what, six-thirty?"

"Okay. I'm going to clean up and do some laundry."

"Get some rest instead," he said, taking a sip of coffee. "You look tired."

"I have two babies," she declared, feeling defensive. "How else should I look?"

He almost smiled again. "I mean no offense."

Allison sighed. "Sorry. Maybe you're right about resting."

"How much longer will they sleep?"

"Maybe an hour. More, if I'm lucky." She smiled. "I'm learning that mothers of babies have to choose between taking showers and taking naps."

Dell leaned against the counter and finished his coffee. "Me or Calvin will watch 'em later, while you clean up." He put his mug in the sink and moved toward the door. He had to pass her on his way out of the kitchen, so he paused and tipped his hat. "See you at supper," he said.

"Six-thirty," she agreed, watching him leave the room. She heard the door bang shut a few seconds later, so she went to the kitchen window and watched Dell cross the muddy expanse between the house and the barns. There were sheds for the calves and bunkhouses for the men, and corrals for the livestock. It looked like a small town, especially when she'd seen it from the back of Gertrude. This Wyoming ranch was like no place she'd ever seen before, and she felt oddly comfortable here in the old ranch house. She thought she would have minded the isolation, but there were people outside. And Dell had told her that two of the summer hands were married, and their wives and children would be returning to the ranch soon. That's what a man like Dell needed, a wife and children. She couldn't imagine why he wasn't married.

DELL WHISTLED as he double-checked the calves. It was amazing what a little bit of warmth could do for them. They perked right up after a few hours out of the wind. He was pleased with the day. Allison had managed to stay on the old mare—anyone would, though—and she'd seemed to have a pretty good time riding around the lower sections. They'd ridden for more than an hour and he'd enjoyed every damn minute, too, until he'd realized the babies would be needing her and turned the horses toward home. Maybe they could do that again. Calvin had surprised him and turned into a damn good baby-sitter. When they'd ridden toward Bunkhouse Two, he'd seen cowboys clustered near the door. No doubt they were teasing the hell out of Calvin. It wasn't often the men had a chance to heckle the grouchy cook and get away with it. Cal would most likely put extra pepper in the meat loaf or cook tomorrow's roast so it tasted like boot leather.

He talked to the men and organized tomorrow's chores. "I need someone to take a truck to Cheyenne in the morning," he told the men. "Anyone feel like making the trip?"

"Sure," Cussy said. "What am I getting?"

Dell avoided Calvin's curious state. "I'll give you a list tomorrow. I've, uh, ordered some supplies."

Calvin kept staring. "What kind of supplies?"

"Just some things I think we need. Now, tell me about—"

"What kinds of things? Women things?"

Dell glared at him. "Things that you don't have to worry about, all right? Just some, uh, decorations to spruce the place up."

"I could use a new lamp," Rob said.

"Yeah," Jed agreed, grinning at his boss. "And a couple of them recliner chairs."

"We could plant some pretty flowers," Cussy suggested, winking at the others. "Since we have a lady visiting and all. Any idea how long she's staying, Dell?"

"No," he snapped. "We done here? Everyone knows what they're doing tomorrow?"

"Yeah," Cussy said, grinning. The others nodded. Calving was just about over, so everyone was perfectly willing to start putting in a normal day's work. Then Dell made sure he was back in the house by six-fifteen, in the shower by six-eighteen, and dressed for dinner at six twenty-nine. He remembered to shave and comb the damp hair off his forehead. He was no beauty, but at least he was clean.

6

"I HATE TO admit that this might be hopeless," Allison said, looking up at Dell with the wide blue eyes. An Alan Jackson song blared in the background, and the babies were propped up on the couch where they could watch the dancing. For the moment they looked content, but Dell figured it was just a matter of time before they cried and he wouldn't have to dance anymore.

"I told you." He glanced over at them, just to make sure they didn't look upset, and then back down at his feet. He'd put on his dress boots for the dancing tonight, but fancy-dressed feet hadn't worked any better than the scruffy ones.

"Maybe it's the counting."

"Maybe," he agreed, looking down at her. She stood beside him, tiny and delicate in faded jeans and that white sweater that made her look like something from heaven. She'd pulled all that yellow hair into a knot at the nape of her neck, and her feet tapped in time to the music.

"One-two-three-four." Allison stepped in time to the music. "Step, step, side, heel. Now you do it."

Dell took a deep breath. He was determined to resist her, but it was pretty damn hard. He wanted to take her in his arms and waltz her around the room. If he could remember how to waltz, that is. He started to move.

"Say it out loud," Allison suggested. "With me."

"Step, step, side, heel." There. He'd done it. Would that please her? "You want to tell me why we're doing this?"

"So you can get out more and go dancing."

"You like to dance?"

"Sure. We—I used to go out once in a while. And they taught line dancing at my health club two nights a week. It was fun."

"I guess you'll go dancing in Seattle."

She chuckled. "I don't think so. I think those days are over." She smiled. "Sophie and Sylvie give me all the exercise I can handle. She looked down at his feet. "What about the two-step? Can you do that one?"

"I don't know." Two steps sounded better than learning combinations of eight or eighty kicks and slides. "I can try." There were a lot of things he could try, like making an excuse and going to bed early. He didn't have to torture himself by standing here breathing in the scent of Allison's hair. He was a grown man with a mind of his own; he could walk away.

Allison left his side to fiddle with the tape player. She walked back to him and stood in front of him. "Okay, here we go." She stepped closer and took his left hand, then put her tiny hand on his right shoulder. "It's one-two-*three*, one-two-*three*, fast-fast-*slow*, in time to the music. Don't worry about moving around too much. It'll come to you, if you listen to the beat."

He put his hand at her waist and wondered how he would be expected to listen to anything while he was holding her in his arms. He was paralyzed with fear and pleasure.

"Now, she said, trying to guide him. He didn't know how he managed to move, but he did. He'd danced at a couple of weddings, long ago, and the two-step was popular even then. He surprised himself by remembering when to move his feet.

"Wonderful," Allison murmured. "You're a natural."

He tripped. "Sorry. Guess you spoke too soon."

Her hand tightened in his. "No, you're doing fine." He managed to guide her around the part of the living room that didn't have furniture waiting to be bumped into. The babies stared at them as they passed the couch, and Allison called to them. "Hi, ladies! What do you think?"

Sylvie frowned, and Sophie's lips formed a little O. Dell stumbled, but recovered quickly. He tightened his hold on Allison's back and kept dancing until the song ended. He released her slowly. Too slowly, he figured, by the expression of surprise on her face.

"You all done?" Calvin called. They turned to see the older man standing in the doorway. He didn't look too happy. "I shoulda taken my hearing aid off before I came in here," he grumbled, rubbing his ear. "Ain't no saloon, you know."

Allison just smiled at him, turned off the tape player and turned to check on the girls. Sylvie sputtered, and Allison sat down on the couch and put the baby on her lap. "Hi, Cal. Would you like to join us?"

"Not me," the man replied, shaking his head. "I just came in to tell Dell something."

That figured, Dell thought. "What?"

"I'm going with Cuss in the mornin'." He took off his hat and sat down in the green recliner. "Thought I could use a trip to the big city."

"What city?" Allison adjusted her hold on the little girl, while her sister looked as if she couldn't decide if she wanted to be held, too. Dell walked over and picked up Sophie. He didn't want her to feel left out.

"Cheyenne," Cal supplied. "That music is gonna hurt the girlies' ears, if you ask me."

"It's not that loud." Dell shook his head. "Turn your hearing aid down."

Cal fiddled with his ear again. "I'm gonna get me another crock pot."

"Fine. Take the money out of the petty cash box."

"Already did." He eyed Allison. "You look like you got some rest. About time. Mothers have to take care of themselves."

"I did," she said, not looking too bothered by Cal's observations. "I mean, I am. Thanks to you."

"Me?"

"You took care of the babies again this morning so I could get on a horse."

"Wasn't nothin'," the older man muttered. "They were good as gold, the girlies were. I think they like our Wyoming air."

"I hope they sleep tonight," Allison said. "I'm trying to keep them awake this evening so they won't be awake half the night. I don't know what got into them last night."

"What d'ya mean?"

"They wanted to be held," she explained, shifting Sylvie's weight against her arm. "Look at her. She's happy now, but if I put her down she's probably going to cry."

"Oh." He studied the baby in Allison's arms, then turned to Dell. "Yours cry, too?"

"Not yet." Dell looked down at Sophie, whose blue-eyed gaze held his own. She was a sweet little thing, but both babies had minds of their own and weren't shy about letting everyone know what they wanted and when they wanted it. They were going to be a handful when they could talk. "When do babies start talking?"

"I'm not sure. I'll look it up in the baby book," Allison offered. "There's so much I don't know."

"You're doing fine," Dell assured her. He walked over to the couch and sat down at its far end. Sophie squawked, which meant she liked being held and walked better than being held on an old brown couch. He looked at his watch. It was after nine o'clock already. "You want help feeding them?"

"Well—"

Cal interrupted. "You done the payroll yet? The men expect their checks tomorrow, you know."

"I know." He'd started it early this morning, in the hour before the sun came up. "It's almost done."

"I'll feed them later. And I can do it by myself." Allison leaned back against the couch and studied the fieldstone fireplace. "I'll bet you have fires in the winter."

"Sometimes," Dell said, fighting the feeling of disappointment. He would have liked an excuse to be with Allison awhile longer. And he didn't mind feeding a baby or two, either. It was nice to have a little life in the house. He thought of tomorrow's delivery and hoped he'd done right. He'd tried to pick out the kinds of things a woman would like, the kinds of things that would make the old place look like someone cared.

Cal gave him a questioning look and Dell ignored him. He would do the payroll later, when he damn well felt like it.

"There's a pineapple cake," his uncle said. "I guess I'm gonna cut myself a piece. Anyone else?" He hauled himself out of the recliner as Allison stood up, too, the baby still in her arms.

"I'll help," she offered.

He shrugged, and Dell could have kicked some sense into him. Just because the old cowboy was terrified of women, didn't mean that he had to be so damn obvious about it. "I will, too," Dell said, rising from the sofa with the baby in his arms. So the five of them ended up in the kitchen, and three of them ended up eating cake piled high with vanilla ice cream. It was the babies' cue to fuss, so Cal took Sophie so Allison could heat up the bottles. She took the babies, one at a time, into the bedroom to change their diapers, and then returned to the kitchen to feed them. Dell silently took Sophie and her bottle, while Cal looked on. If Dell didn't know better, he'd think his uncle was annoyed that he didn't have a baby to feed.

"I'm goin' to bed," the old man said, standing and putting his dirty dish in the sink. "'Morning' comes early, and Cuss wants to be on the road in good time. You want to give us a list or something, so we know what we're getting?"

No, he sure as hell didn't. "JCPenney has the order ready and waiting for you."

"Humph." Calvin shoved his hat onto his head and nodded to Allison. "'Night, ma'am,"

"Good night, Calvin. Thanks again for watching the girls this morning."

"No problem."

He and Allison sat in silence for a few moments. The only noise was the suckling babies, until Allison stopped Sylvie at the halfway mark and lifted her to her shoulder to burp.

It was a strangely intimate situation, sitting at the kitchen table with Allison. Sophie spit out her bottle and Dell imitated Allison's motion of putting the baby against his shoulder and patting her back with the gentlest of motions. The child burped delicately near Dell's ear, so he put her back in the cradle of his arms and tried to interest her in the rest of her bottle, but she pursed her little lips together and closed her eyes.

"I think she's done," he whispered as Allison continued to feed Sylvie. "And I think she's asleep."

"Okay," Allison said, keeping her voice low. "Can you wait a minute while I finish with Sylvie? Then I'll put them down and maybe they'll sleep for four or five hours tonight. I think we might have tired them out."

"Yeah." He looked down at the sleeping baby. "She looks like she won't wake up for a long while."

"I hope you're right." She chuckled, and Dell looked across the table into those beautiful blue eyes. "She can fool you."

"No," he said slowly. "I don't think so." He wasn't fooled at all. He knew animals, and he knew men. He didn't know women, but he'd bet his last section of prime grazing land that Allison was the woman who was meant for him. Up until now, he hadn't thought there was anyone out there for him, or if there was, he wasn't going to meet her in Wells City. He'd wondered how it would happen, and he'd just about given up on it, too.

And here she was, sitting in his kitchen as if she'd always been here.

It damn well took his breath away.

Allison set the bottle on the table, burped the baby, and stood. "I'll be right back," she whispered.

"Is she asleep?"

"Just about. I'm going to try to put her down and see what happens."

He nodded and glanced down at the baby in his arms. Not much bigger than a football, but a thousand times prettier, of course. He carefully stood and the baby didn't wake at the movement, so he walked quietly down the hall toward the bedroom and peeked inside. Allison was bent over the babies' bed, tucking a blanket around the sleeping child. She straightened as Dell walked in and waited for him to bring the baby around to the side of the playpen.

"Should I do it?" he asked.

"Sure. If you don't mind."

He shook his head. "No." He bent over and lay the child near her sister, then moved to the side while Allison fussed with the blankets. She touched his arm when she was finished.

"Thank you for helping," she said. "It's been really hard these past months by myself."

"No problem," he managed to say. She was looking up at him as if he'd given her bags of diamonds. "Glad to help."

She continued to look up at him with those blue eyes. "You would have liked my sister. She would have been a good mother, if she'd gotten the chance."

"You're doing okay," he assured her. And then, he didn't know why, Allison raised on her tiptoes and kissed him on the cheek.

"Thank you," she said. "You're a good man, Wendell Jones."

His face burned where her lips had touched him and before she moved away. Dell tilted his head and met her lips with his own. He didn't know why. It just seemed natural to kiss that warm-skinned woman in the dim light of a room that smelled of baby powder.

She tasted of sugar and ice cream, and her lips were soft and surprisingly responsive under his. He wanted to stand there and kiss her for hours, but instead Dell lifted his mouth from hers after only a few brief seconds. He looked down at her, tried to form the words to apologize, and failed. She didn't say anything, either, so he spun on his heel and left the room as fast as he could without running.

Later, in the privacy of his bedroom, he stared out the window toward the main road. There was nothing to see, of course. There never was. But his own reflection shone back and Dell knew he was looking at the biggest fool who ever called Wyoming home.

OKAY, SHE SHOULDN'T have kissed him. She'd always been told she was too warmhearted, too impulsive, too much of a risk-taker. But she'd sincerely meant to thank him. She'd been overcome with such gratitude for his quiet strength, for his kindness to her and the children. So she'd reached up and kissed his cheek. And then that's when it happened. His dark eyes had widened just the smallest bit, and he'd turned his head just an inch or so, and he'd kissed her. On the lips. Briefly.

Allison closed her eyes again and pulled the covers up to her chin. She'd gone to bed right after the babies, right after Dell had left her. She hadn't bothered to try to read, though the small light from the reading lamp didn't bother the girls. She was only thirty pages or so into that serial killer mystery and it was already scaring her.

And now other things were scaring her, like being attracted to the big rancher. And feeling something when his lips had touched hers. She didn't want to feel anything for anyone. Except the children. Her parents had died; they'd had no business being in that sailboat race on Lake Michigan, but they'd gone anyway. Despite Dad's bad heart and the fact that Mother couldn't swim. And then it had just been Sandy and Allison, for the past three years. Until Sandy was hit by a drunk driver. They'd kept her alive long enough to deliver the babies, and then she was gone.

Allison wiped the tears that dripped silently down her face and turned onto her side, away from the sleeping children. Tomorrow she would find out about her car, she would pin down that enigmatic mechanic and make him tell her when her car would be fixed, and then she would make plans to leave the Lazy J.

It would be for the best.

"WHERE THE HELL do you want all this stuff?"

"Here's fine," Dell answered, and then the rest of his words were muffled by the cursing of another man and the sound of a door banging shut.

Allison, a baby in each arm, couldn't help wondering what was going on in the living room. She came out of the kitchen and peered into the room just as Calvin set down a big cardboard box. Allison watched from the safety of the kitchen as the three men brought in packages and boxes, set them down in the middle of the room and then looked at Dell for an explanation.

"What the hell is this?" Cal handed his nephew a piece of paper as Cussy hurried out the front door. "Here's your receipt. Just a lot of numbers on it, though. Didn't say what anything was."

Dell glanced at the list and tossed it on the couch. "I'm fixing up the house." He waved his arms toward the bare walls. "Thought it was about time."

"Humph," was all Calvin replied. "What for?"

"It looks pretty damn bad, that's why." Dell's gaze met Allison's and he flushed and looked away.

"Well, it's your house," Cal sighed, scratching the back of his neck. "You can do what you want, but I kinda liked this room the way it was. 'Course when your ma was alive I guess it looked better."

"Hard to remember," Dell muttered. "Dad packed up most of the stuff."

"I hope your not making a big mistsake, son." He turned and saw Allison in the doorway, but he didn't smile. He stared at her and the babies in her arms, and then he sighed. "You need some help with the girlies?"

"No, I've got—"

But he took Sylvie out of her arms and held her as if he'd been holding babies all his life. Dell didn't move, but he nodded briefly to acknowledge her presence at the edge of the room.

Allison stood there, feeling awkward. They'd avoided each other all day, or at least that is what Allison figured they were doing. Successfully, too. The house had been empty and quiet when she fed the babies their late morning bottle. They'd woken at four, taken their bottles, and gone back to sleep until nine. So had Allison. The only evidence that Dell had been in the house was the coffee mug in the sink.

"Aren't you gonna start opening these?"

Dell tore his gaze away from Allison. "Yeah, sure. In a while."

"Why not now?" his uncle asked, moving closer to the largest box. "You're making me and the girlie here pretty damn curious."

"Well," Dell drawled, tapping the top of the box with long fingers, "I guess I could do that now."

Allison stepped closer to see. It looked like Christmas in the living room and she couldn't imagine what kinds of things a Wyoming rancher would order in Cheyenne. A new television, perhaps? Or some saddles or blankets? Maybe the boxes were packed with blue jeans and work shirts for all of the men for the summer. Dell pulled a jack-knife from his pocket and began to open the top of the largest box. He slit open one side, then managed to pull out a wide rocking chair.

"That'll come in handy," Calvin drawled. "If you're planning on havin' babies."

"We have babies now," Dell muttered.

Allison peered over the cardboard flaps. The sturdy rocker was a light oak and quite pretty. Flowered blue cushions lined the back and seat. "I hope you didn't buy it just for the girls."

"You needed one," was all the cowboy said. "A big one."

She thought it was time to point out that she and the girls would be leaving soon. She hadn't figured out how to accomplish this yet, especially not after calling the Wells City mechanic this morning. The man had not been very optimistic about receiving a replacement axle anytime soon.

"I talked to the mechanic today," she began.

Dell looked up. "And?"

"He made it sound like the search for the Holy Grail."

"I'm sure he'll find something eventually," Dell said, turning to another box. He started slicing open the top flaps.

"So I've been thinking," she said, watching him remove a pale pink—*pink?*—chest of drawers from the box. "I think I'll rent a car and keep going."

"What about the Probe?" He set the chest against the bare wall by the door, then began opening another box.

"I'll sell it."

"This is a ranch country, Allison. People around here aren't in the market for a car like that." This time the cardboard opening revealed a fancy gold-painted mirror. "What do you think?" He held it up.

Allison saw a tired-looking woman with limp hair and a sleeping baby in her arms. "It's very nice. Where are you going to put it?"

"Your room," he said. "I think that part of the house needs sprucing up, don't you?"

"Well—"

"You're a decorator, right? Wouldn't you say the place needs some spark?"

She gulped. The rocker was acceptable, but the pink dresser and the gold-edged mirror were two things that looked more out of place at the ranch than she did. "I think your house is very nice."

"It's bare," Dell declared. Calvin, looking like he was enjoying himself, sat down on the couch and cradled the baby in his arms.

Allison searched for something to say, something that would make him realize that pink and gold were not right for the ranch. The room was a large one, but the walls needed a fresh coat of soft ivory paint, the stone hearth needed scrubbing and if the couch was moved and that coffee table tossed out... "What about a nice new rug?"

"I thought of that. Got a braided one, like my mother used to have in this room."

"Good."

"Hard to decide between that and an Oriental one, though. I could use some help, I guess," he said. "If you weren't determined to leave, you could—well, never mind."

"I could help you...arrange things," she said, approaching the rocking chair.

"Try it, see if it works," he said.

She did, and it did. "After all, that's what I do—what I used to do—for a living."

"Did you like that kind of job?"

"Sure. Although it's less glamorous than it sounds." She didn't say that her boyfriend had been her partner, or that she'd spent endless hours working on the business only to have to walk away from it. The funny thing was, she hadn't missed working. Maybe, she thought wryly, looking down at the baby in her arms, she hadn't had time to miss much of anything. At least the babies kept her from having the time and energy to think. "Do you have chairs for the dining room table?"

"Yeah. Out in the shed."

"What do they look like?"

"Well..." he looked confused. "Like the table, I guess. Kind of dark and plain."

"Your couch is in good shape, and so are the recliners. A few pillows would brighten things up, and maybe some bookcases, too. In oak, to match the rest of the furniture."

"You want to look at the catalog?"

"Sure." He bent down to his stack of magazines and pulled out a thick JCPenney catalogue.

"Just put it on the couch for now. I'll go through it later. I guess Wells City doesn't have any furniture stores."

"No, ma'am."

"Do you, um, have a budget for this project?"

Cal chuckled. "He don't like to spend money, Allison."

Dell, a fierce expression on his face, glared at his uncle in a way that made Allison want to laugh. If she didn't know him, she might be afraid, but she knew that underneath that giant body beat a giant heart.

"It looks like he spent some today," she said, looking around the room. "What's in the other boxes?"

"Lamps. Some wicker chairs for the porch. I thought we'd fix up the front porch while we're at it. Anything you don't like, I mean, that you don't think is right, can go back."

"All right." That was a relief. She smiled at him and stood. "Let me put the girls down for their nap, and then we'll talk about finding those dining room chairs."

"We never use the table," Cal muttered.

"But it would look nice," she noted. "And the room is

large enough to hold much more than it does. It might make it look homier."

"Homey," Dell repeated, looking almost happy. "That's exactly what I had in mind."

"Good," said Allison, pleased that she could finally do something to repay his hospitality. "I'll get some paper and start making a list while you find the dining room chairs. And do you have a tape measure?"

"I'll find one," Dell promised, and Allison couldn't help but smile at him. The kiss last night had been a silly mistake, an accident in the darkness, and she knew it would never happen again.

"HOMEY," Cal muttered, crossing the muddy yard. He said the word as if it was an evil adjective out to destroy the ranch. He spit in the dirt and kept moving toward the bunkhouse. "Homey, my ass."

"What are you mutterin' about?" Rob called from the porch. "Your face is gonna set in stone like that and you'll scare the girlies."

"Damn fool nephew of mine bought himself some new furniture."

The cowboy's expression brightened. "That means we get the old stuff?"

Calvin shrugged, and pushed the door open. He sat down in the empty chair, stretched his legs out in front of him and adjusted his hearing aid. It had been a long drive to town, but he and Cussy had eaten their fill of chicken-fried steak at that big diner outside of Cheyenne. That, and the mashed potatoes, had been worth the trip. "He's 'decoratin'." And Miss Allison is helping him."

"Well, that's nice. They'd make a right nice couple."

The older man snorted. "She's a beauty, all right, and he's well, he's a good man—"

"Finer man never lived," Rob agreed solemnly.

"But he's not much for looks, and he doesn't know nothing about women and he's going to get his heart broken."

Rob frowned. "I heard in town that she was, well, his girlfriend."

"She ain't. And that's the problem."

"She leavin?"

"Yep. When that silly car of hers gets fixed."

"The boss is sure nicer these days."

"You wait," Cal said ominously. "When she leaves, there'll be hell to pay around here. He'll be like a grizzly with a bullet in his thigh, and there won't be no pleasin' him. She's gonna decorate his house and break his heart and there's not a damn thing anyone can do about it."

"You could," the younger man said. "He listens to you about lots of things."

"Not about women," he muttered. "Not about *this* woman he's not listening."

"Maybe she'll stay. Become the missus. Then the boss would be in a good mood all the time."

Cal shook his head. "Nope. I got a bad feelin'." The other cowboy was silent. Cal's bad feelings were legendary, and to be respected. "I gotta do some thinkin'," the old man declared. "Before all hell breaks loose."

7

"IS THIS WHERE you want it?" Dell tried to hide his smile of satisfaction. This was working out better than he thought. Allison had been busy with the living room for two days. Thankfully she'd been too busy to mind that her car was still in Wells City, too busy to blush when she caught him looking at her and he knew she was remembering that brief kiss just the way he was.

"Over here. I think," Allison ordered, pointing to an empty place in front of her. Dell and Rob picked up the couch and moved it to where she directed, then watched her frown. Her gaze darted around the room as if she was redoing the whole floor plan in her head. Every now and then she'd study the paper she held in her hand.

She pointed to the recliners. "Would you put one to the left and one to the right of the fireplace?" She sighed. "This is a big room, but those recliners are giving me fits. I should put one in the corner with a reading light and a bookcase."

He didn't offer to take them out of the room. No way was he going through football season without his reclining chair, and Cal would feel the same way. And the chairs were only a few years old, so they had some living left to do, that was for sure. Not even for Allison would he give up his chair. She'd moved the stacks of books and magazines out to the porch and, over his protests, she'd scrubbed the wooden floor until it gleamed, and taken the old curtains down from the windows. The place looked better already.

"I don't know," she muttered. She bent over and patted the brown cushions into place, which gave him a heart-stopping view of that cute little bottom of hers. Those faded jeans fit her real well, and Dell considered moving his recliner out to the bunkhouse. There was good reception out there as well.

"I could—"

"No," she said, shaking her head. "We're not moving it again. This is the only spot that takes advantage of the fireplace." The younger cowhand rolled his eyes in relief, but Allison didn't notice. She turned to Dell. "You said you have a fire in the winter, right?"

"Yep." He would build one tonight, just to prove it. He would show her that the room could be warm and comfortable, especially if the lights were off.

"All right, then." She waved toward the rocker and the men backed away from the couch.

"You can go," Dell told the young man. "There's nothing else I can't handle." Besides, he'd seen Rob blush whenever Allison had smiled at him. There was no sense torturing the kid any longer. "Tell Cussy to come get me if he needs me for anything."

"Sure, boss." The cowboy grabbed his hat. "Goodbye, ma'am. You just holler if you need me."

"Thank you." Allison flashed another one of those angelic smiles and the cowboy flushed pink to the tips of his ears before he realized he was supposed to be leaving, not standing beside his boss and grinning like the village idiot.

"I appreciate your doing this," Dell said once again.

"It's the least I can do to earn my keep around here," she answered, giving him another one of those quick smiles before turning back to the chart in her hand. "I wish I had time to paint the walls."

"I can paint."

"Really?"

"Of course. I'm willing to do whatever it takes."

"Why?"

"What?"

"Why are you going to all this trouble now?" she asked. "Usually people redecorate for a reason, like a party or expecting company or for someone new in the—" she stopped and stared up at him. "Are you expecting a lifestyle change?"

"A what?"

"I knew you were just teasing when you said you didn't date."

He didn't know what in hell she was talking about. "I don't."

"Then why are you fixing the place up?"

Dell felt like a cornered bear. He drew himself up to his full height and frowned at the tiny woman in front of him. He'd be damned if he was ready to explain that he hoped she and the babies would stay. He wasn't even sure he was ready to admit it to himself more than once a day, but he was going ahead with the decorating bullshit just in case. The old house needed a good sprucing up, whether he slept alone or not. "Seemed like a good idea," was all he could manage through gritted teeth.

Those blue eyes didn't waver. "Hmm," was all she said, then turned back to her chart. "You wanted the front porch fixed up, too?"

"If it's not too much trouble."

"No, I think that's a great idea. Paint will do wonders for both rooms."

"I'll send one of the men to town. What color do you want?"

She turned to him again. "You have to pick out the color."

He shrugged. "White's fine."

"No, there are too many different kinds. You have to pick."

"No," he countered, putting his hands on his hips. "You're the decorator. *You* have to pick." That made her eyes twinkle and, as a result, he felt his heart beat faster. It seemed to do that a lot lately.

"Okay. Can I borrow a truck?"

"I'll take you myself."

"Are you worried that I'll end up in another ditch?" she teased.

"That's possible. You don't know the roads." He backed up a couple of steps. "You want to go now? I'll see if Cal will watch the girls."

Allison hesitated, but she was clearly interested in buying paint. "You don't think he'd mind? They just went to sleep ten minutes ago, so they should be napping for at least a couple of hours. It won't take me long to pick out paint."

"Hell, Cal won't mind. He's pleased that I'm finally getting around to fixing up this place," Dell lied. "He'll be glad to help."

"He didn't look too happy last night, when we moved his chair."

"I think he likes the rocker better anyway," Dell said.

"We can stop at the station and check on the car," Allison said, picking up a pen. "And I'd better buy some more formula. I'll make a list."

Dell looked around the room and wondered if he would get use to the changes. Was he being foolish hoping he could entice her to stay here on the ranch? Or was he smart enough to know not to let Allison walk out of his life without a fight? Only time would tell, and his time was running out.

"NOVEMBER," Allison announced, tapping the card with the selection of ivory shades striping its surface. "I think that's the best one. Don't you?" She didn't want to push her choice on him, of course, because she didn't believe in bullying clients to accept her taste. On the other hand, she worked hard to ensure the finished projects would be special.

Dell didn't so much as glance at the card. "Sure," he drawled, his gaze dropping to the bin of paintbrushes by his knees. "Get whatever you want."

"I want you to be happy with it," she said, holding up the card in the vicinity of his chin. "You're the one who has to live with it."

"Allison." He gently pushed the card aside and looked down at her with the patient expression she'd seen him use with the younger cowhands. "You're the decorator. I'm the rancher."

"Well..." She hesitated. *Snowflake* would be a good color, too. And she wanted it to be perfect for Dell; she wanted to leave him with a comfortable and pleasant living room that would make him feel good at the end of every long day. She studied the card once again, tilting it to get the best light. "We'll go with *November* then."

Dell waved over the clerk. "Joe? We need ten gallons of something called November."

"Indoor satin latex," Allison added. The man nodded, took the card from Allison and disappeared into the back room. Within ten minutes the paint, mixed and shaken, was stored in the back of Dell's truck, the bag with the brushes, rollers and pads tucked between the cans of paint and a case of baby formula.

"Could we stop and check on my car?"

He hesitated, or at least she thought he did. "Sure," he said, guiding the truck through town. He pulled up across the street and offered to go inside and talk to Pete himself. "If you don't mind?" he added.

Allison was only too glad to let a man handle it. She rolled down the window and took a deep breath of fresh spring air. She still needed to wear a jacket, and her long flannel nightgown felt cozy at night, but there was no doubt that spring was coming, and coming soon. Even to Wyoming. She watched the people going in and out of the diner and wondered who they were, if they lived in town or were ranchers who had come to town to do their errands. They looked as if they were glad that winter was over, too.

Dell came out of the gas station and strode across the street toward her side of the truck. "Come on," he said, opening her door. "I'll buy you a malt. When she hesitated, he added, "Cal and the girlies will be fine."

She stepped out of the truck and the wind whipped her hair around her face. "I saw a used furniture store on the side street by the post office. I thought we could stop and look around before we went home."

"I've got a shed full of that stuff," he muttered, ushering her into the warmth of the diner. "My father never threw anything away, and I guess I'm just like him."

"What did the mechanic say about my car?"

He didn't look at her. "It's going to be a while. No one has the part, and it's looking like it will be faster to take out your axle and rebuild it. If you don't mind."

She hurried to keep up with him. "Did he say how much it would cost?"

"Between four hundred and six hundred dollars." He gave her a sympathetic glance as he opened the door to the diner. "You're to call him when you decide."

Allison's heart sank. That was a lot of money, but she really had no choice. She couldn't stay in Wyoming forever.

"Hey, Dell!"

"Hey, Lucille," Dell said, touching the small of Allison's back and directing her toward a booth by the window. Allison gave the redheaded waitress her best smile and watched as the woman pretended not to notice her again. The waitress followed them, tossed two plastic-coated menus on the table and smiled at Dell once again. She even went so far as to lay her hand on Dell's wide shoulder.

"I see you still have company," she said, nodding to Allison.

"Yep," she said. "I'm still here."

"How long are you going to stay? Dell hasn't scared you out of town yet?"

Allison looked at Dell and touched his arm. "I don't know. Dell, how long am I staying?"

Dell cleared his throat and ignored the question. "I think we're going to have malts. Chocolate or vanilla, Allison?"

"Vanilla, please."

"Chocolate for me, Lucille." Dell handed her the menus and she took her hand from his shoulder.

"That's all? No fries?"

"No. Cal's making enchiladas tonight. I don't want to spoil my appetite."

"A big lug like you shouldn't worry about appetites." Lucille tucked her order pad into the pocket of her pink apron. "Tell the old buzzard that we put him down to bake rolls for the May Day fund-raiser. He'll want to buy raffle tickets, too."

"I'll tell him."

She returned to the counter and gave the order to another woman behind the counter.

"That woman brings out the worst in me," Allison muttered.

"I noticed."

"I don't like the way she looks at you." Dell raised his bushy eyebrows. "Like she's making fun."

"It's just her way, Allison."

"She can keep 'her way' to herself," she muttered, feeling a little ridiculous about the stab of jealousy she'd felt when Lucille touched Dell. There was no reason to feel that way. It wasn't as if she was involved with the big rancher. He most likely had a girlfriend here in the county somewhere, no matter what he said to the contrary. "Please tell me she isn't your girlfriend."

He looked at her and then burst out laughing. "That's the truth."

'Well, then, who is?"

"Who is what?"

"You're fixing up your house, Dell. There must be an ulterior motive."

Guilt flashed across his face for just a second, then he frowned at her. It was a fierce expression, but she knew better than to believe he was really angry. "Don't look at me like that," she said.

"Like what?"

"Like you're going to act like an old dog and start growling at me. I simply asked you a question."

Lucille plopped two empty glasses, two large metal containers and two straws in front of them. "Enjoy," she said. "Now that you're a man-about-town, Dell, you should give me a call sometime, when you're free."

"Thanks," he said, ignoring the invitation. Or maybe, Allison thought, noticing the way he concentrated on pouring the malts into the glasses, he didn't understand that the waitress was inviting him to do more than call her on the telephone. Unless she was teasing again, in which case Allison figured the woman had a mean streak longer than her fingernails.

"Does she give you a hard time every time you come in here?"

"No." He looked surprised. "Is that what she was doing?"

Allison stuck her straw in the drink and took a sip before she answered. She didn't understand why Lucille irritated her so much, except that she knew the waitress was not the right woman for Wendell Jones. "That's exactly what she was doing. And she was flirting with you, too. Do you really think she'd make a good ranch wife?"

"Lucille just teases, that's all. She's been calling me names and giving me a hard time since we were in fourth grade."

Allison didn't like it one bit. The kind rancher didn't deserve to be laughed at. "I don't think that's very nice."

He shrugged. "Honey, when you're as big and ugly as I am, you get used to it. The Joneses aren't known for their great beauty," he added, chuckling.

"You're not ugly." Allison looked into his handsome brown eyes and wondered how anyone could tease such a kind man. There wasn't a mean or vicious bone in his body. He was probably just *too* nice for his own good. "You're the strong, rugged cowboy type of man, that's all."

"You've been watching too many John Wayne movies."

"That's a perfect example. John Wayne. He was a big man, and not exactly the best-looking man in the world, either. But he was rough and tough and had a certain presence. People respected him." She took a sip of the malt and looked past Dell's shoulder toward the counter. Lucille and two older men were joking and laughing and looking in Dell's direction. She didn't know why it amused them all so much to see Dell sitting in the diner drinking a malt with a friend, but if they were so hard up for conversation, she intended to give them something to talk about.

Dell shook his head. "You sure get some strange notions. I'm no movie—"

"Kiss me," she said, leaning forward.

Dell stared at her. "What?"

She moved her glass out of the way and leaned farther across the table. "Kiss me. Right here. Right now."

"Hell, no."

"Please?" She glanced toward the counter again to see that they were still the topic of amusement, then moved Dell's glass out of the way.

"When I make love to a woman, I like to do it in private." He reached for his glass, but Allison stopped him by touching his forearm.

"Dammit, Dell. Just do it." She tugged him forward, and he leaned toward her, a questioning expression on his big square face. "Pretend you want me," she whispered.

She leaned forward as much as she dared, until Dell closed the gap between them, cupped one large hand behind the nape of her neck and touched his lips to hers. He tilted his head, slanting his mouth across hers in a heart-stopping motion. Allison felt that surprising jolt of passion again, wondered where on earth it came from, closed her eyes and stopped thinking. He tasted of chocolate and his lips, cool against hers, sent lovely shivers down the back of her neck. Allison forgot where they were for the long moments of the kiss, until Dell released her. He leaned back against the red vinyl seat, picked up his glass and took a long swallow of chocolate malt. All Allison could do was stare at him. She tingled right down to her toes and in other parts of her anatomy that she didn't want to think about now. She couldn't remember the last time she'd been so affected by a kiss.

The café was silent. So silent that Allison wondered if she'd gone deaf. She forgot to look at Lucille. Instead she watched Dell take a paper napkin from the holder bolted to the wall and wipe chocolate milk from his upper lip. He pulled out his wallet, selected a five dollar bill and tossed it on the table.

"We'd better get going. Are you ready?" he asked.

She nodded. Her hearing had returned, but would her legs hold her up once she'd slid out of the booth? Dell stood, waited for Allison to join him, then called his thanks to Lucille. The expression on his face was impassive, and his tone friendly and casual. Allison gazed at him, but he didn't look at her. How could he be so calm after such a kiss? Maybe kissing was different for men. Or different for men in Wyoming. Or different—

"Allison?" Dell held the door open for her and waited for her to go through it.

He followed her outside, walking to the truck and opening her door. Allison climbed in, watched as he shut the door and strolled around to the other side of the truck. He turned on the ignition, made a U-turn in the middle of the empty street, and headed back to the ranch. Allison waited for him to say something, anything, but he didn't. He fiddled with the radio until a country-western station came in clear enough to whistle to while she looked out the window at the brown, rolling hills. There were barbed-wire fences and the occasional cow, dirt roads heading off from the highway, and once Allison thought she saw an antelope. She thought of asking Dell if that's what it was, but thought better of it.

She didn't really feel like talking. She needed to think

over what had happened this afternoon. As if she didn't have enough to worry about, now she had to decide what to do with her puzzling physical attraction to a stranger. There was no denying the attraction, at least on her part. Those intimate parts of her body were reminding her that she had found that kiss very, very exciting. And unfulfilling. Her body clamored for more, and her heart knew better than to entertain the idea.

Dell turned onto the private road that led to the Lazy J. He slowed down after he'd rounded the first turn and stopped the truck before climbing the hill that led to the ranch house. After he switched off the ignition he turned to Allison.

"Come here," was all he said in that same expressionless voice.

Allison gulped. "Why?"

"Just do it," he said, mimicking her words in the diner.

She inched closer to him, until her hip hit the gearshift's black knob. He put his hands on her upper arms and lifted her onto his lap. Then he kissed her, but this time there was no hesitation in the motion. His lips were warm and demanding, and when he urged her lips apart Allison didn't think to protest the intimacy. His chest was like an iron wall against her breasts, and Dell held her arms so she couldn't move, couldn't wrap her arms around him the way she wanted to. He made love to her mouth for long, body-melting moments, until Allison whimpered with need and desire. He released her then, and lifted her back onto her seat.

Allison took a deep breath. "What was that for?" she asked, embarrassed to hear the way her voice shook.

"I told you," he replied, not sounding too calm himself. "When I make love to a woman, I like to do it in private."

"You're angry about the diner. I'm sorry."

He gave her a look she could only describe as furious, then turned away from her. He gripped the steering wheel until his big knuckles turned white. "I don't like being played for a fool," he told the windshield.

"That's not—"

"And I don't like games."

"I wasn't—"

"And don't ever put your arms around me again and tell me to pretend." He started up the truck and headed home. Allison sat in miserable silence. She would call Mayme to come get her. She would take the babies and go home. She didn't know what else to do, because falling in love with Wendell Jones was something that made absolutely no sense at all.

"THE LITTLE GAL is packing up," Calvin informed his nephew. "You got any idea what's going on?"

"She can't go anywhere," he muttered. He sat on a bale of hay in a corner of the barn and put his head in his hands.

"Is her car fixed? I didn't see it out in the front yard." He tired not to sound as hopeful as he felt.

"No, and it won't be for a while longer." He sighed. "I paid Pete to stall on the repairs to that car of hers. He couldn't find an axle, but he promised to take his time rebuilding hers." He would have to apologize. He knew that, and dreaded it.

Cal was silent as he digested that bit of information. He sat down on the bale of hay beside Dell. "Why is Allison in such an all-fired hurry to get out of here then? She's on the phone gettin' a bus schedule right now."

Dell didn't answer. He wasn't about to explain this afternoon to his uncle. He wasn't sure how he could explain it anyway.

"She can't get on a bus with those babies," Cal continued. "Ain't right. One of the boys could take her into Cheyenne, I guess. But that don't seem like the right thing, either."

No, Allison and the babies all alone again wasn't right at all. They needed a home. Allison didn't need a horny cowboy groping her in his pickup truck. "I should be shot."

"Well, son, I don't think it could be that bad," Cal drawled. "Women are tricky creatures. They get upset and then they get over it in a little while with a little sweet talk."

"No offense, Cal, but how did you get to be such an expert?"

"I've had some experience. When I was in the navy. And before that, too," Cal added, sounding injured. "Hell, son, I'm sixty-five years old and I've sweet-talked a few women in my younger days."

"I'm not much for sweet talking." He winced, thinking of how he'd grabbed her and put her on his lap. She could have bruised from the steering wheel.

"Well, that's true. I thought you were gonna practice with Allison."

He'd practiced a lot more than talking, Dell thought. He'd kissed her twice in less than twenty-four hours. He'd had to grip the steering wheel of the truck in order not to take her in his arms and do it again. "Well, that didn't work out in the way I thought it would."

"Humph."

Dell sat up and eyed his uncle. "I guess I'd better go apologize."

"You?"

"First time for everything," he stated, rising to his feet. "Guess I'd better get to it." He shoved his hands into his pockets and gazed toward the barn door, but he didn't move.

Calvin struggled to his feet and put his hand on the younger man's arm. "You ain't in love, are you, Dell?"

"In love? I don't know." He shrugged. "I think I'm out of my goddam mind." He adjusted his hat and squared his shoulders. "Guess I'd better get to it." He strode out of the barn and into the bright sunlight.

"Supper's gonna be ready in forty minutes," Cal hollered. "You can take it out of the oven yourself."

Dell lifted his hand to show he'd heard him, but he didn't turn around. He had forty minutes to talk Allison into staying. He had forty minutes to redeem himself for acting like a fool so she'd eat supper with him. He wasn't sorry he'd kissed her, though. He was just sorry about the way he'd done it. In anger and frustration.

He was sure going to hate eating alone again. How did you tell a woman that wanting her so much made a man do foolish things?

SHE WASN'T EVEN CLOSE to falling in love with Dell Jones, she reminded herself as she pulled the babies' clean clothes from the dryer and folded them. She wasn't close to falling in love with anyone. She stacked tiny pink sleepers next to the stack of blankets on top of the dryer until there was nothing left to fold.

Therefore, Allison decided, she was in no position to kiss anyone. She had no intention of falling in love again, ever. Except maybe after the girls were grown and life calmed down enough to contemplate marriage. Maybe by that time, in eighteen or twenty years, she'd feel confident enough to make a commitment, to make the right decision.

God knows, her track record making decisions wasn't going to win any awards. Moving to Kansas City, her partnership with Ryan, the resulting engagement and living together; all were examples of bad decisions. She'd hoped to clean the slate with the move to Seattle. Starting over, the three of them, leaving the baggage behind them in the rear-view mirror. She watched out the window as Dell crossed the yard between the barn and the house. His hat shaded his face, but she could tell he wasn't happy. He would be happy when she told him she was leaving. He would be glad to see the last of her, of that she was sure.

He came in the back door and took three steps into the storage room before he realized she was standing there.

He cleared his throat and removed his hat. "Cal said you're packing up to leave."

"Maybe that would be for the best."

Dell's steady gaze didn't waver as he looked down at her. "Maybe, maybe not."

Allison took a deep breath and let it out. "You're angry about this afternoon, and I don't blame you. It was terribly wrong of me to embarrass you in front of your...friends."

"I was angry," he admitted, twisting the brim of his hat. "I thought...well, never mind."

"I'm sorry." Truer words had never been spoken. She piled the babies' clothes in her arms and turned back to the rancher. "It will never happen again. I've called a bus company. If someone could give me a ride to Wells City in the morning, the girls and I can be on the eight-ten bus to Cheyenne."

"And then what?"

"We wait. From a motel. Where we can't bother anyone."

He frowned and looked fierce, but Allison was used to that expression. "You're not bothering anyone here."

"I can't stay here," she said. "We're in the way."

"I, uh, had another idea," he said, his voice low. He looked at her and frowned again. "I want to hire you. Officially."

"To do what?"

"Fix up the house. The porch, the bedroom—yours, I mean, not mine—and the men's bunkhouse. It's about time it got a fresh coat of paint."

"You don't have to *hire* me for that. I was happy to help."

"But you're leaving before the job is finished," he stated flatly, much to her embarrassment. "I'd kinda like to see what the living room would look like with a little paint and some new pillows." He jammed his hat back onto his head as if he were afraid he'd tear it to shreds otherwise. "You did say you would order pillows?"

"Yes. A nice plaid with green and br—"

"Allison."

She stopped and pressed her lips together.

"What happened today will never happen again. You have my word."

Oh, why did her heart fall to her knees with that promise? "It won't?"

"No."

"I'm not going to take your money," she said. 'I'm glad I can do something to help you."

"You'll stay."

It wasn't a question, but she nodded her assent. "I'll think about it." She gripped the clothes tighter against her chest and moved toward the kitchen. "I'd better go put these away. The girls are awake, but I don't think they'll be happy playing in their bed for much longer."

"Cal made out all right?" He followed her through the kitchen and down the hall toward the distant bedroom.

"Just fine. He has such a knack with them."

"Yeah, I've noticed."

Allison paused by the babies' bed and peeked at the girls, who looked up at her with big blue eyes. "Hello, sweethearts. Did you miss me?"

Sylvie smiled and Sophie blew a bubble from her lips. Dell leaned over the bed. "Can I pick them up?"

"Sure." She put the clothes on the bed and waited a few seconds before she turned back to the cowboy who'd promised he would never kiss her again. She turned and watched the careful way he lifted Sophie into his arms.

"Hey, there," he said, not looking fierce at all. "You want your supper, too?" Sophie gurgled her answer.

Allison didn't know why she should feel as if she'd lost something special.

8

"THE BOSS was hidin' in the barn this afternoon," Cussy announced to the other men at the table. "Hidin' like a goddam fugitive, sadder than hell. Never thought I'd live to see the day when a woman brought down a giant like Wendell Jones. In my day a man had better sense than to skulk around a barn feeling sorry for himself."

"How do you know?" Jed asked. "You want to hand that salt down here?"

Cussy slid the salt shaker down the length of the plastic-coated table. "Saw him myself. Ain't that right, Cal?"

Calvin sighed, helped himself to two more enchiladas and debated whether or not to talk to the men about this latest development in the Ranch Romance, as he was starting to think of it. When he could bear thinking about it, that was. He looked up from his meal to see all seven men looking at him and waiting for an answer. "He's in there apologizing to her."

The older men gasped, though the younger ones didn't seem concerned with that particular piece of information.

"No kidding," Cussy said, clearly shocked. "I never heard the boss apologize."

"Well, you ain't never seen him around a little yellow-haired woman, either."

"True," the man admitted. "Guess that would make a difference, all right."

"Women can do that," someone else insisted. "Make a man crazy, don't they?"

They ate in silence while Calvin pondered his nephew's future. He didn't think it looked too bright. Even if Allison forgave him—for what he couldn't even begin to imagine—that still left Dell in pretty bad shape. His poor nephew was in love, and that woman wasn't the one to make him happy either. She was trouble, all right, from the first time he'd seen her. Cal had known that nothin' good could come from her arrival on the Lazy J.

"Is Dell going to be all right?"

Calvin shrugged. "He's in love."

"No way," someone said, scraping back his chair. He went to the sink and refilled his water glass. "Dammit, Cal, that salsa's hot!"

"I didn't make you pour it all over your meal," Calvin pointed out, spearing another forkful.

"She's a nice little gal. Real friendly."

"And I like holding those girlies. What are you gonna do with all the money you're making, Cal?"

He shrugged. "Haven't decided," he lied. He figured he was entitled to his secrets. He adjusted his hearing aid as the clatter of dishes started to hurt his ear.

"I'll bet Dell marries her," a young cowboy said, sounding sad.

Cussy leaned forward. "How much?"

"Five dollars."

"That's all? Chicken feed."

"Hardly worth the effort to bet," someone else added.

"All right," the young man said, sticking out his chin. "Fifty." He dared the older man to take his bet. "I'll bet fifty bucks that Dell marries her. I know I would if I was in his boots."

"Humph," was all Calvin could say. He didn't hold

much with gambling, but that didn't mean he wasn't up for a little friendly bet once in a while. "You're on," he said.

"I'm in," Cussy added. "Fifty bucks says Dell stays a bachelor."

The other men divided up evenly, and Calvin consented to hold the money. "You men have a time limit on this?"

Cussy rolled his eyes heavenward, as if to ask the Lord's opinion. "By the first of June," he said. "A man ought to be able to hog-tie a woman within a month, right?"

There was no answer to that question, as none of the men in the room had successfully hog-tied any women, whether in a month or a year or a lifetime.

"We're a sorry bunch of bachelors ourselves," someone finally declared.

Calvin swallowed the last of his dinner. "Well, misery loves company, I always say."

"Dell looks happier now," the young man, the one whose idea it was to bet, observed. "At least, most of the time."

"You didn't see him this afternoon," Calvin replied. "A sadder sight never crossed the Lazy J."

"I thought you were gonna come up with a plan to make her leave."

"Yeah, well, I'm still thinkin' on it."

"You keep thinkin' any slower, and Dell will be marching down the aisle and I'll be out fifty dollars," Cussy grumped.

Calvin got up and poured himself a cup of coffee. Cussy was right. He had to come up with a plan, and soon. Before his nephew—poor bastard—decided that married life was the answer to his prayers.

"ADVICE?" Mayme shrieked into the phone. "You want advice after you've been living on a stranger's ranch for eight days?"

"Well, I thought—"

"No," her friend interrupted. "You're not thinking at all. I can tell."

Allison almost laughed into the telephone. It was so good to hear a woman's voice after living with all these cowboys for more than a week. "My car is still broken. They have to rebuild the axle. Or something like that. I thought of a bus—"

"You can't take those tiny babies on a bus."

"That's what Dell said, too." She sighed, thinking of Dell's stunned expression when she told him she was leaving. And then he'd apologized, which made her feel worse. Especially since he really didn't have anything to be sorry for. She should have told him that during dinner. They should have talked about more than the weather.

"Well, he's right."

"He's asked me to decorate the ranch house. I'd already started helping him and now he wants to make it official."

"Make *what* official?"

"The job. But I'm not accepting his money, of course. If I stay."

"*If* you stay? Does that mean you want me to come get you?"

Allison hesitated. Of course that would be the sensible thing to do, but she didn't want to leave the ranch. She had come to think of this unexpected detour in Wyoming as a welcome vacation. She'd gone from having no one to help her with the babies to having two men willing to watch them and hold them and feed them once in a while. Just knowing there was someone else to help, if she needed help, eased the stress of being one hundred percent responsible for those little lives. The thought of leaving made her feel a little queasy. "I really don't want to leave. Not yet."

"Allison, is there something you're not telling me?"

She thought of Dell's kisses. "No. I don't mind staying here, that's all. I don't want to return to Kansas City. And I wanted to ask you what you thought."

Mayme was silent for several seconds. "Then stay there, I guess. It's better than being on the road alone with those babies, I suppose. You sound more rested, and if the men are helping with the babies—"

"They are," Allison assured her.

'And you're getting some sleep?"

"Every chance I get."

"Well," Mayme sighed. "I guess that's a good enough reason to remain on the ranch. You're not, um, romantically involved with your cowboy, are you?"

Allison pretended to find that funny. "Of course not," she said, and told her friend that the babies were fussing and she had to go. She said goodbye, replaced the telephone receiver, and returned the phone to its table in the hall. Romantically involved? She walked over to the set of windows on the other side of the dining room table. Dell was out there in one of the barns, but she had no idea what his chores entailed. He might have just made an excuse to leave the kitchen and leave her.

She'd assured him she would have no problems cleaning up the kitchen. She'd bathed, fed and readied the babies for bed as darkness fell and the lights came on in various outbuildings. She'd sat in the rocking chair and hummed "Home on the Range" until their eyes had closed and their breathing had grown even. The house was quiet, except for the occasional humming of the old refrigerator. Allison turned around and surveyed the large room. Tomorrow, she promised herself, she would find out what kinds of things Dell's father had stored in the shed. She would carefully paint a wall or two, polish the furniture and drape the log cabin quilt she'd found in the linen closet over the back of the couch. Painting last was doing the whole thing backward, but she was learning that here on the ranch, you did what you had to do with a minimum of fuss. Whatever it took to get the job done was done, without complaint and without talking it to death, either.

She'd piled newspapers, magazines and books on the front porch and didn't intend to tackle that part of the house until the main room was finished. She'd returned the unread serial killer mystery to the pile of hardcover books, too. There wasn't enough time to sleep, much less read.

And she'd rather spend that precious spare time helping Dell with the house or being outside. Maybe he'd ask her to ride with him again. Gertrude had been very polite and easy to sit on. She'd walked at just the right speed, as if she sensed that Allison wasn't ready to gallop all over Wyoming.

There were a lot of things she wasn't ready for, Allison decided, giving the back of the couch a pat to smooth the cushion into place. She wasn't ready to love again, so she shouldn't be thinking of kissing Wendell Jones. She should keep her mind on paint colors and furniture polish and washing diapers.

Mooning over a cowboy was strictly forbidden from now on. She went into the kitchen, found a pad of paper and a pen in one of the drawers, and sat down at the table to write a note for Dell.

"You have a deal," she wrote, and sighed her name with a flourish.

"BLESS YOU," Dell said, after Allison's delicate sneeze. He carefully picked up a dust-coated chair and showed it to her. She stood closer than he would have liked, if he had his choice, but there wasn't much room in the crowded shed. And he held the only flashlight. He'd known, since he read her note last night, that she was going to stay awhile longer, and he'd slept well for the first time in many nights. "Is this the kind of thing you're looking for?"

She sniffed, sneezed again, and nodded. "That's one of the dining room chairs?"

"Yeah, I think so." He set it down and shone the beam of the flashlight across the pile of furniture to his right. "There are more of them here. How many do you want?"

"Six?" Her voice was hopeful, so he took a closer look.

"Looks like there are at least that many here." They were sturdy oak chairs that didn't look any the worse for wear, but he wondered if Allison realized just how much furniture polish it would take to make them look halfway decent.

"I think they'll be perfect. What's that over there, on your left?"

He swung light where she pointed and revealed some kind of cabinet. "I don't know what it is."

"Could it be a bookcase?"

"Maybe. Or a piece of junk. There's a lot of both stashed in here."

"Dell, you have no vision." She carefully climbed over a trunk to get closer to the piece of furniture.

He had a vision, all right, but it wasn't about arranging old pieces of oak in his living room. Allison's hair was piled on top of her head, revealing the back of her neck above the white T-shirt she'd borrowed from him. He wanted to touch his lips to that soft-looking strip of skin. He wondered if those wisps of golden hair would tickle his nose. She was so tiny that he could rest his chin on the top of her head while he pressed those womanly curves against his hard body. Dell watched her rub her fingers along the scrolled sides of the bookcase or whatever the hell it was, and longed for her to touch him. He would like to feel that touch once more.

But he'd given his word. And since she had stopped packing, he assumed she'd decided to stay. He would offer once again to pay her for her trouble.

"It looks like a Horta, I think. Or a good imitation of one."

"What's a Horta?"

"Victor Horta was a Belgian architect in the late eighteen hundreds. This is probably a very good copy of one of his trademark pieces, a buffet with cupboards at each end. See the scrolls on top? They'll be lovely once they're polished up a bit."

"It'll take four men to get it in the house," he commented. "Are you sure it will look good in the living room?"

She stood back and studied it. "I don't know why not. Those middle shelves give you a place for some books, and so do the glazed cupboards. You can hide your magazines in the cupboards underneath, see? It should hold a lot of your clutter, and be a real centerpiece for the room."

And must weigh hundreds of pounds. Why on earth had his father moved it out here in the first place? "Where?"

"Against the wall, to the left of the front door. We'll center it in the middle of that wall and it will be beautiful. The paint should be dry in another hour or two." She turned and smiled at him again, and Dell wondered if he would ever breathe again.

"How do you know all this?"

She grinned. "I took a class called European Furniture, 1860 to 1920."

"And got an A?"

"No, an A-plus." She shot him a quick grin and turned back to the piece of furniture.

"I should have known." He looked around the shop at the furniture piled to the ceiling. "Anything else you want out of here?"

"I could spend a week sorting through these things. Were they ever in your house?"

"They must have been. My grandmother was a wealthy widow from St. Louis when she met my grandfather. She must have brought this furniture with her, because she didn't want to leave her things behind. I think my mother had it all put away when she and Dad took over the ranch, after my grandparents died. She probably didn't want to have to worry about having anything fancy in the house. Calvin would know where it came from, if anyone would."

"It looks like it's in fine shape. I can't believe the glass isn't broken."

"Yet," Dell reminded her. "We've still got to get it back into the house."

"You won't let anything happen to it," she said. "You never do."

He pondered that statement while she investigated a worn footstool. "Has anyone in your family ever thrown anything away?"

"Not that I know of. Do you want the flashlight?"

"I'm trying to read the writing on this box." She blew at the dust but nothing happened, so she took the edge of her T-shirt and wiped the wood. Dell reached across an old table and handed her the flashlight.

"See if this helps," he said.

"'Marianna's Toys.'" She looked up at Dell. "Who is Marianna?"

"My grandmother." Dell tried to move closer, but didn't

dare. His big feet would break something if he tried to climb over the furniture to see what Allison was looking at.

"Do you think we could open it?"

"Yeah," he said, curious himself as to what was inside the box. "I'll get it out with the rest of the things."

"Isn't this fun? Like a treasure hunt."

Or a challenge to his self-control, Dell thought, noting the way her jeans hugged her bottom when she bent to investigate something else. He was being tortured in the old storehouse and enjoying every painful minute of it. "Yeah," he muttered. "Fun."

The smile left her face. "I'm keeping you from your work, aren't I? I'm sorry, I should have—"

"No," he said quickly. "I have the time."

"Sure?"

"Yeah." He held out his hand. "Here. Let me help you get out of there. I'll come back with some of the men after lunch and we'll get this stuff out of here. If you're sure this is what you want."

"It'll look wonderful in that room, Dell. Really." She beamed at him as she took his hand and balanced on a low table, stepped over a couple of buggy wheels and landed against his chest when she tripped on a broken spoke.

He caught her with both hands and held her again him. He told himself it was just to stop her from pitching head-first into a pile of old saddles, but he knew better. Her breasts were soft against his chest, the skin of her arms velvet under his hands. She smelled of lilacs and he could indeed touch his chin to the top of her head, but she looked up at him with those wide blue eyes.

"Sorry," he muttered, but he didn't release her. He was incapable of moving, as if his giant bulk had been frozen to the dirt-packed floor of the storehouse. If he lowered his head he could kiss her.

But he'd given his word.

"Dell?" she whispered, her voice sounding uncertain.

He didn't know if he should kiss her or toss her over his shoulder and take her to bed. Both actions would get him in trouble, but if she didn't move soon they were both going to be in a hell of a lot of hot water.

She didn't move. "I'm sorry about yesterday."

"Yesterday?" He blinked. What in hell had happened yesterday that she would be sorry for?

"Don't tease," she begged, looking up at him with that expression he never could figure out.

"Aw, hell," he muttered. He grasped her waist and lifted her up so that her lips were level with his. He kissed her for as many seconds as he dared, until the muscles in his arms started to burn with pain. Then he lowered her to the floor, but he kept his hands on her waist so she wouldn't run off before he said what he had to say.

"I broke my word, but dammit, sweetheart, you can't look at a man like that and not expect something to happen."

Allison looked a little dazed, but her arms crept around his waist and she lifted her face to his. "Stop talking and kiss me again."

He didn't need to be told twice. Her parted lips were sweet and inviting, and his tongue possessed her mouth with a longing and need that surprised even Dell. He kissed her thoroughly, until they both gasped for breath once he lifted his lips from hers, but he couldn't get enough. He held her tighter against him and took her mouth again while she held on to his belt as if to keep herself upright. The surrounding world, with its dusty furniture and rusted junk, faded away until Del wondered how long it would take to swing her into his arms and carry her to the house. Doing that would mean having to stop kissing her for a fraction of time, and he wasn't prepared to do that yet.

A shadow crossed the open doorway. "What in the gol-darn hell is going on in here?"

Dell broke off the kiss, but Allison's lithe body was still pressed against a part of him that enjoyed being pressed against. He held her waist and kept her there while he turned toward his uncle. "What is it, Cal?"

The old man looked disgusted, as if such goings-on in the storehouse were illegal or something. "I just came to tell you that the girlies are fussin' and prob'ly want their mama to come give 'em their lunch."

Allison pulled out of Dell's arms and didn't look at him. Instead she made her way through the clutter to the door, where Calvin stepped out of the way to let her pass. "Thanks for coming for me," she said.

"They're on the bunkhouse porch with Cussy," he said. "I haven't sniffed the house to see if that there paint smell has gone away."

"I'll take care of it," she assured him, and hurried off. Dell heard her footsteps in the dirt for a few seconds, then the only sound was Cal's huffing. Dell picked up one of the chairs and came toward the door.

"You gonna hit with me that cuz I spoiled your romantic morning?"

"I'd like to," Dell said, walking past his uncle and setting the chair outside. "But I've got five more of these to take to the house, plus some old cupboard and a box of toys. So I'm too busy to tell you to mind your own business, but if I had the time—" he shot Calvin a warning look "—I'd tell you to mind your own business."

"Humph." Calvin looked at the chair. "Haven't seen these in a long time."

Dell went into the shed and returned with another one, which he set in the dirt. "She likes them."

Dell gave Calvin a look that dared him to say anything before he went back into the shed. Calvin watched him silently, until six chairs and one old box sat outside of the shed.

"Now what?" his uncle said, peering into the dark building.

Dell pointed to the cupboard. "See that? It's going into the living room."

Cal whistled. "Must weigh a ton. You'd better call some of the boys."

"Before we can get it out of there, I've got to clear a path first," he said, rolling up his sleeves. "And I might as well toss out some of the junk while I'm at it."

"You're not going to get rid of anything *good*, are you?"

Dell sighed. Calvin thought every bent nail and old plank ought to be saved, "just in case." "Tell you what, I'll just pile the stuff over on the side and you can go through it and see if there's anything you think is worth saving."

Cal looked relieved, and Dell smiled to himself. Sorting through junk would keep the old man busy and out of his way for the rest of the day.

"You're through kissin' that little gal for a while, then?"

Dell flushed and returned to the shed, but Cal followed him through the door. "You got no business with that little lady," he warned. "She'll be leavin' as soon as that car is fixed up and you'll be standing around with a broken heart for the rest of the summer and we all will have to look at your sad face."

"I've got some time."

"Meaning?"

"Meaning that car won't be fixed as soon as everyone thinks." He shot his uncle a warning look as he moved some tires from around the cupboard. "And don't you go blabbing that around, either."

Cal shrugged. "A man's gotta do what he's gotta do, I suppose. And it's beatin' a dead horse to tell you to be careful, so I won't waste my breath." He peered into the gloom. "What the hell is that, your father's old anvil?"

"Yep."

"What's it doin' out here?"

"I don't know." He lifted it easily and moved it to another side of the shed. "There's enough stuff out here to outfit another house." He eyed the piece of furniture that Allison seemed so delighted with. It didn't look like much, but if it made her happy he'd haul it from here to California and back. Women were strange creatures, all right. Sometimes it didn't take much to make them happy; other times they needed the sun, moon and stars.

He turned to his uncle. "You gonna stand there gawking or are you gonna help?"

Calvin backed up. "You get hold of some of the younger boys, son. My days of bustin' a gut for a woman are over. And if I were you, I'd get on my horse and head to Texas while you still have a chance to escape."

"I don't want to escape." He wanted warm lips and a soft female body and he wanted the scent of lilacs to follow him around. She'd kissed him. She hadn't wanted him to keep his promise. She'd said she'd stay and fix up his living room. She'd had the room half-painted already, before he'd come inside at ten for that second pot of coffee.

He'd kissed her. She'd kissed him. They'd kissed each other. He didn't dare dream that there could be anything better than that.

PAINT FUMES. Dust. Lack of sleep. All of those things could cause her brain to clog so that she did something as foolish as kissing a cowboy in broad daylight, in an old shed, when she should have kept her mind on decorating. After all, that enormous Hortalike cupboard should have occupied her mind for at least ten or twelve hours. It wasn't often that a person entered a shed and came out with such an impressive piece of oak furniture.

Allison heated the bottles for the girls, who sat in their little car seats on the kitchen table and watched her with those now familiar expressions of curiosity and enjoyment. She would have sworn they knew exactly what she was doing and how long it should take before those bottles were in their mouths.

"Well, ladies," she said, putting her hands on her hips. "Your aunt Allison has gotten herself into another fix." The girls blinked, and Sylvie smiled. "Oh, go ahead and laugh," she told the baby, tickling her chin with one finger. "One of these days you're going to be all grown up and you'll think you know everything and then all of a sudden you'll be letting a cowboy pick you up and kiss you till you can't catch your breath and then things won't seem so hilarious."

Allison tickled Sophie, too, making the baby's lips turn upward. "You two better watch out for each other. That's what sisters do, you know."

"Is that what your sister did?" Dell asked, entering the room and taking off his hat.

"Well, she was five years older than me," Allison said, hurrying back to the sink to pull the bottles out of the hot water. She checked the temperature of the formula, glad to have something to do to keep from looking at Dell. "She was in college when I was in junior high. After our parents died, I moved to Kansas City to be with her." Allison didn't add that moving near Sandy was her idea, not her big sister's.

She took the bottles over to the babies.

"You need help?"

"No, thanks. She wished he'd leave. When Dell was around she was all too aware that she was attracted to him, which made life more confusing than she could handle. "I'm going to feed one at a time. Sometimes that works."

She lifted Sylvie from her chair and cradled her in her arms as she sat down at the kitchen table. Dell hesitated, then scooped up Sophie.

"No reason to make her wait," he said, taking the other bottle and putting it to the little girl's lips. He sniffed the air. "Paint smell is almost gone."

"I'll do the other half of the room this afternoon, while the girls are taking their nap. I'll keep the bedroom door shut so the smell doesn't bother them."

"It's a nice day." He walked over to the window and looked west. "You can open the windows."

You can kiss me again. Allison looked down at the baby in her arms and decided that she indeed had gone out of her mind. Round the bend and over the edge, definitely. She was now the mother of two. A month ago she had been engaged to marry someone else, and here she sat lusting over an oversize rancher who probably thought she was a candidate for Idiot of the Year. He walked into the living room and surveyed the east wall.

"Looks good," was all he said, but Allison was pleased with the compliment. She'd sketched out various arrangements for the furniture, and she liked the way the couch and chairs were arranged now. Of course, she'd pushed everything into the middle of the room so she could paint the walls.

"It will be finished in no time at all," she assured him. "And your life will be back to normal."

"I doubt it," he said, and she looked at him, but he turned his head away and said something to Sophie.

She doubted it, too. Allison turned back to the baby in her arms. After eight days on the Lazy J with Dell Jones, she didn't think any of them would ever be back to normal. She would miss him. They all would, of course.

Someday she'd tell them the story of how they moved to Seattle and ended up visiting a ranch in Wyoming, and how the cowboys took care of all three of them. She would send Christmas cards and pictures for a year or two. And someone would marry Dell, paint the walls a different color and get rid of the matching reclining chairs.

Allison sighed. It was too depressing to think about any longer.

9

THEY MANAGED TO AVOID each other. Of course, she didn't know if Dell was avoiding her, but it was a pretty good guess since he didn't come inside all afternoon. Allison played with the children, put them down for their naps, and picked up the paint roller. She was determined to finish painting the walls this afternoon, no matter how much the muscles in her arms would ache later on tonight.

Dell didn't come in for dinner either, though there was a pan of oven-fried chicken and foil-wrapped potatoes in the oven and a salad in the refrigerator. A loaf of Calvin's bread sat on a faded wooden board beside the sink, a serrated knife beside it. Allison served herself and ate alone. She glanced at the back door once in a while, but no one disturbed the quiet of the house.

Except the babies, who decided to be fussy and refused to go along with sitting in their seats and watching their aunt eat her dinner. They cried until tiny tears ran down their reddening cheeks, long after Allison gave up trying to eat with a baby on her lap, long after Allison gave up trying to eat dinner at all. She took turns walking each baby around the living room. She closed the windows against the night air, decided the paint fumes had dispersed, and sat down in the rocking chair with both babies in her arms.

They cried anyway. While Allison rocked the chair in what she prayed would be a consoling motion, the little girls complained. She sang every song she knew, including a couple of campfire songs from her Girl Scout days. She told them stories about Cinderella and Snow White, making up the names of the dwarfs that she couldn't recall. She changed their diapers, looking for diaper rash, but there was nothing to see that could be causing either child to fuss with such gusto. She fed them, she burped then, she rocked them for hours, long after the sky darkened and sunset glowed from the west window. And long after Dell should have come inside for the night. Allison didn't want to admit that she missed him, missed their supper together, missed the hour when he would describe his day and tell about the calves and their mamas, or tell something funny one of the men had done. He would smell of the outdoors, of leather and hay; even after he showered Allison would swear she could still smell that wonderful leather scent.

The girls drifted off into sleep, but Allison was afraid to move and disturb them. Such peace was hard won, and therefore not to be tampered with. Allison, bracing her arms against the rocking chair's wooden armrest, managed to close her eyes and drift off to sleep, too.

DELL DIDN'T SEE her right away. Not until he'd switched on the light in the kitchen and noticed that the food was still sitting on the counter. It wasn't like Allison to leave a mess. He hung his jacket and hat on a peg by the door, then walked through the kitchen and peered down the dark hall. No light shone under the bedroom door. In fact, there were no lights shining anywhere.

Had she left? He felt his empty stomach drop to his feet. Could Allison have been so upset with him that she took the children and left the ranch? She could have found the keys to any number of vehicles; they hung on a board over the washing machine. He turned right, into the living room, and heard the faint creak of the rocking chair on the wood floor. The furniture was bunched toward the center of the room, but off to one side was the rocker. Allison sat there in the darkness, her head resting on the back of the rocker, her arms full of babies. He didn't know how she slept without dropping the children, but as he came nearer he realized they were all asleep.

He wished they were his. He stood there for long moments and watched them. The little girls' faces were blotchy, as if they'd been crying. Allison's hair was loose and waved to her shoulders. She wore a pale yellow long-sleeve shirt and jeans, and her feet were bare. He wondered if she'd missed him at supper, or if she'd been happy to eat without him. Dell tiptoed backward out of the room, grabbed a piece of chicken from the pan, tossed the rest in the refrigerator, and went into his bedroom. He didn't want to wake up Allison and the babies, but on the other hand, Allison didn't look very comfortable and the girls should be in bed. He took a shower and was in the middle of putting on clean jeans when he heard the babies cry. He pulled a white T-shirt over his head and hurried out to the living room.

He would simply offer to help, he told himself, because any woman with an armload of crying babies certainly needed help of any kind, even from a clumsy cowboy who didn't know enough to quit while he was ahead.

"DELL?" Allison blinked and tried to remember where she was. Sophie and Sylvie were crying again, two off-key sopranos screaming for attention.

"Yeah," he said, his voice low. "Let me take one of them."

She felt Sylvie being lifted from her left arm and released her gratefully. She shifted Sophie against her shoulder and rubbed her back, but Sophie bobbed her head and screamed in her aunt's ear. "I don't know what's wrong with them."

"Hungry?"

"Maybe. What time is it?"

"After eleven."

"I'll fix the bottles. They were like this at suppertime, until they finally wore themselves out and went to sleep." Allison hid a yawn and stood, the screaming baby still against her shoulder. She took two bottles from the refrigerator, put them in a pan of hot water, then turned to Dell. "Could you carry Sylvie to the bedroom for me? I'll change them and see if that helps."

"Good Lord," Dell muttered, shifting the screaming twin from the crook of his arm to his shoulder. "She' real upset about something."

"I wish I knew what was the matter." She put the screaming Sophie on the bed and unsnapped the terry-cloth sleeper. Dell usually disappeared during diaper changing, but tonight he stayed in the room and laid Sylvie beside her sister. Allison changed each child quickly and handed one back to Dell. "Do you mind?" she asked.

"No. You think we should call a doctor?"

Allison went into the bathroom, washed her hands and splashed water on her face. From the sound of things it was going to be a long night. "I don't know what to do. I have a baby book. I can reread the chapter on crying."

Sylvie wailed an octave higher. "Good idea," Dell agreed, wincing.

She scooped up the sobbing Sophie from the middle of the bed, tucked her carefully in her arm and picked up *Child Care: The First Year* from the bedside table. "This is a pretty good book."

"It had better be," the rancher muttered, shifting Sylvie

away from his ear. "She's gotta run out of air pretty soon, doesn't she?"

"I wouldn't bet on it," Allison said, hurrying toward the kitchen. "She and Sophie have more energy than I do sometimes, especially at night."

They tried giving the girls the bottles, which pleased them for only a few minutes. They cried around the plastic nipples and the milk dripped down the cheeks toward their ears and puddled in their necks. They burped and cried and carried on, waving little fists in the air and screwing up their faces to show their disapproval of everything around them.

"Good heavens," Dell sputtered, wiping his brow with a red bandanna. "It's midnight and they haven't given up yet."

Allison peered at the baby book. "The only thing I can figure out is that they're overstimulated, meaning their days have been so exciting that they can't get to sleep at night—"

"I can't picture that. Didn't they sleep on the porch with Cal this morning?"

"Yes. Wait a minute." She flipped ahead two pages. "Here it is. Evening colic? No, they're not acting like they have stomachaches."

"How do you tell?"

"They bring their knees to their chests. Let's see..." She ran down the list of things that could cause the babies to cry. "They're happier if they're being held, and they like to be rocked."

"I'll buy another rocking chair," Dell offered.

"Some babies like to be held, period. And then there's warmth." Allison tapped her finger on that column. "It says that some babies cry if they're not warm enough."

Dell eyed the blanket draped around the fussing child. "She looks warm enough to me."

Allison sighed. "They've been fed, burped, changed and snuggled. I guess all I can do is rock them and wait it out." She moved into the living room and sat down in the rocking chair. "Give me Sylvie and I'll do what worked before."

He waited for her to get settled in the rocking chair before handing her the second baby. She noticed he was careful not to touch her when he put Sylvie in her arms.

Dell straightened, taking a step backward. "I'll warm it up in here."

"Go to bed, Dell," she urged him. "I don't want to keep you awake, too." Besides, with Dell around it was only too easy to remember those kisses and the way those strong hands had lifted her up so he could kiss her. He'd made her feel delicate and fragile and desirable. Delicate and fragile she was used to, but desirable was rare enough to be tantalizing.

He left the room, and she heard the outside door shut. Within a few minutes he was back, his arms filled with firewood. The girls' tears had subsided, but they made tiny sobbing sounds every once in a while, as if to remind Allison that they still needed her to hold them. Allison watched as Dell arranged the wood, set a match to the kindling underneath, and the sticks burst into flame.

Dell looked over his shoulder at her. "It's worth a try," he said.

"Anything is," Allison agreed. She wished his shoulders weren't so broad, or his arms so strong. He was the kind of man a woman could lean on, the kind of man who'd driven wagon trains across the prairie and protected his family from harm. She longed to rest her head on that wide chest and sob her heart out, but knew if she did that she'd scare him into the next county. Dell avoided dirty diapers and weeping women, and heaven only knew what else. And she could hardly blame him.

She rocked the babies and enjoyed the fire, letting the warmth surround them. She felt herself relax, despite her careful grip on the children. Dell had bought a rocking chair large enough for triplets. Or one very large cowboy, she thought with a smile.

"Better?" he asked, clearing off a place on the couch to sit down.

"Much better," she assured him. She looked down at the babies, whose eyes had started to lose that miserable expression. "Right, girls?"

Sylvie sighed, a shaky little sound that tore at Allison's heart. "I wonder if they miss their mother. I wonder if they know that I'm not her."

Dell busied himself by pulling off his boots and tossing them aside. "What happened to your sister?"

"A car accident." It was still hard to believe, even when she said the words out loud. "She was driving to a doctor's appointment when a truck ran a stop sign and crashed into her. The babies were born a month early and Sandy didn't live to see them. And they never saw her."

"They're lucky to have you, Allison. That's real important to remember."

Allison held them a little tighter. "I'm the lucky one," she whispered, noting that Sophie's eyes had closed. "Even on nights when they don't want to go to sleep."

He leaned back against the back of the couch and stretched out his legs. The glow from the fire was the only light in the room, and it was enough for Allison to see Dell's profile, though she couldn't tell if his eyes were closed or open. She rocked gently for a long time, while the fire crackled and the man nearby kept her company. If he was asleep, she didn't care. She wasn't alone. She knew if she needed him she could call his name and he would help.

Dell Jones really was a special man. She shouldn't be so attracted to him. A woman with no home, no job and two babies had no business kissing anyone. Still, it was difficult to ignore the attraction she felt for the cowboy. He'd kissed her as if he'd desired her, but maybe cowboys who lived on remote ranches kissed women as if they were trying to turn them inside out. Maybe that was just part of living in the West.

He brought her a brandy without asking her if she wanted one. He set the glass on a table that he slid over beside her.

"Thank you," she said, knowing he didn't realize that she didn't have a free hand with which to pick up the glass. "I'll have to save it for later."

"I was going to offer to take one of the girls."

She shook her head. "I don't dare move them yet, but thanks anyway." she looked around the living room and admired her painting job. "I'll fix the room tomorrow."

"The boys and I will bring in the cabinet, or whatever the hell it is, in the morning."

"I'll polish it," she promised. "You won't recognize it when I'm done. Do you want to arrange your own books on the shelves or should I do it for you?"

He sat down on the empty spot on the couch and took a sip of the brandy. "You can arrange anything you want."

"I want you to like it," she said, smiling a little. "That's the whole point, Dell." She didn't often say his name, and he looked at her with an unreadable expression on his big, familiar face. The flickering firelight threw shadows on his face. She was conscious of the quiet, of the fact that they were alone together after midnight, that there were only two babies between them. The knowledge brought a strange kind of tension and she wondered if Dell could feel it, too. Or if it was simply her imagination.

"They're quiet," he rumbled.

"They're asleep." She kept rocking, afraid to stop the motion and wake up the children. Their small bodies had gone totally limp, heavy with sleep. Their lips were parted in identical shapes, their breathing light and even. Allison knew they must be the most beautiful babies on earth. No matter what it had cost her to keep them, it had been worth it ten times over.

"I brought my grandmother's box to the front porch," Dell said.

"Were there toys inside?"

"I haven't opened it. I was, uh, waiting for you. We can open it in the morning, if you like."

"I'd like that. It must be wonderful to live in the same house all of your life, and to know your parents and your grandparents lived here, too. Not many people have that connection with their family's past."

"You didn't?"

"No. My father's job meant that we moved every year or two. There wasn't much time to put down roots anywhere."

"What kind of child were you?"

"A typical younger sister." She smiled, remembering how quiet the house had been after Sandy left. "A younger sister who was a little bit of a pest, but learned to mind her own business and tried to stay out of trouble. I grew up, went to college, got a job. After my parents died I decided to move to Kansas City to be with Sandy. There was no one left but the two of us and I wanted to be together."

"And your sister?"

"Had her own life. And her own ideas of how it should be lived. And that didn't always include a little sister."

"But you have her children."

"Yes." Her arms tightened around the sleeping babies. "I wouldn't let anything happen to them."

"Come on," he said, getting to his feet and crossing the room. He held out his arms. "Let me help you get them to bed."

"All right," she whispered. "Pick one."

Dell scooped Sylvie into his large hands with the experience of a father of ten, while Allison shifted Sophie with careful movements and followed Dell down the hall. They walked silently to the bedroom, the babies still sleeping in their arms.

"Here's the hard part," Allison whispered, facing the girls' bed. "If we can get them down without waking them up, I'm going to deserve that glass of brandy."

Dell hesitated. "You go first."

She looked down at Sophie, who seemed to be almost unconscious with exhaustion. Allison could relate. She fiddled with the blanket, bent over and placed the baby carefully on the playpen mattress. The blanket went around her, too, and Sophie didn't open her eyes or complain in any way. "Your turn," Allison said, turning to the cowboy. "Or do you want me to do it?"

"Hell, yes." He handed Sylvie to her, and Allison managed to place the second child into the playpen without waking either her or her sister. They stood side by side and watched the babies for a long moment until satisfied that the girls were going to remain asleep, Allison took Dell's hand and led him out of the room. She was halfway down the hall before she realized she held on to him so casually, as if holding his hand was the most natural thing in the world to do in the middle of a dark night. His skin was rough and calloused, his fingers gentle around hers.

This wasn't the first time she'd felt such a strong physical awareness of him, but it was the first time Allison found comfort in it. And something more. The firelight cast an intimate glow over the furniture pushed into the center of the room, and Dell picked up Allison's brandy glass and led her to the couch.

"You'll be warmer by the fire," he said.

She was altogether too warm already, but she sat beside him and kicked off her shoes, then tucked her feet underneath her on the couch. He handed her the glass and picked up his.

"To sleeping babies," he said, touching his glass to hers.

"And sleeping late," Allison added, and took a sip of the most expensive-tasting brandy she'd sampled. "If I'm very, very lucky they might sleep until seven."

He was still holding her hand. Dell lifted their joined hands and looked down at the joining. "This is all very strange," he muttered, then lifted his gaze to her face.

"Yes," Allison agreed, not pretending she didn't know what he was talking about. She tightened her fingers around his.

"Your coming here," he began, keeping his voice low while the fire crackled behind him. "Your *staying* here," he corrected, "was something unexpected. I never thought someone like you would come to the ranch."

"You brought me here," she teased. She wanted to throw her arms around him. She wanted him to kiss her again, the way he had kissed her in the shed. She wanted to run down the hall and lock her door before she made a complete fool out of herself. She kept her hand in his and took another swallow of her drink.

"Ah," he smiled. "That was one of my smarter decisions."

She finished her drink, letting the warmth seep into her bones and pool in her stomach, and set the empty glass on the floor. "Even with your living room in shambles and babies crying half the night?"

"Yes," he replied simply. "Even with babies and chaos. Because I've kissed you."

It was, Allison decided, the most romantic thing anyone had ever said to her. Mostly because Dell meant it, and because he didn't often say romantic things. He didn't often say anything at all. So when he tugged her closer to him, she went willingly. So willingly that it was a little embarrassing, but enfolded in those strong arms of his she felt safe, as she'd never felt so safe before. He smelled of soap and wood shavings. He was everything good and wonderful and solid. She put her arms around his neck and lifted her chin for his kiss.

She was growing accustomed to touching him, after all. His enormous size no longer frightened her. He held her as gently as he would a butterfly and he kissed her with the passion of a man who knew what he wanted was right in front of him. Allison found herself enfolded in an embrace that threatened to take her breath away. Not from the force of the man holding her, but from the intensity of feeling that took her by surprise. She'd expected comfort and instead there was that amazing longing to crawl inside Dell's skin.

He tasted of warmth and brandy. Somehow she was on her knees, to be closer to him. He released their clasped hands and wrapped his arms around her waist while he continued to kiss her.

Allison told herself later that it was inevitable. When Dell scooped her up into his arms and carried her to his bedroom, she was a happy woman. She was also a woman who was being kissed thoroughly the entire time it took to walk halfway down the hall to Dell's room. He nudged the door shut behind him, carried her to a wide bed and paused.

"Now would be a real good time to leave, if you're going to leave," he said. His eyes were dark as he looked down at her.

"No, thank you," Allison said, and kissed his chin. Which made him smile and drop her onto the bed.

"You can change your mind anytime."

"Do you *want* me to leave?"

"Hell, Allison, I'd be a fool to want you out of my sight," he muttered. He sat down on the bed and took her shoulders. 'I'm not much of a ladies' man," he confessed.

"Good."

"I—mean," he stammered, "there've been a few women. But not here at the ranch. And not in a long time." His fingers swept across her cheek in the darkness, and he brushed the wisps of hair from her face. "And there's never been anyone like you."

"You don't usually talk this much," she murmured, placing little kisses alongside his mouth. "I thought you cowboys were men of action."

Even in the darkness she could see him smile. "Lady," he drawled, trailing one large hand gently across her breast, "you ain't seen nothing yet."

Allison inhaled sharply as his thumb caressed her nipple. She didn't know how her clothes came off, but together they managed to unbutton each other's buttons and unzip each other's jeans. It was crazy and right, and in the darkness of a Wyoming night all either of them wanted was to lie naked in a pile of sheets and make love for hours.

She climbed on top of him and buried her nose in the mass of dark hair that covered the largest chest she'd ever seen. She ran her hands along muscled arms, and those arms lifted her and then, with an agonizing slowness, lowered her on top of him. She was ready for him, even as big as he was.

He'd managed, sometime during the tangle of bodies and kisses and caressing hands, to put on a condom. He'd promised not to hurt her, worried that he would, and eased himself inside her with a control that made him grimace in pain and pleasure as he entered her sweet body. She was hot and wet and tight and he was afraid he would come inside of her at the very first thrust. But Dell knew that this miracle might never happen again, and he gathered every shred of self-control he possessed to prolong the lovemaking.

It was heaven and hell, all mixed up in a glorious tangle of silken hair and satin skin and the faintest trace of lilacs. He tumbled Allison onto her back, made love to her as if he would never make love to her again. Her climax caught him by surprise; he felt her tighten and contract around him, heard her sweet sigh of pleasure, and felt himself explode inside of her. He closed his eyes so she wouldn't see how deep the joy went. She didn't need to know that he loved her, though he longed to whisper the words into the soft skin of her neck while he made love to her again.

Dell was careful to rest his weight on his arms. He opened his eyes slowly, as the world settled back into place, to see Allison looking into his face. She touched his cheek, caressed the day's growth of whiskers, and smiled a tender little smile.

I love you, his heart pounded. *Love you, love you, love you.* The rhythm matched the thumping in his chest, but Dell was content to stay silent. He was either in love or having a heart attack from making love to an angel.

Either way, it didn't matter much.

When he thought he could move, he reluctantly withdrew from Allison's body and eased himself away from her. He grabbed a fistful of sheets and blankets, arranged them over their naked bodies, and gathered Allison into his arms. She snuggled against him, her head on his chest, until she drifted off into a sleep.

Dell listened to her even breathing while he counted his blessings.

ALLISON DIDN'T MEAN to kiss him in her sleep, but when she awoke a while later she was half on top of the naked rancher and shamelessly sprawled across his chest as if she were trying to crawl inside of him. She blushed when his eyes opened and he studied her with a curious expression.

"I'm sorry," she whispered. "I must have been dreaming. I didn't mean to bother—"

He took her face in his big hands and kissed her until they were both gasping for air and grasping for each other. She felt him hard against her thigh, leaving no doubt that there were some things she wasn't dreaming at all.

"Stay where you are," he ordered, his voice sleepy. "You're not bothering me." He chuckled as she blushed once again. "Well, not really," he added and reached for a condom.

She rolled to her side, and he rolled with her. He fit himself against her, entered her with a smooth stroke. His large hand splayed across her buttocks and held her tight against him while he moved inside her. Allison wrapped her arms around his neck, tossed her leg over his thigh and hung on. It was insanity to want him this much, but she did. And maybe she was just a little bit crazy.

He moved within her, again and again, creating sensations that made her gasp in pleasure. She kicked the sheet away; he tossed the blanket to the floor. He pulled her on top of him and rolled onto his back. Allison, perched above him, his body filling hers, felt as if she were making love to a giant.

It was a glorious feeling. She leaned forward and licked his neck.

10

"WHAT THE HELL is going on around here? The sun cleared the ridge an hour ago." Calvin's voice was an unwelcome intrusion on Dell's dream. "You sick or something?"

Dell kept his eyes closed and wished his uncle had stayed in the navy. Or better yet, had been stranded on a deserted island and forced to communicate by putting notes in bottles. He played dead and prayed Cal would lose interest and return to the kitchen.

"You ain't dead, are ya?" Calvin yelled.

Dell kept his eyes closed. "You'd be waking me up if I were."

"Coffee's on," his uncle said, "soon as you decide you can drag your sorry ass out of bed and do a day's work."

"You're gonna wake the babies," Dell cautioned. "They had a bad night, so quit yelling."

Cal lowered his voice, but kept talking. "Hell, the girlies have been up for an hour or more. Their mama fed 'em early. You're the only one around here still in bed with his eyes glued shut."

"All right. I'm getting up."

The bedroom door closed and Dell listened to the clunk of Calvin's boots heading toward the kitchen.

Dell rolled over, reached out and touched the empty space beside him. So it could have been a dream, he thought wearily, his eyes closed against the dim light of dawn. Except that his body was spent and if he wasn't tone deaf, he would surely break into song. He couldn't feel this damn good and have a dream be responsible.

Loving Allison had been real. He grew hard just thinking about the way his fingers had slid over that satiny skin, the way her legs had wrapped around his. She had been so delicate, and yet she had taken him inside her and turned his heart inside out.

He'd have to get out of this bed and find her. Or maybe not, he wondered, opening his eyes and surveying his empty room. She could have taken one look at him in the daylight and figured she'd made a big mistake. He scratched his whiskered chin and sat up. His room wouldn't win any prizes. A queen-size bed—the only new furniture he'd bought in twenty years—and a couple of old oak dressers were the extent of the decorations. He hadn't bothered with curtains for years and it was anyone's guess what the original color of the bedside rug had been.

Dell, naked and suddenly nervous, made his way to the bathroom. Hell, he'd shower and shave and get ready to bust his ass for the rest of the day, until he was too tired to think about Allison and her golden hair and soft skin and sweet-tasting lips, until he was too exhausted and bone-weary to wonder if Allison would come to his bed again tonight.

He wondered if he would be able to live without loving her again.

ALLISON DIDN'T KNOW if she was happy or disappointed that Dell wasn't in the kitchen when she fed the girls their early morning bottles. He was usually gone before the early feeding, then she put the girls back to bed and had some time to drink coffee, clean up the kitchen—if Calvin wasn't around to sputter—and shower.

This morning she'd managed to take a quick shower

while the bottles heated up. The girls had been surprisingly patient and content to amuse themselves while waiting for breakfast and clean pants. Now they were fed and dry and still cheerful. Allison heard Calvin hollering at Dell to get up and quietly shut her bedroom door so the girls wouldn't cry for him. They seemed to like the old man; Allison swore they saved their best smiles for him. They seemed fine this morning, with nothing wrong at all. Allison sat on the edge of her bed and looked at them as they gurgled at each other in their playpen. If they would close their eyes, she could crawl—clothes and all—under the covers of her own bed and go to sleep.

Heaven knows she hadn't had much sleep last night. Allison smiled to herself and laid back on the bed. She had been made love to. Thoroughly, and with great passion.

She never would have suspected the big rancher would be such a lover. Of course, she hadn't had too much experience in that department. One brief fiasco in college had left her leery of young men with groping hands, and then much later there was Ryan. That had been a pleasant relief, but it didn't compare with what happened last night.

She didn't know how to explain last night. She couldn't blame it on the brandy, or the fire. She couldn't tell herself that she was lonely; who could be lonely taking care of twin infants? Allison closed her eyes and remembered Dell's large body filling hers. She didn't know how to even describe what happened last night, even to herself. It must have been lust, because falling in love didn't happen in eight days. Except in books, or in romantic movies. This was no romantic movie. This was her life, and she had most likely screwed it up royally.

Allison drifted off to sleep, but not before wondering how on earth she would face Dell later on in the morning. She would hug him, she decided, because that would be a good way to show him that last night meant something special.

"ALLISON."

Allison opened her eyes to see Dell looking down at her, his beautiful mouth turned into a grim line. She tried to remember where she was as she struggled to sit up. "What time is—"

"Your fiancé's here." His voice was cold, the expression in his eyes wary. "I think his name is Ryan Conway?"

Allison blinked. "My fiancé?"

"You have one?"

"Ryan's *here?*"

He gave her a disgusted look. "Yeah, he's here, all right."

"In Wyoming?"

"In the living room."

"I can't believe this." She stared up at Dell and waited for him to tell her that this was a joke, but he turned away and headed for the door.

"You didn't answer my knock," he explained. "And I didn't want to wake the girls. Sorry for invading your privacy. Your *fiancé* said you were expecting him."

"He's not my fiancé, not anymore," Allison managed to say, but Dell had left and shut the door behind him with a quiet click. She looked over at the girls, whose cheeks were rosy with sleep, then glanced at herself in the mirror above the dresser. She smoothed her hair, tucked her shirt inside her jeans, and decided there wasn't time to find her shoes. Ryan Conway and Wendell Jones in the same room—in the same state, even—was something she had to see for herself.

Before Dell killed him.

Allison hurried down the hall and rounded the corner to see Ryan standing alone beside the rocking chair. The furniture was still pushed to the middle of the room, making the place look worse than it deserved to, although the dust-covered cabinet had been moved into place against the east wall. Dell had promised he'd have it moved in the morning, and there it was.

"Ryan?"

He turned around, his ivory windbreaker unzipped over a powder blue crew neck shirt. She'd bought him that shirt last Christmas, because it matched his eyes. He was tall and slender, with windblown light brown hair.

"Allison," he said, his handsome face breaking into a smile. "I was beginning to wonder if you were really here."

"What are you doing here?" She stopped four feet away from him and shoved her hands in her jeans' pockets. "How did you find me?"

"Mayme told me you were stranded on a ranch near Wells City. I stopped in town and asked directions."

She'd always thought he looked like Robert Redford's son, if Robert Redford had a son. She waited for the familiar thrill that seeing him brought, but nothing happened except strong feelings of annoyance and disbelief. "But why?"

"To see you, of course." Once again, that smile. He stepped forward and put his arm around her shoulders. "To ask you to come back."

"I've already moved away," she felt it necessary to declare, and stepped out of his embrace.

He chuckled. "You didn't get very far." He glanced around the room. "Redecorating, Allie?"

"Yes." Her chin lifted. "I've been hired to redo several of the rooms, plus a bunkhouse."

"A bunkhouse," he repeated, looking incredulous. "One of the most sought-after decorators in Kansas City is redesigning a bunkhouse."

"I don't work in Kansas City any longer." Allison looked around for any sign of Dell or Calvin. Dell might stomp off and leave her with Ryan, but Calvin would have his hearing aid firmly in place and would take up a position in the kitchen so he could listen to every word being said.

"Could we talk about that? Maybe I was hasty."

"Hasty? You bought out my share of the business, Ryan. We signed the contracts Mayme drew up and you gave me a check." She stared up at him, trying to figure out why Ryan had come to Wyoming to find her.

"That can all be rectified."

"And the children?" She wondered how on earth he would have figured out how to deal with the babies. "What about them?"

"We'll hire a nanny. And we'll build a house. Didn't you always want to decorate your own house?"

"I always wanted a home of my own. That's different."

He looked around the room and frowned. "Could we sit down somewhere and talk? I have a proposition for you."

"How about a cup of coffee? Come on."

She led him into the kitchen, where Calvin stood at the counter kneading bread dough. "Cal, I'd like you to meet Ryan Conway. Ryan, this is Cal Jones, the cook here on the Lazy J."

Calvin held out one flour-covered hand, and Ryan reluctantly shook it.

"Nice to meet you," the younger man said.

"Yep." The old man nodded, and Allison noticed his hearing aid was in place. "Who are you?"

"A friend of Allie's. From Kansas City."

Calvin turned back to his bread dough and pounded it against the wooden board. "What the hell are you doing in Wyoming?"

Ryan smiled, but Cal didn't see it. "Trying to talk Allie into coming home with me. It was good of you to give her a place to stay on your ranch."

"Ain't my ranch." It was said with great belligerence.

Allison decided against the coffee and steered Ryan back

toward the living room.

"Whose ranch is it?"

"Mine," Dell said, standing in the doorway. He held both babies in his arms and his expression was deliberately bland. "I'm Dell Jones, owner of the Lazy J." He turned to Allison. "They were crying."

Ryan looked surprised, then chuckled. "*You*'re Dell Jones?" He turned to Allison. "You wouldn't believe what a waitress in the café told me."

"And what was that?" Dell planted his feet on the floor and held the silent babies with steady arms.

Ryan shook his head, obviously rethinking what he was going to say. Allison could guess. Lucille must have been flapping those red lips of hers. "Never mind." He turned to Allison. "Is there someplace where we can talk privately?"

Allison wished Dell would look at her. She wished he'd smile or wink or something, just to show he didn't believe that she would make love to him while she was engaged to marry someone else. She ignored Ryan's question. He hadn't acknowledged the children or asked how they were doing. All he could think of was hiring a nanny and resuming life as usual. "I'll take the girls," she said, stepping closer. "They must need to be changed."

"Yeah," Dell said. "I'll take them back to the bedroom for you."

She turned back to Ryan. "Have a seat. I'll be back in a few minutes."

He grimaced, barely glancing at the babies. "Guess some things don't change."

Allison ignored him and followed Dell down the hall and shut the bedroom door behind her. "He's not my fiancé," she said to Dell's broad back. He set one girl, then the other, on the bed.

"Then why does he think he is?"

"He *was*. Once. Before the babies came."

Silence. He moved aside so she could unfasten the girls' sleepers. Neither Cal nor Dell had ever stayed in a room where there was diaper-changing going on, so Allison figured the silent rancher was willing to listen to her. "We were partners in a decorating business. He specialized in business environments and I did houses. We were engaged for two years, living together for six months, and then the babies came. And Ryan left."

Which, she wanted to add, was exactly what the girls' father had done, too.

Dell cleared his throat. "Why?"

"Why did he leave?" Dell nodded, a grim expression clouding his face. "He didn't want children. At least, he didn't want someone else's children. He didn't like the noise or the mess or the fact that I wanted to stay home and take care of them and not display carpet samples anymore." Allison swallowed hard, hoping to dislodge some of the bitterness she heard in her own voice.

"You loved him."

"Yes. At least, I thought I did." Looking back now, she wondered if the marriage would have worked. They most likely would have done fine, unless she decided that what she wanted was different from what Ryan wanted.

Ryan usually got what he wanted.

Allison changed the diapers slowly, giving Dell as much time as she could to say something. Anything. She would have settled for a smile or a pat on the back. A brief kiss would be nice, too. But the stubborn rancher simply leaned against the wall, his arms folded across his chest, his gaze on a spot above the headboard.

"Would you watch them while I wash my hands?"

He nodded, so Allison gathered up the dirty diapers and went into the bathroom. When she returned, Dell was sitting on the bed tickling Sylvie's chin. He stopped when she stepped into the room.

"What does the son of a bitch want now?"

"To take me back to Kansas with him."

"And the girls?"

"I don't intend to go anywhere without the babies."

Dell nodded. "Yeah, I can see that. You think *he* will?"

She wanted to touch him. She wanted to stand in front of him and put her hands on either side of his face and kiss those frowning lips of his. She wanted to kick him in the shins and make him beg for mercy. "Move over," she said, her voice brusque. "I can't stall in here much longer."

He moved, and she sat down beside him on the bed. Their thighs touched, but neither moved to break the contact. "I'm not going back with him."

"I wouldn't blame you if you did."

Allison turned sideways to face him. He looked as if he'd blame her for the rest of her days if she walked out that door this morning. She touched the back of his hand. "You must have chores to do."

"Are you trying to get rid of me?"

"I'm trying to tell you that I have to talk to Ryan. He came all this way. It's the least I can do."

"Yeah, well." He shrugged and moved off the bed. "He doesn't want the girls?"

"No." And he never would, no matter how hard she tried, Ryan was not ready, willing or able to be a father. When it came right down to it, no one was.

Dell picked up Sophie, who started to cry. "He can stay for lunch."

"Thank you." She gathered up Sylvie, who was about to burst into tears, too. "I guess everyone's hungry."

"We'll feed 'em," Dell said. "All of 'em, and then maybe we'll have some peace around here."

"And I've got some furniture to move," Allison said, suddenly feeling more cheerful. "I can't keep you in a mess." She opened the door and headed down the hall. Ryan could talk until he was blue in the face, but that wouldn't change anything. She wasn't going back to business as usual.

"I NEED YOU, Allie. I've fired three assistants in three weeks." Ryan put his hands on his hips and surveyed the living room furniture. "Tell me you're not going to keep that sofa."

"I'm putting a quilt on it."

"A *large* quilt, I hope." He helped her push the green recliners into place by the east wall. "These hideous things should have been banned years ago."

"They're comfortable, and the men like watching football."

Dell almost said something, like *get the hell off my property*, but Allison didn't seem to be bothered by her ex-fiancé's comments, so he leaned against the doorway of the kitchen and watched the two of them move the furniture into place.

"Where on earth did you find that cabinet?"

"The Horta? Out in the shed."

The clown from Kansas shook his head. "It's not a Horta. Not enough detail on the scrolls. And the wood is all wrong."

"You sure?"

"Positive. But it's a nice piece all the same. Made in New York, not Belgium." He turned away from the cabinet and surveyed the rest of the room. Dell watched to make sure he didn't lay a finger on Allison. He expected the man to keep his distance or pay the consequences.

"Don't you have somethin' better to do?" Calvin asked, coming up behind him.

"Nope."

"You've been standin' here for an hour. You think she's gonna fall into his arms if you're not standin' here to make sure she doesn't?"

"I'm making sure he doesn't try anything."

Cal shook his head. "You've been acting pretty strange, son. Sleepin' late don't agree with you."

Dell thought about what had happened last night and wondered if his uncle was right. Making love to Allison had agreed with him, all right. It was just the morning that had been tough to take. "That slick bastard isn't going to take Allison away with him."

"You don't have a choice, Dell. That ain't up to you."

"It should be," he growled. He had tasted heaven last night and this morning he was chewing dust. His fists were clenched tight and he wanted to pound something, but Allison wouldn't like it if he messed up her guest. Hell, he'd been the idiot who had invited him to stay for lunch. The man had been personable and charming, grateful for the invitation and curious about the ranch. He'd eaten Dell's beef and thanked Calvin politely for the meal.

And Dell, sick with visions of that man making love to Allison, wanted to stomp him into the shape of a cow pie.

"But it ain't up to you." Cal patted him on the shoulder. They watched Allison and her friend argue over the placement of the couch as if they'd argued over furniture a thousand times before. "She's not yours, Dell. She's a woman with a broken car and two babies and she's not gonna stay here on this old ranch takin' care of a bunch of sorry cowboys."

"Shut up," Dell said, his voice deadly quiet. He watched Allison stand beside the handsome blond man. They made a good-looking couple, like a magazine advertisement for toothpaste or vitamins or yuppie running shoes. Yellow hair and blue eyes, perfect in every way.

Except, Dell thought in grim satisfaction, Conway didn't want the babies. And Wendell Jones, big ugly cowhand that he was, did. He wanted Allison, too. And she was here, her car being repaired slowly and painstakingly by a guy whose freezer was going to be full of beet come fall. He'd had ten days to show her what her life would be like if she stayed. He'd thought he'd had a chance, until Conway showed up with his offers of business deals and nannies and a new house.

Dell turned his back and walked through the kitchen, picked up his hat and left the house. Maybe it was time to give up. A smart man knew when he'd been beaten.

"LAST CHANCE," Ryan said, smiling that charming smile of his. The blue eyes looked a little sad, though. He waved his arm toward the ranch buildings. "I could still take you away from all of this."

Allison kissed his cheek and took a step away from the car. "Thanks, but I'm going to stick with my original plan."

"Looks like you've gotten sidetracked."

"Temporarily," she insisted, knowing sooner or later she'd have to leave the safety of the ranch.

He hesitated before getting into his car. "We could have made it work, I think. I do love you."

She shook her head. 'You don't want the babies, Ryan. You never did, and our staying together and raising them isn't fair to them or to you. Sooner or later it would have fallen apart."

"Well, I'm sorry about that." He grimaced. "Babies and diapers and bottles are a bit much. And if I ever decide to have a child, I want him to be my own."

"I know," Allison said, wishing he would just get in his car and leave. She felt as if the children had been rejected once again, but at least she knew now, without the smallest doubt, that she had done the right thing by starting over. The girls would never have to find out that "Uncle Ryan" would prefer they talk to the nanny, that their father didn't want them, that their half brother and half-sisters lived in the most expensive section of town and didn't know the twins existed.

He got in the car, started up the engine and within a few minutes was just a cloud of dust on the long drive to the · main road. *If I ever decide to have a child, I'd want him to be my own.* The words echoed in Allison's head as she walked up the steps to the front porch. She tiptoed down the hall and checked on the sleeping girls. She'd done the right thing by leaving, but now what? She was in danger of falling in love with the big rancher, and there was no reason to believe that Wendell Jones was interested in anything more than a brief affair. He was the kind of man she could love with her whole being, depend on till her dying day, trust with her heart.

She didn't know whether to run into his arms or hitch-hike to town to buy a station wagon.

THE IDIOT COWBOY didn't come inside for supper. Allison picked at her food, oven-fried chicken and baked potatoes, until she pushed the plate aside. She couldn't leave the babies alone while she searched the ranch for one Wendell Jones and the man knew that.

Allison waited for Dell, knowing he'd have to come inside eventually. The girls were tired tonight and easily went to bed after baths and bottles. She cleaned up the kitchen and watched out the window as lights glowed in the outbuildings. The men would be gathering around the scarred oak table for their nightly games of cards and Scrabble. Cal told her he was the ranch champion. She didn't know whether to believe him or not.

It was after ten when Dell entered the kitchen. He looked tired, which was no surprise. Neither of them had gotten much sleep last night.

He glanced in her direction, took a glass of water from the cupboard and poured himself a drink of water.

"Long day?" Allison asked.

"Yeah." He drained the glass in one long motion, then refilled it and leaned against the counter. "Real long."

He was jealous, Allison realized. He actually thought that Ryan could snap his fingers and she'd grab the girls and the diaper bag and go running back to Kansas. She didn't stop to wonder why she was pleased that Dell was acting this way. She waited for him to ask where their visitor had gone. "More calves today?"

"Just a few. Nothing to speak of. The season's over, 'cept for the surprises." He took another drink of water and gave her a level look. "Speaking of surprises, where's Conway?"

"In Cheyenne, I guess."

"Heading east?"

"Yes."

"Without you?"

"Yep." She waited for a reaction, but didn't get one. Dell stood quiet and calm, drinking his water. They may as well have been talking about the weather. Had she imagined the flicker of jealousy?

"You were together a long time."

"Yes."

"Shouldn't you be crying or something?"

"Not if I'm not sad." She stood. "I called the garage today and checked about the car. He said to give him another week."

"A week," he muttered, setting the empty glass in the sink as she crossed the kitchen to stand in front of him. Allison put her arms around his waist and looked up into his face.

"Seven days. Do you mind?"

"No."

His arms started around her, then stopped. "I'm dirty and covered with—"

"That doesn't matter," she said, laying her head on his chest. "I just need you to hold me." She needed him for a lot of things, but she wouldn't tell him so. She would stay for seven more days. She would wrap her arms around him and show him that he shouldn't stay up here alone on the ranch for the rest of his life. She would teach him to dance and show him that he was attractive and help him get out of his isolated rut.

"You smell like furniture polish," he said, wrapping her into his embrace.

And she would love him, Allison added to her mental list. Heaven knows, he was a man who deserved it.

11

MIDNIGHT FOUND HIM lying naked, Allison tucked against his chest. Her hair was spread across Dell's shoulder, the curls tickling his neck. He thought he might have dreamt the past hour, except she was soft and warm against him. She'd taken his hand and led him into the bedroom. They'd showered together and she'd scrubbed his back. He took her to bed and kissed that lovely body in places that drove them both crazy with desire. When she'd taken him inside her body, the pain of the day had receded and Dell had realized that he'd been given the gift of another night.

Allison lifted her head and kissed his mouth.

"Smile," she commanded, looking down at him. "You haven't smiled at me all day."

He hadn't felt like smiling. He'd felt like drowning himself in the old horse trough behind the barn when he'd seen that handsome son of a bitch grinning down at Allison. Dell knew damn well that the Conway character wasn't worthy of Allison and she was better off without him, but he was sure surprised that Allison knew it, too.

She continued to look at him. "You're still not smiling."

"Sorry." He forced his face into what he hoped was a pleasant expression. "That better?"

"Mmm." Allison tilted her head and didn't look impressed. "I'm sorry about today."

'There's nothing to be sorry for." It wasn't her fault that Conway found his way to the ranch.

"You didn't get a chance to look at the living room, did you?"

"No."

She nodded. "That's what I thought. Tomorrow you can tell me if you like it or not."

"It'll be fine." He closed his eyes so she wouldn't see the love he felt. There was no sense in acting like a lovesick fool.

"Do you want me to leave?"

"Leave?" He opened his eyes and studied her face. He thought they'd settled that. She would stay for another week and he would try like hell not to make a fool of himself.

"Calvin came to your room this morning. I don't want him to find me here tomorrow."

"That was because I didn't get up. Stay," he said, tightening his arms around her. "I'll set the alarm clock."

"I have to open the door so I can hear the babies. They'll never sleep through the night since they went to bed so early."

"We can sleep in there," he offered.

She shook her head and his heart sank until she added, "Not if we're not going to sleep." She smoothed the palm of her hand along his chest, then lower. Her small fingers found him, then hesitated. "And I don't think we're going to sleep right away."

He shook his head and felt himself grow larger against her fingers. "No."

Allison caressed him with her hand until he thought he would disgrace himself by passing out from the pleasure. She'd never touched him so deliberately before. After several of the most enjoyable minutes he'd experienced in his life, Dell rolled Allison onto her back. She wound her arms around his neck.

"You're smiling now," she told him.

"Am I?"

She nodded and kissed his chin. "Now I know the secret."

"I am making love to a very smart lady."

"And a very happy one," she added.

Dell paused. "Are you, Allison? Happy, I mean?"

"Yes." Her hand caressed his face. "And happiness is a welcome change from the past months, believe me. I'm glad it was you who rescued me."

He entered her with a single stroke, feeling that sweet, tight warmth encompass him. Her arms tightened around his neck and he heard her gasp as he moved within her. He moved slowly, prolonging the sensations, until neither one could delay the inevitable climax that swept them both.

When Wyoming settled back to earth and Dell remembered his name and other details of their conversation, he gathered Allison into his arms. "I'm glad I rescued you, too," he lied, though a sinking feeling accompanied the words. Calvin was right. Allison was going to break his heart. He was a goner, all right. He'd fallen for the first pretty woman to enter the Lazy J and now she was in his bed and her babies were down the hall.

She would move on to Seattle and marry a guy who looked like that Conway character. They would have beautiful babies who would wear booties, not boots. He would never see the girlies again, or feel Allison's skin against his.

He'd learned a lesson today, Dell decided, and it had nothing to do with making love or figuring out where the couch should sit.

"How are things in the big house?" Cussy called as Cal made his way across the yard. Cussy was saddling up his horse and preparing to check fences in the western hills. "Who's gonna win the bet?"

Cal lifted his hat, scratched his head, and replaced his hat low on his forehead. "Don't rightly know. Things are sure heatin' up." He hadn't liked what he'd seen this morning. Dell had that tired look again, yet he didn't seem sick. Allison had blushed her morning greetings while she fed the girlies.

"You got the inside track, Cal. We heard her old boyfriend came to visit."

Yep. He wanted her back but she sent him packin'."

"Yeah?"

"Yep. She made him help her move all the furniture first, though. Smart gal, that one."

"Smart enough to know a good man when she's found one? The boss could use a wife."

Calvin shrugged. "She ain't ranch material. Hell, she's painted the walls and moved my chair."

"You'll get over it," the cowboy said. "And you like them babies."

Cal couldn't deny that. Them girlies were a lot of fun, and as long as no one expected him to change diapers he was happy to sit with them and read his magazines. He'd collected quite a piece of change, too, with all the baby-holdin' goin' on, too. "Don't know what they'd do without me," he boasted.

Cussy gave him a solemn nod. "Damn right. You'd make one hell of a grandpa, that's for damn sure."

"Grandpa?" He stared at the other man, who had swung himself onto his horse and gathered the reins. "*Grandpa?*"

"Well, isn't that what you'd be if Miz Allison stuck around?"

Calvin scratched his head as Cussy trotted toward the fence line. A grandfather. He hadn't thought of that.

'Course, Dell had been like a son to him. Always had. He'd never figured Dell for a family man, so he'd expected the two of them would go on as they always had. He turned and gazed toward the house. So little Allison was blushing and Dell had circles under his eyes. That could only mean one thing.

There was more goin' on in the ranch house at night than midnight bottles.

Which meant the girlies might leave or the girlies might stay. Could be trouble either way, Cal figured.

Hell, now he had to do some more thinkin'.

"WHAT DO YOU THINK?" Allison waved toward the living room and waited for Dell's reaction. He surveyed the cabinet that she'd turned into a bookcase, the antique quilt that covered the back of the couch, the dining room chairs that surrounded a gleaming table.

"Real nice." He took a step backward, into the kitchen, and poured himself a cup of coffee. Cal looked up from kneading dough and gave Allison a wink.

"Real nice," he said, echoing his nephew's words. "I can still see the TV from my chair."

"I'm glad." She turned toward Dell, who didn't look at her. She told herself she shouldn't be disappointed. She knew he was a man of few words, but she'd expected a little more than "real nice." "You don't like it," she said, following him to the kitchen table. The girls gurgled and kicked from their car seats, but Dell didn't seem to notice.

"I like it just fine."

Maybe he was disappointed that she hadn't hung the gold mirror in the living room. She'd debated about returning it, but put it in the bathroom instead where it brightened up the small area. "I saved the little pink dresser for the front porch," she said, trying to get his attention. "I might paint it forest green and do the porch in green and white."

Dell nodded. "All right."

Allison wiped a dribble from Sylvie's chin and watch as Dell moved to the sink. He poured his coffee down the drain and set the mug on the counter. She wouldn't have thought this was the same man who made love to her two nights. Twice. He'd withdrawn since then, as if he were trying to distance himself from her and the children. Yesterday she'd been too busy with the babies and the decorating to take it personally. She'd slept in her own bed because he was late at the barn, but this morning he was avoiding her. And that hurt.

She tried one more thing because before he escaped outside into the bright spring sunshine, she wanted to finish the living room. "Would you mind if we opened the box?"

He frowned. "The box?"

"One of the men brought it in with the cupboard and the chairs. It's the box of your grandmother's toys."

"Go ahead."

"You don't want to see?"

He hesitated. No. Go ahead. Surprise me."

"Okay."

"Nice day," Cal declared, looking out the window at the cloudless sky. "S'posed to be a good weekend, too."

"Thanks for the update," Dell muttered, heading for the door.

"Kelly Beatrice called. She wanted to know if you could donate a hundred dollars toward the raffle. I told her, hell yes. Don't you always?"

"Fine." He grabbed his hat.

"She wanted to know if you and Allison here would be going to the May shindig on Saturday, and if you wanted to sit with her and Jack for supper. I told her yeah, that was fine. You're to meet them there at six o'clock."

Allison turned to Dell. "What's going on?"

His gaze flickered over to her. "May Days. Used to be a party after calving season. Got out of hand."

"Raises a nice chunk of money, too," Calvin added. "Just about everyone in the county shows up." He turned to Allison. "I'll take care of the girlies, of course. I'll get Cussy to help."

"I haven't been invited," she pointed out.

"Aw, hell, you're going with that grouchy nephew of mine. And it's potluck. You're s'posed to bring a dish. And then there's the dancin'." he winked at her. "Figures that now that Dell can dance, he oughta take you to town and show off a little bit."

Dell glared at him, but Cal didn't seem to notice. He turned back to his work and kept kneading that dough until it was silky and smooth. "I'm not making a fool of myself in front of the whole town," he declared.

Allison smiled at him. "It would be fun to go," she mused. "We wouldn't have to dance."

"Hell."

"Unless you already have another date?" In which case, she'd have to do something drastic, like tie him up in the barn so he couldn't go to town and dance with anyone else but her.

He shot her a disgusted look, jammed his hat on his head and left the room. She heard the back door bang shut, then watched out the window as Dell crossed the yard and headed toward the barn. She didn't envy the men who had to talk to him today.

She left the window and turned to Calvin. "What kind of dish?"

The old man shrugged. "I usually bake up a few pans of

rolls, but since this is your first time you oughta bring something yourself. You have any favorite recipes?"

"Not exactly."

Calvin, a painted expression on his face, sighed. "Guess I'll have to teach you something then."

"HELL AND DAMNATION. He'd been roped into going to a goddam dance. Here he thought he was doing such a good job at staying away from her, and now he was taking her to town. Dell glared at himself in the bathroom mirror and parted his damp hair with the comb. He'd been trying to act civilized by not making love to her every night. And he'd managed to avoid his bed for two long nights, but there'd be no helping him now. After an evening of looking at Allison and breathing in her perfume and dancing with her, he'd have a hard time walking to the truck without embarrassing himself.

Dell sighed and adjusted his string tie. He wanted her all the time. He wanted her beside him when he rode out to check the cattle or talk to the men. He wanted her across the supper table. He wanted to drink his morning coffee and watch her feed the girls. He liked the way she teased him and he liked his new living room.

He was a sorry lovesick mess of a man. Anyone in town tonight would see that right off. They would point and say, "There goes old lovesick Jones, dancing over there with the beautiful blonde."

And someone else would say, "Wonder what the hell she sees in him." And no one would have an answer. Not even the guy they were talking about.

"You ready yet?" Cal hollered.

"Almost." Dell stuck his head out of the bathroom as his uncle approached.

"The little gal is out in the kitchen with the girlies." Cal surveyed his polished boots, pressed slacks and white shirt. "You look right nice. Better 'n usual."

He winced. "Thanks."

"I see you've got your dancin' shoes on."

"Yeah, for what it's worth. I'm gonna look like a fool."

"You're gonna look like the luckiest man in the county," Cal assured him. "The little gal looks real pretty, and she's made your favorite food."

"Apple pie?"

"Nope." Cal looked disgusted. "Enchiladas. I gave her the recipe and taught her how."

Dell's mouth dropped open. "You gave her a recipe? You let her cook in your kitchen?"

His uncle shrugged. "Yep. So what?"

He brushed by him and took a sport coat from the closet. "Just wondering if you were feeling all right, that's all. Guess you're getting soft in your old age."

"She's a nice little gal. Mebbee I was wrong about her. About women. Mebbee you should sweet-talk her into stayin' around here, be on your best behavior tonight, dance real nice."

Dell shook his head. "I feel like I'm going to my own funeral."

"What the hell are you talkin' about? You're goin' to the supper dance with the prettiest gal in Wyoming. You'd better perk up, soon."

"People are going to wonder what she sees in me."

"You always were sensitive about your looks." Cal shook his head. "You've grown into that nose, and all that weight on you is pretty much muscle. It ain't as bad as you think. And the little gal seems to like you."

Dell closed his eyes against the vision of a naked Allison sliding on top of him. Yes, she seemed to like him, but there was a world of men out there. He opened his eyes and forced himself to face reality. "She could have her pick of any man in Wyoming, and you and I both know it."

Calvin winked at him. "But it looks like she's picked you, son. If I were you I'd quit bellyachin' and start enjoyin' life. You ain't the prettiest cowhand around, but you're a decent man, with a good head on your shoulders and not a mean bone in your body. That little gal should thank her lucky stars you came along when you did."

"You're not kidding me, are you?"

"Not about this," Calvin said, his voice solemn. He fiddled with his hearing aid. "Sure glad I got to wearin' this contraption. I kinda like this baby-sittin' job."

"They're a handful. Is Cussy coming over to help?"

"Yeah. We're gonna watch the fights and I'm gonna stick him with changin' diapers."

Dell shoved his wallet into his back pocket and took a deep breath. "I guess we're ready then."

"Yep." Cal gave him a pat on the back that threatened to shove him out into the hall. "You go on now, and show that little gal a good time."

"DANCE?" Dell asked, standing and taking her hand in his.

Allison smiled. She'd been hoping he'd quit looking nervous every time the band played a slow song. "Sure."

He led her from their table and onto the dance floor, the center of the community center where a large crowd of people of all ages were dancing. He took her into his arms and managed a respectable two-step around the dance floor.

"Anyone looking?" he asked.

"Just Lucille. She's green with envy because I'm dancing with you and she's not." She smiled up at him. "I'm glad you're dancing."

"Yeah, until I step on your foot and cripple you for life."

"I'll take my chances."

He held her closer, and Allison pretended that she belonged here, in Wells City, Wyoming, population 8,243. She wondered what it would be like to shop for groceries and run into friends. She would like to know some other mothers and take the girls to preschool in a few years. She'd like to drive carpools and learn to bake and ride a horse as calm as Gertrude.

Everyone had been so kind tonight. The enchilada pan had been scraped clean by seven o'clock. Dell, unaware that she had made the casserole herself, had two helpings. Kelly's husband, a lean rancher with an easy smile, also went back for seconds, so Allison was pleased that she hadn't hurt Cal's reputation as a cook. She'd brought a couple of plastic bags filled with homemade rolls and delivered them to one of the ladies working behind the serving tables.

"I still can't believe how you know everyone. I've never lived in a small town like this. No wonder you don't want to leave."

"Most everyone has asked me if you're the same gal who's living with me."

"Uh-oh."

He looked down at her and chuckled as the music stopped. "You brought it on yourself, you know, by teasing Lucille the way you did."

"She deserved it." She waited for him to release her, but he only tightened his hold as the band started to play a waltz.

"I can waltz," he informed her. "It might be my one and only accomplishment."

She gave him a wicked smile. "I think you have a few others." When he winked at her, she blushed. The couple beside them laughed.

"Lady, are you flirting with me?"

"I'm allowed. After all, I'm your date, aren't I?"

"Yes," he murmured, holding her tighter. "You sure as hell are."

Allison liked his reaction. They danced in silence, and every once in a while Allison could hear Dell counting under his breath. When the music ended, he released her, touching her back to guide her back to the table.

"Speak of the devil," he said.

"Who?" She couldn't see through the crowd.

"Your favorite waitress. Be nice."

"I'll be nice as long as she's nice to you."

He gave her a warning look, but his dark eyes twinkled. "Don't start trying to kiss me. I'm not going to fall for that one again."

His hand tightened around hers and Allison chuckled as they neared the table. Lucille, in a bright green Western shirt, looked up from her conversation with Kelly's husband and smiled.

"Hey, there," the redhead drawled. "You through dancin', Dell? I didn't know you had it in you."

"Allison's been giving me lessons." Dell pulled out a chair and Allison sat down on the other side of Jack Beatrice. She planned to stay as far away from Lucille as possible. If Dell wanted to dance with her, he was welcome to and she wouldn't do anything to embarrass him. After all, now that he was becoming more social, he might meet someone he'd like to date. Allison decided she wouldn't think about that. The big rancher sat down and Jack handed him an unopened bottle of beer and Allison retrieved her plastic cup half-filled with white wine, from the center of the table.

"Where's Kelly?"

"Calling home to check on the kids," her husband said, stifling a yawn. "We've become old fogies now."

Dell turned to Lucille. "You want a drink, Lucille?"

"Pete's bringing me one, thanks." She turned to Allison. "He has some good news for you."

"About my car?"

Dell nodded at the group of people still dancing. "Good turnout this year. How much money do you think it made?"

"Plenty," Jack said. "More than last year, I'll bet. How'd you make out this spring? Never saw such weather."

Allison leaned forward. "Lucille, do you think Pete fixed my car?"

"He can tell you himself. He's coming round the dance floor right now." She scooted her chair closer to Allison. "I know you and me got off on the wrong foot, honey. I just want you to know I never meant no harm. Dell's a good man and I wouldn't have minded hooking up with him, but he was never interested."

"And Pete is?" The women shared a smile.

"Oh, he sure is. I thought he was too young for me, but I've decided I like his...energy. Come by the diner sometime and I'll buy you a cup of coffee."

"Thanks. I'd like that."

"Here, honey," Pete said, setting a drink in front of Lucille. He hooked a chair rung with his foot and moved it into place beside his date. "Hey, there, everybody. Dell. Jack. Allison." He nodded at each one in turn. "How y'all doing tonight?"

Allison said hello, but didn't ask about her car. She decided she didn't want to know if the Probe was ready. She wanted to pretend that she was part of Dell's life for just a while longer. She couldn't stay unless he asked her to stay and there was no way to tell if the man was serious or not. But she knew that men didn't want to raise babies—sometimes not even when they were their own—and she didn't expect Dell to want them, either. It was a hard lesson, but she'd learned it well.

The band finished the song and announced that they were taking a break, so the noise level subsided enough that no one had to holler across the table.

"Tell Allison about her car," Lucille said, nudging Pete with her elbow.

Pete glanced at Dell and gulped. He turned to Lucille and put his arm around the back of her chair. "Not much to tell, honey. Besides, I don't feel much like talking business at a dance."

"Since when? You just told Jim McGregor you'd have to order him some new shocks for that old truck."

"That's okay," Allison said quickly. "We don't have to talk about it right now." She scooted her chair over to make room for Kelly, who returned to the table and greeted everyone.

Dell cleared his throat. "So you got that axle rebuilt?"

"Yeah. Came in yesterday. Everything should be set by Monday afternoon."

'Thank you," Allison said, wishing she meant it. She didn't dare ask how much the repair was going to cost and besides, she didn't want to know. She didn't care if she never saw the car again. She wanted to go back to the home that wasn't her home and feed the babies who weren't her babies, crawl into the bed that wasn't her bed next to the man who wasn't really her man at all.

Allison took a sip of her wine and felt completely, one hundred percent pathetic.

NO ONE HAD LAUGHED at least not to his face. A couple of ranchers from north of town told him they were glad to see him finally getting out. One of their wives said that Allison looked like a nice young woman and wasn't it wonderful of her to take in her sister's children like that.

Obviously, word traveled fast.

He glanced over at Allison as he drove the miles back to the ranch. She had her head back against the seat and he couldn't tell if her eyes were closed or not. The radio played an old Vince Gill ballad, one of those sad songs about lost love. Hell, he'd be singing those tunes himself in a few days.

Allison would bundle up those girls and leave. Unless he did something to stop her, of course. And then she'd politely turn him down and they'd both be embarrassed. A woman like Allison didn't belong on the Lazy J.

"Dell?" Her voice was soft in the darkness.

"I thought you were asleep."

"No. Just thinking."

He waited for her to continue since she sounded like she had something on her mind, but she didn't say anything. "Thinking about what?" he asked after another mile passed.

"About the car being ready."

She would be anxious to get going. She would want to be on her way to Seattle and her fancy life. "I'll pick it up for you on Monday."

There was a silence. "Thank you," she said, and that was all she said until they pulled up in front of the house. They walked in quietly, through the back door, to find Calvin sprawled on the couch and snoring like an old bear. Allison went right to the babies' room and came back to whisper that they were still asleep. Dell saw from the kitchen clock that it was after midnight already.

"I guess I'd better leave Cal on the couch," Dell said.

"I hope the girls didn't wear him out too much."

"Don't worry about it," he said, following her to the hall.

"He's like a mother hen with her chicks. I never would have guessed."

"Me, either." She paused before walking down the hall. "That was a really nice evening. Allison hesitated in the hall. "I guess I'd better get to bed."

"Yeah. Me, too." He stood looking at her and trying to memorize the way she looked in the dim light. She was all shadows and golden hair. He couldn't tell if she smiled when she said good-night, but he stepped toward her anyway. She came into his arms and he bent his head to touch his lips to hers. He didn't intend to kiss her with anything but a casual good-night, but he couldn't help but kiss her with all the passion and longing that was in his heart, as if he could tell her that he loved her with only one kiss in only one moment.

It would have to be enough, he thought, releasing her. There was no question of making love to her tonight, not with Calvin on the couch and no telling when the children would wake and need their mother. It was better that it ended now, before he got in so deep he couldn't get out. Before he drowned from the pain of losing her.

Unless, he thought, going into his empty bedroom and shutting the door behind him. Unless there was a way to convince her to stay. A way that would give them all what they needed.

12

"WHAT'S GOIN' ON, Cal?" Cussy, his horse trailing behind him, stopped the older man as he came out of the main barn. "Heard the boss has gone to town to get the little gal's car."

"Yep." Cal sighed. "He took Rob with him to drive the truck back."

"We've all got money ridin' on this one." Cussy shook his head. "Dell didn't look too good this mornin'. He didn't say two damn words to anyone, 'cept to tell Rob to meet him out front after lunch."

"We might as well get used to it. When Miz Allison and those babies leave the ranch, Dell could turn mean."

"Rob's gonna be out fifty bucks. And you and I are gonna be the big winners," Cussy drawled, but he didn't look any happier about it than Calvin felt. "From the looks of things, looks like we'll be the only ones... Shoot, Cal. That little gal shouldn't leave. Can't you do anything to stop it?"

Lord knows he would if he could. "Dell's the only one who can ask her to stay, and don't you think that boy has too much pride. He's sure she'd turn him down. You know how he is."

Cussy sighed. They all knew how Dell was. Stubborn. And no lady-killer, that's for sure. "The poor boy never could figure out how to sweet-talk a woman."

"Nobody's talkin' to anyone else this mornin'. It's a damn morgue in there." Sure, the babies smiled at him, but they didn't know what was going on. Allison had thanked him for the enchilada recipe as if he'd given her a sackful of gold. He'd been glad to see the dish come back empty. He'd be glad to teach her how to make cinnamon rolls, too.

If she'd stay.

Cussy swung himself onto his horse. "I gotta get back or the boys will figure I've gone to Cheyenne. When's she leaving?"

"In the morning. First thing, she says."

"Damn. Well, it was fun while it lasted."

"Yep. Sure was." Cal watched Cussy ride off, then he shook his head and walked back to the house to see if Allison needed any help with the girlies. It was a sorry deal when a man could win fifty dollars and feel sorrowful about it. Calvin pulled his handkerchief from his back pocket and wiped his nose.

He must be getting old.

THE PROBE returned at two-thirty, but Dell didn't. He'd taken the truck and gone on to Cheyenne, Rob explained. He gave Allison the repair bill to pay on her way out of town tomorrow, tipped his hat and hurried outside. Allison figured the sight of a teary-eyed woman scared him half out of his wits.

SHE'D SPENT the afternoon watching the girls play on her bed. She wanted to keep them out of their car seats today; they'd be in them long enough this week. So she watched them kick their chubby legs and wave their hands in the air trying to catch hold of the matching pink rattles she'd bought in Kansas City and she'd blinked back tears and told herself she must be coming down with a cold.

It wasn't one of her better days.

"I put one of them frozen chicken pot pies in the oven for

you," Calvin said at suppertime. "Takes about an hour to cook through." He picked up his hat and jammed it on his head. "Don't let it burn."

"I won't." She knew better than to ask him if he wanted to stay and share the meal with her. He liked the social life of the bunkhouse in the evening, unless there was something special that he wanted to watch on Dell's big-screen television.

"Dell will most likely be home pretty soon." Cal glanced at the clock and shoved his hands into his jeans' pockets. "It's not like him to be gone this long without tellin' anyone where he's goin'."

"He probably had business to do." That's what she'd been telling herself all day. Dell wouldn't be avoiding her, avoiding any potentially embarrassing conversations about the future, would he? He needn't have taken the trouble. She certainly wasn't going to bring up the fact that she'd fallen in love with him.

Who'd believe it? Mayme sure wouldn't. Or maybe she would, but Allison wasn't calling her again until she reached her destination. She'd left a message on Mayme's machine telling her not to encourage Ryan to drive to Seattle next week. Two months ago she'd been engaged to marry someone else, she'd helped run a successful business and she'd thought she had her life all planned. Then Sandy died, the babies came and Ryan bowed out. And now she'd fallen in love with a rancher who'd picked her up on the side of a muddy road and brought her home.

It wasn't as if he was in love with her. Oh, he'd appreciate any woman who smiled at him and treated him nice. Living the way he did, the man was a walking target.

Allison walked through the living room and on to the front porch. It had been cleaned up and Dell had had one of the men slap on a fresh coat of white paint. She shouldn't leave before selecting the furniture and finishing the project, but it was better for everyone if she left. The box marked Marianna's Toys sat, still unopened, by the door. That old shed probably contained a lot of treasures that everyone had forgotten. Allison looked toward the road, hoping to see Dell's truck heading her way. She didn't get her wish, though she waited on the porch for a long time.

Allison shivered and, taking a deep breath so she wouldn't cry, turned around and went to her room. He wasn't coming, and that was that. Besides, she had to finish packing. It was time to move on with her life.

EVERYTHING HAD GONE wrong. Everything had taken too much time. Dell drove up late to find the house dark. They would all be sleeping, getting ready for a big day of traveling tomorrow. Hell. Hell and damnation. He cursed salespeople who figured he had lots of time to kill and lines at the bank and a truck that blew a rear tire thirty miles from home.

He parked the truck next to Allison's Probe and gave the little car a fierce look. The little son of a bitch better take good care of Allison and those kids. Dell went inside through the back door and listened hard to hear if Allison was awake and feeding the babies. Nope, he'd missed her.

But she was still here. He patted his front pocket to make sure it was still there, and smiled when he felt the little circle. Yep, she was still on the Lazy J. There was still a chance to keep her here.

"ANYONE SEEN HIM?" Allison asked Cal. She poured herself a cup of coffee and looked outside at the dawn. The girls had been awake since five and were impatiently waiting to be fed.

"Nope." Sophie let out a shriek and Calvin hurried to adjust his hearing aid. "Though I sure as hell would like to have a little talk with him myself."

"Do you think he'll say goodbye?"

The old man shrugged. "I dunno. I finally figured out that I don't know anything."

"Me, too," Allison sighed. "All I know is that I've got two kids to take care of and a job waiting for me in Seattle. It's a good job, too. With benefits."

Cal nodded. "Sounds nice. I heard it rains a lot there, though. The girlies aren't going to go outside and play."

"It's not *that* rainy," she assured him. "It's a beautiful city. I went to college there."

The old man didn't look impressed. He picked up Sophie and told her to be quiet. Allison handed him a bottle and then turned to Sylvie, who opened her mouth to scream. "Stop that. You don't want to wake up Dell."

"I'll wake him up," Cal muttered, frowning. "I'd sure as hell like to know where he was yesterday."

"He must have had business in the city." *He must have been avoiding me.*

"Business." Cal shook his head. "He had business *here.*"

Allison found a paper napkin and wiped her eyes. *I'm sure it was something important, Cal. It takes a lot for Dell to leave this ranch.*

"Humph," was all the old man had to say. Allison carried Sylvie into the living room and sat in the rocking chair to feed her. She admired the way the large cupboard gleamed from the three polishings she'd given it. Even the battered coffee table looked better with a layer of polish and a good scrubbing. She'd debated about whether or not to keep it, but it was the kind of table that was accustomed to boot heels and beer bottles, wet glasses and warm plates. It belonged here.

She didn't.

HE COULD HEAR them out in the kitchen. Cal was grumbling and making more noise in the sink than was necessary. Dell almost smiled. The old man was most likely trying to wake him up without banging on the door and making it obvious. His uncle would be happy thinking he was going to have the kitchen to himself again.

Well, he could think again. Dell looked at the alarm clock by his bed. Still early. He had time to clean up and make a good impression. He took a long shower and put on a clean shirt. He made sure his hair was combed, and he waited for the nick on his chin to stop bleeding.

Thirty minutes later he stood in the kitchen doorway and said good morning. "Where are the girls?"

"They've gone back to bed," Allison said, taking a sip of her coffee before arranging empty bottles on the counter. She was already dressed and her hair was pulled back in a low ponytail. He wondered how long she'd been up. He wondered if she was packed, but then realized she would need help carrying all that stuff to the car. And if the babies were asleep, Allison couldn't put their playpen in the Probe. He still had some time.

"You're still leaving this morning?"

"Yes."

"When?"

"After the girls wake up. After I pack the car."

"I took it for a test run. Pete did a good job."

She opened a can of formula and didn't look at him. "Rob gave me the bill. I'll stop in Wells City and pay it on my way out."

'It's out of your way."

Allison shrugged. "That's all right."

Calvin muttered something under his breath, grabbed his hat and stomped out the back door.

"What's the matter with him?" Dell asked.

Allison opened another can. "I don't know. He's a little edgy this morning, I guess."

Dell poured himself a cup of coffee, but set it on the counter without tasting it. He moved a few steps closer and figured it was now or never. His heart pounded like he'd just lifted one end of a horse. He wondered if he was having a heart attack or if this was just part of dealing with women. He took a deep breath.

"Are you okay?" Allison asked. "You look a little pale."

"I could use a wife around here," Dell announced. Allison was at the counter fixing baby bottles. Some of the milk spilled and she grabbed a sponge and started wiping it up.

"I'm sure you could, she replied, not looking at him. "It's not healthy to live in such an isolated place and be alone all the time." She snapped the plastic nipples and caps on the bottles and took them over to the refrigerator.

Dell figured he hadn't phrased that right.

"I meant you," he said, standing there as helpless as a newborn calf in a ditch. "You need a husband and I need a wife. It could work. Marriage, I mean."

Allison shut the refrigerator door and turned to face him. "What are you saying, Dell?"

He stood his ground. "I'm asking you to marry me."

Those blue eyes blinked. "Because you need a wife?"

He nodded. Thank goodness she understood. "Yep."

"And you think I need a husband."

"You do," he agreed. "You need someone to take care of you and those babies."

She looked at him as if she was waiting for him to say something else.

"You need *me*," he explained. "And you know it."

"I see."

"It could work." He didn't tell her how much he loved

her. He didn't want to scare her off. "It's worked so far, hasn't it?"

Allison didn't answer his question, but instead asked one of her own. "Why do you want me to marry you, Dell?"

Because I love you so much that the thought of losing you makes me want to throw myself in front of a herd of stampeding horses. "A lot of reasons. Those girls need a father. You need a husband. I hate to see you taking off all by yourself. It's a long way to Seattle."

"I'll be all right. I have a job waiting for me when I get there." Her voice was quiet.

"You and the girls could have a good home here," he countered. "You'd never have to worry about anything, 'cept maybe the weather. I wouldn't mind having a son or two, but it's okay, too, if it's just the girls."

She didn't say anything, but her face had gone pale.

Dell took a swallow of hot coffee and hoped he hadn't scared her. "Think it over."

"I don't have to." He noticed her hands shook as she reached for the sponge and wiped the already clean counter. "I can't stay," she said. "Not like that."

His heart grew cold in his chest. "Well, hell, I guess I should've known better than to bring it up."

"You just feel sorry for me," she said.

Dell found he couldn't speak. He'd counted on her staying. He'd counted on her seeing the practical reasons why it would be for the best. He hadn't thought she'd say no just like that.

He walked by her and took his hat off the peg. It took every ounce of self-control he had not to gather her in his arms and carry her off to bed. He wanted to make love to her until she agreed to stay. Until she smiled and kissed him and told him to put the Probe in one of the sheds because she wouldn't be needing it right away.

Instead Dell kept walking, through the storeroom and out the back door. He'd made her a fair proposal. He'd done all he could do. Saying anything about love would just be making himself look like a fool.

ALLISON STOOD at the counter and watched out the window as Dell hunched his shoulders against the wind and strode toward the large bunkhouse. He'd left her alone in the kitchen. He hadn't told her he loved her or taken her in his arms. She gave him credit for not being a hypocrite.

She watched until he disappeared from her sight, until the tears that she refused to shed blurred her vision. He didn't love her. Oh, he needed her. Just like Ryan needed her to help run the business. Well, she'd told him no and she told Dell the same thing. Wendell Jones needed a wife. Any woman would do. He hadn't come down from his ranch to go search for one, but having a woman come right into the ranch made the job easy.

Damn the man.

She loved him. And if she married him she'd love him even more. She'd fix up the ranch and the bunkhouses and she'd have a few more children and she'd learn how to ride a horse faster than a trot. She'd be happy to stop decorating other people's houses and concentrate on her own. She wanted to bake cupcakes for birthday parties and talk about babies with the other young mothers in town. She wanted to be in love with her husband, and she wanted to be loved by him so much that when he smiled at her she'd known she was the most important person in his life.

She couldn't settle for anything less. Allison turned from the window and wiped her eyes on a paper napkin. It was time to leave.

SHE WAS LEAVING, but he'd be damned if he was going to make it easy for her. Cussy and Jed were still around, so they were given the job of carrying Allison's belongings to the car. Calvin banged pots and pans in the kitchen and gave Dell dirty looks whenever he got the chance. Like it was his fault Allison and the girlies were leaving.

Allison's eyes were rimmed with red, but she talked with Calvin about the days of traveling ahead. Dell hung back, afraid to open his mouth and say the wrong thing. And yet, things couldn't get much worse.

Until Allison hesitated on the front porch and pointed to the unopened box that had belonged to his grandmother. "Don't you want to know what's inside?"

"It doesn't matter," he said, folding his arms across his chest. He had no use for toys, and never would. Allison turned away and hurried outside for yet another trip to check the car while Dell stood on the porch and felt completely helpless. He wanted to put his fist through the freshly painted wall. On the next trip, she carried the babies, and this time Dell's heart rose to his throat and threatened to choke him. He didn't dare touch them or say a word.

When the Probe was loaded, the babies fastened in their car seats and the cooler filled with the baby bottles, he thought saying goodbye to the girls would kill him, but he managed to stay upright as the pain radiated through his body.

'Thank you," she said. "For everything." She gave him a quick hug, but moved away before he could make his frozen arms wrap around her. Allison kissed Cal on the cheek.

"I've got copies of all your best recipes," she said. "Thanks for sharing."

"Just do 'em justice," he growled. "Though you might want to go easy on the hot sauce when the girlies are old enough to eat my food."

"I will," she promised. She turned to Jed and Cussy, who removed their hats and accepted her thanks for all of their help. Then, with car keys in hand, she stepped toward Dell, raised up on her toes and kissed him briefly on the lips. He got a quick glimpse of tears before she slid behind the steering wheel and shut the door. The engine roared to life, the men stepped out of the way so she could back the car up and head down the drive.

Cussy and Cal took out handkerchiefs and blew their noses loudly. Jed gulped as he glanced at Dell and turned away.

"Doesn't anyone have work to do around here?" Dell roared.

"Hell, yes," Cussy said, backing up. He grabbed the younger man's arm and hurried him out of the line of fire. Dell stomped back into the house, with his uncle close behind.

He hesitated on the porch and turned to watch the cloud of dust behind the Probe. She was driving slowly, but the car was heading in a direct line to the main road.

"What're you bawling for? I thought you didn't want a woman around here."

Cal sniffed. "I could've been a grandpa. I could've been, too, if you had asked that woman to stay."

"I asked her to stay," Dell muttered.

"Well, you musta messed it up then," the old cowboy grumped. He wiped his eyes and kicked the unopened box out of his way. "Open the goddamn thing or let me put it back in the shed."

"Got no use for toys," Dell snapped. He watched the little car continue slowly on its way out of his life as Cal took out his pocketknife and slit through the tape holding the box together. "Never will."

Cal unwrapped a wad of newspaper. "Why, it's two little

wooden animals. Sheep, I think." He reached in and continued to unwrap sets of animals, and lined them up two-by-two under the window. He pulled out a large wooden boat and showed it to Dell. "I think it's s'posed to be Noah's ark. The girlies would love it, when they get a little older."

Dell barely glanced at the wooden figures. The car had slowed down. It may even have stopped, but he couldn't tell. "Put the damn things away," he said. "Where the hell are the binoculars?"

"Hangin' on that nail over there," Cal said. "Two by two," he muttered, struggling to his feet. "Just the way it should be. Not right for a woman to go off alone into the world when there's a man who—"

"Cal, shut up and take a look at this." He handed his uncle the binoculars. "What do you see?"

Calvin adjusted the binoculars and squinted. "She's gone off the road."

"That woman can't drive for beans," Dell declared, a smile crossing his face. "She's stuck."

The older man handed him the binoculars. "So what in hell are you going to do about it? Bring down the tractor and pull her out and send her on her way again?"

"She wouldn't stay. I asked."

"Did you sweet-talk her a little?"

Dell hedged. "I offered her a home."

"Did you tell her you loved her?" Cal shouted. "I'll bet a hundred dollars you kept your mouth shut and that pride of yours right safe, didn't you, son?"

"She couldn't love me. Nothing could be that good."

"Why the hell not?"

He picked up the binoculars again. The car wasn't moving. "Why the hell would she?"

"She didn't care about that face of yours. I think she kinda liked it, myself. That little lady thought you walked on water," Cal declared. "Why, those blue eyes would shine when you came inside for supper and she'd watch you out the window when we was cookin'. I may be deaf, but I'm sure as hell not blind. That woman loves you."

Dell fought the surge of hope that took his heart from his throat and settled it back where it belonged. "She never said anything."

"Why should she? She's been hurt bad. Prob'ly has as much foolish pride as you do." Cal sighed and shook his head. "Young fools." He pointed toward the road. "She's about a mile and a half away. What're you gonna do?"

He readjusted his hat and pushed the door open. "Why, hell, Calvin. I'm going to find out what the lady wants."

ALLISON KNEW she should get out of the car to see what had happened. One minute she'd been speeding down the gravel road and the next thing she knew she'd wished she'd been going slower. The car had shimmied and slid on the dirt, then pitched into a low ditch. She didn't want to get out and see what she had done. Not yet. Not until she'd found a tissue and wiped her nose.

Not until she stopped crying.

The babies had protested at the bumps and now screamed their discontent with life in the back seat of the Probe. Allison didn't try to calm them with soothing words. She felt like screaming, too. She wanted to kick her feet and kick the car, too, while she was kicking things. She wanted to get out of Wyoming and she couldn't even get off the ranch.

She rested her arms against the steering wheel, put her head down and sobbed until she could hardly breathe.

"Hell, Allison," a familiar voice drawled. "You don't drive any better than you ride a horse."

She didn't lift her head. She was a mess and he didn't

have to see it. "I do okay on pavement." She heard him open her car door. He bent over so close that she could smell his shaving lotion. The girls stopped crying when they heard his voice, but the pounding pain in Allison's temples continued. She hated goodbyes and she hated dirt roads.

"I thought you might have changed your mind about leaving," he said.

Changed her mind? She wanted to run back to the house and into the safety of his arms. "No."

"I thought you might have decided you need a husband after all."

"Go away, Dell."

He cleared his throat. "Truth is, Allison, I've never asked anyone to marry me before. I guess I messed it up pretty bad. I've never been in love before, either." She heard him take a deep breath and his boots crunched in the dust as he crouched to be at the same level. "Cal says I've got too much pride, and I guess he's right. So if you don't love me, just tell me. I'll get the tractor and pull you out of here and you can be on your way to wherever it is you want to go. But you should know that I'll love you till the day I die and I'll do my best to make you and those babies happy if you marry me."

Allison lifted her head and turned to look at him. Had he really said he loved her? "Why would you marry me even if I didn't love you?"

He gulped. "No, I guess I wouldn't want that, after all. I'd sure as hell want someone who loved me, but I'm willing to bet that you'd come to love me, in time."

"Yes," she said, wiping her eyes. "That would be easy enough. You're a good man, but you should marry someone who knows how to ride and cook and take care of animals."

He frowned. "Why? I have the men for those things."

Allison couldn't help smiling. "Yes, I guess you do."

"Tell me you love me," he said. "One way or the other and we'll go from there."

"Truth is," she said, touching his face with her hand. "I do love you, Wendell Jones. I'm not sure how it happened, but I know I don't want to leave."

"Then get the hell out of that car and come home," Dell said, but Allison didn't move except to put her arms around his neck and kiss him for long, wonderful moments.

"All right," she agreed, stepping out of the car. She resisted the urge to dance with joy. "Which baby do you want?"

"Makes no difference," the cowboy said. "I'll take them both, if you want."

"I guess you're taking all three of us." She paused. "Are you sure, Dell?"

He nodded. "I've got a diamond ring in my dresser drawer. A man doesn't go into a jewelry store in Cheyenne unless he's sure."

"Is that where you were yesterday?"

"Yeah." He waited for her to unbuckle the children from their seats and took Sylvie from Allison's arms. "But I made a mistake."

Allison paused, giving him a worried look. "What do you mean?"

He waved at the car tilted into the ditch. "I should've bought you a truck instead."

She laughed. "First thing, you're going to have to give me driving lessons."

"No, ma'am," Dell said, kissing her once again. "That's not the first thing we're going to do at all."

If the woman needed to

. . . into

"For all I know, he's s

. . . one has to take responsib

". . . No lecture, lady," . . .

. . . chair as the music starte

. . . bility, and now I prop th

Baby Mac's lookin' to rope himself a dad...

The Next Man in Texas

1

DON'T FALL IN LOVE with a cowboy.

The words echoed in Grace Daniels's head as she drove toward Locklin, Texas, with a sleeping baby and a carload of baby apparatus. Her neighbor Lucy had loved to give advice. She would shake her head sorrowfully, blow a perfect smoke ring and roll her blue-shadowed eyes toward the ceiling.

They'll always break your heart, honey. Just like the song says.

Well, Grace figured, that much was true. At least in Lucy's case. Lucy, a thirty-something redhead with azure eyes, had had more experience with cowboys and broken hearts than Grace could imagine in her wildest dreams. In fact, Grace didn't have wild dreams, had never loved a cowboy, and her heart was nicely insulated from aching of any kind. And she intended to stay that way, too, though at times she had envied Lucy's breezy life-style and live-for-the-moment attitude.

But living for the moment didn't fit with raising a child. Lucy had done the best she could under the circumstances. She'd lived long enough to make Grace promise to deliver little Mac to his cowboy daddy. Lucy could convince anyone to do practically anything, even a shy computer programmer who preferred plants to people.

Grace turned up the air-conditioning, made sure the vents weren't directed toward the baby and headed south on Interstate 35. The sooner she got there, the sooner she could go home. All she had to do was find someone called McLintock, give him his son, break the news about Lucy and tiptoe quietly back to her car. She wasn't good at emotional moments, but she'd do her best.

He was a real charmer, that man was. Just about broke my heart when he left, but I got over it soon enough. Hearts mend, Gracie. They always do, sooner or later.

Grace squinted against the afternoon sun. She was tired of driving. She hadn't had much sleep last night; she'd been worried about driving close to three hundred miles with a six-month-old baby, but little Mac had been as well behaved as always. He went to sleep with a smile on his chubby face and woke up that way, too. Grace yawned. She would find a nice hotel room in San Antonio and tour the Alamo in the morning before heading back to Dallas. She didn't know why she'd never taken the time to see it before.

Mac gurgled, so Grace looked over to him and smiled. "Hey there, sweetheart. You ready to meet your daddy?"

The baby smiled as if he knew what she was talking about.

"He's going to be real happy to see you," she promised. And hoped she was right.

He told me he liked the idea of having sons. Guess he should get the chance to raise this one, don't you think, Gracie?

Yes, Grace definitely thought Mr. McLintock should raise his own son. Lucy had come to the right person to agree with that particular statement. While it wasn't like her to leave home without a Triple A map and one of those thick books of hotel listings, Grace knew she had been given a mission to carry out. Mr. McLintock was about to get his baby back.

"PUT THE LITTLE son of a gun in the barn." Jack McLintock had run out of patience. "I've had just about enough for one day."

"Yes, boss." Jethro grinned and led the prancing two-year-old gelding out of the corral. "Anything you say, boss."

"Shut up, Jet."

"Yes, sir." He saluted as he walked past, and his battered hat tilted to reveal a pale forehead and a shock of dark hair.

Jack shook his head. "They're not going to know what to do with you in Nashville, you know."

"They'll learn," his brother assured him. "Don't you think?"

"Yeah," Jack said. "They'll learn, all right." He stepped back as the horse passed by him. Yesterday he'd learned that the gelding had a mean kick, and he didn't need to be reminded again.

Jethro called over his shoulder. "I'm cleaning up and going to town. You want to come? There's always a steak special at Nellie's on Friday night, then we're playing at the Stampede from nine to two."

"No, thanks. I've got—"

"Work to do," Jethro finished for him. "You work too hard."

"We all do."

"We all *did*."

"It's not over yet." Jack shrugged away the feeling that nothing was going to be the same again. They'd waited a long time for this summer to arrive. In a few weeks—exactly two weeks from today—everything would change. For the better. The relief almost made him dizzy. The anticipation was sometimes too much to bear.

"'It's All Over But the Shouting,'" Jethro said.

"Is that the name of your latest song?"

"Yep. I wrote it last night. Gonna try it out on the crowd

during the second set, before everyone's too drunk to know what they're listening to."

"Sounds like a plan."

"Hell, yes," Jet agreed. "You should come down, have a beer, hear the band. We've got some new songs."

Jack shrugged. "Yeah, maybe," he said, but he knew he wouldn't.

"Well, think about it," Jet said, moving away. He whistled as he led the horse down the road to the largest barn on the place.

Jack turned away and headed toward the house. He could taste the dust, but that was nothing new. Just part of the job. He'd been running this ranch for so long that he'd gotten so he almost liked the taste. Jack tried to whistle, but his mouth was too dry to come up with anything but a pathetic rasping sound. He didn't know how Jethro did it, but that boy could make music in the middle of a dust storm.

Isabella sat fanning herself on the back porch. "Lord, it's hot," she said. "Too hot for June."

"It's always hot in June." He pushed his hat off his forehead and leaned against one of the posts. "I smell something good."

The old woman fanned herself with her apron and shrugged. "I would cook you something that smelled bad?"

Jack smiled at the familiar question. "No, Bella, in twenty years you have never cooked anything that smelled bad. 'Cept for that time you burned the—"

"Oh, hush your teasing."

"What are you going to do when you retire, Bella?"

The old woman gave him a dark look. "I don't like that word. And I'm not going to discuss it with a dirty, sweaty cowboy."

He bent over and brushed some of the dust from his jeans. "Better?"

She nodded. "You've got company. In the living room."

"Who?"

Isabella smiled. Jack figured she was seventy, easy. Maybe closer to eighty. "I don't know. I'm just an old cook who burns things."

Jack sighed and walked past her. "You and Jet are in good moods today. The two of you could get more work done if you weren't looking for ways to tease people all the time."

She muttered something, but didn't leave her seat on the porch. Jack went into the kitchen and peered into the pot on the stove. Ah. His favorite. Next to the oven, a stack of freshly made tortillas sat under a cotton cloth. He turned away from the food and walked down the hall to the large room that ran the length of the house. He stopped when he reached the doorway and saw a slim young woman standing in front of the fireplace. She was looking at the framed photographs that lined the wooden mantel, but when his boots clicked on the tiled floor, she turned around.

"Hello," he said, removing his hat. "What can I do for you, miss?" Gray eyes studied him. She didn't smile at first, but then a rose-tinted pair of lips turned upward and she moved forward, holding out her hand. He didn't recognize her, and wondered if he should. She could be one of Old Bill's lawyers, but he knew he hadn't seen her before. He would have remembered.

"Hi. I'm Grace Daniels."

Not a lawyer, or she would have said so. He took her hand as gently as he could and released it quickly. He didn't want to get her dirty. "Jack McLintock."

She nodded. "Yes, that's what I thought."

"You did?"

"Absolutely. I'm sorry to come here with no warning, but I tried to call from Locklin. The line was busy."

"Isabella takes it off the hook when she's fixing dinner."

Her expression clouded. "Oh. Your wife. I hadn't thought of that."

"Hadn't thought of what?" He ignored the mention of a wife and gestured at the brown leather couch. "Would you like to sit down?" He hoped she would. The woman, this Grace Daniels, had a fragile look about her. Maybe it was the flowered sundress, or the way her chestnut hair brushed her bare shoulders, or the white sandals that encased her tiny feet. She was pale and slender, the kind of woman who didn't spend much time outdoors and made a man feel hot and sweaty just to look at her.

"I'm sorry," she said again. "I'm just realizing how complicated this could be, and I can't believe I didn't think of it sooner."

"Complicated?" He could think of other words to describe having a beautiful stranger sitting in his living room on a Friday evening.

She waved her hand toward the overstuffed chair that sat by the window. "This is Mac. I brought him as soon as I could."

Jack's gaze dropped to the floor, where a chubby baby sat nestled in one of those thick plastic car seats. His eyes were closed, and his head was tilted at an angle that looked anything but comfortable.

"Mac looks tired" was the only thing he could think to say. Maybe Grace was one of Jet's friends, though she didn't look like the type to hang out in cowboy bars.

"We've come from Dallas today," she explained. "I thought it was best that I bring him to you right away. Before I got too attached to him."

"Excuse me," he said, moving toward the couch again.

He waited for her to sit down before he sat in the rocking chair across from her. "You're saying you brought this baby here? Why?"

"Lucy Bagwell passed away three days ago. Of cancer." She cleared her throat and hesitated, almost as if she expected him to say something. "Before she died she asked me to make sure that Mac got to his father. She didn't want him to end up in foster care."

He waited for her to continue, but she just looked at him. "And?" he prompted.

"Lucy Bagwell. You don't remember her?"

"I'm sorry, but I don't think I know anyone named Bagwell. Maybe you have the wrong place. Or the wrong man."

"No, I don't think so. I looked in the phone book and yours was the only McLintock listed." She flushed. "I'm really afraid I've done this the wrong way, but hiring a lawyer seemed so cold and impersonal, and I wanted to see for myself that Mac would be all right with his father."

Jack leaned forward. He dreaded the answer to his next question, but it had to be asked. And answered. "And exactly who on this ranch is supposed to be his father?"

"You, of course."

He couldn't say anything for long seconds. Then he drew in a deep breath and prayed for patience. "Lady, you're barking up the wrong tree."

"You're saying you didn't *know* about him?"

"If I were a father, I'd think I'd know it."

Grace gulped and reached for a large tote bag. She reached in and pulled out a piece of paper, then leaned forward to hand it to him. "All this time I thought you knew. Here, I think this explains it," she said, her voice soft. "It's Mac's birth certificate."

Jack took the paper and examined it. *Mother: Lucy Ann*

Bagwell, birth date April 23, 1961. Place of birth: Dallas, Texas. Father: J. McLintock. Place of birth: Locklin, Texas. No birth date for the father, which sure as hell complicated things. He didn't know if this was a fraud or not. He didn't know which brother to tar and feather. "Are you sure about this?"

"As sure as I can be. It's the only record I have. Lucy didn't leave much else."

He held it up to the light. Sure enough, the damn thing had a seal pressed in the corner. Though, that didn't make the information on it 100 per cent accurate, either. "Mind if I make a copy?"

"No, of course not."

Jack stood up. He was going to make several copies and present them to each of his brothers before daybreak tomorrow. "I'll be right back. I have a copy machine in the office."

Grace stood, too. "Do you mind if I come with you? That's an original."

"Of course not." He didn't blame her for being careful, but he had no intention of destroying the damn thing and making a bad situation worse. She bent over and picked up the sleeping baby, plastic seat and all, and followed him down the hall to the office.

"It'll take a minute to warm up," he said, switching the button on. He took the baby, seat and all, from her and sat him on top of the papers on his desk. "How old is he?"

"Almost six months."

Add nine months to that, turn the clock back fifteen months, and see where the boys were. Should be simple to find out what was going on a year ago last March. That is, if one of them was involved. It was hard to imagine any of the boys being so careless. Damn it, he'd lectured them often enough. Jack examined the birth certificate again, this time looking for where and when the boy was born.

Mac started to cry, and the woman had him out of the seat and into her arms within seconds—she obviously cared for the boy. Jack turned away from them and made his copies. He handed her the original. "I'll look into this," he said, motioning for her to precede him into the hall. "Why is he crying like that?"

"He must be hungry."

"Do you, ah, have something to give him?"

"I have bottles in the cooler in my car. I also brought his fold-up bed and high chair, plus two boxes of clothes. Would you take him, please, so I can get him something to eat?"

He didn't want to take the child, but before Jack could protest, Mac was thrust into his arms. Twenty pounds of sobbing baby didn't faze Jack. He'd changed more diapers than he could count. He adjusted his grip on the boy. "Hey, kid, go easy on my eardrums."

Mac hiccuped and stared up at the stranger. Two tears ran down his red cheeks, but he stopped screaming.

"Thanks," Jack told him. "It's the end of a long week, and I could use a break, all right? You're going to have your dinner, and pretty soon I'm going to have my dinner." *Then in the morning I'll find your father and figure out what to do about you.* Jack walked over to the window and watched as the woman fumbled in the back seat of the Ford Taurus sedan. She didn't seem like the type to run off and leave the kid, but it wouldn't hurt to keep an eye on her, just in case.

She might be telling the truth. Or she might not. He wasn't going to take any chances. Locklin was a small town. People talked. And he was sure not going to give anyone anything more to say about the McLintock family.

GRACE HURRIED TO THE CAR and retrieved a bottle and a blanket. The inside of the ranch house had been air-conditioned. She didn't want Mac to catch cold. Meeting Mac's handsome father had been an experience, especially since the man seemed sincere when he'd said he didn't even know he had a son. What on earth had Lucy been thinking, if she hadn't told the father that he *was* a father? And the fact that he was married had been another surprise, but maybe Isabella would fall in love with Mac and want to keep him.

And maybe Santa would put diamonds in her stocking this year, too.

She arrived back in the living room to find Mac comfortable and quiet against the rancher's wide chest. Yes, Lucy hadn't exaggerated. From his dusty boots to those chiseled cheekbones, the McLintock man was clearly the kind of cowboy that would make a woman like Lucy salivate.

"He settled right down," the man said.

"Mac's probably happy to be out of that seat." Grace lifted her gaze to Mr. McLintock's chin. Sure enough, there was a cleft there. Mac had it already. In fact, they had the same dark brown hair, the same questioning expression in their dark eyes as they looked at her.   "What's wrong?" the man asked.

"Nothing." She attempted a smile. "I need to heat this bottle."

"Follow me."

He led her out of the room, past an enormous dining room filled with thick pine furniture and down a hall to a bright kitchen. Life wasn't fair sometimes, which wasn't exactly a revelation. She hadn't wanted to get involved in this situation. She knew she could have called the state authorities and let them handle this, but she couldn't risk Mac being put in foster care. Early this morning she had spent an anxious hour drinking a pot of coffee and wrestling with her conscience. Her conscience had won. She had promised Lucy to deliver Mac to his father and that is what she would do. Had done.

If Mr. McLintock refused to raise his own son, he would have a fight on his hands. Mac deserved to have a father. His *own* father.

"Isabella," the rancher called. An old woman, her gray hair hanging in a braid, stood by the stove stirring something in a steaming pot. The woman turned and stared at the baby in his arms.

"Ah," she sighed, reaching one bony finger to touch the child's chin. "Another McLintock. Whose?"

"I don't know," McLintock muttered. "This is Grace Daniels. She has quite a story to tell." He didn't smile. "Grace, come meet Isabella Moniz. She runs things around here and also makes fifty-eight different kinds of chili."

"Fifty-nine," the woman said. She smiled at Grace but didn't move from the stove. "You are staying for supper, miss?"

"No, but thank you for the invitation." So Isabella wasn't the wife, after all. Grace knew she had to stop jumping to conclusions. "Can I put this bottle in some hot water, please?" Mac whimpered and squirmed when she held up the bottle, but Mr. McLintock didn't seem to be the least uncomfortable holding him.

"Sure," he said, moving out of the way so she could reach the sink.

"A pot," the woman said, placing one battered pot in the sink. Grace filled it with water and put the bottle inside to warm.

"Where are you going?"

"Back to Dallas."

"Tonight?"

"No. I'm going to San Antonio tonight. I always wanted to see the Al—"

"With or without this child?"

"Without." Her gaze dropped to Mac, who gave her that *where's my supper* look. She ignored the pang in her heart and turned back to the bottle. It would be warm enough by now. She sprinkled a few drops on her wrist just to make sure. "I've done what I promised to do."

He put the baby in her arms while Isabella watched with undisguised interest. "No, lady, I don't think you have."

"Meaning?" Grace didn't wait for an invitation to sit down. There were several pine chairs arranged around a long trestle table, so she sat in one and gave Mac his bottle. The rancher took a chair and placed it across from her, then sat down.

"Meaning, I'm not the boy's father."

"You want dinner now?" Isabella called.

"No. Not yet. Not till I get this straightened out."

"Hah," the cook snorted. "You'll have to wait a long time for *that*. That boy has the chin, he does. And there's no telling where he got it, either." She shook her head as she looked at Mac, then she went outside through the back door.

Grace was hot and tired and thirsty, and she had to go to the bathroom. She wished she had stayed in Dallas. She wished Lucy was still around to tell stories and give her advice that she would never need to use. Mac drank with noisy slurps, then she sat him on her lap and awkwardly burped him.

"What do you want?" the man asked.

"I want what's best for Mac. I promised to bring him to his father." She studied the man's expression. He was handsome, with those dark eyes and short brownish black hair. Jack McLintock looked the part of a Texas rancher, all right. He was covered in dust, dirt streaked one side of his face, and his jaw was square and set in an uncompromising position. *That boy has the chin,* the old woman had said.

He sure did.

"Are you his father?" It was a simple question. Grace assumed he'd tell the truth.

"No."

"Are there any other McLintocks I could talk to about this?"

"I'll take care of that," he said.

"I can't leave him until I know he's going to be all right. I have to contact Lucy's lawyer when I get back and—"

"Lady, you're not going anywhere. Not until this is straightened out."

"I really can't do that."

"You don't have any choice. I'm not the baby's father, so you haven't delivered him to the father. Right?"

"How do I know you're telling the truth?"

He smiled grimly. "You don't. But you and I know you can't leave this child with strangers. You drive out of here and I call Children's Services and have that boy put in their custody until we get to the bottom of this."

"You would do that?"

He leaned forward. "I'm sure as hell not going to babysit someone else's kid while a woman I've never seen blackmails me into taking responsibility for him."

"He's not yours?"

"The McLintocks aren't known to be family men. You've walked into the wrong place."

Grace's arms tightened around the child. She had done her best. She could take Mac and go home now. And she would do her best to make sure that little Mac grew up safe and happy and healthy. "Okay," she agreed. "I'll have my lawyer call you if there are any problems with the adoption process."

His eyes narrowed. "Adoption process?"

"Yes." She put Mac up to her shoulder and stood. "If you don't want him, I'll find a nice childless couple who does."

"I didn't say I didn't want him. I said I wasn't his father." He stood, too, and looked down at her as he put his hands on his hips. "I'm not a liar, and I never heard of Lucy Bagwell, but I intend to find out who's going around writing 'McLintock' on birth certificates."

"If you're not his father, you can't—"

McLintock smiled, as if amused by her innocence. "Lady, there are other McLintocks here. You're staying and Mac is staying until we figure out what the hell is going on."

"*Other* McLintocks?" Oh, heavens. What on earth had she gotten herself into?

"Yeah."

Grace pretended that she was still in control of the situation. "Can I talk to them, please?"

"You'll meet them all soon enough, but for right now, this little problem stays between us. I don't want everyone in town talking about the McLintock bastard."

Grace gulped. "I'm sure I don't want that, either, Mr. McLintock."

"Jack," he corrected her. "Call me Jack. I don't want you talking this with the boys, either. That's my job. From now on you're a distant cousin of my mother's from Dallas who's here for the party. Mac here is your son. You've just gotten a divorce."

"I have?"

"Yeah. If anyone asks, just say that Jess McLintock was your mother's third cousin."

"Who's that?"

"My mother."

"She won't mind?"

"She's dead," he said, and the tiniest shadow of pain crossed his face.

"I'm sorry."

He shrugged. "It happened a long time ago. Now, people won't be coming here for the party yet, but as far as my brothers are concerned—"

"A party?" Grace wished she could retrace her steps, reconsider this morning's decision and fade quietly back into the woodwork.

"My youngest brother is turning twenty-one in a couple of weeks. We're having a big shindig to celebrate."

Brothers. She hadn't thought of that, either. Grace sighed. She had been spending too much time at her computer and not enough time in the real world. There could have been a wife, but thank goodness there wasn't. There could have been other McLintocks, and there were. Brothers. Jack McLintock could be lying about not fathering a child or he could be telling the truth, but she really had no choice but to go along with this. For Mac's sake, anyway. If he had a father here on the ranch, then he should have the chance to be seen by him.

Grace squared her shoulders. "How many brothers?"

"Three."

She had a sinking feeling in her chest. "And their names?"

He leveled that steady gaze on her. "Jethro, Jimmy-Joe and Jason," the McLintock man drawled. "Not going to be as easy as you thought, is it."

"What about cousins, uncles, brothers-in-law?"

Jack McLintock shook his head. "Nope. It's the four of us. We're the last of the line."

"Not exactly."

His eyebrows rose. "Maybe. All you have is a baby and a birth certificate."

"And that baby has the McLintock chin. Anyone can see the resemblance."

"We'll see," he said. "Let me show you to a room."

"I could stay in town," she offered, not comfortable with the idea of staying in a stranger's house.

"No way. The less you and Mac are seen in town, the better. I don't want any of this to get out and spoil Jason's party. He just graduated from college. With honors. And a chance to study in England."

"Really? That's impressive."

"He's the smartest McLintock I've ever seen. Takes after my mother. She liked to read, too. When she had the time."

Before Grace could ask him anything else, he led her down a hall into a separate wing of the house and into a bright corner room on the first floor. The floor was tiled and dotted with faded rag rugs. There was a single bed covered with a bright blue cotton spread, a pine chest of drawers and a ladder-backed chair.

"I'll bring in the baby's things from your car," McLintock said. "Do you think you'll need anything else?"

She needed a glass of wine and a few days' vacation, but she'd settle for a washcloth and a chance to change Mac's diaper. "Can you tell me where the bathroom is?"

"Down the hall, the second door on your right. Ask Isabella to get you anything you need." He glanced at Mac, who rested his head on Grace's shoulder and stared at the cowboy with big brown eyes.

"Just Mac's bed for now, thank you."

He nodded. "I'll be right back." And he left her there, holding the baby and gazing out the window into an enormous courtyard. *Courtyard?* Grace stepped closer to the window, which she noticed was actually a narrow door that led outside. A wheelbarrow stood in the middle, as if someone had been weeding or digging. Pots of flowers sat to one side as if they were waiting to be planted. The house was a Spanish design; the walls were adobe and appeared old. It was the kind of home she'd dreamed of as a child, the kind in magazines where beautiful mothers and handsome fathers smiled at each other and their sweet-looking children. It was the kind of place she'd longed to belong to, but that had never happened, and never would.

"How about that?" she asked the baby. "You might be living in a real hacienda." Mac's head lay heavy on her shoulder, and he seemed content to be held. His little legs were relaxed, and one hand played with her hair. "Your name will be Mac McLintock. You'll have a daddy and maybe your own horse. Won't that be nice?"

Grace wished Mac could talk and agree with her so she would feel better about leaving him. There was nothing to stop her from leaving and taking the child with her. Nothing but a birth certificate, a promise to Lucy and a very large cowboy. He could call the sheriff, could accuse her of kidnapping. He might not want a scandal, but he wanted the truth.

She would stay for tomorrow, until she found Mac's father. She wasn't leaving until she'd done what she'd promised Lucy. Little Mac was going to have a family.

2

"WHERE'S JET?"

One of the men looked up from his supper. "Gone to town, I guess. He's playin' at the Stampede tonight. You goin'?"

"No." Jack hid his disappointment. "I just thought I'd catch him before he left."

"Aw, he was outta here like a streak of greased lightnin'. He always moves fast on Fridays."

"Yeah, well, I'll catch up with him tomorrow, then." Jack backed out of the bunkhouse and left the men to their supper. They'd be heading to town as soon as they cleaned up. Friday night in Locklin was almost as good as Saturday night in Locklin.

No way was he spending all weekend trying to figure out this mess. No way was he getting stuck with a baby at this time of his life. Hell, he'd raised enough boys. He would have to talk to all three of them, though, just to make sure. Jimmy-Joe had taken off early, and Jason was late getting his college-educated ass home.

And he was left dealing with the Dallas woman and the McLintock baby. *"Hell,"* Jack swore out loud. He was already thinking of little Mac as a McLintock. Surely there were other babies with brown eyes and an unmistakable cleft in their chins. He walked back to the house and tried to convince himself that there were worse things in the world that could happen now. If that little boy was Jet's, then he could damn well support the child. He would be able to do that, at least financially, in two weeks.

He wondered if Grace Daniels knew about the Mc-Lintock trust fund. Or if Lucy Bagwell knew she was sending her baby to a family who would now be able to afford to feed one more.

Well, he wasn't going to sit around all night worrying about it. He knew exactly where Jet was going to be at nine o'clock tonight. As much as he hated hanging out at the Stampede, he was going to get this mess straightened out as soon as possible. Before people started to talk.

"Supper," Isabella said. She stood in the doorway to Grace's room. "Come. It's ready."

Grace hesitated. Mac was sleeping peacefully, his thumb tucked in his mouth and his freshly diapered bottom up in the air.

"He will be fine," the old woman assured her. "I will come back and listen for him while you eat."

"Are you sure you don't mind?"

"I like babies," the woman said. "I have seventeen grandchildren."

"That's wonderful." Grace followed her down the hall. "Do any of them live around here?"

"Some. My two oldest girls live in town. Another is married to one of the hands here on the Double L. The other three are grown and have moved away."

"You have six children?" Grace wondered how the woman had managed. Just taking care of Mac these past weeks had turned her life upside down. "That's wonderful."

"You'll meet them. They are all coming next week, for the party."

Grace didn't point out that she would be leaving tomorrow. "That's nice," she said as Isabella led her back through the living room, dining room and kitchen.

"You can save yourself some steps and walk across the courtyard next time, if you want. Be careful where you walk, though. We are cleaning it up for the party."

"Sounds like it's going to be quite a celebration."

Isabella nodded, her face solemn, as she pointed out a place at the table that was set with bright pottery. "We have all waited a long time for this."

Jack McLintock shot Isabella a stern look. "Jason has worked hard to graduate from school," he said.

"Yes," the old woman said. "He is such a smart boy, always writing things on paper, always reading."

And making babies, too? Grace sat down at the table and put her napkin in her lap. "Where are the rest of your brothers, Mr. McLintock?"

"Call me Jack." He frowned, knowing exactly what she was asking. "Jet has gone to town. His band is playing in Locklin tonight."

"Could we go see him? The sooner we clear all this up, the better."

Isabella placed a large bowl of chicken stew in front of her. "Clear up what?"

"Thank you," Grace said. "It smells wonderful."

Jack shook his head. "Never mind, Bella."

The old woman laughed. "Oh, you're wondering where that baby got his McLintock chin, aren't you?"

Grace looked at Jack and waited for him to answer, but he ignored the question and Isabella returned to the table with a bowl for him.

"Green chicken chili," she said. "Not too hot."

"'Not too hot' could mean anything," the rancher warned. "So go easy on the first bite."

"Okay." She scooped up a small spoonful and tasted a

piece of chicken and green sauce. It was spicy enough to make her throat burn, but the sensation wasn't unpleasant.

Isabella returned with a plate of tortillas and two bottles of beer. "There," she said, setting the bottles between them. "I'm going to sit with the little one while you eat." She turned to Jack. "I'll stay here tonight if you want to take the lady to meet Jethro."

"Thank you," Grace said, pleased that it was going to be easy to talk to another McLintock. "Are you sure you wouldn't mind?"

The housekeeper chuckled. "No, I love babies. I'll sit with him in his room while he sleeps. You'll like Jethro. He's a fine boy."

"No one's going anywhere," Jack said.

Grace ignored him and looked at Isabella. "Jethro is the singer?"

"Here." Jack twisted the top off of the beer bottle and handed it to her. "If you're going to eat Bella's chili, you're going to need something cold."

Grace wasn't a beer drinker, but she took it, anyway. She didn't usually eat chili with cowboys or take care of babies, either, so what difference did a bottle of beer make? She took a couple of sips and then got back to the subject of the conversation. "I'd really like to meet your brother."

He waited for the cook to leave the kitchen before he answered. "I don't want you asking anyone any questions."

"I know that. But you're not exactly calling the shots."

"You're in my home, accusing me of fatherhood. I'd say that gives me the right to get to the bottom of this mess."

"I'm not leaving until I deliver this child to his father. I promised his mother, and that's what I'm going to do."

"And if you can't find out who the father is?"

"There are lawyers and blood tests and DNA."

"You're prepared to go that far?"

He didn't have any idea how far she was prepared to go. If he'd spent a couple of months in a bad foster home, he'd understand. Or even worse, if he'd ever been taken away from a loving foster mother and placed somewhere else, he'd know.

"If he's a McLintock, he should be raised as a McLintock," she declared.

Jack laughed. "That's a curse, not a blessing, sweetheart. We're not exactly the most stable family in Texas. Ask anyone in Locklin. My father was in jail—twice—and took off after Jason was born. My mother died of overwork and a broken heart. Sure you want Mac to join this family?"

"He deserves to have a name. Let me talk to Jethro tonight."

"No."

"Why not?"

"It should be done man-to-man. In private."

"So the two of you can cook up some story? No way."

Jack opened his mouth, but no sound came out. He inhaled and exhaled slowly before answering. "You're questioning my integrity?"

"I'm just saying that if you two are going to talk, I should be there to listen. I won't say anything unless I have to, but I should be there."

"How do you know I haven't already talked to him?"

"You wouldn't be arguing with me if you had."

"If the boy is a McLintock, I'll see that his father takes responsibility for him."

"Will he give him a home?"

"He doesn't have a home to give him. You want that child raised on a tour bus?"

"Will he sign away his rights, then, so Mac can be adopted?"

"By you?"

"No."

The man's eyebrows rose but he didn't say anything. "Are you married?"

"No."

"Children?"

"No."

"And yet you're concerned about the little boy. Why?"

"His mother was my friend. It was important to her, my taking Mac to his father."

"But you haven't found him yet."

"I will."

"And then what?"

"Then I leave here and go back to Dallas."

"Promise?"

She nodded. "Promise."

"All right. We'll head to town at eight and see if we can talk to Jet before the first set."

"Good," she said, picking up her spoon. "I've never met a country-western singer before. Has he been doing it for a long time?"

"Yeah. He's going to Nashville in a couple of weeks."

"Is he famous?"

"Only around here."

"He's never played anywhere else in Texas?"

Jack McLintock drained his bottle of beer. "Save the questions for later, lady. Jet goes on stage at nine. We'll get to him before then."

Grace helped herself to a tortilla. She was on the right track now. It had taken her a little longer than she thought it would, but Lucy had loved honky-tonk bars and men who played guitars. Jethro McLintock had to be the one.

"HELL," JACK SWORE, pulling Grace into the crowded bar. The jukebox volume must have been turned to high. "You can't hear yourself think in this place."

"I should have worn jeans," she muttered, hanging back. "I'm not dressed for this."

"You're fine." He glanced down at her and hid a sigh. She was too damn pretty for this place. Jack surveyed the room and caught two or three men staring at Grace as if they'd never seen a woman before. He glared at one guy until the man turned back to his shot glass. Jack tightened his grip on Grace's hand. "Come on. I'll find a table for you, then I'll see if I can find Jet."

"You're going to leave me here alone?"

He released her hand and pulled a chair over to a small corner table for two. "You'll be fine. Just don't talk to anyone except the waitress."

She gave him a strange, questioning look, so he added, "Look, honey. You wanted to come here, so you're going to have to do things my way. Sit down, and by the time you order a drink I'll be back with Jet."

Grace sat down and surveyed the crowd. "Your brother must be very popular."

"It's like this on Friday nights whether Jethro is playing or not. Don't move. I'll get him and be right back."

"You won't talk to him about Mac?"

"Not unless you're hanging on every word."

She smiled, which made Jack even sorrier he'd brought her to a dump like the Stampede. She was the kind of woman a man took to a fancy restaurant with candles on the table and violin music. Of course, there weren't any places like that until you got to San Antonio. He tipped his hat to her and made his way through the crowd. He had to keep his mind on business, not on a pretty brunette with soft gray eyes.

Two of the guys were busy setting up the equipment when he approached the stage. "Hey, Tim, Gus."

Gus, the bass player, turned and grinned. "Hey, Jack. Jet didn't say that you were comin' tonight! You come to hear the new songs?"

"Not exactly. I've got to talk to Jet for a few minutes. Where is he?"

"He was out back unloading, but he came inside a few minutes ago and went off to talk to a couple of people." Gus looked at his watch. "We're going to start getting tuned up as soon as I get all this stuff plugged in. When I see him I'll tell him you're here."

"Thanks. Maybe I'll get lucky and find him first."

Tim chuckled. "Look for a group of women and he'll be in the middle."

Jack turned back to survey the room. The place was starting to fill up even more, the overflow moving onto the dance floor, where a handful of couples danced the two-step to the jukebox. They were lined up three deep at the bar on the other side of the building, and more were spilling in through the door. He couldn't see Grace; a group of cowboys stood showing off for a hard-looking blonde and blocked his view of the corner table. Either folks in the county were desperate to party or Jet and his band were drawing a big crowd. Jet should have been easy to spot, but the light was dim and the air smoky.

Jack made his way back to the table to find Grace talking to the waitress.

"One beer and one whiskey on the rocks, please."

"I don't drink whiskey," Jack said.

"Usually, neither do I," Grace informed him. "But this seemed like a good place for me to do it, don't you think?"

"Bring the lady a Coke, too," he told the waitress, then he pulled out a chair and sat down.

"Is it always like this here?"

"I wouldn't know. I'm not much for hanging around in bars."

She actually looked disappointed. "Neither am I. I thought I was with an expert and could learn something."

"What exactly did you want to learn?"

She shrugged those pretty shoulders, and Jack's gaze drifted down to her breasts for a brief, appreciative second. "I don't know," she said, looking around the room. "Lucy used to talk about the noise and the fun and the people. She worked as a cocktail waitress in a lot of places like this."

Which was exactly the right place to meet a guy like Jet, Jack thought. "Was she a big drinker?"

"Not that I know of. What are you getting at?"

"I was just thinking that she could have misunderstood the name of who she went to bed with."

Grace glared at him. "Lucy wasn't like that."

The waitress returned and set the drinks in front of them. Jack started to pull out his wallet, but the girl stopped him. "That's already been taken care of," she said.

"By who?"

"Me," a tall young man declared, stepping up to the table. He tucked a bill in the woman's apron. "Thank you, darlin'. I'll take over from here."

"Don't forget my song," she said, clearly impressed that Jet McLintock was taking the time to flirt with her.

"I won't. 'I Still Believe In You,' right?"

"That's the one." She moved away reluctantly and was immediately stopped by a group of rowdy cowboy look-alikes.

Jet grinned. "Everyone wants me to sing like Vince Gill."

"Sit down," Jack said, not smiling at his younger brother. He wanted to ask some questions, and he wanted some answers. And then he wanted to be able to send Grace and Mac back to Dallas to find the child's *real* father.

"Can't," Jet said. "We're starting at nine. If we're late starting we don't get free drinks during the first break." He turned to Grace and held out his hand. "Hi, there. I'm Jet, the good-looking McLintock."

She laughed and shook his hand. "Grace Daniels," she said. "You two look so much alike."

"But I'm the best-looking one. And I didn't know Jack had a date tonight." He released her hand and grinned at his brother. "Thought you weren't going out."

"It's not—"

"Hey, guys and gals!" a voice called over the microphone. "You all ready for a good time? You know who's here! Jet and the Naked Ladies!"

The crowd cheered and Jet laughed. "Gotta go." He tipped his hat toward Grace and winked. "They can't start without me. I'm the lead guitarist and singer."

"I need to talk to you." Jack gave his brother an I-mean-business look, but Jet stood up.

"I'll catch you between sets," he promised, turning to Grace. "Any requests from the lady?"

She looked surprised. "Really?"

Jet winked. "Yep. If I know it, I'll play it for you."

"How about 'Crazy'?"

"Willie Nelson?"

"Yes. But if you don't know it, then that's all right. Anything would be—"

"No problem, darlin'. One of my favorites, in fact." He grinned at Jack one more time. "You ought to date this lady again."

Jack ignored the romantic advice. "We'll wait for you."

"Right," he agreed, walking away, but Jack thought his

brother could have taken the command a little more seriously.

"So that was Jet," Grace murmured. "Definitely Lucy's type, though a little on the young side."

"He's twenty-six. And, according to the birth certificate, Mac's mother would have been the same age as I am, thirty-six."

"That's a big age difference."

"Some women prefer it," he said, watching the way the women in the crowd watched Jethro hop onto the stage.

"I meant between the two of you."

"Yeah, well, my father was doing time in the state penitentiary for a few years. Kind of interrupted his family life."

Grace took a sip from her whiskey glass. "And you and your mother worked on the ranch?"

"Yep. When the old man came home, he stuck it out for a few years. The boys were born and he took off again." He took a swallow of beer and studied the woman beside him. "Still sure you want that baby of yours to be part of the family?"

"He's not mine," she pointed out, but she gave him a look that made him feel guilty for being so blunt. But damn it, the woman needed to know what that child was getting into.

"For all I know, he's yours," she added. "Or Jet's. Someone has to take responsibility for him."

"No lectures, lady," Jack drawled, leaning back in his chair as the music started. "I wrote the book on responsibility, and now I'm on the final chapter."

"I'D LIKE TO DEDICATE this next song to the little lady who's crazy enough to go out with my older brother," Jet announced, waving one arm toward their table. People stared. Grace tried not to laugh at the expression on Jack's face. He wasn't happy being the center of attention, that was certain.

"Honey," Jet continued, "I hope you know what you're getting into."

The crowd applauded as Jet broke into the first verse of "Crazy," and the dance floor quickly filled with couples who wrapped themselves around each other for the slow dance.

"I suppose you want to dance to this one," Jack said, standing up.

He didn't have to sound so reluctant. "With you?"

He held out his hand. "There are two guys waiting to see if you're going to dance with me. If you refuse, they'll think you're fair game, and they'll be over here as soon as I excuse myself to go, uh, outside for a few minutes. You want that?"

Grace stood. "I'd like to dance, thank you."

"Thought so," he said, guiding her away from the table. She stopped short. "Where's your beer bottle?"

"On the table. Why?"

"Could you bring it?" She pointed to the men dancing, their beer bottles hanging from their fingers behind their ladies' backs. "I've always wondered how that works."

"I usually don't drink and dance at the same time," he muttered, but he took his bottle and her hand.

"Me either," she said, but she figured she was going to like it. He led her onto the dance floor and took her into his arms. His right arm, bottle in hand, dangled from her shoulder, and his left encircled her waist. Grace was impressed.

"I'm not much of a dancer," McLintock said.

"You seem to be doing all right." She liked the way he held her. He seemed a lot larger now that she was touching him. When someone bumped her and pushed her against Jack's chest, she felt the warmth beneath his shirt and that hard chest. "Sorry," she said, righting herself.

"My fault," he said. "I should have seen him coming."

Grace, feeling shy again, fumbled for something to say. Dancing this close to such a big cowboy was turning her from an intelligent computer expert into a tongue-tied teenager. She looked over and saw Jet smiling at her. "Your brother is watching us."

"My brother has some explaining to do."

Grace hoped that Jet would take the news of his fatherhood well. She didn't think he seemed like the kind of man who would ignore the existence of a child, but since she'd only spoken to him for five minutes, she probably didn't have much of a handle on him. "Does Jet like children?"

"He likes everyone. And everyone likes him. Women, kids, horses and dogs, you name it and Jet will charm them."

"You don't call him Jethro?"

"Sometimes."

Grace listened to Jet's deep voice as he sang the song. He sounded just as good—or even better—than the singers she listened to on the radio while she worked. Add the McLintock good looks, including that square McLintock chin with the appealing cleft. He wore black jeans and a black T-shirt, with a black Stetson perched on top of his dark hair. He was tall and lean, not as wide-chested as Jack, but maybe a little taller. And definitely more outgoing.

The song ended, and the band went right into a faster number, something that made enthusiastic couples crowd the dance floor. Jack led her back to their table and politely held her chair for her.

He looked at his watch and then at her almost-full whiskey glass. "Jet should be through with this first set pretty soon. Want another drink?"

"No, thanks."

They sat in silence, waiting for Jet to return. When the set ended with a loud guitar flourish and a crashing of the drums, they watched Jet hop off the stage, grab a beer from a passing waitress and head their way. He hooked his foot around a chair leg and pulled it toward him, straddled it backward and grinned at Grace. "What'd you think? Saw you two dancing out there."

"You have a great band," Grace told him. "Jack said you're going to Nashville soon?"

"Yep. In a couple of weeks. We've got the name of a guy to contact, we're going to make a demo tape, and then we're going to start making music. Stick around for a while. We're going to do some of the new numbers in the second set." He looked at his watch. "I gotta get back pretty soon. The owner doesn't like long breaks."

"I'll bet you'll be famous some—"

"Jet, do you know a woman named Lucy Bagwell?" Jack had leaned forward, his gaze on Jet's face.

The younger man shook his head. "Nope. I don't think so. Is she an agent or something?"

"No. She had a baby a few months ago, and she put a McLintock down on the birth certificate as being the father."

Jet chuckled. "Not me, Jack. I don't go around taking chances like that."

His brother didn't smile. "Not even once?"

"No." He turned to Grace, but this time Jet wasn't laughing. "I thought your name was Grace."

"It is," she said, scooting her chair closer so she could hear over the sound of the music coming from the jukebox. Jet looked so sincere that she almost felt sorry for him.

"Lucy was my neighbor. She left the baby with me before she died. I came to town to bring Mac to his father."

He took a drink from the beer bottle. "What does this have to do with me?"

She had to give Jet credit for looking calm. "Where were you a year ago last March?"

Jet shrugged. "I don't know. I'll have to look it up. Gus keeps a record of where we've played and for how much."

"Find out" was all Jack said, but Jet looked as if he'd been given a command from up above.

"First thing in the morning," he promised.

"Grace is staying at the ranch," Jack added. "With the baby."

Jet's eyebrows rose as he turned to his brother. "No sh— kidding. You think there's a chance this could be legit? Have you talked to Jimmy?"

"Not yet."

"Damn. He can't take a baby with him to L.A."

Jack didn't look sympathetic, Grace noticed. "If it's his, he'll have to figure out something."

"Could you and Isabella keep—"

"*No.*"

"I gotta get back," Jet said, swinging his leg over the chair. "The crowd gets ugly in between sets, and there'll be a fight in the parking lot, sure enough, if the music doesn't start soon." He hesitated, then leaned closer. "I'm not anyone's father, Jack. I swear."

"We'll talk in the morning," his older brother said. "We'll get to the bottom of this."

"Ma'am." Jet tipped his hat. "I wish you luck, but I'm not your man."

Grace wondered. She'd give a lot to see a record of where that band had played. Anyone with a band called the Naked Ladies must like women. And Jet had the kind of easy charm that Lucy would fall for.

"I'll finish this beer and we'll leave," Jack said.

"I'm in no hurry. I'd like to hear some of your brother's songs," she said. When else would she get the chance to hear a real country-western singer perform? Grace watched as Jet stepped up on stage. A group of young women hovered nearby and watched him with adoring expressions.

"You may want to hang around here, but I don't like crowds."

"Do you think he's telling the truth?"

"He's never lied to me before. Least, not since he was grown."

Jet's band roared to life and Grace couldn't hear the rest of what Jack said to her, but she thought she heard him ask her if she really wanted a McLintock to raise that child.

"DAMN, MAN, YOU CUT IT close. Old Burley gave me the evil eye for five minutes," Gus complained.

"I was talking to Jack," Jet said, slipping the guitar strap over his head. He tried out a few chords. Jet waved to the sound man, and got the thumbs-up sign. "He's here with a woman, a *pretty* woman."

"You know her?"

"Never saw her before." He looked over toward the table, but the shadows hid Jack's face. *Never heard of her friend Lucy, either.*

Gus chuckled and practiced a riff on the bass. "There's a pretty woman in Texas that you don't know? I can't believe it."

"She's from out of town. Jack didn't say from where." He wondered if that was deliberate.

"Maybe he's getting married. Now that you all are going on your way and all, he's found himself a woman."

"Jack? He doesn't go anywhere to meet women." Hell, his older brother sure wasn't being accused of fathering a child. "I don't remember the last time he had a date."

"We starting with 'All My Exes' or one of the new songs?"

"One of the new ones. Let's do 'Can't Take It Anymore.'" Gus nodded and told the rest of the guys. Jet glanced toward his brother one more time as the band started the intro. He didn't know how this was going to turn out, but he was sure glad to see Jack getting out and having a good time. Jack must like the little lady or he wouldn't have danced with her.

Everybody knew Jack didn't dance.

Jet launched into the opening bars and sang, "I can't take it anymore, but I want all you have to give," into the microphone. He kept his voice low, the way he knew the women liked it, and scanned the crowd.

"I can't take it anymore, when there's nothing for which I have to live." He made sure he looked tortured. Women loved it when a man looked like he was suffering from love.

A scuffle broke out in the corner near Jack's table, but Jet couldn't see through the crowd to find out what was going on. Then he spotted his brother, and a man fell against a table. He heard glass break and saw the two bouncers shove their way through the crowd.

"I can't take it, no, I can't take it."

Jet forgot about looking tortured and grinned. Friday night in Locklin, and Jack was finally getting into the swing of things.

3

"I'M SORRY." And she really meant the words. She'd said them at least three times since they'd left the bar, but the tall rancher hadn't said anything in response but *Don't worry about it.*

"Don't worry about it." Jack opened the refrigerator and rummaged through the contents. "Damn."

"Let me get it for you," Grace said. "I'll fix an ice pack."

"Not ice." He took out a flat package. "Steak."

"You're hungry?"

He sighed, shut the refrigerator door and turned around. "It's for the swelling." He tossed his hat on the table and sat down, then leaned back. He rested his head against the kitchen wall and held the white paper package of meat to his eye.

Since Jack looked like he had everything under control, Grace left the kitchen and hurried to the bedroom to check Mac. Isabella sat knitting in the chair while the baby slept in his little bed. The old woman put her finger to her lips.

"I just fed him," she whispered. "He ate like a Mc-Lintock, all right."

Grace had to smile at the woman's description. "Thank you for taking such good care of him."

"He's a sweet one." Isabella gathered her yarn and stuffed it into a faded tapestry bag, then followed Grace into the hall. "You found Jethro?"

"Yes." Grace shut the bedroom door behind her with a

quiet click, and the two women walked back down the hall toward the other wing. They walked into the kitchen, and Isabella clucked her disapproval. "But there was a little bit of a problem before we left."

"Oh." The woman sighed. "There usually is."

Grace decided that Isabella's observation was probably true, at least from what she'd experienced tonight. Jack still leaned against the wall, but he took the steak from his face and peered at them through the eye that wasn't swollen shut. "You call this a 'little problem'?"

Isabella shrugged. "We've all seen worse. But I thought you were too old for bar fights. Thought you were old enough to know better."

"Yeah. Seems like there are a few things we all thought we knew better than what we did," he muttered.

Grace supposed that remark referred to Mac's arrival on earth.

Isabella sniffed. "Won't hurt you much to get out and have some fun, I suppose. If you can hold your temper."

"Last time I take Grace to a bar, I'll tell you that."

"The black eye isn't my fault," Grace protested, wishing she could back out of the kitchen and go to bed. She should have stayed with Mac, but she'd thought she should say good-night to her host.

Jack put the meat back on his face. "You smiled at the guy."

"I was being polite." The big man had said hello to her, and she had thought he was a friend of the McLintocks. She hadn't wanted to be rude, despite the leer on his big square face and the way his gaze had dropped to her chest.

"He thought you were encouraging him."

"You didn't have to hit him."

"Oh, yes, I did." He wiggled the fingers on his right hand. "I hope I didn't break anything."

"You didn't," Isabella said, winking at Grace. "I'm going home now. You'll have to tell me all about your troubles in the morning."

"I'm sure as hell not going to discuss that again," Jack muttered.

"Thank you again," Grace told the woman. "I hope Mac wasn't any trouble."

"He's a good boy," Isabella assured her, pushing open the back door. "Does he belong to Jet?"

Jack answered for her. "I doubt it."

The housekeeper hesitated. "That child has a McLintock look about him. Looks like Jason did when he was that age."

"All babies look alike," Jack muttered.

"Not really," Grace said. She was beginning to realize that Jack McLintock was all bark and no bite. He grouched quite a bit, but he had defended her honor and protected her from a half-drunk cowboy. He'd been quite heroic, even though he would look a little worse for wear for the attempt. "Not all babies have a cleft chin," she added, just to annoy him.

His lips thinned.

"McLintock babies do," Isabella called as she stepped into the night. Grace poured herself a glass of water. She would say good-night, then she would go to her room and crawl into bed. It had been a long day, and tomorrow promised to be even longer.

"She always gets the last word," her host said.

"I'm going to bed."

"So soon?" His tone was sarcastic. "Are you certain we've had enough excitement tonight?"

You'll have to get excited all by yourself, she longed to say. "Unless you have any more brothers I can talk to, I'm going to bed." She set the glass in the sink and moved toward the door.

"Tomorrow," he said, lifting the meat from his face. "We'll get answers tomorrow."

"I'm sure we will," Grace said, though she wasn't sure at all. The brothers were handsome devils whose charming smiles could cover up just about anything.

Even a son.

Grace hurried to her room, unpacked her small bag and used the bathrooom. Mac slept, completely unaware of the questions swirling around him. He was a good baby, patient even with a woman whose only experience with children had been years ago. She'd been a child herself. A child old past her years. A child who had seen too much and whose heart had been broken too many times.

Grace crawled into bed. She'd been smart to bring her overnight things. Of course, she'd thought she'd be sleeping in a San Antonio hotel tonight. She hadn't counted on a ranch. Or four McLintocks. But despite everything, she'd enjoyed herself. Once she settled Mac, life would return to normal. That would be fine, she assured herself right before falling asleep. Normal was quiet. Normal was peaceful.

Normal was lonely, a voice inside reminded her. She was accustomed to lonely, Grace argued. There were worse things in life.

"HELL, JET, YOU'VE GOT to give me more to go on than that." Jack tapped the copy of the birth certificate. "There's a McLintock name on there, and someone has to be responsible for that little boy."

Jethro poured himself a cup of coffee and eyed his older brother. "You look like hell. What happened last night? Can't hold your liquor?"

"No. Greg Enders couldn't. He made some remarks to our houseguest and I warned him to shut up."

"And he hit you."

"He flapped his mouth again, hit me and I hit him. He was still on the floor when I left the bar." Jack couldn't help the pride that crept into his voice.

"Guess you haven't lost your touch."

Jack drained his coffee mug and leaned forward. "You want to cut the small talk and tell me about Lucy Bagwell?"

Jet stared into his coffee as if the answers were there in the bottom of the cup. "Nothing to tell," he said after a long moment. "The kid isn't mine, though I wouldn't mind too much if he was."

"You've seen him?"

"Not yet."

"Just wait. He looks like Jason did at that age."

"I'm not sure I remember." Jethro sat down across from his brother. "Those years are a blur, and it's not like Ma had a lot of time to take pictures."

"I want the truth, Jet. Are you—is there any chance in hell that you're this boy's father?"

There was a long silence. "We played in a place outside of Dallas a year ago last March. Gus looked it up."

"Do you remember anyone named Lucy?"

"Hell, Jack, that was almost a year and a half ago."

"Fifteen months is not that long."

"It is when you play in a different bar each weekend. You know the schedule we keep—"

"I don't want to hear it, Jet. I just want to know if you slept with anyone that weekend, and if that kid could be yours."

"He's not mine."

"This Grace woman might want blood tests," Jack warned.

"Fine." Jet's gaze didn't waver. Jack held it long enough to make his point, then got up and refilled his coffee cup. His eye was sore, the skin still hot and puffy, but he wasn't in bad shape. He'd almost enjoyed popping that big mouth of Enders. Maybe he wasn't as old as he thought.

"What about Grace?"

She wasn't cut out to deal with drunk and horny cowboys, that was obvious. "What about her?"

"She seemed nice. Pretty, too."

"She's not your type."

Jet looked surprised, then he laughed. "And my type is?"

"Skinny blondes with big attitudes and bigger—"

"Good morning," Grace said, making Jack close his mouth. She stepped into the kitchen, the chubby baby tucked against her hip. The child surveyed the two men and then grinned. "This is Mac," Grace said to Jet.

"Call me *Uncle* Jet," the young man told the wide-eyed baby.

Jack glared at him. "This isn't the time or place to tease."

Jet ignored him. "Where'd that boy get that chin?"

"That's what I'm here to find out," Grace said as Jet stood up and held his arms out to the child.

"Will he come to me?"

"Let's see." She gave Mac a chance to go to Jet, and the boy leaned away from her and into the cowboy's arms.

Jet looked comfortable holding him, but he turned to Jack with a worried expression. "Does Jimmy know about him?"

"No. He's spending the weekend in town while the play is on." Jack saw the likeness right away as Jet and the child were almost at eye level. Now he understood why Grace had given him such a strange look when he'd held Mac yesterday. She'd seen it, and so had Isabella. "Does he have a last name?"

"I guess he's a McLintock now," Jet answered, grinning as the baby patted his face.

"I think Lucy used 'Bagwell,'" Grace said.

Jack got up and poured another cup of coffee, then handed it to Grace. "Here," he said, figuring her for a woman who needed caffeine in the morning. Her grateful expression told him he'd guessed right.

"Thank you." She went to the refrigerator and took out one of the bottles of formula that were stacked neatly on the door. Jack watched as she hid the bottle from the baby's sight while she held it under hot tap water at the sink. Mac hollered the minute he saw Grace wipe it dry with a nearby dish towel.

"I'll take it," Jet offered. He sat down in a chair, stuck the bottle in the baby's mouth and grinned. "I always knew I'd be one heck of a fine uncle."

Jack took a sip of his coffee. "Getting ahead of yourself, aren't you?"

"Hey, he's not mine," Jet said. "But that doesn't mean he isn't ours." He gave his older brother a questioning look. "Are you sure he's not yours?" And this time he didn't smile after he asked the question.

Jack figured that didn't deserve an answer. Grace, looking real pretty in white shorts and a pink T-shirt, brought her coffee cup to the table and sat down.

"Who do I talk to next?"

Jack and Jet looked at each other.

"Jimmy-Joe," Jack said.

"Is he here on the ranch?"

"Not this weekend. Not until tomorrow night."

"He's an actor," Jet explained. He lifted the empty bottle from Mac's mouth and tilted him into a sitting position. "He's in a show in town. *Paint Your Wagon.*"

Grace looked confused. "Isn't that a movie?"

"It was a play first," Jet said. Mac coughed, and Jet looked at Grace. "Now what?"

"He needs to be burped."

"Oh. Yeah. I forgot."

Jack sighed. Didn't Jet remember how to take care of a baby? "Sit him up a little higher and pat his back."

Jet did as he was told, and the little boy let out a burp that would rival anything heard in the bunkhouse. "Hey, kid, nice going. Jimmy-Joe takes his acting real serious," Jet said after he stopped chuckling. "He's going to Hollywood in a couple of weeks."

One week and six days, Jack thought silently. In less than two weeks they would all go their separate ways. He wondered what it would be like to stand out in the yard and wave goodbye. He wondered if he would wish he was going, too. No, he wouldn't. He would find one of those old plastic lawn chairs, and he would open a beer and sit in the shade and watch the grass grow.

Life would be good, all right.

"Jack?"

He blinked and realized the gray-eyed woman was looking at him as if she was waiting for an answer. "Yeah?"

"Can we go to town and talk to your other brother? I'd like to get Mac settled as soon as possible."

"Settled?" he repeated. "With Jimmy-Joe?" The woman didn't realize that Jimmy-Joe didn't know the meaning of the word.

"Yes," she said in that soft voice that made him feel like some kind of brute. "The sooner Mac finds his father, the better."

"I don't think—"

"He shouldn't be too hard to track down," Jet said, interrupting his older brother. He grinned at Jack, but Jack sure didn't feel like grinning back. "And I want to be there to see him find out he's a daddy, too."

"This isn't something that needs an audience."

"Well, how about moral support?"

Mac held his arms out to Grace, and she leaned over and scooped him into her lap. "I really don't care how you decide to talk to your brother," Grace informed the two men. "But it needs to be done soon. A child's future is at stake."

She made him feel like the kid in kindergarten who went around telling everyone else that there was no Santa Claus. Still, Jack cleared his throat and tried to explain. "I'm not trying to make things difficult for you," he said. "And I want what's best for the boy, too. It's just that Jimmy-Joe is an actor. He's got some fancy agent in Los Angeles, and he's heading there in a couple of weeks. I don't think he's the man you're looking for." And if he is, Jack added silently, he'd be tied to the barn and made to live up to his responsibilities.

"Don't you think we need to find out as soon as possible?"

"I'm not sure where he's staying," Jack hedged. J.J.'s womanizing was legendary, and there was no telling where he'd slept last night. And Jack wasn't going to start calling various Locklin women to ask, either.

"We have tickets to the show tonight. Grace can have mine, since I've got a gig."

Jack tore his gaze away from the brown-eyed baby and looked over at Jet. He was getting pretty damned tired of his brother's suggestions. "I thought you were going to see the first half."

Jet shrugged. "I went to the dress rehearsal on Thursday and saw the whole thing. Didn't know Jimmy-Joe could sing that well."

Grace looked uncertain. "I can't take Mac to the show."

"One of Isabella's daughters can watch him. Lord knows we have enough people around here to take care of one more child." He might as well tell the woman what she wanted to hear, and that was she would get her chance to talk to another McLintock.

"Yes," Grace said. "That's exactly what I've been thinking, too."

Anxious to escape, Jack stood up. "I've got work to do. Guess I'd better get at it." He nodded at Isabella, who had entered the kitchen to start cleaning up the breakfast dishes.

"Take Grace with you," Jet said. "I'll bet you've never been on a ranch, have you, Grace?"

"No, but—"

Isabella patted Mac's head. "I'll take the boy. We'll go visit Lina for a little while. The girls will love playing with him."

Jack knew when he was being backed into a corner. "I'll be out back. You might want to change. That is, if you've brought clothes fit for a ranch." He hoped she hadn't.

"I have jeans," she said. "Is that all right?"

"Yeah."

"I'll wait for you," Jet offered. "Jack has to see if he can get the truck started."

"All right," she said in that soft voice that did funny things to Jack's heart. He left the kitchen, jamming his hat on his head as he made his escape. A woman had no business here on the ranch, and neither did a baby. There was no room for either one, not on his ranch or in his life. He was through with all that, but Jimmy-Joe might not be. Jack took a deep breath of the humid morning air and hurried to the barn. He hated to think that his younger brother's dreams were about to be postponed or, at the very least, complicated beyond belief, but that's what happened when a man didn't think past what hung between his thighs.

OKAY, SHE SHOULDN'T BE having fun. Grace knew she should be back in Dallas where she belonged. Her compact apartment held a desk piled high with work; she had deadlines for two computer programs and their manuals and one more waiting as soon as she signed the contract. Her job was to explain the unexplainable, at least in layman's terms. What she couldn't explain was why she didn't mind staying another day—and yes, another night—on the McLintock ranch.

She could leave. She could take the child home with her, let the lawyers decide what to do with Mac. But then Mac's future would be out of her hands; her promise to deliver Mac to his father would have gone unfulfilled. Lucy deserved better than that.

And so did Mac. So Grace handed Mac into Isabella's plump embrace, changed into her jeans and prepared to tour the ranch. With a handsome cowboy, of course.

Lucy wouldn't believe it.

"IT'S THE ANSWER to everything," Jet said, following Isabella to the clothesline. He set the heavy basket of wet clothes at her feet. "Don't you think?"

She shook her head and reached into the basket. "You always had such an imagination, Jethro. Ever since you were a little boy."

"But it's simple," he said, stepping back to avoid a flapping shirtsleeve. "We've all been worried about Jack, and now here comes a beautiful woman, right to the front door. It's clear he likes her."

"And how do you figure that?"

"He danced with her last night at the Stampede." To Jet

it was simple. Jack had held a woman in his arms. Jack had danced with her, defended her honor, brought her back to the ranch and installed her in a spare room. Once there was a woman on the ranch, well, hell. Anything could happen.

Isabella's eyebrows rose. "You think that is a sign?"

"Yeah, I do. If we play our cards right." If nothing was left to chance. "If Grace stays, if she and Jack get, uh, together, that means that Jack won't be alone when we leave. He'll have Grace and the baby."

"Maybe he *wants* to be alone," the old woman pointed out. "Maybe he is looking forward to being on his own, too, just the way the rest of you are."

Jet shook his head. "I don't believe that for a minute. I think he's putting on a good show so the rest of us don't feel bad about leaving."

Isabella shrugged and reached for another shirt. "You can't make two people fall in love, Jet."

"I do it all the time." He shoved the bag of clothespins farther along the line so she could reach them. "I sing the songs and they get closer together and pretty soon they're rubbing against each other and he's whispering in her ear and she—"

"Stop it," Isabella laughed. "I don't want to hear any more of your nonsense."

"It's not nonsense," he protested, his feelings injured.

"Then you are going to sing to Jack and Grace?" She waved toward the west. "They are a mile away by now. I don't think they're going to hear you."

"Very funny. I hope that mule gets loose again and takes down the clothesline."

"No, you don't. You lost two shirts last time."

Jet shrugged. "They were old."

"You carried on for hours about having to spend money

buying new ones," she reminded him. "Tell me, Jet, what are you going to do about the baby?"

"Where is he?"

"Lina and the girls are fussing over him while I get the clothes hung out. Everyone loves a baby. No matter who he belongs to."

"He's not mine, Bella."

"I know that, but you should talk to Jack and tell him why. And maybe you should talk to Jimmy, too. That little boy is a McLintock. Anyone with eyes can see that."

"Yeah. Jimmy has a lot to answer for. Or Jason. I guess he's no saint, either."

Isabella stopped working and put her hands on her hips. "I raised that boy better than that. He's not the kind to hang around bars and pick up women."

"Are you saying that I am?"

"It's your life-style. Not Jason's."

"I don't take chances. And I don't have as many women as you all like to think I do."

Isabella shrugged. "Maybe. Maybe not. But Jason isn't like you. Once he gives his heart, he will give it forever. And I don't think he'll sleep with the girls just to have a good time."

Jet sure as hell didn't want to discuss his sex life with the woman who had practically raised him since he was ten. "I thought we were talking about Jack's love life."

"You were. I am talking about the child. He belongs here, to one of you. And one of you must raise him."

"Exactly. And Jack is the perfect one to do it, too. He raised all of us, and he did a pretty good job."

"He may not want to. He is buying some new cattle, hiring some new cowhands, talking about going fishing in Montana. He does not talk about women and babies and becoming a father."

"He'll get used to the idea," Jet declared. "I think we all have to help him."

"Not me," the woman said. "I am minding my own business."

"Since when?"

"Since I decided to retire and sit in the shade and watch the grandbabies play," she said.

"Yeah, right." He didn't believe the retiring talk for a minute. Jet adjusted the brim of his hat and looked toward the west. "Jack likes this woman. All I'm saying is that we ought to give him some help."

"You have work to do," Isabella reminded him. "Unless you want to help me hang clothes?"

Jet backed up. "Think I'll ride over to the east pasture and see if everything's all right." He left the old cook shaking her head, but he wasn't about to let her comments bother him. She knew as well as he did that Jack wasn't going to know what to do with himself once the brothers went their separate ways. Once the money was distributed and they were all free, things would never be the same.

Which would make a good song title. "Never the Same Again." He liked it. Jet began to whistle, which set the birds flying off the electrical wires as he walked by.

HE HAD GIVEN HER A HAT. Battered, with an odor of sweat rimming the dark-edged inner band, it wasn't a great-looking Stetson, but Grace wasn't about to complain. In fact, she thought it gave her a certain cowgirl flair. It also protected her face from the sun that already blasted the Texas landscape.

And there was lots of landscape. For a couple of hours, Grace obediently looked in whatever direction Jack pointed. She admired the red-and-white cattle, smiled at the sight of the calves frolicking across the pastures and squinted at the brand, until she realized that what looked like an *M* with an extra flip was actually an *ML* stuck together. She tried to remain remote, but it wasn't easy, especially since she'd never been on a cattle ranch until now. "How many cattle do you have here?"

"Hundreds" was the clipped answer. "'Course, there are more now, with the calves," he added, shifting the truck into a higher gear. Grace braced herself by holding on to the dashboard as they bounced over the rutted dirt road.

"This is a big ranch. I don't have to see it all in one day," she managed to say between bounces.

"You couldn't," he replied, glancing at her. "The truck doesn't hold that much gas."

"Oh." Grace looked around at rolling fields topped with a cloudless blue sky. She took a deep breath and felt worlds away from Dallas. She'd almost forgotten what it was like to be without Mac. She'd cared for him for the past couple of weeks, while Lucy was in the hospital, and, though she'd grown to adore the chubby child, it felt good to be free from worrying that she was doing the right thing for him twenty-four hours a day.

"You've never been out on a ranch before?"

"No," she admitted. "I'm pretty much a city girl."

"Yeah? You grow up in Dallas?"

Grace hesitated. She didn't like discussing her personal life, especially not with strangers. "Pretty much," she replied. "What about you?"

"I've lived here all my life," Jack said.

"On this ranch?"

"Yep. The four of us have never lived anywhere else, except for when Jason went to college."

"You're very lucky. Not many people have that kind of stability."

He chuckled. "Growing up around here wasn't what

you'd call 'stable,' lady. We worked our butts off trying to keep this place going."

"And it looks as if you succeeded."

"Eventually," he admitted, slowing the truck as they came to a muddy stream. "For now."

"That's all I want for Mac, that kind of stable life," she said. "That's all Lucy wanted, too, was for her child to be raised with his family."

"And if he's not a McLintock? What then?" He stopped the truck, turned off the engine and turned to look at her.

"I don't know. I never thought the birth certificate would be wrong."

He looked as if he felt sorry for her. "Honey, people lie all the time."

She met his gaze. "Exactly."

"No one here is lying to you."

She raised her eyebrows. "No?"

"No."

"If he doesn't belong here, I'll take him back to Dallas with me. I'll make sure he has a family who loves him, and I'll see that he is happy and safe." She paused, then added, "But there's nothing that makes me believe he *doesn't* belong here."

Jack McLintock's gaze didn't waver. "And there's nothing that makes me believe he does."

"I guess we have our work cut out for us, then," she said, wishing he would stop looking at her as if she was out to con the entire family.

"Yeah," he agreed, "I guess we do." He looked away and turned the key in the ignition. "Guess we'd better head back. It'll be lunchtime soon, and I wouldn't want to be accused of starving the city folk."

Grace grabbed the dashboard again as Jack backed up the truck, then headed back the way they came. He'd been honest with her. That was more than she'd expected, especially after last night and Jet's denial of fatherhood.

Not that she was going to trust any of these McLintock men, of course. It was her job to find out the truth and deal with it. If these cowboys thought that she was easily fooled, a person who could be conned into believing anything and everything they said, well, they were wrong.

Grace Daniels was nobody's fool.

"THANK YOU FOR SHOWING me around." The truck bounced to a stop in front of a weathered barn where a couple of curious horses lifted their heads and looked over the corral fence toward them.

"You're welcome." He almost smiled. "It was safer than taking you back to the Stampede."

"I had a good time last night. Until the fight, that is." Grace opened the door and, grateful to have made it back to the ranch with all of her bones still connected, stepped out. She looked at the horses and wondered if touring on horseback would have been easier.

"Do you ride?" he said, coming around the front of the truck.

"No." Riding horses was another one of those dreams that she'd shelved, along with Thanksgiving dinner at Grandmother's house and teenage sleepover parties.

"How can you be a Texan and not know how to ride a horse?" he teased.

Grace tried to keep her tone light. "Didn't I tell you I was a city girl?"

"I guess you did," he drawled, but as she turned to go back to the house he touched her shoulder. "Look, Grace, we might have gotten off on the wrong foot, and I take my share of responsibility for that. But you could have given the family some warning before you came driving up with a baby and a birth certificate. You can't blame a man for being surprised or for trying to defend himself. We're not so bad," he said, looking down at her. "If it weren't for Mac, you might even like us a little."

"I can blame a man who doesn't take care of his child."

"And if he didn't know the child existed?"

"Lucy spoke as if he knew."

"You're sure about that?"

Grace paused. "Not exactly. It was just an impression I had."

"Pretty big impression," he pointed out.

"And raising Mac is a pretty big responsibility. The right person ought to do it."

"And that is?"

"His father. Or a loving adoptive family."

Jack frowned. "Strangers?"

"Adoption is a wonderful alternative." *Adoption* was a magic word, another dream that had never happened.

"Then, why don't you adopt him yourself?"

"It's not that easy." She shoved her hands in her pockets and gazed at the horses. "I wish it was, but it's not."

"It might be easier than finding Mac's father," he pointed out.

"Meaning it might be easier for one of your brothers if Mac was adopted by someone else."

"That's not what I meant."

"I'll find Mac's father, no matter who he is," Grace said. "I made a promise and I intend to keep it."

Jack started to say something, but then looked as if he'd changed his mind. "Have Isabella fix you some lunch. Tell her I'll get my own later."

Grace watched him walk toward the barn. She would talk to his brother tonight, and they would decide what would be done about Mac. Jimmy-Joe the actor would have attracted Lucy, especially if he was as good-looking as the other men in the family. Jason, the young college graduate, would have been too young for her neighbor. But then again, it was hard to tell. It wasn't up to her to decide which brother was Mac's father—Jack was taking care of that. It was simply up to her to deliver the baby when his father was identified. Getting more involved with the family wasn't part of the plan.

And Grace always followed the plan. She'd learned a long time ago that everything was easier with a plan. And her plan right now included leaving the ranch tomorrow. By tomorrow she certainly should know more about Mac's parentage and what to do next. He belonged with his own flesh and blood, if possible. That's what Lucy had wanted. That's what Grace had promised.

She returned to the house, and Isabella showed her where Mac was playing. She collected the baby from Isabella's giggling granddaughters and thanked them for watching them. She met Lina, a quiet woman with a shy smile and short dark hair, on the steps of a small white house a few hundred yards from the main house.

"Bring him anytime tonight," she offered. "The girls and I will take care of him while you are at the show."

"Thank you." She balanced the baby on her hip and winced as he tugged a lock of her hair. "I appreciate the help."

"Mom told us about his mother." The young woman reached out and stroked the baby's soft arm. "He will be all right now, I'm sure."

"If I can find his father."

"You will." Lina smiled. "Who would not want such a beautiful son?"

Grace could think of two particular men. "I hope you're right."

"The McLintocks are good men. They will see that he is taken care of."

"Well, I hope so. That's why we're here." She shifted the baby's weight on her hip and unwound her hair from his grip. "Come on, Mac. You look like you need a bath."

"The girls tried to feed him," Lina said, handing Grace a half-empty bottle. "I think he was too interested in everything going on around him to bother with lunch." Lina smiled again. "Don't worry. My mother says that Mac belongs here, and she's never wrong."

"Thanks," Grace said. "I'll keep that in mind."

"TELL HER WE HAVE to leave here at six-thirty." Jack moved through the kitchen and into the living room, Isabella following him as best she could.

"Tell Grace?"

He sighed. "Yeah. Since she's so all-fired anxious to see Jimmy in action, she can be ready on time."

"You were late for dinner," she pointed out. "We ate without you."

"Not the first time." He walked swiftly down the hall and turned the corner toward his bedroom, with Isabella right behind him. When he reached his door, he stopped. "Bella, what are you doing?"

"I want to talk to you," she said, poking him in the chest with one plump finger.

"I'm about talked out." Between Grace and Jet, Jack had just about all he could stand. "Can this wait?"

"No."

He leaned in the doorway of his room and prayed for patience. He was hot, tired and hungry. He had to clean up to go to town. He had to sit through another one of Jimmy-Joe's plays, and then he had to find out if the boy had been making time with some Dallas woman last year. All the while he'd have Grace hanging on every word, her very attractive little body distracting him every time she moved. She was lovely, but she didn't belong on the ranch. She needed to leave before he forgot what cows were. Before he forgot that he didn't have the energy for pursuing beautiful women. Or the money.

"The child doesn't belong to Jet and he doesn't belong to you. Which leaves Jimmy."

Jack folded his arms across his chest. "Not necessarily. Jimmy has more sense and less time than Jet. I don't think Jet would lie to me, but then again, I don't think he remembers all the women he, uh, meets."

"Men." Isabella rolled her eyes. "Don't you remember when Jet was so sick with the mumps?"

"He missed out on a pretty good fishing trip."

"He was fourteen. And his private parts swelled up like watermelons."

Jack hid a grin. He'd forgotten about that. Jet hadn't known whether to be embarrassed or proud. "And?"

"Mumps can cause sterility."

"You're saying *Jet* can't have children?"

"I'm saying you should talk to him before you jump to any conclusions, that's all." She looked as if she wanted to say something else.

"And?" he urged. "I assume there's more you have on your mind."

"The young lady is very pretty. And very kind."

"Which has nothing to do with me," he pointed out. "Nothing at all," he felt obliged to repeat.

"When's the last time you were with a woman?"

"That is none of your business." There was no way in hell he was going to admit that it had been well over a year. Before the librarian had moved to San Antonio, though. Come to think of it, he hadn't had much time to read, either.

The cook sniffed. "Everything around here turns out to be my business sooner or later. I think *you* should think about taking advantage of having a lovely woman in your home."

"Seduce the houseguest? I don't think so."

Isabella shot him a disgusted look. "I am not talking about seduction. I'm talking about enjoying a woman's company. For once."

"I'll 'enjoy' when and where I damn please," Jack sputtered. With that said, he turned around and shut his bedroom door. Privacy was all he asked for, and there was little of it here. But that was going to change. In one week and six days.

He stripped off his shirt and headed for the bathroom he shared with Jet. Seduction wasn't a bad idea. In fact, he was planning to look around and start dating. He would have the time and the money and, hell, even the energy. He would be free to sample the pleasures of San Antonio, look up the librarian, flirt with pretty ladies who gave him an interested smile. Once he paid off the mortgages on the ranch, he might be free to sow some long overdue wild oats. Or at least sleep at night without wondering if he would be able to pay the real estate taxes.

Jack leaned forward and examined his face in the mirror. He hoped he wasn't too old to have fun.

He hoped he still remembered what it was.

SHE'D FORGOTTEN MOST of the story, but remembered that Lee Marvin had played the experienced gold miner in the movie. Jimmy-Joe McLintock—Jim McLock on the program—was the younger farmer, accidentally involved in the discovery of gold and eventually in love with the wife of the older miner. Jimmy-Joe had an easy singing style, but his deep voice and impressive stage presence made him look like a star.

And Grace had no doubt that Jimmy-Joe McLintock was going places.

He was taller than Jet and not as heavily muscled as Jack. Or so Grace guessed. She watched in fascination as the first act ended and the crowd erupted in cheers for Jimmy and the others.

"Well?" Jack turned to her as the lights went on for intermission. He'd rolled up the paper program as if he was going to hit someone with it. "What did you think?"

"It's a good show. I love the music." She didn't know what to say about the third McLintock brother. He looked like the kind of man who would have women dropping at his feet. Lucy would have loved him. And probably had.

Isabella struggled to her feet and, her enormous purse hanging over her arm, fanned herself with her program. "I'm going outside to get some air."

Jack rose. "We'll join you in a few minutes."

Grace fanned herself with her program and stood, too. The crowd was hurrying outside, presumably toward the bar that was set up on the front lawn of the old theater. She'd worn the sundress she'd worn yesterday, but even the lightweight cotton fabric felt uncomfortably hot against her skin. Jack wore a short-sleeved white shirt and beige slacks, but for some reason he still looked like a cowboy.

"I'll buy you a drink," the rancher said, touching her elbow to guide her out of her seat and up the aisle. "I think we could both use something cold."

She sipped iced tea from a plastic cup while Jack settled for something with bourbon and ice. They stood on the shaded side of the building and sipped their drinks. Isabella was nowhere to be seen, but several people smiled at

Jack and gave Grace a curious look. A short, stocky man hurried over to Jack and shook his hand.

"Two weeks to go, huh, son? I expect you'll be sowing your own wild oats afterward." He looked down at Grace and grinned, his face red from the heat. "And who is this lovely lady?"

Grace held out her hand and the man held it. "I'm Grace Daniels. A...family friend."

Jack cleared his throat. "The man who is holding your hand is Harry White, vice president of the only bank in town."

"Yes, ma'am," Harry said, finally releasing her hand. "I'm right pleased to meet you. I'll bet you're here for the festivities."

"Festivities? You mean Jason's party?"

"That's right, among other things." He winked at Jack. "A big time ahead for all of the McLintocks, right, son?"

"Yeah," Jack muttered. "A big time."

"Heard Jet's heading to Nashville." Harry took out a kerchief and wiped his brow.

"That's what he says."

"Well, you tell him that the Whites will buy all of his records. Janie can't wait to hear him on the radio someday."

"Thanks, Harry. I'll tell him."

"Nice meeting you, Miz Daniels," the banker said. "See you at the party!"

"It was nice meeting you, too," Grace managed to say before the little man disappeared into the crowd.

"You're supposed to be a cousin," Jack said.

"I forgot. I just went blank."

"Well," he drawled, "that I can believe, all right. You wouldn't make a very good spy. Otherwise you wouldn't have driven into the middle of my property claiming to have brought me my son. You would have checked us out first, I think."

Grace bit back a laugh. "I guess you have a point. I *could* have been sneakier, I suppose, but I never thought that Mac's father didn't know he existed." She looked at her watch. "I hope Lina didn't have any trouble putting him to bed. He had such an exciting day."

"Did you know his mother well?"

"She was my neighbor. I didn't know her until she moved into the apartment next to mine. She was very pregnant at the time, and we became friends after she had Mac. I didn't know she was sick."

He took a sip of his drink. "What happened?"

"She'd refused to have any treatment that would endanger her pregnancy. It ended up costing her her life."

"I'm sorry," he said. "She must have been a very brave person."

"She was. And she was funny, too. Even when she was suffering, she wouldn't let anyone feel sorry for her."

The bell rang to announce the end of intermission, so Grace and Jack walked with the crowd back to the theater. Jack remained silent long after they had tossed their empty cups into the trash bin and taken their seats in the fifth row from the front. Isabella was already in her seat, and she smiled at them as they sat down.

"You are having fun?" she whispered as the lights dimmed.

"Yes. Very much."

"Good," the older woman said. And the curtains opened on the second half of the show.

Fun, Grace thought, was all relative. She'd never thought that delivering Mac to his father would be classed as "fun." She hadn't intended to have fun when she came to the ranch. She'd intended to do what she had to do and then leave. Since arriving in Locklin, she'd danced in a country-western bar, ridden in a pickup truck, eaten green chili, and now sat watching the Locklin Playhouse version of *Paint Your Wagon*. With Mac's father as one of the stars?

She would know in another hour or two. Unless someone was lying.

JIMMY-JOE HAD BETTER not lie to him. None of the boys had pulled that in years, not since they'd left elementary school. And there was Grace, who would be listening to every word. He wondered if he could figure out a way to get her to stand quietly off to one side while he handled Jimmy. Yeah, right. Grace would be right in the middle of it. He had to admire her devotion to the baby, but he sure as hell wished she would let him handle this his own way.

Which would be in private. He managed to squeeze through the crowd backstage until he reached the center of attention. As usual, there was Jimmy, his makeup still on, his shirt unbuttoned and a grin a mile wide on his handsome mug. A couple of real pretty women clustered around him, which explained Jimmy's satisfied smile. Jack didn't know how his brothers found the time to romance women, between their ranch work and their careers.

"Hey, Jack!" Jimmy waved when he saw him approach. "How'd you like the show?"

"Great," he managed to say, moving sideways to avoid a couple of men covered in makeup and holding full champagne glasses.

"Act 2 might have been a little slow," Jimmy said as Jack shook his hand. "Could you tell I missed a line near the end?"

"Not at all. The show was great."

"Thanks. What happened to your eye?"

"I got into a fight with Greg Enders at the Stampede last night."

Jimmy burst into laughter. "No, really, what happened to your eye?"

Jack sighed. "Never mind. But I got in the last punch."

His younger brother grinned, then looked past Jack. "Did you bring a date?"

"Well, not exactly." He reached over and helped Grace make a hole through the crowd. "This is Grace. She's visiting us for the weekend."

"Really? Nice to meet you!"

"I enjoyed the show," she said, raising her voice over the sound of celebrating actors. "You were wonderful."

"Thanks, Grace." He almost looked as if he was blushing, but Jack was sure that was the stage makeup. "Are you two coming to the party at Nellie's afterward?"

"No, but I need to talk to you tonight, because—"

"Jimmy!" A pretty blond woman threw her arms around Jimmy and kissed his cheek. "I *loved* the show! I couldn't take my *eyes* off you!"

"Thanks, Chrissy." He put his arm around her waist. "Darlin', meet my brother Jack and his girlfriend Grace."

"Hi, y'all. Isn't Jimmy here just the *greatest?*"

Jack ignored the "girlfriend" comment. "Yeah. The greatest." He looked at Jimmy. "Are you coming home tonight?"

"I wasn't planning on it," he admitted. "But I can be home first thing in the morning."

"Good enough," Jack agreed. He wasn't about to discuss illegitimate children in the middle of the backstage chaos, and he wasn't sure that Jimmy's dressing room would be any more private.

Grace tugged on his arm. "Couldn't we find a place to talk now? I really need to get back to Dallas. My work—"

"Just a minute," he told her, then turned to Jimmy. "You have a minute?"

Jimmy's smile died, and he unwound the little blonde's clinging arms from around his neck. "What's the matter, Jack?"

"Nothing that can't wait," Jack said, realizing a bit guiltily that he was going to spoil Jimmy's big evening. He had been so damned careful to avoid any discussions before the show that he hadn't thought about ruining the fun afterward. He should have realized that the cast would be in a state of euphoria after the curtain had come down. "I'll see you in the morning."

"But—" Grace sputtered.

"Later," he told her, gently moving her backward and out of Jimmy's hearing. "We don't have to do this now."

"But of course we do," she insisted. "I can't take any more time away from my work. Tomorrow's Sunday and I need to be home."

"You'll be on your way soon enough," he told her, taking her elbow and hustling her out of the backstage area toward the stairs. "Jimmy will be home in the morning. We can talk to him then. I don't know why I let you talk me into doing this now."

"Because I can't stay here forever, that's why. I have to get back to work. I have projects to—"

"Lady, your work schedule is the last thing I'm thinking about right now." They were outside and alone at the side of the theater. "I've been letting you call the shots here, and now that's going to stop. I've got a black eye and—"

"You like it," she said, lifting her chin to meet his gaze. "Don't expect me to feel sorry for you. You didn't mind punching that other cowboy at all."

"That's not the point." He hid his smile, remembering the surprised expression on Enders's big mug as his fist connected with flesh and bone. "I'm not ruining Jimmy's big night tonight. I'm not changing my life around because some city woman thinks one of us is the father of that child. I've got things to do, and I'm not getting them done."

"Like what?"

"What?"

"What *things* are you not getting done? What *things* are more important than finding Mac's father?"

"For all I know, Mac's father is some bartender in Dallas who thought it was funny to make up a name one night. For all I know you have no business on my ranch." That seemed to shut her up. "I'm a busy man. With a business to run. And I'm getting ready to give one hell of a party. Jason turns twenty-one, remember? And that birthday means a lot more than blowing out a few candles." He wasn't about to explain the trust fund to a stranger. Lord knows she didn't need any more reasons to think that one of the boys would make a great father. A rich father.

"Look," she said, keeping up with him as he strode down the sidewalk to the parked truck. "I don't care about your birthday party. I care about Mac. And I want to know that he is safe, with his father, before I leave. Why do I have to keep saying this over and over again?"

"You're asking a lot, lady." Jack began to lose his temper. "You can't just come into Locklin and start pointing fingers at people, saying, 'Are you a daddy?'"

He opened the door of his old Cadillac and motioned for her to get in.

She did, and Jack caught a glimpse of shapely legs before the flowered dress was smoothed into place. "You don't have to yell," she said.

He walked around the car to the driver's side and counted to ten. Yell? She hadn't heard him yell. Not yet. He was still using his calm voice, damn it all to hell. Jack slid behind the wheel and slammed the door shut with more force than he intended. Grace jumped a little and put on her seat belt. "I'm not yelling."

"*If* you're telling the truth, then Jimmy-Joe or Jethro is Mac's father. I think Jason is too young. Lucy never talked about her boyfriend being younger than she was."

"Which might let Jimmy and Jet off the hook?" he asked as he put the car in gear and headed home.

"No. They both look older. And Lucy was in her late thirties, I think. It was hard to tell, because she'd had a pretty hard life."

He sighed. "Great. Lucy was a hard-living woman with an eye for cowboys. Jet and Jimmy were hard-living cowboys with an eye for women. That doesn't mean any of them actually got together."

Grace gave him a who-do-you-think-you're-kidding look. "Which brings us back to the matter of Mac's chin."

He didn't answer. In fact, he didn't feel like talking for quite a few miles. He thought he might not talk until tomorrow. Or maybe not until August. In two weeks he would have paid off the ranch. The place would finally be his, without threats from the bank.

He told himself it was foolish to worry about one small woman and one chubby baby. Everything would work out. Jimmy-Joe, the only candidate for daddy now, would take responsibility for his son. Everything else would go along as planned, including the party. Including the distribution of the trust fund money. Little Mac could afford those fancy diapers with the cartoon characters on them. Hell, he could have his own horse and a fancy Hollywood nanny. Jack turned onto the ranch road and headed toward the house. There were lights on; Isabella had arrived home before them.

"I hoped to do this without lawyers and blood tests,"

Grace said into the darkness. "You're not making this easy."

"Easy?" he repeated. "What in hell is easy about any of this?"

"You don't have to start yelling again."

"I'm not—" He stopped and made a conscious effort to lower his voice. "I'm not yelling," he said once again. He parked the Cadillac beside Grace's Ford, then shut off the engine. He turned to Grace and met her gaze. "I don't need this in my life right now."

"And you think *I* do?"

"Why on earth are you involved? Surely there were authorities—"

"No way," she interrupted. "Not if I could help it. I spent most of my life in foster homes, and I don't want to see Mac in the same situation. He has a chance to grow up with a family, and I'm not going to let anyone take that away from him."

"Growing up in this family might not be the best thing for him. Have you thought of that?"

"Not yet."

"You might give it some thought," he said, his voice quiet.

"You're all flirts," she whispered. "Real charmers."

"Yeah," he said, reaching out to pull her into his arms. "I know." He touched her lips with a gentle kiss, enough pressure for her to know that she was being kissed, but not enough to scare her. He didn't want to part her lips and touch her tongue. He didn't want passion; he merely wanted her to know that she should go back to Dallas before she got into trouble.

But her lips were sweet. And warm. And incredibly soft. He inhaled the light scent of flowers and drew her closer into his arms. She didn't pull away, but she didn't move into his arms, either. She let him kiss her, returning the kiss slightly but almost with more curiosity than passion.

He lifted his head and looked down at her. "Maybe you'd be better off in Dallas."

"Maybe *you* would," she said, her gray eyes large in the dim light. "But I'm not going anywhere."

"That's what I was afraid of," he muttered, releasing her from his arms. "But you can't blame a man for trying."

"I don't blame you for anything," she said, and got out of the car. "You're the kind of man who would tell the truth, no matter what." She turned around and walked to the house without waiting for him to follow. And of course he didn't follow her at all. He stuck his hands in his pockets and looked up at the moon.

He was the kind of man who told the truth, all right. But he was also the kind of man who wanted nothing more than to follow his houseguest to her bed and make love to her.

5

GOOD HEAVENS, WHEN WAS the last time she'd been kissed?

This really was becoming more complicated than she wanted to admit. She thanked Lina's daughter for baby-sitting, paid her enough to make the teenager smile with surprise, and then shut the bedroom door. And locked it, just to make sure. Not that she thought that the oldest McLintock would force himself into her bedroom. He wasn't that kind of man, and it hadn't been that kind of kiss. She didn't know exactly what kind of kiss it was, but it hadn't been threatening. It had been...intriguing. And exciting.

And something to forget as quickly as possible.

Grace tiptoed over to Mac's bed and adjusted his blankets with a careful motion. Thank goodness he slept through the night, though he awoke at sunrise hungry and wanting company. Good thing she was a morning person and liked to see the sun come up.

Mac slept, oblivious to the questions surrounding his future. Grace wondered if she was any closer to finding the baby a home. She could take him back to Dallas, but would that be fair? He had a chance to grow up on a ranch, to know his relatives, to take his rightful place in the family. If she packed up the car in the morning and returned to Dallas, she would be depriving Mac of the chance to be a McLintock. Jack had warned her that none of them would make good fathers, but she wasn't so sure. Nothing she'd seen so far made her doubt her decision to come to Locklin.

If she continued to do what was best for Mac, how could she go wrong? Unless she kept kissing charming cowboys, of course. That part could never happen again. She was too smart to make the same mistake as Lucy.

"ALL I WANT TO KNOW is did you have an affair—or something like that—with a woman named Lucy Bagwell?"

Jimmy eyed his older brother warily. "Jack, it's six-thirty in the morning, and I've had two hours' sleep, and even though it's Sunday you've probably got a list of chores for me to do that are gonna take till sunset, and you're asking me about who I've slept with?"

"Yes." Jimmy's moaning and groaning didn't affect him in the least. "And I want an answer." He'd been up for an hour. When he'd heard Jimmy's truck in the drive, he'd headed for the back porch. They would have privacy out there even if Isabella decided to get up early or Grace had to feed the boy.

Jimmy sat down in one of the plastic lawn chairs and closed his eyes. "Lord, that was one hell of a party."

"Jimmy—"

"And I don't know anyone named Lucy. Can I go to bed now? If I could get two more hours' sleep I—"

"Were you anywhere near Dallas a year ago last March?"

"You and I went to the stock show, remember?"

"A *year* ago last March."

Jimmy frowned and opened his eyes. "Why are you asking?"

"Because Lucy Bagwell had a baby boy. He's six months old, and he's sleeping in the spare room waiting for someone to figure out who his father is."

"And you think he's *mine?*"

"It's sure looking that way."

Jimmy groaned and closed his eyes again. "I can't believe this. What does this Lucy woman want?"

"Could the baby be yours?"

"I don't know. I doubt it. I'm pretty damn careful."

"You don't remember where you were that March? Supposedly she met a McLintock in a bar outside of Dallas and they had a brief affair."

"Maybe if I see her I'll remember. What does she look like?"

Jack hesitated. He knew Jimmy was going to feel even worse when he heard what was coming next. "She's dead. The woman you met last night—Grace—was her neighbor. She promised Lucy to take the baby to his father."

"Which is supposed to be me," Jimmy said, sitting up straight and staring at his brother. "You think I'm a *father?*"

"It's not me and it's not Jet. And Jason isn't home to ask, though I think he's a little young for side trips to Dallas bars."

Jimmy shrugged. "The rest of us managed to get to Dallas when we were that age."

"I can't picture Jason, though."

"No—" Jimmy sighed "—neither can I." He brightened. "Hey, I'm a father! I don't think I'm gonna mind too much."

"You can't take a baby to Hollywood," Jack pointed out.

"Sure I can. I'll take Isabella with me and we'll manage just fine."

"Isabella isn't going to leave her family to go traipsing off to California."

Jimmy's face fell. "The little guy doesn't have anybody but me, does he."

Jack told him the truth, or as much of it as he knew. "Not

that I know of. If you're his father. The name on the birth certificate just gave the first initial of J, so that could be any one of us. Or else the name on the birth certificate isn't the correct one."

"Sure it is," Grace said, opening the screen door and stepping onto the porch. The little boy was tucked against her hip, and he looked at both men and smiled. "That's why Lucy named him Mac. She said he should have his father's name."

"Hey," Jimmy said, staring at the boy. "So you're the little guy we've been talking about."

Mac held out his arms, and Grace let him go to the young man. "I guess he wants to say hello," Grace said.

"He sure looks like a McLintock," Jimmy said, holding the baby on his lap and looking at his face. "But I don't remember anyone named Lucy."

"She was a tall redhead with blue eyes," Grace said. "She had a low, raspy voice and a big laugh."

"I've, uh, never exactly been attracted to redheads," he admitted, looking embarrassed. "I think I would have remembered." He turned to Jack, a hopeful expression on his face. "Jethro likes redheads. Remember the waitress over in El Paso that came all the way out here to—"

"Never mind," Jack said, cutting him off. He didn't think Grace needed to hear the details of his brothers' exploits with women. "I've got my reasons to believe that this little boy isn't Jet's."

"What do you mean?"

Jack shook his head, hoping Jimmy would get the message. He wasn't going to discuss Jet's experience with mumps while Grace was listening.

Jimmy bounced the baby on his knee, and the child gurgled as if he was enjoying it. "And he's not yours, Jack?"

"No." If he was, he'd know it. He'd sure as hell remember having sex with someone. It wasn't something he got to do every day. Or night. He avoided looking at Grace. She hadn't said anything to him yet, probably figuring he was some kind of oversexed Texas stud who spent his evenings groping women inside his old Cadillac.

"Can I get anyone coffee?" Grace asked.

Jack frowned. "You don't have to wait on us."

"I was trying to be helpful," she said, meeting his gaze. "I thought we could sit here like civilized people and discuss Mac's future."

"You know," Jimmy said, a puzzled expression on his face, "I don't—"

"Coffee, then," Jack said, ignoring his brother. Grace was wearing those shorts again and that knit shirt that showed off some tempting curves. He wondered why she wasn't married. "We'll all have coffee."

Jimmy tried again. "I have to check—"

"Black, right?" Grace asked.

"Right."

Jimmy stood up and plopped the baby in Jack's lap. "You take him for a sec. I have to see something."

"Hey," Jack said, gripping the child securely. "Where are you going?"

"I'll be back," he called, the screen door banging shut behind him. Jack looked down at the baby, who eyed him with a solemn expression. "Hey, kid. Remember me? Uncle Jack. That's not so bad, is it?" The child continued to stare at him, so Jack tried the bouncing-knee trick, but Mac still stared up at him until Grace stepped outside. She carried two steaming mugs and set them down on the old pine table that was shoved up against the outside wall of the house.

"Jimmy said he'd get his own," she said, explaining the two cups. She left him alone on the porch once again, and in a few minutes returned with a streamlined version of a stroller. "You don't have to hold him. He likes his stroller." She lifted Mac out of Jack's lap. Jack noticed she was careful not to touch him. He told himself he wasn't disappointed.

He watched as she settled Mac into his stroller, adjusted the safety straps and fixed it so he could look at both of them while they talked.

"I guess we've found Mac's father," she said.

"I guess so." Though he wasn't completely convinced. "A lawyer might tell Jimmy to get a blood test first, just to make sure."

"You'd want them to have DNA tests?"

"I don't know. It seems like there should be some way to make sure, though."

"That's fine. I want Mac to have the right father just as much as you do."

"That I doubt," he murmured. His gaze dropped to the child. He was kicking his bare feet as if he was trying to get somewhere. McLintocks walked by the time they were nine months old. His mother used to say she wondered why they were in such a hurry to get someplace they'd never seen.

"I think those kinds of tests can take weeks to get results," she cautioned.

"We'll figure it out."

"I'm sure you will." She leaned back in the chair and took a sip of the hot coffee. "I have to admit that I'm relieved. I think Jimmy is willing to take care of Mac, don't you?"

Jack didn't think that his brother had a clue about what it would take to be a father, but he didn't say so. It would be his job to educate Jimmy-Joe on his responsibilities, not Grace's. "Have you ever been married?"

"Uh, no."

"No?"

"No." She took another sip of her coffee and looked toward the outbuildings. "Aren't you usually working by now?"

"It's Sunday," he pointed out. "We try to take it easy."

"Oh."

It was easier making conversation with a six-month-old baby. Jack wiggled his fingers at the child, and the little boy moved his fist in the air. "I think he's trying to wave."

"He's too young," Grace said.

"But he's smart."

She started to smile. "You're saying that runs in the family?"

"Well, I—"

"Jack, you've got to see this," Jimmy-Joe said, bursting onto the porch. "Excuse me," he said, stepping in front of Grace and handing Jack a scrapbook. "See that review?"

Jack turned the book right side up and looked at a newspaper photograph of Jimmy dressed as a middle-aged man. "*The Odd Couple*?" he asked. "I remember that one."

"In San Antonio," Jimmy pointed out, tapping the page with his index finger. "A year ago last March. Every weekend for four weeks. I *knew* something didn't seem right when you said 'March.'"

"You could have met Lucy then," Grace suggested.

"Except I was dating a little gal who lived outside of San Antone. She, uh, kept me pretty busy. And gave me a place to live. I couldn't have been in Dallas, not even for one night." He turned to Jack. "Remember how I used to come home on Mondays and fall asleep when I should have been helping you guys with the calving?"

"I remember." And he did, now that Jimmy described it.

Jimmy sprawled in his chair and looked at Mac. "Sorry, kid, but I guess I'm just your uncle." He looked at Jack.

"We could keep him, anyway, you know. You and Isabella could—"

"That's what Jet thought, too. Does it ever occur to anyone around here that Bella and I have raised enough kids? She's going to retire, and I might, too."

"You can't retire," Jimmy scoffed. "You're only thirty-six."

"I can do any damn thing I please," he pointed out. "In one week and five days." Which wasn't exactly the truth, but he figured he had a right to his privacy.

"Excuse me," Grace said in that soft voice that made him want to take her to bed. "Could we talk about Mac, please? Could someone explain what we should do next?"

"*We* do next?" Jack asked.

She wasn't intimidated. "Where were you a year ago last March, Mr. McLintock?"

He figured she'd called him 'Mr. McLintock' to annoy him, so he plastered a smile on his face to show her he wasn't bothered at all. "Calving, I would imagine."

Jimmy hopped to his feet. "Want me to check the book?"

"What book?" Grace asked.

"No," Jack said. "I will."

"What book?" Grace asked once again.

Aw, hell. He didn't want to explain the book to a city girl. "I keep a record of all ranch business. That way we can tell what we sold, when we bred the cows, when we bought the new tractor, things like that."

Jimmy nodded, a smile on his face. "And it would tell what Jack was doing that March, too, I'll bet."

"I don't write down everything," he felt obligated to point out. "I sure as hell don't put personal stuff down."

"You don't *have* any personal stuff," Jimmy said. "You wouldn't have anything to write down."

"Thanks for pointing that out."

"Hey, no problem." Jimmy flashed Grace a movie-star smile. "He's grumpy in the morning. Have you noticed?"

"I'm catching on," she said. She pulled the stroller out of the way as Jack headed for the door and went inside. "This is turning out to be a busy morning."

Jimmy yawned and stretched. "Here I thought I was coming home to go to bed, and in about twenty minutes I find out I'm a father and then I'm not a father and then maybe I'm an uncle." He closed his eyes and yawned again. "Wake me up when you find out what my official title is going to be, okay?"

"It might take a while."

"That's okay," he mumbled. "I could use the rest."

With that he appeared to go to sleep. Grace smiled as Jimmy started to snore. He seemed like a nice young man; he'd been willing to take Mac to Hollywood with him. He'd suggested, as Jet had, that they keep Mac, anyway. It was easy for them to assume that their older brother wouldn't mind taking care of one more person, but Grace had seen the expression on Jack's face. He was a man who wasn't interested in fatherhood. So Grace sipped her coffee, listened to the birds, made smiley faces at the baby and waited for Jack to return with the mysterious book.

"You were in Dallas," Jethro pointed out, following Jack onto the porch. "That has to mean something."

"Shh," Grace whispered. "Jimmy's asleep."

"It means I was in Dallas, that's all. It doesn't mean I went to bed with a stranger and fathered a child." Jack sat down, took a sip of cold coffee and tossed the rest into a sad-looking flower bed. He glanced toward Jimmy. "That boy could sleep through a dynamite blast."

Jet tipped his hat to Grace. "Good morning, Grace. Mornin', Mac," he said to the child, then sat down in the remaining chair. He tilted his hat back and looked around him. "This is a pretty sorry place for a family meeting. Now, if the courtyard was cleaned up, we could have ourselves some better scenery."

"Feel free to go back there and dig, weed and plant during your spare time," Jack told him. "No one would mind."

"Isabella would have my hide."

"Why?" Grace couldn't help asking.

"She thinks we'll put all the flowers in the wrong places," Jet said. "And she figures she's going to get it all done by herself in the next two weeks."

"It will be beautiful for the party," Grace said. "Isabella told me you were going to have it there."

"Yep. If it gets done in time."

"It'll get done," Jack declared. "Everything will get done."

"The band's coming early to help."

Grace wanted to laugh at Jack's expression. He didn't look at all impressed with that news.

"Why?"

"To help out."

"They get kicked out of another apartment?"

"Well..."

Mac let out a loud wail, Jimmy stopped snoring, and the other two men looked at Grace for help. She unhooked him from the seat belt and lifted him into her arms.

"What's the matter with him?"

"That meant he was tired of sitting by himself when there were lots of people with laps."

Jack nodded. "Smart kid."

Jet agreed. "Yep. But what are we going to do about him?" He looked at his older brother. "You're sure you didn't have a little too much fun in Dallas at the equipment show?"

"I'm sure," he said through gritted teeth. "I looked at tractors. I had a couple of drinks with some of the boys from Santa Fe. I went to bed. Alone."

"So, if it's not you, not me and not Jimmy, then—"

"We're not a hundred percent sure about you."

Jet nodded. "I'll take care of that. Then what?"

"We're going to talk to Jason."

Jimmy opened his eyes and struggled to sit up. "Jason? Where is he?"

"We don't know. He called a few days ago and said he had things to do and wouldn't be home right away."

"What kind of things?"

Jack shrugged. "I didn't talk to him. Bella did."

Grace bounced Mac to make him giggle. "I can't stay here much longer." She looked at Jack; after all, he sat in the chair closest to her. "Should I take Mac with me?"

He didn't hesitate, just looked at her with those dark eyes. "We'll wait for Jason. Can you do that?"

"How long?"

"I don't know. Soon, I would think. Today, tomorrow, maybe."

Grace looked around her. Jet winked, Jimmy smiled, and a horse whinnied from somewhere over by the barn. There was an entire courtyard to weed and teenaged baby-sitters to hire. There was Jack, who had kissed her last night as if he found her irresistible. "All right. I'll stay until you talk to Jason, but if he's a McLintock you have to make plans for him."

Jack didn't smile. "Agreed" was all he said.

Mac chuckled and pulled her hair.

"WHAT THE HELL is she doing?"

"Weeding."

"I can see that," Jack said, standing with his hands on his

hips. He and Jet watched Grace from the glass doors of the living room. The wall of doors was designed to open onto the courtyard, but that part of the house had been neglected since Jess McLintock died. "But why?"

"I guess she felt like it" was all Jet could come up with. He didn't have any idea why their houseguest wanted to pull weeds, but if she did, why would Jack want to stop her? He was always trying to get people to work.

"She's not even wearing a hat. She could get heat stroke."

"Well, get the woman a hat." Jet tried not to smile at the expression on Jack's face. He looked like a man who couldn't have what he wanted, a rare thing for their oldest brother. Jet couldn't wait to tell Isabella that he'd caught Jack pacing in the living room.

"We don't need a sick woman around here," Jack grumbled. Jet turned back to watch Grace dig weeds from between flat stones. She wore an old pair of gloves and was on her knees digging with a small spade. Mac sat in his stroller in the shade of the porch. He was most likely sleeping, since his head was tilted to the side. "Especially not now."

"Less than two weeks to go." Jet clapped his brother on the back. "I'm going to Nashville, Jimmy's heading for Hollywood, and Jason is going to grad school. What are you going to do with your money, Jack? Buy some more cows?"

Jack didn't answer for a few moments. "I don't know," he said. "I haven't decided what I'll do. I'll give Isabella enough so she can retire."

"We'll all chip in for that," Jet agreed.

"And then, we'll see. I can't shake the feeling that something is missing. I don't have the talents the rest of you have. All I know is ranching, and yet sometimes I want to get into my car and drive away. Far away."

Jet didn't know what to say. He'd always pictured Jack as the solid older brother, the brother who would always be on the ranch, always available to solve any and all of his younger brothers' problems. "Maybe you spend too much time alone. You should get out more."

"Like I did Friday night?" He pointed to underneath his eye where the skin was still bruised and swollen. "I don't think so."

"Hey, you got to dance with a pretty woman. And you got to hear one of the new songs."

"I heard half of it," he said. "Until Greg Enders decided to fight."

"I'll play the rest at the party," Jet promised. "We don't have a gig next weekend so we have lots of time to practice. We decided not to take any more gigs until we hit Nashville. And we're all yours until the party."

Jack didn't seem to be impressed with that information. "Have you told Isabella that?"

"Oh, they're bringing their own food. And their own beer. Gus has an old trailer he's pulling behind his truck, so the guys won't be any trouble."

"I'll believe it when I see it," Jack said, still watching Grace. She'd made quite a pile of weeds.

"Maybe you should help her," Jet pointed out. Jack needed a woman. Anyone could see that. "You could bring her a hat. And you could push the wheelbarrow."

He could tell Jack was thinking it over by the way he was scowling. Jack never looked happy when he was thinking. "I thought I'd take the truck and go out and check on the cows up north this afternoon. Unless you want to do it."

"I'll do it," Jack said. "Only I'm going on horseback. Last time I was up there the road was washed out."

"Why don't you take Grace up there with you? Show her

another part of the ranch, keep her from working herself to death out in the courtyard."

"What about the baby?"

"I'll watch him."

Jack turned and looked at him. "You? You don't know anything about babies."

"Hey, I'm going to make a pretty damn good uncle."

"You sure you want to have that test tomorrow?"

Jet shrugged. "I need to know if I'm shooting blanks or not. But I'm damn sure I haven't had sex without using a rubber, so there's no chance of my being Mac's father."

"I've got to find out who is." They both looked over to the sleeping child. "If he's not one of ours there's no sense worrying about it."

"And if he is?"

"We'll do what we can," Jack promised. "Whatever that is."

Jet chuckled. "I think Grace is going to make sure of that."

"She's a pain in the neck."

"You like her."

Jack shrugged. "I don't have a lot of experience with women."

"At least you recognize a pretty one when you see one." Jet nudged his brother toward the door. "Go see if she wants to go riding with a cowboy. Quit worrying about the kid and concentrate on being with a woman."

Jet strolled out of the living room to the kitchen. It was Bella's day off, but he'd find her. He couldn't wait to tell her that he was right, after all: Jack had his mind on something else besides cattle.

"YOU DON'T HAVE TO DO that," a low voice said. Grace had seen Jack's shadow before he spoke, but she didn't stop pulling weeds. She liked to pull weeds. She liked plants, although she was used to plants in pots. She'd have to call her neighbor and ask if she would water her plants.

"I don't mind," she said without looking up. She could see the toes of his dusty brown boots near the pile of weeds. "I can't just sit around doing nothing."

"You don't have to work," he insisted.

"I don't mind. This is a beautiful courtyard. Isabella said you're having the party out here."

"Part of it," he said, stepping in front of her. He sat on his haunches so she had no choice but to look at him. He was better-looking than his younger brothers. More solid, with less charm and more substance. She liked the younger boys, but they still seemed like young men. Jack McLintock was very much a grown man.

Don't fall in love with a cowboy. There was little chance of that, Grace decided. This particular cowboy didn't spend much time talking or smiling. She waited for Jack to say something else, and when he didn't she looked down at the skinny row of weeds between the flat stones.

"If you're going to be outside you should be wearing a hat," he said, holding out a worn brown Stetson. She took it and put it on. And felt like Annie Oakley.

"Thanks."

"Now you're ready." He stood and held out his hand. "Come on."

It was ridiculously easy to put her hand in his and let him help her to her feet. It was ridiculously hard to pull her hand away from those rough, warm fingers. She brushed the dirt from her jeans. "Ready for what?"

"You said you've never been on a horse." He waved toward the direction of the barn. "I have a couple saddled and ready to go."

"But Mac—"

"Will be with Isabella. She and her granddaughters are arguing right now over who is going to get him first."

"They are?" She looked over to the baby, who still slept peacefully in his stroller. "He's going to wake up soon."

"They're prepared. And eager."

"And very nice," Grace added. "They've been a big help."

"That's what families are for," Jack said. "And Isabella and her family have been on this ranch longer than I have."

"You're very lucky."

"Yeah," he said, adjusting the brim of his hat. She couldn't see the expression in his eyes now. "Now and then."

"Is it a very tame horse?"

She thought she saw him smile. "And old, too. We'll take it slow."

Grace somehow doubted that.

6

"PUT YOUR LEFT FOOT in the stirrup and swing yourself up."

Easy for him to say. Grace eyed the animal, who suddenly appeared to be three stories high. The horse shook his head and stomped one foot. "What does that mean?" She pictured the horse thinking, *No way am I going to let that woman from Dallas climb on top of me.*

"Flies."

"Oh." The horse looked forward again and stood patiently while Jack held his reins in one hand. Grace grabbed the saddle horn, stuck her booted foot in the stirrup and managed to sprawl against the animal's side.

"Throw your right leg over and you're all set."

She did and she was. Barely. And she hadn't looked graceful, either. "I wish you'd given me a shorter horse."

"Cobble may be a little on the tall side, but he's as tame as they come. And almost twenty years old."

"That's good?"

"That's old." He handed her the reins. "Hold these in one hand, like this. You are right-handed, aren't you?"

"Yes."

"Okay, then hold the reins in your right hand. When you want to go left, press the reins against the right side of his neck. When you want to go right, press the reins against the left side of his neck. When you want him to move, nudge his sides with your heels. Those boots okay?"

She'd borrowed them from Lina. "Fine. And what do I do when I want to stop?"

"Pull back. Gently. If you do it too hard, he'll stop short and you'll fly over his head."

Grace gulped. "Well, I wouldn't want to do that."

"No. Not your first time in the saddle, anyway." Jack swung easily onto a heavily muscled palomino and gathered the reins. He looked exactly like every cowboy in every western movie she'd ever seen.

"Hi, Cobble," Grace said, patting the horse nervously on the neck. He was a nondescript brown color; his mane and tail were sparse and a shade darker than the rest of him. "Is he named for apple cobbler?"

Jack looked over his shoulder and gave her a strange look. "No. He came to us as Cobble. I don't know why." He brought his horse around to stand beside hers. "We'll walk for a while, until you get used to being in the saddle."

"A while" had better be about six hours. Her horse started up on his own as soon as Jack nudged his into a walk, so Grace hung on to the saddle horn with one hand and the reins with the other. She refused to topple from the saddle. If she broke any bones she wouldn't be able to take care of Mac. She didn't want to think about how much she'd miss him when she left. Instead, she looked at Jack's broad back. His horse kept pulling ahead, and Jack kept bringing him back to fall into place beside Grace and Cobble.

"Sorry," he said, reining the prancing horse. "He likes to be first, and he likes to go fast."

"You won't go fast, will you?"

"No." He smiled, which made him look much younger. "I'll stay here with you."

Grace didn't know why the simple sentence gave her a

lump in her throat. Maybe because no one had promised such a simple thing before.

"What's wrong?" He drew closer. "If you're that scared, we don't have to ride. I thought you'd enjoy—"

"I'm fine," she managed to say. "I was just thinking about something else, that's all."

"Keep your mind on your riding," he said. "Or you'll wind up sitting in the dust."

Grace laughed. "Okay, cowboy. I'll pay attention."

"See that you do." He smiled again, only this time Grace's heart pounded just a little bit faster. Which, she told herself, was silly. She was twenty-nine years old, and much too mature to react this way to a set of wide shoulders and a Stetson.

They rode in the opposite direction from where they'd been yesterday. This time he guided her north, over some gentle hills and along a trail lined with the occasional mesquite. A hot breeze blew against her back and sent tendrils of hair against her cheeks. The old hat shaded her from the relentless sun, and the long-sleeved shirt she'd borrowed from Isabella protected her skin. She began to relax, especially since Cobble showed no signs of wanting to race the restless palomino. She loosened her grip on the saddle horn. Jack pointed out various cattle and their little calves, explained how the ranch was run and described how hard he and his brothers had worked to keep the place going over the years. He seemed to want her to understand what a hard life ranching was.

So she listened. And she thought of Mac growing up on this Texas ranch. He would work hard, but he would have a father and uncles and the grandmotherly Isabella to love him. He would be where he belonged, and he would grow up knowing it. No matter how difficult this weekend had been, Grace knew that she was doing the right thing.

They rode for more than an hour, until Jack halted before a shaded spot by a shallow pond.

"You ready for a break?"

"Yes." Her thighs were protesting the hour on the saddle, but she didn't want to complain. Cobble had behaved himself nicely. She attempted to pull back on the reins, but the horse stopped voluntarily before she said, "Whoa. Will he hold still while I get off?"

Jack swung out of the saddle and walked over to her. "He's not going anywhere," he assured her. "Just get off the opposite way you got on."

"That's easy for you to say." Her muscles refused to cooperate. "You'll have to give me a minute."

"Here," he said, lifting up his arms. Grace let him help her from the horse and stand her on her feet in the grass. He didn't release her until she told him she was fine. It took only a few minutes for her feet to work, and Jack returned to his horse and unpacked his saddlebag.

Grace took off her hat and ran her fingers through her hair. She stayed in the shade, then sat down with her back against a tree trunk when Jack came over with a canteen.

"Have some water," he said, handing it to her. He unwrapped a package of sandwiches and cookies and put it between them. "I brought lunch," he declared. "It isn't much, but it was the best I could do on short notice. I'll bet you were too busy to eat breakfast."

"This is great," she told him, surprised at how hungry she was. She'd made herself some toast after she'd fed Mac, but she hadn't thought about lunch for herself. She helped herself to what looked like a roast beef sandwich. "I'm impressed that you thought of it. Thank you."

"No problem." He sat down and took a sandwich for himself. "We always carry water when we head out."

"Why are you doing this?"

"Doing what?"

"Taking me out here. Showing me more of your ranch. Fixing lunch."

He didn't answer right away. "I guess I wanted you to know what kind of life Mac is going to have here."

"That's what I thought." She took a bite of her sandwich. Okay, she was right. It was because of Mac and not because he liked her. It was a ridiculous thought, anyway. "I think he'll have a good life here with one of you. Were you hoping I'd take him back to Dallas?"

"I don't know." He ate half of his sandwich before speaking again. "I guess I was hoping to get to know you better. It's not easy to try to figure all this out. I've never been faced with anything like this before."

"What do you want to know?"

He studied her with that familiar serious expression. "Why did you get involved in this?"

"I told you. I made a promise."

"But why? Surely it was up to the state authorities to find the child's real father."

"And put him in a foster home until they figured it out—if ever? No." She said it more emphatically than she would have wished, because his dark eyebrows rose.

"You have something against foster homes?"

She lifted her chin. "I've lived in a few. Some were wonderful and some weren't."

"Where were your parents?"

"No one knew." It wasn't hard to say it anymore. Not really. If she kept her tone very matter-of-fact, then Jack wouldn't think it bothered her. "No one ever found out."

"How old were you?"

"Four. I never knew who my father was. I don't even know if my mother knew. One day she left me at day-care and never came back to get me. No one ever found her or discovered what happened."

"People don't just disappear," he said, clearly bewildered.

"Of course they do." She set the remaining section of her sandwich on the aluminum foil and took a sip of water from the canteen. "It happens all the time."

"Were you eventually adopted?"

"No." She slapped a fly that landed on her leg. "By the time anyone got around to figuring out that my mother wasn't going to come back, I was too old for anyone to want to adopt me."

There was a long moment of silence. "And that's why Mac is going to have his own home."

"That's right." She looked toward the horses, who grazed on the sparse grass under the trees. "When you and your brothers get around to figuring out what to do with him, I'll go back to Dallas knowing I did the right thing."

"I see." And he looked as if he did. He climbed to his feet and held out his hand to help her up. "I just hope it works out the way you think it should."

"It will," she promised, putting her hand in his. He helped her stand, but he didn't release her. They were very close to each other and neither moved.

"You're very sure of yourself," he whispered, his head dipping toward hers.

"I have to be." He had a beautiful mouth, she thought as his lips touched hers. She should have expected to feel that tug of longing, that irresistible pull toward him. Grace moved into his embrace and felt those solid arms wrap around her. Her breasts were against his chest, her hands on his shoulders, her mouth on his. It wasn't the tentative kiss of last night. He urged her lips apart; she wanted him closer. He explored her mouth; she gripped his shoulders to keep from falling as her body turned soft and hot.

He slowly withdrew and gently set her away from him. She didn't know what to do with her arms, so she smoothed her palms on her jeans and looked around for her hat. Jack picked it up from the grass and handed it to her.

"We'd better get back." He stood there and didn't move.

"Yes," she managed to say, but her heart pounded loud enough to scare the horses.

"I guess you've seen enough."

And felt enough. Her gaze went to his lips, then higher, to those dark eyes that gave her no clue as to what he was thinking. "Yes."

He brought the horses over and helped her mount Cobble. He paused, his hand touching her leg. "I'm not going to apologize," he said.

"Good." She adjusted her hat and attempted to hide how much he affected her. "I've never been kissed by a cowboy before. Not until this weekend, that is."

He smiled, just a little. "I don't dare ask you how cowboys compare to the men in Dallas."

"There were no men in Dallas," she told him. She wanted him to know she didn't go around falling into the arms of any man who kissed her.

Jack shook his head, climbed onto his horse and picked up the reins. "Sweetheart, I can't believe they're not falling at your feet."

"Now you're teasing."

He winked at her and swung his horse toward home, leaving Cobble and Grace to follow. Grace smiled. She liked it when he didn't look as if he had the weight of Texas on his shoulders. She eyed those shoulders and remembered how strong he'd felt under her fingers. No wonder women loved cowboys. They *felt* so darn good.

NAKED WOMEN DECORATED the side of the old school bus. Black curtains covered the windows, and blue smoke poured from the exhaust pipe as the bus bounced into the yard. Jet stood in the yard and directed the bus driver to an empty area where the chicken house used to be before it burned down, and Jack reined in his horse and watched the monstrosity find a home next to the best outhouse on the property.

Cobble brought Grace up next to him. "What is it?"

"Can't you guess?"

"How?"

"From the painting." He sighed. "That's the tour bus for Jet and the Naked Ladies."

"You're kidding."

"No. They've come for the party, Jet said, but they've actually been kicked out of another apartment."

"They're going to stay here?"

"I'm afraid so. Probably until they leave for Nashville."

"In two weeks."

"Yes."

"Why is everyone leaving in two weeks?"

Jet waved and called to them, so Jack was saved from having to explain. Their grandfather's strange trust fund was pretty much public knowledge, and the folks around town were ready to help the McLintocks celebrate, but Jack hesitated to explain it to Grace. He didn't think she was here for the money anymore, but he couldn't take the chance. And he didn't have time to discuss his crazy family, not when his brother's crazy band was spilling out of the bus.

One of them went inside the outhouse, but the other four gathered around Jet and began to walk in their direction.

"I don't think I've ever seen anything like that," Grace said, still looking at the side of the bus. "It's obvious the ladies are naked, but the guitars hide everything so well."

"Yeah," Jack said, climbing off his horse. "It's real art, all right." He came over to her side. "You need some help getting down?"

"Sure."

He touched her for the first time since they'd headed for home. Since he'd put her out of his arms instead of making love to her. This time Grace managed to dismount with less awkwardness, but Jack still had the pleasure and pain of taking her by the waist and holding her steady as she touched the ground. She was small and delicate under his palms. Beads of sweat broke out on his forehead, and Jack took his hands away from that tempting little body. He had no business kissing a woman from Dallas, or kissing anyone, for that matter.

"There," he said, backing away from her. "I hope you're not sore tomorrow."

"I'll be fine." She flexed her knees a couple of times and continued to hold Cobble's reins. "Do we take the horses to the barn now?"

"To the corral," he said, "but I'll take care of—" Jet and his friends approached them, and the drummer hurried out of the outhouse and caught up with the others.

"Hey, Jack!" Jet grinned at both of them. "First you'd better say hi to the guys in the band. They want to thank you for letting them crash here."

Jack shook hands with the men while Jet introduced Grace as a "friend of the family." She told them she liked their bus and Jack winced. Isabella was going to pitch a fit over that chunk of rusty metal being parked within sight of her grandchildren.

"We're going to set up in the slaughterhouse and start practicing," Jet said.

"No one's been in there in years. You sure you want to put expensive equipment out there?"

"I've been cleaning it up," he replied, taking Jack aside.

Grace was asking the men about Nashville, and they were practically tripping over themselves to answer her. The horses stood there patiently, which was more than Jack could say for himself.

"I've got it looking pretty good," Jet was saying, "but we're going to need some more extension cords."

"In the east shed, on the wall over by the window."

"Thanks." Jet glanced over at Grace. "How was your ride?"

"Fine."

"She looked at you and blushed. That's a good sign."

"Like hell."

"Seriously," Jet insisted. "I saw her when you helped her from her horse. Which wasn't exactly necessary. She looked capable of climbing down from old Cobble without you holding on to her."

"I didn't mind."

Jet chuckled. "No, I'm sure you didn't mind at all."

Jack looked over his brother's shoulder as a truck and trailer pulled into the yard. "Looks like Gus has arrived."

"Great! He's got the food." Jet hurried over to talk to him, and Jack returned to the group of men gathered around Grace. He'd known most of them since they were teenagers. They were a decent group, just a little rowdy. And they loved to play music. Jack took the reins from Grace as the men hurried over to greet the bass player.

"I'll take care of the horses," he said.

"Thanks." She smiled at him again, and his heart did strange things in his chest. "I'd better go check on Mac." She hesitated before walking away. "Thanks for teaching me how to ride."

He tipped his hat. "Any time."

Jack watched her walk toward the house before he turned away and led the horses to the corral. Their ride hadn't exactly been much of a workout, but he felt like he'd been put through the wringer. He couldn't believe she'd only been here three days and already he was worn out.

"YOU DON'T THINK he's too little?"

Isabella folded her arms across her chest and studied the baby as he sat in the high chair. "I think he likes it."

"Really?"

"Look at him." Isabella smiled with grandmotherly pride. "He likes being a big boy and sitting there."

Mac grinned as if he understood what she said and slapped his little hand on the plastic tray. When he realized it made a noise, he did it again. Several times.

"I guess you're right," Grace said, keeping a careful eye on the child. "He can't fall out?"

"No. There are safety straps, and I put a little pillow around him to prop him up." She clapped her hands and made the baby chuckle. "Oh, what a big boy you are!"

Mac proudly banged the tray again, as if to show her just what a big boy he was.

"He's a McLintock, isn't he?" Grace asked.

"I think so," the older woman agreed. "He looks like the boys did when they were little."

"But none of the men are claiming him."

Isabella motioned for Grace to sit down. "They will have to," she said, pouring two glasses of lemonade. She brought them to the table and sat down opposite Grace. Mac practiced slapping the tray.

"Thank you."

"You and Jack had a nice ride?"

Grace smiled. "It was more like a 'walk,' but I got to see more of the ranch. It's a big place, isn't it?"

"Yes. And it means a lot to Jack. He's worked hard to keep it. You are going to stay?"

"For a little bit longer. Until Jason arrives."

"Jason isn't Mac's father," Isabella declared, her brown face creased with worry.

"Then, one of the others isn't telling the truth."

Isabella shrugged. "Jet is not the one. And Jimmy-Joe told me that he was in a play that month. He didn't even have a car that winter, and he already had a girlfriend."

"Having a girlfriend doesn't necessarily mean that he didn't, um, meet another woman."

"No, but Jimmy is loyal when he is in love. And he thought he was in love, until the girl left him for someone else."

"Why are you sure it's not Jet?" Mac squeaked, and Grace patted his soft little hands. He patted hers back.

"That is for him to say, but I think the chance is only very slight."

"Which leaves Jack." Grace could picture Lucy with Jack, but she didn't like thinking about it. Any woman would find him attractive and sexy and appealing, and Lucy had liked cowboys. She'd said they knew what they were doing and they took their sweet time doing it.

"I don't believe that, either," Isabella said, "but there's no denying the boy's chin. He had to get it from somewhere." She studied the child's face again. "But none of those boys would lie. That is what puzzles me."

Jason, Grace decided. He was the youngest and would

have been intrigued with an older, experienced woman. She couldn't blame him. Lucy had been a woman who lived life to the fullest and enjoyed her men the same way. Now she was gone and here was Mac, a little boy who needed his daddy. "I should go back to Dallas," she said. "Maybe I should take him with me until all of this is straightened out."

"With Jet in Nashville and Jimmy in Hollywood? No." Isabella shook her head. "There is not enough time. They will all be gone soon, and whatever is decided has to happen in—"

"I know. Two weeks."

Isabella nodded and drank the last of her lemonade. "I don't have much time to get the courtyard ready. I heard you like to weed?"

Grace smiled. "I hope you don't mind."

"Mind? Of course not. Come," she said, standing up. "I'll show you what I have planned. You can help, I think."

"I'd like that. If you don't think I'd be in the way."

"In the way?" Isabella scoffed. "You're practically one of the family now."

Grace watched the woman extricate Mac from his high chair. *One of the family.* She liked the sound of that. At least for now.

"IT'S JASON," JET SAID, holding out the telephone receiver. Everyone at the long table stopped talking. Isabella had cooked up an extra pot of chili and had made sure all of the band members joined them for supper. Jack stood up and tossed his napkin on the table.

"I'll take it in the office."

"He wants to talk to Jimmy first." Jet spoke into the phone again. "Yeah, kid, we're eating chili. Isabella outdid herself again." He paused. "Yep, we're all set. Don't forget to bring it."

"Bring what?" Jack asked, moving around the table.

"His diploma," Jet said, then listened into the receiver again. "Yeah, okay. Sure."

Jimmy scraped his chair back and took the phone from Jet. "Hey, kid, how are you? Still smarter than the rest of us?"

Jack held up five fingers so that Jimmy would know that he was getting five minutes to chat with Jason and no more. He left the kitchen and hurried down the hall to his office to pick up the extension. He gave Jimmy a few minutes, then picked up the phone.

"Anytime," Jimmy was saying.

"Jason?" Jack wanted to hear the kid's voice. "Where are you?"

"Hi, Jack. I'm on my way home, don't worry."

"I *am* worried," he said, but hearing Jason's voice made him smile to himself. The kid sounded just fine. "We figured you got lost."

"Nah. I just had some stuff to do before I got home, that's all."

"What kind of 'stuff'?"

Jimmy broke into the conversation. "Hey, kid, I'm going back to eat my dinner before anyone else gets it. See you later."

"Yeah, later," Jason said.

Jack heard a click, and then the connection became louder. "So, why aren't you here yet? We can't start the party without you."

"I've been packing, getting things together, you know. I've got a lot of things to talk to you about."

"Yeah? Well, get your butt home, then."

Jason laughed. "I'll be there. Tell me again when we meet with the lawyers."

"A week from Friday. At 9:00 a.m."

"I'll be there."

"You'd better be home before that, Jase. We could use you around here." He could hear Jason laugh.

"You can't wait to put me back on a horse and make me fix fences," he said. "How is everybody there? Everything okay?"

"It's fine," Jack fibbed. "Jet's band is here getting ready for the party. When are you coming? It better be soon."

"I'm bringing a surprise, too." Jason's voice grew serious. "Jack, I've got a lot of news."

"About going to England?"

"More than that. I'll tell you when I see you."

"Tell me now." He wasn't too thrilled with surprises, especially after the last few days.

"Nope. Can't. You have to see for yourself."

"I don't want—"

"I'll be home in a few days."

"When, exactly?"

"As soon as I can," Jason promised. "Tell everyone I said hi and tell Isabella that I can't wait to have chili again. Do you think she'll make my favorite?"

"She will, once she knows you're heading home."

"I'm on my way. Just give me a few more days."

"Okay, buddy," Jack said. "Take care, and don't be too long."

"See ya, Jack."

"Okay, kid. Take good care of yourself and come home safe."

He heard the receiver click, and then the dial tone. Then he realized Jason hadn't said where he was. He was bringing a surprise. He was on his way home.

Jack shoved his hands in his pockets and looked out the window. He knew he should rejoin the group seated around the kitchen table, but he really didn't feel like talking right now. He wanted that boy home. He needed to know if there was any chance that Jason was Mac's father. Because if he wasn't, there was only one other possibility.

And that didn't bear thinking about.

7

ON MONDAY MORNING Grace worked out a plan for the courtyard, one that involved flowers in big pots. Of course, the weeding had to be finished first. Isabella said that Jack planned to drape strands of little white lights along the porch eaves, and there would be tables filled with food lining the side that opened onto the kitchen.

"You must stay for the party," Isabella said, pushing the empty wheelbarrow beside her. "It is going to be so beautiful."

"I'm not very good at parties," Grace admitted, though she wanted to stay. She also knew she should leave, but she couldn't use work as an excuse. Work could wait; seeing that Mac was settled and cared for couldn't.

"Then, it's a good thing for me that you are good at planting flowers."

"Flowers are easy," she said, attacking another set of weeds. She looked over at Mac, who lay on a blanket in the shade where Marta and Mica watched over him. "Easier than children."

"You don't want to have children?"

"Oh, it's not that. I would love to have a family, but I worry that I don't know how to take care of Mac. I worry all the time that I'm doing something wrong."

"You are not," Isabella insisted. "He is a happy child, and a healthy one. The size of those thighs! My goodness!"

"He's going to be a big boy."

"And he will be fine," Isabella assured her. "You have nothing to worry about, except what you will wear to the party."

Grace shook her head and sat back on her heels. "I'll be long gone before then, so I'm not worrying about it." But she was running out of clothes, even though she'd washed the few things she brought with her. A sundress, a pair of shorts, jeans, some underwear and two shirts weren't getting her very far. "I wish Jason would show up soon."

"Jack told him to get home as soon as possible, but I don't think that boy was paying attention."

Grace thought he sounded irresponsible, but she didn't say so. Clearly Jason was a favorite of Bella's. The woman's face lit up whenever she talked about him.

"Well, it would sure help to talk to him."

"He has a scholarship to go to school in England. Did Jack tell you?"

"Yes. He said Jason was smart."

"And he writes poetry, too," the woman added, attacking weeds a few feet away. "His poems have won prizes at college."

"Maybe that's his surprise. A book of poetry."

Isabella's brown eyes lit up as she looked at Grace. "Oh, do you think so?"

"If he's a poet..."

"Of course. He's bringing us his first book. I never thought of that. I wonder if Jack thought of it."

"Thought of what?" a voice asked.

They turned around to see Jack tickle Mac's tummy. Grace answered, "We've been talking about Jason's surprise and what it might be. I thought of a book of poetry."

"Could be, I guess." He stood up. "I'm going to town. Do you need anything?"

"Take Grace," Isabella said. "She needs some clothes if she's going to stay here and wait for Jason."

"I don't—"

"Sure you do," the older woman said. "And this is your big chance to see Locklin. You don't want to miss out on that, do you?"

"I'm not ready to go to town."

"I'll wait for you to clean up." He looked at his watch. "If you hurry. I have a meeting at eleven-thirty."

Isabella shooed her away. "Go," she urged. "The girls and I will spoil your boy while you're gone. And you can pick up some groceries for me while you're in town."

Grace couldn't say no, not when Isabella needed groceries. She stood up and tried to brush the dirt from her jeans. "All right. I'll shower and put on my dress."

"I'll wait here," Jack said, and tickled Mac again.

Grace hurried as fast as she could. She grabbed her purse, made sure she had her credit card and checkbook and was back in the courtyard twenty minutes later.

Jack looked at his watch, then at her. "Not bad" was all he said.

Grace thanked the girls, promised to bring them something special from town and kissed Mac's soft cheek. "Be a good boy," she told him, inhaling the sweet scent of baby powder. She'd bathed him this morning, the part of the day he loved the best. And she'd kissed his toes and tickled his feet and made silly noises on his belly so she could listen to him laugh.

"You're going to miss him," Jack said.

Grace didn't think it was very nice of him to point that out.

ARTIE BALLARD HELD UP one huge hand. "Stop right there, son," he drawled. "I am *not* hearin' this."

Jack glared back. "Then, how in hell am I supposed to tell you what's going on?"

"I'm your lawyer," Artie said, leaning forward in his huge leather chair. "But I can't tell you to break the law. It's against the rules." He leaned back, gave Jack a wink and said, "Let's speak hypothetically. About a rancher in Oklahoma. Let's call him John Wayne. Why don't you tell me a story about John Wayne?"

"I don't want to talk about anyone called John Wayne. I need some advice and I need it now. And I am *not* breaking any laws, by the way."

Artie sighed. "All right, boy. Go on."

"Like I said, she arrived with a baby and a birth certificate with the McLintock name on it."

"You have it?"

"Here's a copy." Jack took the folded paper from his shirt pocket and handed it to Artie. The stocky lawyer, who looked more like a cattle auctioneer than one of the smartest lawyers north of San Antonio, unfolded the paper and examined it.

"What does she want?"

"She wants to give the baby to its father. Trouble is, none of us seems to be the father."

Artie chuckled. "That Jet oughta be more careful with his women. He's going to have to pay for this one."

Jack shook his head. "Jet had trouble with mumps when he was fifteen. I think he might be out of the fatherhood department. Jimmy-Joe was doing a play in San Antonio during the month that the baby was, uh, conceived, and his truck was broken. He had a girlfriend, too, so I don't think he was making trips to Dallas."

He put the paper to the side of his desk. "May I keep this?"

"Sure. I made extra copies."

"This woman showed you the original?"

"Yep."

"So that leaves you and Jason. And I'm goin' to assume that neither one of you should be called 'Daddy'?"

"If I'd made love to a redhead in Dallas, I'd remember," Jack declared.

Artie sighed. "So would I, son."

"But I didn't."

"I did," the lawyer said. "Twice. Only it was in Fort Worth, on the fourth of July. I always liked redheads, and this one was no exception."

"Her name wasn't Lucy Bagwell, was it?"

"No. And I'm thinking of something that happened twenty-one years ago."

"So, you'd understand that I'd remember something that happened a year ago last March."

"Yep. Now, Jet, on the other hand, might have so many women he doesn't remember them all, but you—" Artie shrugged, making Jack feel more like a monk than a rancher. He tried to get the conversation back on track.

"I haven't talked to Jason about this, but he's been in school in Oklahoma. I can't picture him going to Dallas and, uh, getting into trouble."

"Neither can I, but boys will be boys."

"Not Jason. He's more serious, more into his books and his poems."

Artie's eyebrows rose. "You're saying—"

"No, that's not what I'm saying. As far as I know, he likes girls just fine. But he would have been too young for this woman."

The lawyer shook his head. "I've seen it all, son. No rules about young or old, as long as they're consenting adults."

"Jason's not the baby's father."

"Then the birth certificate's a fraud. You want me to send someone to Dallas to check it out?"

Jack took a deep breath. "Not yet. First I want you to send someone to El Paso to find my father."

"Aw, hell," Artie swore. "You're tellin' me you think that old son of a bitch is still alive?"

"He's the only McLintock, other than me, who could have been in Dallas a year ago March. I haven't seen him in years, but if anyone was going to get someone pregnant and then leave her high and dry, it would be J.T. He took off and left my mother often enough."

Artie stood up and went over to the bar. "I know it's early, but I don't give a good goddamn about the time. You want one, don't you?"

"No, I'd better not." He didn't want whiskey on his breath when he met Grace at Nellie's. He'd offered to buy her lunch, and right now he couldn't remember why he'd thought that was a good idea.

"How about coffee, then?"

"No, thanks."

Artie returned with his drink and sat down at his desk. "I don't want to scare you, Jack, but if your grandfather's lawyers get wind of this, there could be hell to pay." He pushed a button on the intercom. "Sally, bring me the McLintock files. All of them, please." He took a sip of his drink and turned back to Jack. "Have you decided what you're going to do about the ranch?"

"I planned to use the trust fund money to pay off the loans."

"Conner's offer still stands, far as I know."

"Yeah, I know. But I don't want to sell."

Artie shook his head. "That place has been in your family for what—eighty, ninety years?" Jack nodded. "Seems a shame to let it go now." He paused as the secretary brought the papers he'd requested, then left the room and closed the door behind her. "Let's see," he muttered, flipping through the papers until he found what he wanted. "Give me a minute, Jack. I want to check something here."

"He's probably not alive," Jack muttered. "No one's seen or heard from him in fifteen years."

"Hold on," the lawyer said, studying the papers in front of him.

"Someone must have shot him by now." Jack walked over to the window and pulled back a section of the vertical blinds. Locklin was busy at noon, despite the heat. He looked down from the second-story window and wondered where Grace had disappeared to. He wished she'd walk by. He wouldn't mind looking at her, though he'd have been better off if she'd never come to Locklin.

"I thought he was in prison."

"He got out years ago," Jack said, turning away from the window and letting the blinds fall back into place. "Biggest mistake Texas ever made."

"His crime wasn't that bad," Artie reminded him.

"He wasn't your father."

The lawyer sighed. "Sit down, Jack. Why do you think this baby could belong to J.T.? He must be in his sixties by now."

"Fifty-six," Jack replied.

Artie tapped the papers piled in front of him. "I'll go through these line by line. I don't want you to worry until we have something to worry about, but you and I both know that your grandfather's instructions were pretty damn clear. I'll have a friend of mine, an investigator, do a little checking. Nothing official."

"Fair enough. And what do I do in the meantime?"

"You wait."

Jack figured he'd been waiting for sixteen years, and he

was getting damn sick of it. "What about Grace Daniels and the baby?"

Artie reached for his whiskey and drained the contents of the glass. "You keep her away from lawyers, that's for damn sure. You don't let her out of your sight, and you sure as hell don't let her know that J. T. McLintock might still be catting around Texas. Can you do that?"

"I can try. She seems to like the ranch."

The lawyer winked at him. "See that you keep her happy, son. At least until Jason turns twenty-one and all you boys have cashed your checks."

Jack shook Artie's hand and left the building. He'd never been comfortable lying, but there was more at stake than just his future. The boys had waited a long time, and as long as there was no hard information about Mac's father, Jack would have to hope that Jason wasn't the shy poet everyone thought he was.

Until he found out what the hell was going on, he'd be nice. Even if it killed him.

"EVERYONE IS SO FRIENDLY," Grace told the salesclerk. She stepped closer to the mirror and turned to see if the shorts fit her properly.

"It's a nice town," the young woman agreed, then made a face. "Sometimes it's too small, if you know what I mean. Those shorts look good on you. Nice color."

"Thanks." So far she'd found another sundress, three T-shirts and these cotton shorts. She hadn't intended to buy so many clothes, but everything was on sale and there was lots to choose from. She returned to the dressing room and changed back into her sundress. Then she decided what she was going to buy and carried the items over to the register. "I guess I'm all set."

The young woman stopped folding T-shirts and started ringing up Grace's purchases. "Where are you from?"

"Dallas."

"And you're shopping in Locklin?"

Grace chuckled. "I didn't have much choice. I've ended up staying here longer than I planned."

"We don't get a lot of visitors out here," the young woman said, smiling. "But I'm glad you came. At least it will look like I did my job today."

"Do you know the McLintock family?"

"Everyone in town does." The girl looked at her with some awe. "Is that who you're visiting?"

"Yes."

"Are you some kind of relative?"

Grace hesitated. She couldn't remember what Jack had told her to say, so she opted for something close to the truth. "I'm a family friend."

"Wow. Lucky you, getting to stay with Jet McLintock. Have you heard him sing?"

"Yes, last Friday. I bet he'll be a big star someday."

"My momma won't let me go to the Stampede, so I haven't heard his new songs." The salesclerk sighed and finished punching the numbers into the cash register. "Cash or charge?"

"Charge." Grace handed her a credit card.

"Thanks." She completed the sale, handed Grace the card and the receipt and started putting the clothes in a bright pink bag. "I guess you're here for the big party they're having. Sure is nice they're finally getting their money. Everyone in town thought Old Man Freemont was crazy for writing up his will the way he did."

"Really?" Grace tucked her wallet in her purse and hoped the girl would continue.

"Oh, yes. My grandfather said Mr. Freemont couldn't

take his money with him when he died, so he wasn't going to let anyone else have it, either. 'Course, he hated old J.T. and the way he treated his daughter.''

"He did?" She knew she shouldn't listen to gossip, but anything that concerned the McLintocks concerned Mac, and naturally anything that concerned Mac concerned her.

The girl handed her the bag and lowered her voice, even though there was no one else in the small store. "The second time Jet's father landed himself in prison was the last straw for old Mr. Freemont. My grandpa said that everyone in town was talking about the will for days, how Mr. Freemont didn't want his grandsons to turn out like their father and waste all his hard-earned money."

The bell rang as another customer walked in, so Grace thanked the girl and left. She blinked against the harsh afternoon sun and reached in her purse for her sunglasses. Well, that had been interesting. She'd bought herself a summer wardrobe and learned that the McLintocks were going to inherit some money. No wonder Jack thought her arrival with Mac was suspicious. He must have thought she and Mac were after his money. Jack and his brothers could keep it, for all she cared. All that mattered was that one of them came forward to take care of Mac. Grace looked at her watch and then crossed the street. She had an hour to shop before meeting Jack for lunch, and she didn't want to waste any time.

HE TOOK HER TO NELLIE'S for hamburgers and chocolate shakes. He carried her packages, though he couldn't figure out how she could find so much to buy. He bought her an ice cream cone at the Dairy King outside of town. And when she congratulated him on inheriting his grandfather's money, Jack almost drove the car into a ditch.

"I think it's wonderful," Grace continued. "Now I understand why everyone is leaving and why you're having such a special party."

"Who told you?" was all he could manage to say.

"A salesclerk in the—" she rustled through her bags and read the name from the pink one "—Crystal Butterfly. Nice store, too. They were having a sale."

He should have known that people would talk. No one said much to his face, though George at the hardware store had clapped him on the back and said, "See you next Saturday."

"Jack?"

He glanced over at her. She wore that flowered dress that he liked, and her hair was loose and wavy. It looked soft, like her skin. Artie had said to keep her happy. She looked happy, even though she knew something about Grandpa's will. He wondered just how much. "What?"

"What's the matter? Was it a secret?"

"Nothing in Locklin's a secret, Grace. But I didn't think people were talking about it to strangers."

"She—the salesclerk—said everyone was really happy for you. It wasn't said in a mean way."

"Fine." He told himself it didn't matter, that as long as no one knew that J.T. might still be alive then everything would turn out fine.

"And she didn't think I was a stranger, since I said I was staying at the ranch. I told her I was a friend of the family."

So much for the "cousin" explanation. "You didn't mention Mac, did you?"

He saw her frown at him. "Of course not."

They rode in silence for a few miles until she spoke again. "Did you think that I came here for the money?"

"The thought did cross my mind."

"Mac doesn't need your money," Grace said, her voice low and quiet. "He just needs a home."

"If he belongs to one of us, he'll get what he needs," Jack said. He didn't know how he could promise anything more than that. Even to Grace.

"IS THIS SOME KIND of trick?"

"Just get into the truck," Jet hollered. Jimmy-Joe had to have an explanation for everything. He opened the door and got in.

"Damn it, Jet," he grumbled. "What's your hurry?"

Jet put the truck into gear and stepped on the gas. A flock of chickens scattered out of the way and ran for their lives. "We have work to do."

"*Work?* Jack's gone to town and I just finished cleaning out the barn. Jack got me up at five-thirty."

"You had yesterday off," Jet pointed out, steering the truck toward the north pasture. "And I spent most of my day working with those horses Jack wants to sell." He'd also spent twenty minutes in a doctor's office, but he wasn't about to start talking about *that.* Talk about embarrassing, especially with Doc Reynolds's pretty nurse giving him a plastic cup and leading him toward the bathroom.

"Where are we going?"

"The road's washed out up here. I thought we'd dig it out and put some boards in so Jack can get the truck up to those pastures. It'll be faster that way."

"Faster for who?"

"Jack."

Jimmy yawned and pushed his hat back. "You want to tell me why Jack needs to do things fast?"

"Well, for one thing, he's going to be doing the work alone. Except for Lina and Ed. Isabella's talking about retiring and growing flowers, so there's going to be a lot of work for one man."

"I thought Jack was going to hire more help."

"He hasn't said anything lately." Jet guided the truck over the hill and then gave it some more gas. "Maybe he's changed his mind."

"Jack doesn't change his mind."

That was true. "It's not important," Jet said. "Right now, I'm trying to give Jack time to find himself a woman. So he won't be lonely after all of us leave. He's never been alone."

Jimmy took some time thinking that over. "What about Grace? She seems nice enough, and she's pretty good-looking, too."

"Yep. Bella and I already talked it over. Jack seems to like her, and she even seems to like him. So all we have to do is give them time to be together."

"That's why we're fixing the road?"

"Yeah. And I'm gonna come up with some other ideas, too. Like takin' over Jack's chores." He looked over to his brother and grinned. "Pretty good thinkin', huh?"

"I don't know where you get your ideas," the younger man groaned.

"I get 'em all the time. That's why I've written so many songs and why the folks in Nashville are going to love me."

Jimmy leaned back and closed his eyes. "Hollywood's going to be a piece of cake compared to ranching in Texas."

"GIVE HIM TO ME," Jimmy said. "I'll tell him a story."

Jet reluctantly placed Mac in Jimmy's arms. "He'd rather hear me sing. You'll just put him to sleep again."

"He's a baby," Jimmy pointed out, settling Mac against his wide chest. "He's supposed to go to sleep at night when people tell him stories." He looked across the living room to where Grace sat on the couch. "Right, Grace?"

"Well, I don't—"

"Stop it, you two," Jack drawled. He handed Grace a small plate that held a generous piece of chocolate cake.

"Don't let them bother you, Grace." He smiled, and her heart melted a little bit more. "They may look grown up, but they're just big kids."

"Jet's just upset 'cause he's sitting home on a Friday night," Jimmy teased.

"They're not bothering me," she insisted. And, remembering the plate in her hand, she added, "Thank you."

"Isabella's in a baking frenzy this week." With his own dessert in his hand, Jack sat down beside her. He looked over to his brothers. "You two can get your own, right, Bella?"

The old woman sat down in the rocking chair and patted her empty lap. "Give me the baby, Jimmy, and go get your cake."

He did as he was told, Jet following close behind. Mac snuggled against Bella's ample bosom and closed his eyes. "There, there," she crooned. "You dream sweet dreams, little man."

Oh, dear. What Lucy had warned her about was happening, and Grace looked around the living room and realized she should have left days ago. She should have gone home to her empty apartment and rejoiced in the solitude. She shouldn't be helping Isabella clean up the kitchen or be spending the dark evening hours relaxing with men who had worked hard all day and enjoyed something to eat before heading to bed. Soon, too soon, she would return to Dallas and curse the silence.

"Grace?" Jack's voice broke into her thoughts, and she turned to face him.

"What?"

"Is something wrong?"

"I was thinking about work," she said. "I can't remember the last time I've been away from the computer for so long." Jack had gone out of his way to be nice these past few days. She'd watched the way his brothers respected him, the way they helped one another with all of the ranch chores. The McLintock brothers were a close-knit family. And they were still waiting for Jason, waiting for the last piece of the puzzle to fall into place.

"What do you do?" Jack asked.

"I design software programs for small companies. Do you have a computer with a modem here?"

He shook his head. "I've got something I bought years ago. It works okay, I guess, but none of us ever got into it. What's a modem?"

"I guess you don't know what e-mail is, either," she said, trying not to laugh at the confused expression on that hand-some face of his.

"Nope. And if it has to do with computers, I don't want to know."

"I could teach you," she offered, taking another bite of her cake.

Jet stretched out on the floor by her feet. "You might as well teach a skunk to sell perfume, Grace. Jack's not known for trying new things."

"That's not true," Jack said, winking at Grace. "Didn't I install indoor plumbing in the bunkhouse?"

"Yeah," Jet drawled. "And I wrote that song about it. Gets a laugh every time, too."

"Oh, Jet." Isabella chuckled. "You should stop with the silly songs. Your love songs are the best of all."

"That's what all the ladies say," Jet said. "Right, Jimmy?"

His younger brother shrugged. "I don't listen to what the ladies say about you. I'm too busy listening to what they're saying about *me*."

Jack set his empty plate on the table and picked up his

glass of iced tea. "You two are going to be famous some day, I guess, but you'll never grow up."

Jimmy leaned in the doorway. "Do you have any brothers to boss you around, Grace?"

"No," she said lightly. "I always envied my friends who had older brothers, though."

Jack shook his head. "Wait until you meet Jason. He might have a few things to say about older brothers that you've never heard before."

"We've been good to the little guy," Jimmy said.

"Most of the time," Jet added, then they both began to laugh.

Isabella shushed them all. "You'll wake up the baby," she said. "And you two played too many tricks on Jason. I'm surprised he never got even with you."

Jack touched Grace's shoulder. "You don't have to answer any questions," he told her, his voice low. "The boys don't mean any harm."

"Of course they don't," she said. "I think they're great."

"Yeah," he agreed. "They're pretty good guys."

"You're lucky."

"Hey," Jimmy said, looking at the window behind them. "Someone just drove up."

"Probably one of the band," Jet said. "Gus said he was going to town."

"It's not a truck. It's a—hey, I think that's Jason's car!"

Grace turned and looked out the windows as the headlights of a small car went dark. She couldn't see much in the darkness, but two car doors slammed shut and the three McLintocks rushed out of the living room door.

8

"I TOLD YOU I WAS bringing a surprise." Jason, the tallest and thinnest McLintock brother, introduced his family to the tall, slender woman by his side. "I'd like you to meet Anne Carter, my fiancée."

"Fiancée?" Jack echoed, exchanging a quick look of concern with Grace. He was sure she was thinking the same thing he was. Another complication. A big one. *"Fiancée?"*

"Yep," Jason said, a worried look in his eyes. "I wanted it to be a surprise. I mean, I thought you guys would be happy for me."

"Hi," Grace said, shaking the young woman's hand. "I'm Grace Daniels, a friend of Jack's, from Dallas."

"No kidding?"

"Of course we're happy for you. That's great," Jack said to Jason, managing to hide his surprise and give his brother a hug. Then he turned to Anne. "It's our pleasure to meet you. And we're happy to welcome you to the family."

Jason took Anne's hand and led her over to Isabella, who had stayed in the rocking chair while she cradled the sleeping child.

"Welcome home, honey," the old woman said. "It's been too long."

"Bella, I'm going to get married in a few weeks."

"That is wonderful." She patted Jason's cheek as he bent to kiss her, then she took Anne's hand. "We had no idea!"

"I thought he should have warned you," Anne said.

"Who's the baby?"

"Shh," Anne told her future husband. "You'll wake him up."

"He belongs to Grace," Bella said. "His name is Mac."

"Hi, Mac," Jason said, keeping his voice low this time. He looked at Bella. "Does he ever wake up and play?"

"Yes, and then you have to fight your older brothers to get near him."

Anne touched the baby's hair with one finger. "He's so sweet," she murmured.

"So, you're really engaged?" Jet asked.

Jimmy smacked his youngest brother on the back. "I can't believe it. You?"

"Hey," Jason protested. "I'm twenty-one as of Friday, and I'm going to England for two years. We decided not to wait." He looked over to his older brother. "You don't think it's a bad idea, do you, Jack?"

He opened his mouth, then closed it again. He sure as hell didn't know what kind of an idea it was. "I'm glad you brought Anne home for the party," he managed to say. "I'm a little surprised by this whole marriage idea, though, but I'm sure we'll have a chance to talk about your plans in the next few days." He took Anne's hand. "It's a pleasure to meet you, Anne. I hope this bunch of cowboys doesn't make you crazy. And welcome to the family." And please, he added silently, be an understanding woman if your future husband is already a father. He'd seen the tender look she'd given Max. It could be worse. The young couple would have a nice nest egg once the Freemont money was released, Jason had his future ahead of him, and Anne seemed to like babies. Maybe, just maybe, there was hope.

Now all he had to do was pray that his youngest brother had had sex with a redhead in Dallas.

It was a strange prayer, Jack thought later, long after

everyone else had gone to bed and he sat alone in the living room. But it sure as hell beat the alternative.

GRACE FIXED MAC'S MORNING bottle when the kitchen was empty and tiptoed back to her room to feed the baby in private. She didn't want to face the rest of the family right away. In fact, she wanted to stall for as long as she possibly could. She needed time to decide what to do next.

"I think it's time to leave," she told the baby, who fixed his brown-eyed gaze on her as he sucked down his breakfast. "I tried, sweetheart, but I'll be darned if I can figure out who your father is."

She gazed out the long windows to the courtyard. Yellow flowers in brightly colored pots lined the perimeter now. She and Isabella had made a lot of progress by working together the past few mornings, while it was still cool enough to weed and plant. They were ready for that party, if Isabella's cooking frenzy was any indication. Jason would celebrate in style, while she would take Mac and return to Dallas.

Jason wasn't involved, not that she could tell. That nice young man with his nice young fiancée couldn't possibly have had a weekend affair with Lucy. He was too young, for one thing. And even if he had, would Anne be willing to mother a child who wasn't hers?

Maybe or maybe not, but Grace had begun to wonder if what she'd thought was the right thing for Mac wasn't the right thing at all. She'd wanted to give him a father, a family of his own. She'd wanted him to grow up knowing where he belonged, but so far she hadn't been able to discover where that was. So she would take Mac and leave the McLintocks to their celebration and their reunion and their dreams of fame and fortune.

"Saturday already. We've been here a week," she told

the baby, lifting him to a sitting position. "You're getting a tooth and learning how to sit in a high chair, and I've ridden a horse and been to a country-western bar. Haven't we had an exciting time?"

Mac smiled at her, drool escaping from his bottom lip and sliding past the cleft in his chin.

"But I don't know if we should still be here. Maybe I should have let the lawyers sort everything out from the beginning." She wiped Mac's distinctive chin with a tissue. "I guess it was pretty dumb of me to think I could take care of this myself."

Mac grabbed for the tissue and managed to rip a small section and put it into his mouth. Grace fished it out and wiped his damp chin one more time. "I guess you're stuck with Auntie Grace for a while longer, sweetheart." She gathered him into her arms and walked over to the window. "At least until I can decide what to do."

The baby patted the glass and chuckled. He wanted to touch everything he saw lately. The world was an exciting place when you were discovering it for the first time. "Window," Grace told him. "And see the pretty flowers out there?"

He patted the window again and left a sticky handprint on the glass. "Uh-oh," she said, making him smile. "Guess who will be cleaning a window today? Come on," she said, opening the door to the courtyard. They would take the shortcut to the kitchen. Perhaps she would see Jack. If he had some answers from Jason, then the two of them could sit down and make a decision about Mac's future.

And then she would leave. It was time. If she stayed any longer, she risked falling in love with cowboys and ranches and courtyards. It meant hoping that a handsome rancher would kiss her good-night and smile at her in the morning. She couldn't keep her heart safe much longer.

"HAVE YOU STARTED drinking?" Jason asked, giving Jack an odd look. "It's only nine in the morning."

"Lucy Bagwell," Jack repeated. "Did you have an affair with her in Dallas a year ago last March?"

Jason smiled. "This is a trick, right? Jet put you up to it, didn't he?"

"Look," Jack said, praying for patience as he sank into his office chair. He'd managed to pry Jason away from his exuberant brothers and his quiet fiancée this morning, and now the darn kid thought he was playing a joke on him. "A lot is at stake here, Jay, and I'm not playing games. You saw that little boy last night?"

"Yeah. Cute kid."

"Well, he's got 'McLintock' on his birth certificate and none of us know how it got there."

"And you think it's *me*?" Jason turned red all the way to the tips of his ears. "You think I'm his father?"

"It has occurred to me, yes."

"Heck, Jack, I'm not doing stuff like that. I'm engaged to be married."

"I'm talking about fifteen months ago, not now."

"Fifteen months ago I was up to my neck in English Lit classes. I wasn't in Dallas having, uh, you know. I sure wasn't making babies."

Jack leaned forward and made sure that Jason looked him in the eye. "If there ever was a time to tell the truth, Jason, this is it."

The boy didn't flinch. "It couldn't be me."

"You're positive? I have to be sure."

Jason turned even redder, but he held Jack's gaze with a steady look. "I've never, uh, done it."

Oh, shit. "Never?"

Jason shook his head. "I came close a few times, but

nope—never. With all the talk of disease and everything, I never found a woman who was worth it."

"You don't have to be embarrassed," Jack said. "You made some safe decisions. But you and Anne haven't, uh, slept together, either?"

"We decided to wait until after we were married." He grinned. "Which is why we decided to get married. It's getting harder and harder to stay apart."

"Yeah," Jack said, thinking of living here in the house with Grace for the past week. He'd watched her walk and smile, he'd smelled her cologne and he'd listened to her laugh and he'd wanted to kiss her so badly that he'd had to excuse himself and go out to the barn and hide. "I understand."

"Anne wanted to go to England, too, because she was a history major, so we thought it would work out better this way, getting married and all."

"And I'm sure it will." He hesitated, wondering the best way to phrase his next question. "Have you told anyone about, uh, this part of your life?"

"You mean my brothers?"

"Yes, that's exactly who I mean."

Jason made a face. "Hell, no. They'd rib me until I fell over into the dust."

"Let's keep it between us for now, until I figure out what to do about Mac."

"Whose son is he, then?"

"I don't think he belongs to any of us. There must have been a mistake," Jack assured him. "I talked to Artie on Monday, and he's going to look into it for me."

"Good. I didn't figure that Jet or Jimmy would do something like that."

"But what if they didn't know there was a baby? Those things happen."

Jason shrugged. "Which is another good reason for me to, well, you know, but I'll be real glad after the wedding's over."

"And when is the wedding going to take place?"

"In a few weeks. We're still trying to figure it out."

Jack stood up and held out his hand. "I don't know if I had a chance to say it last night, but congratulations."

Jason took Jack's hand and smiled. "Grandpa Freemont's money is going to come in handy. You guys have waited a long time for me to be twenty-one."

"I was congratulating you on your upcoming wedding."

"And I'm congratulating *us* on making it through. I know it wasn't easy."

"No," Jack said, releasing his young brother's hand. "But it was sure worth it."

He meant it, too. He sat in his chair long after Jason had gone to find his future bride and take her for a ride around part of the ranch. He hoped they would end up kissing in the barn. Which was something he wouldn't mind doing, either, come to think of it. With Grace.

And Grace hadn't seemed to mind when he'd kissed her by the stream that day. She'd kissed him back, an encouraging reaction. He'd had all he could do to get on his horse and lead her back home.

Jack leaned back in his chair and closed his eyes. If he were free to do whatever he wanted, he'd take Grace to bed. He wouldn't worry about who Mac's father was, or wonder in what part of Texas old J.T. was causing trouble. He'd let all the boys go off on their adventures, he'd pay off the bank loans, he'd admire the sunset, and then go make love to Grace.

He'd be a satisfied man, yes, sir.

Oh, Lord, how he wished the next few days would pass quickly. There were too many secrets for one cowboy to keep track of. He wished he could stop being a brother and simply act like a man who wanted one particular woman, but now he had to tell her that Jason wasn't Mac's father.

And she would want to know who was, he wouldn't be able to tell her, and she would leave. Jack paused in the living room and remembered when Grace had stood there and told him in no uncertain terms that she was bringing Mac to his father.

If Mac's father was an aging, hot-tempered cowboy with a taste for women and whiskey, a man with more wanderlust than common sense, what then? Would she give that boy to him, anyway?

He couldn't take the chance. Damn it, he didn't want her to leave. He wanted a date for his own party. He wanted someone to dance with and someone to talk to. Someone special. Someone like Grace.

Jet or Jimmy would know how to convince her to stay. They knew what to say to women, how to behave. One of them would have to tell him what to do.

"YOU MIGHT SMILE MORE often," Jet said, restringing his guitar. "Women like it when you smile at them."

"I don't know about that." Jimmy shook his head. "I think women like that brooding look. You know, like you have dark secrets and pain. They always fall for a man who looks like he's in pain."

"Pain?" Jack clearly didn't get it. "I could do the 'dark secret' thing, but I'm not real sure about the pain."

Jet grinned. Old Jack was finally starting to notice that there was a beautiful woman in the house. "You have some dark secrets, Jack? You keeping something from us?"

"Another thing, Jack. You've got to spend some time with her."

"I work all the goddamn day."

"Jet and I have been doing some of your chores. Didn't you notice?"

"Yeah, but I thought you were trying to get caught up before you left."

Jimmy sighed dramatically and rolled his eyes at Jet. "I told you he wouldn't notice."

"We were trying to give you more time. Time to spend with Grace."

Jimmy nodded. "Jet figured you're going to be lonely after we leave, and having Grace around would help."

"Lonely?" Jack roared. "You make me sound like some old retired geezer. I'm only thirty-six and I have a life."

Jet set his guitar aside. "Okay, Jack. Tell us about your life. When's the last time you had a date? Before Grace came, that is."

"I don't remember."

"It was the librarian," Jimmy pointed out. "A year ago? Didn't you take her to see me in *Fiddler on the Roof?*"

"Not one of your better performances, either," his oldest brother pointed out.

"You think it's easy dancing like that?"

Jet held up his hands. "Okay, so maybe we'd better not talk about the past. Have you kissed Grace yet?"

"That's none of your damn b—"

"He has," Jimmy declared, nodding toward Jet.

"How do you know that?"

"He almost smiled. Means he's kissed her. Probably a couple of times, right, Jack?"

"Well, I don't think it's right to talk about—"

"You're not down at the Stampede, Jack. You're in the slaughterhouse with your brothers. You asked our advice. We're giving it to you." Jet tried not to laugh, but it wasn't easy to keep a straight face when his older brother looked so confused. "Spend some more time with her, Jack. Take her riding. Or take the truck and go have a picnic. Women love picnics, and you'll have the built-in advantage of lying on a blanket with her, and the whole time she'll think you're being sensitive."

"Why?"

"Why what?" Jet picked up his guitar and tested the new strings. It would be kind of fun to write a song about picnics and sex, something upbeat for dancing.

"Why do they think you're sensitive if you're eating on a blanket?"

Jet shrugged. "Beats me."

Jack turned to Jimmy, who didn't look any more enlightened. "I don't know, either, but I agree with Jet. Have Bella fix a lunch for you. Women are always happy if you're feeding them."

Jack didn't look convinced, but Jet figured it was sinking in somewhere in his brother's thick skull. "One more thing," Jet said. "It's about time you stopped worrying about that baby and started wondering how to impress the lady. Everything else will take care of itself."

"I wish you were right," Jack said.

Jimmy nodded. "Good, Jack. You've got that 'dark secret-pain' look down perfect."

"Have you seen her anywhere?"

Jet nodded. "She was here a few minutes ago. She said something about going back to Dallas." He watched his older brother turn pale.

"When?"

"About half an hour ago."

"No, I meant when did she say she was leaving?"

Jet shrugged. "I don't know. I've offered to teach her a song, so she might come back when we rehearse. If Lina's girls will watch Mac while he takes a nap."

"Teach her a song?" Jack repeated, as if he couldn't believe it. "Grace?"

"Yeah. She was real surprised when I asked her, but then she said okay. But she said she was leaving, so she didn't know if she'd have time."

"She's not leaving," Jack said. "Not until after Jason's birthday."

Jimmy cleared his throat. "Is he, uh, you know, Mac's father?"

The guys in the band walked in the door, so Jack stood up to leave. "We'll talk about that Friday. If you see Grace, tell her I'm looking for her."

"My pleasure," Jet said, nodding. Jack was going to do just fine. He picked up his guitar and looked at Gus. "You guys ready to rock and roll?"

"Where the hell is she?"

Isabella didn't turn around but continued to mix batter in a huge bowl. "Who?"

"Grace, of course." Jack leaned against the counter and waited for Bella to give him an answer. "I've looked all over the house."

"She went outside with the baby."

"And where did she go?"

"I don't know. Perhaps to visit Lina. The girls were here earlier wanting to know if they could have Mac for a while." She looked over and smiled. "He is a sweet boy. The girls love him. We're keeping him, aren't we?"

"No. I don't know."

"He's not Jason's child, then."

Jack debated whether or not to tell her about Jason's denial, then decided against it. "I don't know yet."

"You are the only one who was in Dallas that month," Bella declared. "The others are not his father."

"And neither am I."

The old woman went back to stirring the cake batter.

"Go ahead," Jack said. "Say whatever it is you're thinking."

"No." She shook her head and rested the spoon against the side of the bowl. "I think I will be very quiet and pretend to know nothing. Like you."

Jack turned away. "I'm going to keep looking."

"You're in a hurry to find her?"

"I thought she might want to go on a, uh, picnic."

Bella chuckled. "I will fix you something to take with you. She is a pretty lady, and very kind, too. Maybe you should think about settling down."

He looked over his shoulder to see the old woman laughing at him. "I've lived on this ranch all of my life. How much more settled could a man get?"

"Oh, it takes a woman to settle a man," Bella said. "Didn't you know that?"

Jack kept walking. He didn't figure that deserved an answer. He'd been unsettled since Grace Daniels walked into his life.

"Try the courtyard," Isabella called. "She's usually out there in the morning."

Jack didn't point out that it was almost lunchtime. He'd tried the courtyard before, but it had been frustratingly empty except for all of those flowers in their pots. The courtyard had looked ready for the party. He wished he felt ready for a party. He heard the Naked Ladies start practicing in the slaughterhouse, which meant they were getting ready for the party, too. Jet had promised they wouldn't practice late at night and disturb Lina and Ed, so they'd adjusted their hours to something closer to normal.

If you could call a group of guys who named themselves the Naked Ladies normal.

She was there, in the courtyard where Bella said she would be. She wore white shorts and a shirt the color of the bright flowers she touched with her fingertips. He watched her and she didn't know it, and he wondered once again if the surge of longing that filled him was simple loneliness or something else. His brothers said he was lonely; he didn't feel lonely. Or at least he hadn't felt lonely until Grace arrived and he'd realized that he was indeed alone. Even in a house filled with noisy brothers.

Which didn't make sense.

Bella would tell him that things didn't have to make sense, that sometimes things just are the way they are.

He wanted to take her riding. He wanted to see her smile, and he wanted to kiss her again. He needed to make her stay. There was no telling what would happen when she returned to Dallas and called a lawyer. She had six days to stir up trouble; he had six days to prevent it. But lawyers and paternity suits fled his mind as Grace looked up and saw him in the doorway. Her smile warmed him, and he smiled, an idiot smile, in return. He opened the door and walked outside, across the courtyard to the woman who stopped touching flowers and put her hands in her pockets as he approached her.

"The courtyard looks good," he said. "Bella said the two of you have been working hard."

"I enjoyed it."

"And so did Bella."

"I thought you were working," she said. "You're not riding the range today?"

"Not yet. I came to ask you if you wanted to go with me. Bella will fix us a lunch."

She hesitated. "I don't think I should be going anywhere but back to Dallas, Jack. I've been here too long with nothing settled. I have to go back and find a home for Mac."

"Come riding with me," he urged. "We'll talk about it."

Grace didn't budge. "Jason and Anne have Mac, but I don't know how long they're willing to watch him."

"You go change into your riding clothes and I'll find out."

"Jason's not his father, is he?"

"We'll talk about it later, all right?"

"All right." She took her hands out of her pockets and swept her hair from her face. "Do I get to ride that nice, slow horse again?"

"I'll saddle him myself," Jack assured her. "I'll meet you at the barn in thirty minutes. Do you still have the hat I loaned you?"

"Yes."

"Good." He hesitated, then turned away. She'd said she'd go with him. At least he'd gotten that far.

THIS WOULD BE THE LAST day, she promised herself. Her last day at the ranch, her last day with Jack. She planned to enjoy herself, without a repeat of the embarrassing kiss they'd shared last time they'd gone for a ride. This would be strictly business, a private lunch to discuss what would happen to Mac. They were two adults who should be able to come up with an acceptable plan.

Just because he was handsome and looked about as sexy as a man could get in those jeans and boots didn't mean a thing. She would keep her mind on business and babies and the important things in life. They rode for more than an hour. The ever-present breeze kept Grace from feeling the afternoon heat. He stopped before a grove of trees nestled near a shallow watering hole. Several head of cattle lazed in the heat and looked at them with curious brown eyes as they dismounted.

He came over to help her from her horse, barely touching

her waist to make sure she didn't fall. This time her feet held her up, so she turned around to tell him that she was getting used to riding, after all. One minute she was looking up at him and the next she was in his arms. She didn't intend to put her arms around him, but he bent to kiss her, and she didn't stop to think that she shouldn't be kissing him, or anyone, really. She should be back at the ranch packing up her car and saying goodbye to everyone.

Her hat fell to the ground. His hands gripped her waist and held her to him while his mouth tasted hers. It was the kind of kiss that made her forget where she was. She wanted to sink to the ground and have him follow her down, but he held her upright and kissed her neck, the sensitive skin below her earlobe, the hollow at the base of her throat, before returning to her lips. His tongue teased hers, made her cling to him even harder. After long moments, during which Grace figured she would gladly spend the rest of her life kissing this man, he lifted his lips from hers and caught his breath.

"Oh, hell," he muttered, and kissed her again. Then he scooped her into his arms and carried her to the shade. Grace wrapped her arms around his neck and hung on.

"Why are you swearing?"

"Because," he said, setting her carefully on the dry grass, "I was going to wait until after lunch to kiss you."

She smiled. "I thought we were going to talk about Mac."

He sat beside her and leaned against the tree. Their thighs touched, turning Grace's skin warm. "I lied."

"I didn't think a McLintock ever lied," she couldn't help teasing.

"I did, this one time," he admitted. "To get you to come out with me. Jet told me that women like picnics, so I figured I'd give it a try."

She smiled at him. "So far, so good."

He leaned over and kissed her on the lips. Their embrace began simply and ended with half of Grace's clothes unbuttoned and Jack lying on top of her. It was a few minutes before either one of them could speak.

"I guess I'd better get the food." He stood up and walked over to the horses and retrieved the saddlebags. He returned to the base of the tree and spread out a large cloth, then placed plastic containers and silverware in the middle. "There," he said. "Bella packed enough stuff for five cowhands."

"Should I start opening them?"

"Yeah. I'll pour us something cold to drink." He sat down, rummaged through the bag and found two tin cups and a bottle of wine. He fiddled with a Swiss Army knife and found the corkscrew, uncorked the bottle and poured them each a glass of wine. "Now, this is what I call living."

The containers held shredded lettuce, chopped vegetables, cheese, sliced grilled chicken breasts and homemade corn tortillas. "You don't usually have tacos on Saturday afternoons?"

"No, Grace." He handed her a cup. "But I'm not complaining."

"Neither am I." She took a sip of the white wine and then looked down at the food in front of them. "Bella went to a lot of trouble."

"She likes you." He took paper plates from the other bag, then rummaged to the bottom and found paper napkins.

"I like her, too. She's been very kind to me, and she treats Mac like one of her own grandchildren."

"Then, why are you talking about leaving?"

"It's time."

"Nothing's been decided."

"Exactly," Grace said. "Nothing's been decided and

nothing is going to be. It's time I went home. I probably should have never come here in the first place. Jason's not Mac's father, and the rest of you deny knowing Lucy."

"We've told you the truth," he insisted, but she noticed he didn't look at her when he said the words. "Stay," he said, lifting his gaze to hers. "Why don't you stay and be my date for next weekend?"

Don't fall in love with a cowboy, Gracie. Grace ignored the words of advice echoing in her head. If she stopped to think about it she'd probably have to admit it was too late. "I'd like that."

"Good. Do you think we could pretend that we're just two people who have gone out to lunch?" He looked down at the food spread between them and handed her a paper plate.

Considering the way she'd kissed him, Grace wondered if she was capable of pretending anything. "Yes," she said, hoping for the best. "I think that's a good idea."

He smiled, and Grace wished he'd kiss her again. Tacos were tempting, but kissing this particular cowboy was much better. She took the plate and concentrated on food.

9

"STAND HERE AND SING into the microphone."

"I can't sing," Grace said, standing where Jet told her to stand. The slaughterhouse was a strange building, with large hooks hanging from the ceiling and stains on the cement floor. It certainly didn't look like a great place to break into song.

"Sure you can," he insisted. "Just sing 'Take off your boots' whenever I point to you and Gus. Jack, too. You're the chorus."

"I've never been in a chorus," she said, just so he'd know she had no experience singing alone or in a group. She'd been so shy as a teenager that she'd been afraid to sing along with the songs on the radio for fear someone would listen and make fun of her. She hadn't felt like singing much in those days, either.

"You are now," he said, and waved Jack over. "Jack, come on over here. Stand beside Grace and get ready to sing 'Take off your boots' when the time comes."

Jack stepped over to Grace's side. "This must be a new song."

"Yeah. I wrote it this morning, and I'm real anxious to hear how it's going to sound." He tried out a few chords on the guitar. "I think this is the right key," he muttered, then turned around to the band. "It's fast, but it should have a pretty good beat. You guys all set?" They nodded. "One-two-three!"

The crash of chords made Grace jump, and Jack touched her back to steady her and smiled. It was too loud to try to talk to him, so she smiled back as he took her hand. Jet started singing about a man who couldn't find love and how sad he was about being alone.

Jack cleared his throat.

Jet winked, then launched into what Grace figured was the chorus. "Take off your boots!"

"Take off your boots," Grace echoed, along with Jack. He had a surprisingly mellow baritone.

"Come over here and see me," Jet crooned. "Take off your boots!"

Grace was ready. "Take off your boots!" she sang, louder this time.

"I've got a little more to say, so take off your boots," Jet sang, then pointed.

"Take off your boots," they sang.

"Come a little bit closer."

"Take off your boots!"

"I'm never goin' away."

Grace stepped back from the microphone and laughed. Jet winked at her, continued with the second verse and nodded to the drummer. She couldn't believe she'd just sung a country-western song with the man who'd written it. She couldn't believe that Jack had sung along with her.

Jack nudged her. "Take off your boots," he sang near her ear. Grace joined in as quickly as she could.

She didn't know how this weekend could get any better. Yesterday afternoon had been the picnic. And the kissing. She'd spent Saturday night in the midst of the family, with Jet playing his guitar and singing everyone's requests. This morning Grace and Mac had slept late. She had awakened to hear Mac gurgling and cooing in his bed. She'd heard the comforting sound of someone watering plants in the courtyard and muffled laughter in the hall. Now it was Sunday and she was singing with a band.

And Jack was still holding her hand. "Take off your boots," she sang, right on cue this time.

She was really starting to have a good time.

"WHAT'S THE MATTER with him?" Jason ruffled Mac's hair as the baby sat screaming in the high chair, but the child refused to be distracted.

"I think he's getting a tooth. That's what Grace says," Jack answered.

Jason grinned. "Well, if Grace said it, it must be right."

"What's that supposed to mean?"

His youngest brother chuckled. "Nothing. Where'd she go?"

"To her room to get something for Mac." Jack looked at his watch. It was after two, and Isabella had promised she'd give him a list that he could take to town. She knew he usually went to town on Mondays, and this was supposed to be a major shopping trip. He'd hoped to talk Grace into going with him, but if something was wrong with Mac, Jack knew she wouldn't be able to leave him.

"If you're going to stay with him, then I'll go out and help Jet with the horses. Isabella went over to Lina's for a few minutes."

"Go ahead. I need to talk to Grace, anyway," Jack said as Jason grabbed his hat and hurried from the kitchen.

"Come here, kid." Jack lifted Mac from his chair and held him in his arms so the child, now a little quieter, could look around the room. The phone rang, and Jack answered it. "McLintocks," he said.

"Jack?"

"Yeah." The baby tugged at the cord.

"This is Artie. Can you talk?"

"Not exactly," he replied, watching Grace step into the kitchen. She smiled when she saw the baby in his arms. "Just a minute," he told the lawyer, and managed to hand Mac to Grace without dropping him or the telephone receiver. He spoke into the phone. "But I'm coming into town this afternoon. How about if we get together later?"

"Good." The man sounded relieved. "I'll be free any time after four."

"I'll be there." Jack hesitated. "This is important?"

"I wouldn't have called you otherwise, Jack. Did you have any luck talking to Jason?"

"No."

"I was afraid of that. See you later."

"Yeah. Thanks." He hung up the phone and took a deep breath before plastering a stupid smile on his face. *Did you find him* was what he'd wanted to ask, but he couldn't, not with Grace fussing over Mac a couple of feet away.

Grace looked over to him. "Is something wrong?"

"No. I just have some business to take care of in town."

"I heard you were going to pick up supplies. Would you mind getting Mac some more formula? I'll pay—"

"Don't worry about it." He could certainly afford to feed his nephew. Or his brother. Jack studied Mac's now-familiar face. *Brother?* "Just write down the name so I get the right kind."

"Okay. Thanks." She hesitated. "Would you like some help with the groceries? Mac's pretty good in the car."

And take the chance that he'd be recognized? No way. "No, I'm fine," he said, a little harsher than he intended. He tried to smile, but he could tell by the look on her face that he didn't look like he was smiling. "But thanks for offering," he said. "I have some business in town to take care of, and I don't know how long it will take."

"Okay. I just thought I'd ask." She busied herself putting medicine on Mac's gums while he fussed and drooled.

He had five days. Four, really, if he didn't count Friday. Friday morning at nine-thirty the four McLintock brothers would be standing in the office of Locklin Federal Savings Bank while the trustees wrote out checks for large sums of money.

If there were five McLintocks, no one would get a dime. And it would be J.T.'s fault, of course. Most things were.

"HE'S STILL ALIVE, all right." Artie handed Jack a manila file. "Read it and weep."

Jack sat down and opened the file while Artie poured whiskey into two glasses and put one on the desk in front of Jack. Instead of sitting behind his desk, he sat beside Jack in the vacant leather chair. "He's living in El Paso," Jack said. "The rumors were right."

"When's the last time you heard from him?"

"Oh, it's been years. I told him he was welcome to stay if he wanted to work for me." Jack took a sip of his drink. "He didn't, so he left." He turned the page to see a detailed description of J.T.'s whereabouts the past three years. "How the hell did you get all this?"

Artie shrugged. "I hired the best. Turn to page two. That's where it all hits the fan."

Jack turned the page. It was easy to see, about a third of the way down the page. "He was in Dallas during the winter Mac was conceived."

"Yep. He had a job there, but it didn't work out. So he went back to El Paso. Alone. There are some copies of interviews conducted with the people he worked with in El Paso, also interviews with three women and one man who worked with Lucy Bagwell. Nothing unusual, and they all expressed sympathy for Lucy's death."

"So another nice lady was conned by J.T."

"Looks like it. If you're sure none of your brothers is responsible."

Jack took another drink of the whiskey, then another. "I guess I'm as sure as I'm going to get."

Artie shook his head. "Damn shame."

Jack took the folder and placed it on Artie's desk. "Now what?"

"You take that folder out of the office, for one thing. This was a private matter."

"All right. And what about the child?"

"That's up to you. You and your brothers are going to be rich men on Friday morning. As soon as all of the 'McLintock boys' have turned twenty-one."

"Chances are that Mac is one of the boys."

"And he's not even a year old. You want to wait another twenty years for your money?" Artie got up and returned with the whiskey bottle while Jack debated how to answer that question.

"I'd be lying if I said I wanted to wait. But I don't want to do anything illegal. Especially if Mac is my brother. Would I be lying by letting the trust money be disbursed on Friday?"

"Not necessarily. You don't know for sure who Mac's father is. You don't even know if he's J.T.'s kid. You'd have to find your father and have DNA tests to be positive. That could take months, even years. Does the woman who brought him here have any legal rights?"

"Not that I know of."

"Then the state of Texas would have to get involved, but I doubt if they'd go to the trouble and the expense. They'll most likely declare him a ward of the court and see about getting him adopted."

"Which I could do myself."

Artie shook his head and poured some more whiskey. "Not without some claim to him. And why would you want to take care of a baby, anyway?"

"If he's one of the family—"

"Pretty big 'if,'" the lawyer pointed out. "And it would open up a pretty big can of worms."

Jack leaned back in the chair. "I wish it was Friday."

"You and me both. You're going to lose the ranch if you don't pay off those loans. I'd hate to see everything you've worked for go up in smoke."

"Yeah," Jack said. "Me, too."

"I'm going to assume the woman and the baby are still with you."

Jack nodded. "Fortunately. She wanted to leave, but I talked her into staying."

"Good." Artie sat back in his chair. "If you can keep things quiet for a few more days, I think you'll get through this just fine."

"Yeah," Jack agreed, but he wished he was miles away from Locklin right now. He didn't like being in the middle, and he wasn't much for subterfuge. He wanted to explain the trust fund to Grace, but she was so damned insistent on Mac having a father that she'd probably deliver the child to J.T. in El Paso. And that was the last thing the little fellow deserved.

No, he'd have to keep his mouth shut for the time being. He'd get the money and pay off the ranch. The boys would take theirs and follow their dreams. Everyone would get what they deserved.

Except Mac. If the kid was really a McLintock, he was coming out of this with the short end of the stick.

Jack took another swallow of the whiskey, which had begun to warm his insides. If he didn't take his inheritance, the only thing he could offer Mac was a debt-ridden ranch and a good bunch of calves.

"BUT HOW DO YOU WRITE a song like that?" Grace sat outside in the evening shade at the edge of the courtyard and watched Jet water the flowers. Mac lay on the blanket beside her, his bare feet kicking hers. "Where do you get your ideas?"

Jet turned off the water and flopped down on the blanket near Mac. "They just come to me. Sometimes Jason sends me lyrics, and all I have to do is put them to music."

"He sends you his poetry?"

"Sometimes. I have some real nice slow songs that we're working on now. Nice ballads, which aren't exactly my style." He smiled that devastating smile. "I'm a honky-tonk man, but it doesn't hurt to have a few belly-rubbin' songs for the ladies."

"Belly-rubbing?"

"Yeah. You know. Slow songs."

Grace laughed. The young man was outrageous. "I've never heard that phrase."

"Now, why doesn't that surprise me?" He tickled Mac's bare belly. "I wish I was that little again, so I could just lie around in my underwear and stare at pretty flowers."

"Your mother must have had her hands full with four boys. I can barely manage one boy for a few weeks."

Jet's smile faded. "Our mother worked hard, that's for sure. I don't know what any of us would have done without Jack. He was older than the rest of us, and we looked up to him. He always had all the answers."

"He seems like the kind of man who will always be there," Grace said, touched by Jet's obvious love for his older brother.

"Yeah. He's that kind of guy." He looked at his watch.

"He should have been back by now. It's not like Jack to miss supper."

"He had errands in town."

Jet frowned. "He shouldn't be this late. It's starting to get dark."

"And time for me to put Mac to bed," Grace said, scooping Mac into her arms. She grabbed his blanket with her free hand and stood up.

"I wonder where Jack could be," Jet muttered. "The boys and I are going to San Antonio to meet a friend of Gus's who spent a couple of years in Nashville. Will you tell Jack that we might just spend the night there if it gets late?"

"Sure." She hoped she'd see Jack tonight, though he'd been aloof this afternoon. He hadn't wanted company when he went to town, that was certain. He hadn't even said goodbye. Grace told herself it was foolish to be disappointed. "Are you leaving now?"

"Yeah." He looked at his watch again. "And I'm late. You need any help before I take off?"

"No, but thanks."

"Did Jase go to the movies?"

"He and Anne left a while ago." She held Mac up for Jet to kiss good-night. "Have a good time in San Antonio."

"Thanks." He hurried through the courtyard and out of one of the side doors. Grace made her way to the kitchen to get Mac's evening bottle. He started to fuss when she took it from the refrigerator. He was still fussing when she ran hot water over the bottle and the phone began to ring. He fussed while she turned the water off and reached for the telephone.

"McLintocks," she said, imitating the way Jack answered the phone.

"Hey, honey, could one of you come out here and pick up Jack? He's here at the Stampede, and he can't exactly drive himself home tonight." The man's voice was almost drowned out by country-western music and conversation.

"Excuse me, but who is this?" She wondered if it could be a joke that one of the boys was playing on her.

"Ed Burley. You want to send Jet or someone to get his brother?"

"Sure. Thank you very much for calling."

"Yeah. Just come get him out of here before he causes any trouble."

Grace hung up the phone and, still holding Mac in her arms, gave the baby his bottle while she looked out the window for Jet. She couldn't see the Naked Ladies bus, so she walked through the house to the living room in time to see a cloud of dust swirling around the back of the bus as it lumbered down the driveway. "Darn," she said softly, and almost jumped out of her skin when a man spoke.

"You need help, Grace?"

She turned to see Jimmy in a corner chair with a thick sheaf of papers on his lap. "A man just called from the Stampede and wants someone to go get Jack."

Jimmy looked confused. "Get Jack?"

"It seems he's had too much to drink and they don't think he should drive home."

"Get Jack?" Jimmy repeated. "No one's ever had to get Jack. He hardly ever drinks. Doesn't approve."

Grace adjusted her grip on the baby, took the empty bottle out of his mouth and lifted him to her shoulder. "That's what the man—a Mr. Burley—said. I was trying to catch Jet before he left, but I missed him. Jason and Anne went to the movies."

"Yeah. They sure are cute together."

Grace smiled. "Yes, they sure are. Can you get Jack?"

"Sure, I'll—" He stopped, then cleared his throat. "Oh,

shoot, Gracie. No, never mind." He rose from his chair and put the manuscript on the floor. "I'll do it."

"What's the matter?"

"Nothing."

But she could tell something was wrong. "Were you leaving, too?"

"I was waiting for a call to discuss this project," he admitted, pointing to the thick stack of paper. "It's something I hope to audition for in L.A."

Grace hesitated. "Is there anyone else who can go?"

"Nope. Unless you could help me out?" He reached for Mac and gently took the child into his arms. "I could stay here and read some stories to Mac until he went to sleep."

"Well, I—"

"Do you know where the Stampede is?"

"I was there once, but I don't—"

"It's on the highway. Turn left when you leave the ranch, like you're heading to town. Just stay on the road for about thirty miles and it's on the west corner of the first intersection."

"That sounds easy enough." She watched as Mac lay his head on Jimmy-Joe's shoulder. "And Mac's tired. He should go to sleep without much trouble."

"He's never any trouble," the young man assured her. "He's a good little guy." Jimmy flashed that charming smile. "You go get Jack and don't worry about a thing."

"I'm not sure I can handle this," Grace said, still uncertain.

"There's no one else," Jimmy insisted. "And you're just the person to talk to Jack and find out why he's sitting alone in a bar on a Monday night."

"Why me?"

Jimmy gave her a wink and pushed her gently toward

the hall. "Because, sweetheart, you're probably the reason he's there."

JACK BLINKED AGAINST the sight before him. Grace Daniels, her gray eyes worried and her sweet, rosy lips curved into the gentlest of frowns, stood before him in that flowery dress. Once again she looked out of place, but he felt a strange sense of comfort at the sight of her. And the immediate stirring of pure lust.

"What the hell are you doing here?"

She sat down on the bar stool next to him, set her car keys on the counter and swiveled in his direction. "I've come to take you home."

"How did you know I was here?"

"Mr. Burley called me and said you couldn't drive and that someone should come get you."

Jack looked at the empty glass that sat in front of him. He'd asked Burley to call home for him, but he hadn't expected Grace to show up. "It's not that I can't drive. A friend of mine brought me here. My truck is still parked in town."

"He left you here all by yourself?"

"I insisted." He'd insisted on feeling sorry for himself. Now all he felt was empty. And alone.

"Well, I'm glad you did."

The bartender wiped the counter in front of Grace and asked her if she wanted anything.

"No, thank you," she said in that soft voice of hers. The man looked as if he wanted to stay and talk to her, but Jack gave him a dirty look that sent him looking for another customer. "You don't look drunk," she said, studying his face.

"I'm not." All he had to do was look at her and he felt dizzy. It wasn't whiskey causing his problems.

"Mr. Burley said you couldn't drive home."

"I told you, my truck is in town. I asked Burley to call home and see if anyone was coming into town who could give me a lift. I didn't think they'd send you. Who's taking care of Mac?"

"Jimmy. He volunteered because he had to stay home and wait for a phone call from Los Angeles."

"Yeah, I'll bet he did." Jimmy-Joe was matchmaking as much as Jet was. "I'm just surprised they sent you."

"No one else could do it." She picked up her keys and slid off the stool. "Shall we go get your truck, then?"

"No."

She returned that cute little bottom to the stool.

"Why not?" she asked.

"You can drive me home," he said, reluctant to let her out of his sight. "After we have a dance."

"There's no band."

"There's a jukebox. What do you want to hear?"

Grace shrugged. "Whatever you want."

He climbed off the stool and walked over to the jukebox. Two quarters and three minutes later he'd found the songs and pushed the right buttons. Then he returned to Grace and led her onto the empty dance floor. She looked as if she was humoring him. He wasn't drunk, though he wondered if he'd feel better or worse if he was. Old J.T. was alive and still causing trouble. If that wasn't a good excuse to drink himself into oblivion, he didn't know what was. But he wasn't drunk, or even tipsy. He was warm and a little on edge, but that was because he'd caught a whiff of perfume when Grace hopped off the stool and handed him the car keys.

Jack inhaled as he took Grace into his arms. He'd punched in a slow tune, an old Willie Nelson number meant to make a man want to dance with a woman against him. She was warm and soft in his arms. His fingers spread across her back, his hand held hers. He could feel her breasts touching his chest. It sure as hell didn't feel like either one of them had much clothing on, and he'd like to take off the stuff that was in the way.

"What's wrong?"

Jack liked the way her hair tickled his chin. "What?"

"You sighed. Twice. Is something the matter?"

"No."

"This is nice," she said after Willie sang another verse.

"Yeah." He urged her another half inch closer. She felt so damn good against him. He heard himself sigh, and winced. By the time the song ended, he was a man on fire. He released her enough so he could look down into her face. "There's another song. Do you mind?"

She didn't take her hand from his shoulder. "No. Not at all."

He'd chosen another old song, this time about making love for just one night. The words took on new significance as he gathered Grace in his arms again. Several other couples joined them on the dance floor, and Jack noticed that the men gave him sympathetic smiles. He must look like a real goner, but he didn't care. He danced with Grace's tempting little body warm against his, their thighs touching, her breasts brushing his chest. He would have danced until his boots wore out, but the music eventually stopped. Some idiot had paid for a fast tune, so Jack took Grace's hand and led her off the dance floor as the music blasted.

"Are we leaving now?" she asked.

He paused at the edge of the crowd. "Do you want to?"

"I should get back."

He noticed she didn't sound any more interested in going home than he was. "Yeah," Jack said. "Thanks for the dances."

She smiled and didn't take her hand from his. "Anytime."

He gave her the keys. "You should drive."

"Okay."

"I'm not drunk," he insisted. "But you can't be too careful."

"Right," she said, taking the keys. He held her hand until they reached the door and he had to drop it to open the door to the outside. He was surprised that it was dark. He must have been sitting in there a long time. No wonder old Burley thought he was too plastered to drive. He'd nursed a whiskey or two, but his presence in a bar must have reminded Burley of old J.T.

He'd been told they looked a lot alike, and he'd never taken that as a compliment. He climbed into the Ford's passenger seat, rolled down his window and watched Grace as she drove them back to the ranch. He liked looking at her, even though he couldn't see much in the faint glow of the dashboard lights. Her hair blew around her face, and once in a while she glanced over toward him.

"Did you get all of your errands done in town?"

He winced, remembering Isabella's groceries. "Not exactly. I'll have to run in tomorrow, or send one of the boys. Where is everyone, anyway?"

"Jason and Anne went to the movies, and Jet and the band headed to San Antonio to meet with a friend from Nashville. Isabella went home right after dinner, though she was grumbling about needing supplies."

He didn't want to talk about supplies. He didn't want to think about brothers, and how he might have four instead of three. When they finally reached the house, only one light in the living room glowed through the windows and the porch light illuminated the front door.

"I guess everyone is in bed," Grace said, parking the car in the shadow of the toolshed. She turned off the ignition.

Everyone was in bed but the two of them, he thought, remembering the way she'd felt against him while Willie Nelson sang. He cleared his throat and managed to say, "Thanks for the ride."

"Thanks for the dance."

It was foolish to smile at her. And it didn't make sense to reach for her in the darkness, but that's what he did. She went into his arms as if she was made for him, and he kissed her cheek and brushed her hair away from her face so he could find her lips. She tilted her head and wrapped her arms around his neck as Jack managed to avoid hurting himself on the gear shift.

It was one hell of a kiss. It continued until it was clear to both of them that the car wasn't the best place to make love. And, Jack decided, making love was exactly what was on his mind.

SHE'D BEEN WARNED, Grace realized. She'd been told by one of the best advice-givers in Texas, and she'd done it, anyway. She'd fallen for the first real cowboy she'd met outside of Dallas. He was helping her out of her car and kissing her at the same time, which might have been because she still had her arms around his neck. He backed her against the car, his wonderful mouth on hers, his hands on her shoulders, his body warm and solid against hers.

"Crazy," he muttered, lifting his mouth.

"Us or the place?" She was afraid he was going to step away, and her heart sank as he did exactly that.

"Both," he said, taking her hand and leading her toward the house. "I don't want to make love to you against a car."

She wondered if he was teasing. "No?"

"No." She thought she heard tenderness in his voice. "I like beds or haymows, take your pick."

Grace hurried to keep up with his long strides. "Both, I suppose. I've never made love in a haymow before."

He stopped in the middle of the driveway and looked down at her with a fierce expression in his dark eyes. "Tomorrow," he promised. "You'll have your haymow tomorrow."

"And tonight?" The question was out of her mouth before she could take it back. She'd never been bold before.

He started walking again, but he kept a gentle grip on her hand. "Tonight, Gracie, we use a bed. That is, if you're thinking what I'm thinking."

She wasn't thinking at all. That was the problem—or the wonder of it all. She decided that question didn't need an answer, especially since they were now through the front door and in an empty living room. Jack left the corner light on, tugged her down the hall and stopped in front of Grace's room. "Mac," he said.

"I'll check him," she whispered. She pushed the door open and tiptoed into the room, dark except for the wedge of light that shone from the hall. The baby was sleeping quietly, and Jimmy was sprawled on top of the bed. He was fully clothed and snoring, which presented another problem.

"Jimmy-Joe," Jack whispered, standing beside Grace. He shook his brother's shoulder until the young man opened his eyes and blinked.

"Hey," he muttered, struggling to sit up. "Must've fallen asleep."

"Thanks for watching Mac," Grace said, hoping Jimmy wouldn't notice that her cheeks were flushed and that Jack had his hand on her waist. She needn't have worried, because Jimmy muttered something about going to bed and staggered out of the room.

"Does he wake up in the night?"

She knew he was talking about the baby. "Not usually."

"My room is at the end of the hall," Jack said. "Unless you've changed your mind about the haymow."

She ignored his teasing. "I could hear Mac if he cried?"

Jack turned her toward the door. "I've heard him more than once."

"Your room, then," Grace said, knowing she'd fallen in love and it was too late to do anything to prevent it. She'd done what she'd thought she'd never do, what she was afraid would never happen to her, what she'd given up looking for. She had fallen in love for the first time in her life with a handsome rancher, a man with a gentle touch and a way of kissing that made her forget her name. She followed him down the hall and thanked her lucky stars for Texas cowboys.

The room was dark, illuminated only by an outside light that shone across the courtyard. He kicked a chair; she stumbled over the rug. Grace didn't know how they managed to get their clothes off, but it was an exciting process. He unzipped the back of her dress and eased the fabric from her shoulders. She let her dress fall to the floor while she unbuttoned Jack's shirt and kissed the base of his throat. He kissed her and caressed her, removing the remaining pieces of her clothing, until Grace stood naked near the bed. Between kisses, he somehow removed the rest of his clothes. She heard the dull thud of boots hitting the rug.

He started to lead her toward the bed, then hesitated. She wondered if he'd changed his mind. She wondered if she'd be able to face him in the morning if she had to turn around and walk, her clothes clutched to her body, back to her room. Grace braced herself for certain disappointment.

"Grace?" he whispered, fingers trailing across her rigid shoulders. "What's wrong?"

She felt foolish. She couldn't say something pathetic like *I thought you had changed your mind.* "You, um, stopped."

"I just remembered the words to Jet's song," he said, a thread of laughter running through his voice. "'Take off your boots.'"

"'Come a little bit closer'?" Grace recited, her tension easing.

"Yes, ma'am," the man said, enfolding her against his hard, warm male body. "You've got the right idea."

She should have felt self-conscious, but she didn't. Not when the backs of her knees touched the mattress, not when Jack swept the covers back and she slid between cool sheets. She didn't want to talk about boots or songs or anything else. He gathered her into his arms and ran gentle fingertips over her breasts and abdomen, then lower. Grace urged him closer. She wanted him inside her and she didn't want to wait. She'd thought she might die if she had to wait.

It was a perfect fit.

Grace didn't hide her sigh of pleasure. Jack, propped above her, brushed her lips with his. "I knew it would feel this good," he whispered.

"I didn't."

He moved within her. "No?"

She shook her head. "No."

"It gets better," he said, a smile touching his lips.

She kissed the cleft that marked his chin. "Maybe you'd better show me."

"Yes, ma'am." And he did, moving in and out in a tantalizing rhythm. Grace slid her hands to his hips as the passion built to an exquisite peak. It seemed like hours or minutes; Grace lost all sensation of time. All she knew was pleasure, loving the man whose body loved hers with such skill. She climaxed first, with Jack following with deep strokes until he shuddered into her warmth.

Long minutes later she lay snuggled against Jack's shoulder and thought about the past hour. Everything Lucy had said about cowboys was true.

10

McLINTOCKS WEREN'T FAMILY men. Everyone knew that. There were generations of McLintocks who couldn't figure out how to stay in one place and take care of their womenfolk. They didn't fall in love and crave to be in the same bed with the same woman till the day they died.

Which was why Jack couldn't believe that he was naked and alone in his bed and very unhappy about being naked and alone in his bed. He and Grace had made love twice, and were working on the third when the baby's cries had sent Grace scrambling into her dress and out the door. Jack was left with the disappointing acceptance that further lovemaking would have to wait until later, and, for what it was worth, that he had fallen in love with his houseguest.

And he was pretty crazy about Mac, too. After all, the little guy was probably his brother. He couldn't let him go to strangers, and he couldn't let Grace find out about his father, either. No, he would have to figure out what was best for the child without revealing a truth that would hurt everyone.

It was Tuesday. Three more days and then it would be Friday morning. Jason would turn twenty-one and the lawyers would hand out checks. The party was Saturday. Grace wouldn't think about leaving until Sunday, so he had plenty of time to think over what he should do. The first thought was to keep them both here, if such a thing was possible. He and Grace could take some time and figure out just exactly what they were doing together. Yep, he might have lucked out, after all. He might have found the right woman at the right time.

Jack stretched and reached for his jeans. He might as well get some work done, now that he was awake.

"Now, THERE'LL BE no teasing," Isabella said, shaking her spatula in Jet's direction. "It's not your business."

Jet grinned, pleased with the world today. The Nashville connection had proved to be legitimate, and the new songs were going to be recorded on demo tapes. "Can I help it if I came home in time to see Grace running out of Jack's room?"

Jason shook his head, and his fiancée smiled as if she thought the McLintocks were pretty funny. "Maybe they weren't, uh, doing it."

Jimmy nodded. "I thought I set it up pretty good, making up that story about having to stay home so she'd have to go pick him up. Do you really think old Jack spent the night with her?"

"What else would she be doing in his room at five o'clock in the morning? They hadn't been talking about the weather, I'll bet you that." Jet grinned as Isabella deposited another helping of eggs on his plate. "Thanks, Bella. I'm mighty hungry this morning."

"You're mighty mouthy, too," she said. "Talking too much about things that aren't any of your concern."

"My future sister-in-law is my concern." He winked at Anne, who gave him a shy smile. "Right, honey?"

Anne didn't answer, but Jason rolled his eyes heavenward. "You get worse every day," he said.

"Nope." Jet took a hefty swallow of coffee. "I get better. And having Jack and Grace sing together was a stroke of genius. Sending them off on a picnic was a pretty good idea, too. Our big brother needs all the help he can get in the romance department. The rest of us don't have any trouble." He shook his head. "Jack's different from the rest of us, that's for sure."

"He's had more responsibility," Isabella said. "You can't meet women when you're raising three boys."

"Well, we're raised now," Jimmy declared. "And I'm happy for him. I like Grace."

"So do I," Anne said. "But what about Mac?"

Jason met Jet's gaze. "I told her. We don't have any secrets."

His little brother had never had a secret in his life. Jet hid a sigh. "Jack could adopt him," Jet said, but even as he said it he didn't know if that was possible. There was a mystery there, a mystery that shouldn't be pried open and solved. He had the uncomfortable feeling that he didn't want to know which McLintock had been with Lucy Bagwell.

Jet picked up his coffee cup. Whatever the problem, Jack would take care of it. They all knew that.

THE MAN STEPPED OUT from behind the horse barn, causing Jack's horse to shy at the sudden movement. Jack easily brought the horse under control, then squinted at the figure in the shadows of the building. The man lifted one hand in greeting and stepped forward out of the shadows.

"Howdy, Jack."

He didn't want to see what he was seeing. It wasn't possible. He'd been out in the sun all day long. He should have come in for lunch, but he hadn't wanted to take a chance on seeing Grace and carrying her off to bed in front of all the family. He'd ridden himself so hard he was having hallucinations.

"I hear you've been looking for me," the old bastard drawled.

Jack opened his mouth, but no sound came out. He swallowed and tried again. "What are you doing here?"

"Thought I'd wish Jason a happy birthday. Friday's his

big day, isn't it?" J. T. McLintock reached into his shirt pocket and lit a hand-rolled cigarette. "Gotta quit one of these days," he muttered, giving Jack a fleeting smile.

"Smoking's the least of your problems," Jack said, dismounting. "What the hell are you doing? The last time you were on this property was after Ma died."

"She was a good woman."

"She died of overwork and a broken heart," Jack reminded the man. It was like looking into a mirror, and he hated seeing the resemblance. Thick, dark hair, wide chests and shoulders, dark eyes and heavy brows—they all matched, though his father was heavier from too many bottles of beer, and his skin was weathered and lined. He was still a handsome man; Lucy Bagwell must have thought so.

"And her father left all the money to the grandsons. My sons," the older man pointed out.

"Is that why you're here, to see if you can figure out how to get some of it?"

"Not exactly." J.T. smiled and leaned against the barn as if he had nothing better to do on a Tuesday evening. "But I hear you've been looking for me."

Jack knew better than to reply.

His father took a deep drag on the cigarette. "Yep, it seems like some lawyer's been nosing around, asking questions about me and a trip to Dallas and a redhead I once knew. Interesting questions like that." His dark-eyed gaze held Jack's. "So I got to thinking, what if this tied in with my boys' inheritance?"

Jack kept his voice and his gaze level. "I don't know what you're talking about."

"Don't you?" J.T. tossed the cigarette butt to the dirt and rubbed it out with the scuffed toe of his boot. "I thought to myself, Why would my boy be asking questions about me and that redhead? And I came up with some real interestin' answers. You want to hear them?"

"I guess you're going to tell me whether I want to hear them or not." He braced himself, but surely there was no way J.T. could know about Mac's existence.

"I saw a pretty woman holding a dark-haired baby this morning. Spittin' image of you at that age."

Leave it to J.T. to see Grace and Mac. The old man didn't miss a damn thing. "So?"

J.T. smiled and nodded, as if he'd heard what he wanted to hear. "According to Burley down at the Stampede, I don't have any grandchildren, and there's a little gal from Dallas visiting, so that brings me to what you could call a 'logical conclusion.' And I think you don't want anyone to know what that conclusion is, either."

Leave it to J.T. to get all his information while sitting on a bar stool. Jack looked over his shoulder. Last thing he needed now was any kind of an audience. The fewer people who knew J.T. was still alive, the better for everyone. "I suppose you're going to tell me."

"I ain't gonna tell anyone," he promised. "I'm going to go away nice and quiet-like."

"That always was your specialty."

"'Course, a little going-away money would help. And you and the boys are going to have plenty of it, come Friday, as long as no one knows that there's a fifth McLintock who ain't even close to being twenty-one years old."

"You're pretty sure he's a McLintock."

"Hell, son, have you taken a good look at that boy's chin? I could see it from fifty yards away."

Jack stiffened. "You can go to hell."

"I'm sure I will, someday—" the man smiled "—but I'm not goin' poor. Old Man Freemont worked me to death on this place and I never saw a dime. Seems only fair that I should get my share now. And maybe I should get my son, too. I hear Lucy died a few weeks back and that little boy is an orphan."

"What do you want?"

J.T. smiled. "So you're not denying it."

Jack cursed himself for being a fool. "I asked you what you wanted."

"Let's see, old Freemont was leaving each of his grand-kids fifty thousand dollars. I'll take your share. You ended up with the ranch, anyway."

"My share of the money is going to pay off the loans." And keep the wolf from the door. And invest in some new equipment.

"Thirty thousand, then," the older man bargained. "Or I'll have a little meeting with Old Man Freemont's lawyers and see if they want to meet my fifth son."

"You're a real piece of work, J.T." He had no choice. Thirty thousand dollars was a small price to pay for his brothers' freedom. All four brothers. "Thirty thousand it is, then. But stay away from town."

"Sure. No one will ever know that there was another McLintock boy."

"And you'll stay away from here, too." He didn't want J.T. anywhere near the child or Grace or any of the boys, for that matter. "I'll get the money to you on Friday."

Jack mounted his horse. "Meet me here Friday afternoon at five."

J.T. nodded. "Nice horse."

"Yeah."

"And the ranch looks pretty good, too. You've put some money into this place."

"I've had to."

"This dump always sucked up money."

Jack looked down at his father and felt very tired. "Yeah, well, some things don't change."

MAKING LOVE WAS ONE of the world's greatest pastimes, Grace mused, watching Jack ride into the yard and dismount. Last night had been an education in just how much pleasure one woman could experience in an eight-hour period of time. They'd been quiet enough to prevent anyone from hearing them, careful enough to protect themselves against an unwanted pregnancy, and discreet enough to avoid each other today.

Everyone had been quiet today except Mac. She'd taken him for long walks outside, which seemed to please him for a while, but he was drooling and fussing again. She didn't know what she could do to make him happy. She stood by the entrance to the courtyard and held the heavy baby in her arms.

She didn't know how she was going to give him up. None of the McLintocks had come forward to claim him, which meant Mac was going to have to be given to the state authorities when she returned to Dallas. She could try adopting him herself, but an agency wasn't going to give a child to a single woman when there were so many childless couples waiting to adopt.

No, Mac needed a father. She would have to leave this wonderful home and return to Dallas. Grace didn't look forward to going back. She hadn't missed anything about her apartment. She'd called her answering machine and picked up her messages. She'd made some calls and postponed a couple of unimportant meetings. Her work could be delayed awhile longer. No one would know she was away, except the neighbor who watered the plants and collected the mail.

Jack walked the horse toward the corral and disappeared from view.

"What's my big brother up to now?" Jet asked, coming up behind her.

"I don't know. I haven't seen him all day."

"Ranching is a full-time job."

"You're not going to miss this place when you go to Nashville?"

Jet grinned. "It's my home, but I'm ready to move on."

"All of you are ready to move on but Jack."

"He loves this place more than any of us." Jet shoved his hands in his pockets. "He's told you about the trust fund?"

"Yes. After Jason turns twenty-one. I heard about it in Locklin."

Jet chuckled. "Yeah, I guess the whole town would be talking about it. I'm glad you're staying for the party. You're good for Jack. You and Mac should stay."

Grace felt her face grow warm. She was saved from trying to come up with an answer as Jack rounded the corner of the house. His steps slowed as he noticed them waiting for him.

His gaze dropped to the sleeping baby. "Something wrong?"

"No. I think he's getting a tooth. We've been walking all afternoon."

"Give him to me." Jack moved to take Mac from her arms.

Grace hesitated. "He might wake up."

Jet stepped back so he could see Mac's face. "He's out cold. He's even drooling on your shoulder."

"He's always drooling on my shoulder." She helped Jack ease the baby out of her arms and into his. Mac blinked, made a little sound of protest, then went back to sleep. Grace rubbed her aching arms. "He's getting bigger—and heavier—every day."

Jack started toward the kitchen door. "Did I miss supper?"

"No, but Bella made five big pans of enchiladas. The Naked Ladies are joining us for dinner." Grace hurried to keep up with both men as they headed inside.

"How was San Antonio?" Jack asked, stepping into a kitchen that smelled of peppers and cheese.

"Real interesting," his brother said. "How was everything here?"

"Real quiet." Jack glanced at Grace and winked as soon as Jet turned away. "I guess I'll go clean up before supper. Want me to put Mac in his bed?"

"Sure. I'll go with you." She kept her voice casual and attempted to erase the smile from her lips. Jimmy-Joe stopped them as they left the kitchen.

"I read that screenplay," he announced. "There's a part that's perfect for me."

Grace stared up at him. If anyone was going to be an overnight sensation, it would be the handsome young cowboy standing in the kitchen doorway. "That's wonderful."

"No kidding?"

Jimmy nodded. "I talked to my agent today. He set up a meeting for me for next Thursday. Can you believe it? My first Hollywood meeting."

"Is that like an audition?"

The young man shrugged and turned to Jack. "I guess so. They look at me and I look at them and everyone discusses the part. Boy, is this gonna be great. I can't believe it's really happening. Jimmy-Joe McLintock is going to Hollywood."

"I'd better get your autograph before you leave." Grace stood on tiptoe and kissed him on the cheek. "Congratulations. You'd better call me when you're on television so I can watch."

"I will," he promised. "I'll phone everyone I know."

"Call everyone for supper," Bella said, coming up behind him. "By the time you find everyone, it should be ready."

"Yes, ma'am."

She frowned at Jack. "You have time to clean up, if you don't dawdle."

"I'm heading that way right now," he assured her.

"I'll be right back to help," Grace said, hurrying to follow him. "I'm putting Mac to bed."

Isabella peered at the child, whose head rested heavily on Jack's shoulder. "Looks like he finally settled down," she called after them. "Maybe you'll get some sleep tonight."

Jack kept walking, but he tilted his head toward Grace. "Don't count on it," he whispered.

"DO YOU THINK they know?"

"Nope." He unbuttoned her shirt and smoothed his hands over her lace-covered breasts. "They don't suspect a thing."

Grace loved the way he touched her. Loved the way he made her feel when he touched her. "Everyone was smiling at me tonight."

His lips found the top of one breast. "Everyone always smiles at you."

"Shh. Keep your voice down. This was different."

Her shirt fell to the floor, and her bra quickly followed. Jack turned his attention to the snap of her jeans. His fingers sent erotic sensations through her abdomen as he released the zipper and smoothed the fabric, including her underpants, past her hips. "Different?" he whispered. "How?"

"Oh, I don't know." It was getting hard to think. Especially with his lips tickling her abdomen while his fingers explored lower. It was getting pretty difficult to stand, too, when her knees threatened to dissolve from underneath her. "Take off your boots," she managed to say.

"Are you singing or giving me something to do?"

"I'm not singing. Take off your boots."

"I already did. You weren't paying attention."

Maybe not. She'd been a little mesmerized after he'd

tossed his shirt over a chair and unzipped his own jeans. "Take me to bed," she whispered. "And that's not part of the song."

"Sweetheart," he said, lifting her into his arms. "I'm happy to do anything your little heart desires."

And he kept his word, too, doing things to her body that caused her to gasp with surprised pleasure. They'd made love for the longest time, as if neither one wanted it to end. Much later, he'd come to her half asleep and she'd welcomed him into her arms and into her body. Twice in the night Grace had pulled on a nightgown and tiptoed out of the room to check on Mac. If she ran into anyone, she hoped they'd think she had been to the bathroom. But she didn't think she'd fool anyone. She looked like a woman in love, which is exactly what she was.

She'd fallen in love with a cowboy and she'd never been happier. She refused to think of the future, of what would happen after the party. The present was much too good.

"AREN'T YOU GOING to open your gifts?"

Jason grinned at his fiancée. "I will, in a minute. I want to enjoy being twenty-one."

"We *all* want to enjoy that," Jet said. "This is one hell of an important day."

"We've waited a long time for you to grow up, Jase," Jimmy added.

They were seated around the dining room table, a place reserved over the years for special occasions. And this was special, all right. It wasn't every day the entire family gathered for a birthday breakfast. Jack glanced toward Grace, who sat to his right. Mac was in his high chair, between the two of them. Jack leaned over and wiped the boy's chin with his napkin.

"I have an announcement," Jason said, standing up.

Isabella, seated at the other end of the table next to him,

patted his arm. "I can't believe you are all grown up." She shook her head. "It isn't right."

"Now, Bella, I'll always be the baby of the family," he assured her. "You know that." Jason grinned as he turned to the rest of his family, including Grace in his smile, Jack noted. What on earth was the boy up to now?

"Spit it out, Jase," Jimmy said. "Before my coffee gets cold."

"Anne and I are getting married."

Jet didn't look impressed. "You told us that before, Jase."

"We're getting married tomorrow."

"Tomorrow?" Jack echoed. *"Tomorrow?"*

"Yes." Jason and Anne nodded and blushed. "We got the license last week, and we arranged for a justice of the peace to arrive tomorrow at noon."

"My parents are coming, too," Anne said. "We thought it would be easier this way."

"Married. Tomorrow." Jet grinned. "I'll have to start practicing 'Here Comes the Bride' on the guitar, now, won't I?"

Jason nodded. "That's a real good idea. I figured since we already had the party and the music and the family all in one place, we might as well make the most of it. Jack, is that okay?"

All eyes turned to the head of the table. "It's a fine idea," he said. If he could keep J.T. off the ranch, it would be one heck of an event. "If you're sure about getting married, I guess that's what you'd better do."

Relief swept across Jason's face, and he sat down and put his arm around Anne. "Thanks, everyone," he said, his grin widening. "I told Anne you guys wouldn't mind."

Grace looked down the table at Anne. "What about a dress?"

"I saw one in town yesterday, but I didn't have time to try it on. I thought I'd go in this morning and shop."

"Do you want company?"

Anne smiled her familiar shy smile. "I'd like that."

Isabella nodded. "I'll keep Mac with me so you girls can shop. Buy Jason a new shirt, too, will you?"

"We will," Grace promised, looking happy.

Jack shook his head. Leave it to women to be happy about shopping.

"What about you, Jack? Do you want to celebrate your good fortune and a wedding by getting a new shirt?"

"No. I have plenty of shirts."

Grace shot him a questioning look, which he tried to ignore by picking up his coffee cup.

"I thought you'd be happy today. What's going on?" she asked him.

"Nothing." He'd spent yesterday afternoon in his office, trying to figure out how to make twenty thousand dollars pay off thirty-five thousand in bank loans. The drop in cattle prices, the 1993 tornados and Jason's education had taken their toll. He'd kept the place afloat for twenty years. He would have to sell the east section to his neighbor now.

"I don't believe you."

"Drop it, Grace. Nothing is wrong."

"It's Mac, isn't it." She kept her voice low while the others teased Jason about becoming an old married man. "You know something."

"No." But he heard the lie in his own voice and he couldn't meet her eyes.

"Jack? Who does Mac belong to?"

The voices silenced as the others heard her question and looked to him for an answer. Jack looked at his brothers, at the sympathetic expression on Bella's lined face, at the surprise that flitted across Anne's. He couldn't look at Grace, but he turned to Mac. He'd planned to protect him. He may as well start now.

Jack took a deep breath and met Grace's eyes. "He's mine."

"Yours."

"Mine," he repeated, a little louder this time. "Mac is mine. He's a genuine McLintock."

The genuine McLintock started to cry, so Grace lifted him from the high chair and into her arms. "He can't be. You said—"

"I was wrong."

No one else at the table dared contradict him.

Grace stood up and put Mac in Jack's lap. "Then you might as well start taking care of him." She sat down and picked up her coffee cup as if nothing had happened. Mac reached for Jack's napkin and tried to put it in his mouth.

"Hey," Jack said. "Stop that." Mac looked up at him and smiled.

"I'll bet you found your dress in the Crystal Butterfly," Grace said to Anne.

"Uh, yes, I think that was the name."

Jack stood up, Mac secure in his arms. "We have a meeting at the bank in two hours, boys. I suggest we be on time."

The brothers nodded and almost knocked each other down trying to leave the table.

"YOU'RE LYING," GRACE said, poking her finger at Jack's chest. "And don't think I don't know it."

He backed up a step. "Why would I lie about this?"

"I don't know." And she really didn't, though she had a few ideas. "You're protecting one of the boys, and that's not right. One of them should be made to accept responsibility for his actions."

"Jet had the mumps and can't have kids," Jack reminded her. "And Jimmy-Joe was in a play *and* had a jealous girlfriend at the time of Mac's conception."

"Which leaves you and Jason."

"Jason doesn't count," Jack said a little too quickly.

"You're taking Mac so Jason can get married and live happily ever after? Isn't that a little extreme? Anne would make a great mother, and Jason would be a wonderful father. He reads stories to Mac all the time. They're a little young, but—"

"Mac is a McLintock and he's mine. And Jason might not be the only McLintock who wants to settle down."

"Meaning?" He couldn't be saying what she thought he was.

"Meaning," he said, giving her a brief kiss, "I need to get these next two days over with before I can start thinking about myself. And us. And Mac."

"Us?" She loved the word *us*.

He put his large hands on her shoulders and made her look at him. "Let me get the boys on their way. Then you and I will sit in the courtyard and talk about the future, okay, Grace?"

She could do nothing else but nod her head yes. "And then, the truth."

"When the dust settles, Gracie. Then I'll tell you everything."

Grace watched him walk out of the bedroom. She planned to hold him to that promise.

11

"Why are you doing this, Jack?" Jet stood beside his older brother in the lobby of Locklin Federal Savings Bank.

"Doing what?"

"Is Mac really Jason's, after all?"

"No."

"And he's not yours," Jet said. "I'd bet my own mother that you didn't leave Lucy What's-her-name pregnant and alone."

Jack smiled wryly. "Why not? It seems to run in the family."

"Not this generation."

The brothers stood in silence and watched the younger boys at the bank tellers' windows. Jet patted his shirt pocket. "I have a check in here that will finance a year or two in Nashville, more if I'm careful. Jason has his studies in Europe. Jimmy should be able to make it in L.A. What are you doing with your money, Jack? Putting it back in the ranch?"

"Yeah, you could say that." Along with a fat donation to Father of the Year.

"You could take Grace somewhere nice. You could go to New Orleans. I'll bet she'd like all those old buildings with the balconies. Or what about heading up to the mountains, to Utah?"

"You have some pretty strange ideas, Jet."

"You're not in love with her, then?"

Jack looked at his watch. He could still get in a few hours' work if they could get home. "I didn't say that."

"You have an odd way of showing it, brother. Are you taking Mac to make Grace happy?"

"Not exactly, but that's part of it, I guess." Jack took a deep breath. "I'm going to ask Grace to marry me, soon as the party is over and the place gets back to normal. She takes good care of that baby, but I don't know if she wants to be his mother permanently. And I'm not real sure how she feels about me."

"Have you told her you loved her?"

"Well, no."

Jet shrugged. "Guess I can't blame you there. That's getting in pretty deep."

"I'm going to do my best to convince her to take on an old cowboy and a less-than-profitable ranch, but she has a business in Dallas. She has a whole life I don't even know about."

Jet clapped him on the back. "Looks like you've got plenty of time to find out, once you've walked down the aisle."

"Shut up," Jack said, but there was affection in the command. He looked around to see if anyone had overheard Jet's comment about walking down the aisle. "There's just one McLintock getting married right now, and he's coming toward us with a grin plastered all over his face."

"I can afford to buy a ring now," Jason proudly announced.

Jack tried to keep a straight face. "That sounds like a good idea."

"Can you afford to buy your brothers a beer, too?"

"Yeah," Jimmy said, joining them in time to hear the last suggestion. "We need a bachelor party."

"Just one beer," Jack cautioned. "I have cattle to feed."

"Sure, Jack." Jet winked at the other three. "We'll feed those cattle as soon as we're through in town."

Jack nodded toward Harry White, the banker, who gave him the thumbs-up sign from his corner office door, and followed his brothers out of the bank. On Monday he'd take care of business; a check for thirty thousand was folded in his shirt pocket. A small price to pay for Grace and Mac's happiness, the check would be delivered at five o'clock to J.T.

And then Jack would start the rest of his life.

"I NOW PRONOUNCE YOU husband and wife."

Grace blinked back tears as the justice of the peace—who looked more like Johnny Cash than Johnny Cash—finished conducting the courtyard wedding ceremony. Anne looked lovely in a simple white sundress and a white cowgirl hat decorated with satin ribbon and pink rosebuds. Jason wore a new pair of blue jeans, a white western shirt and a black string tie. Both the bride and groom, now kissing each other with shy pleasure, wore cowboy boots.

The audience applauded, with several members of the Naked Ladies hooting their approval. Jet strummed a few chords on his electric guitar and began an instrumental version of "Look At Us," Vince Gill's anniversary ballad. Fitting, Grace decided, reaching for a tissue while balancing Mac on her hip. The baby was fascinated by all of the people. He didn't seem to mind being passed around to Isabella's daughters and granddaughters, all of whom claimed the right to care for him. Isabella, resplendent in a bright pink dress, openly wept into a large handkerchief while Jimmy-Joe tried to comfort her.

Jack, the best man, stood near the Johnny Cash lookalike and watched Jason and his bride wade through the crowd. Everyone wanted to congratulate Jason and kiss Anne. Anne's parents, a sweet couple from Austin, seemed to be enjoying the boisterous celebration. Grace's gaze returned to Jack, who looked too serious. Worried, even, as he scanned the crowd as if searching for someone in particular. She didn't understand what was going on, but she looked forward to hearing his explanation.

He'd stayed away from her bed. And she'd stayed away from his. There was an unspoken agreement that everything—even sex—was on hold until the weekend was over. She missed him. And she would miss the baby in her arms, too. Going back to Dallas was starting to feel like punishment. She didn't dare let herself think that she would stay with Jack, here in Locklin, with Mac and maybe several McLintock children with dark hair and charming smiles.

She'd never thought she'd be one of the lucky ones, those women with adoring husbands and happy children and a house that rang with excited chatter. She'd only dreamed of a large family, with uncles and aunts and cousins arriving on holidays.

Well, dreams were dreams, and reality was that little apartment in Dallas.

But love was here on the ranch, here with Jack McLintock. She blinked as he stepped closer and stood by her side.

"Is everything all right?" he asked.

"Just fine."

"Are you having a good time?"

He was treating her like a casual guest, instead of someone who'd strung lights across the eaves and rearranged the pots of flowers this morning. "It's a lovely party."

"It's just getting started." He pointed to Jet and the band. "They're going to set up out back and turn up the volume now, so hang on." Jack peered at the baby. "Hey, kid. How do you like your first party?"

"He likes it, especially when Lina's daughters take him for walks."

"Want me to take him?"

"Not yet. He needs his diaper changed, so I'm going to go clean him up and try putting him to bed at Lina's for a while. The girls said they'd stay with him, and it's a little quieter over there."

"Good. You'll come back and dance with me?"

Grace smiled. He sounded like an unsure teenager. "After I help Bella put the food out, sure. How about one of Jet's belly-rubbing songs?"

"Jet's *what?*"

"A slow dance," she explained, happy to have flustered him. She moved toward the house. "I'll see you in a little while."

He nodded and looked relieved. "Hurry back. There are some folks I'd like you to meet."

"Okay." She would meet the devil himself if Jack would keep looking at her with that tender expression on his face.

"THAT'S A PRETTY good-looking woman you've got yourself. And that's another fine-looking boy I sired," she heard a man drawl from outside the door to the courtyard. Grace leaned over the bed and slipped the plastic pants over Mac's chubby thighs. So far he showed no sign of being sleepy, which didn't bode well for his afternoon nap.

"Stay away from both of them," Jack said, sounding angry. At least, Grace thought the voice belonged to Jack. She'd never heard him sound that upset before, except maybe when the man at the Stampede had threatened him. What on earth was the visitor talking about? Obviously this wasn't one of the people Jack wanted to introduce her to.

"Why didn't you show up yesterday? I waited at the barn for over an hour before I started thinking you finally grew a conscience and changed your mind."

"I got a little sidetracked in San Antonio."

"You have no business being here today when half the

town is wandering around. What if someone recognizes you?"

Grace sat down on the bed and listened carefully. She didn't know what was going on.

"You kidding? Everybody's gathering around the food and the beer, or they're off dancing to Jet's crazy music. I'll keep my hat low and my sunglasses on, son, if that makes you happy."

Son? Grace tried to remember what Jack had said about his father. She'd assumed he was dead, but had Jack said that exactly?

"Thanks," the man said. "You boys enjoy the rest of Freemont's check, you hear?"

"Get out," Jack said, his voice low. Grace strained to hear his next words. "You sure as hell don't belong here."

"I loved your mother," the man said, sounding a little sad. "But I wasn't the right man for her."

"Get out," Jack repeated, sounding as if he was talking through gritted teeth. "*Now*, before I change my mind."

There was a chuckle. "You won't change your mind. You've got what you want, too, and so do your brothers. As long as I don't tell anyone that kid is mine, you and the boys are rich. Looks like we're both going to have a good weekend. I'll think I'll get a beer. For the road."

"Out," Jack repeated. "And don't talk to any of the others."

"See you around, kid."

Grace hurried to put Mac in his bed so she could go to the window and see the man Jack had been talking to. She didn't dare think what the words had meant. She couldn't let herself think that she'd heard that Mac was that man's child. *Another fine-looking boy I sired* were his words. *You and the boys are rich.*

She opened the door to the courtyard before she thought better of it. Jack turned, his mouth in a grim line.

"Oh, hell."

"So there's another McLintock, after all," Grace said, her voice sounding calm. He couldn't know her heart was threatening to pound so hard she couldn't hear her own words. "I guess I should have figured it out for myself."

"I thought you went to Lina's," he said, sounding resigned.

"No." She waited there in the shade of the overhang, in between two pots of yellow chrysanthemums, for some kind of explanation, but Jack simply stared at the crowd of people by the kitchen end of the courtyard. "That man is your father?"

He hesitated, then replied. "Yes."

"I thought all along you were protecting Jason."

Mac started to cry, so Grace turned toward her bedroom. She looked back over her shoulder at the tall rancher. "You've been lying all along."

"Yes, but I had my reasons." He didn't bother to deny it. "We need to talk."

"No," she said, going inside to the crying child. "We don't have anything else to say." She shut the door, muffling the outside noise and effectively shutting Jack outside. He could have opened the door and followed her, but she didn't think he'd really want to start confessing how he'd known all along who Mac's father was. It didn't take a genius to figure out that none of the McLintocks wanted to wait another twenty-one years for their inheritance, and if Jack's father announced he had another son, then that's exactly what could happen. The party would be over. And so would Nashville, Hollywood and Oxford.

One little baby would have changed everything.

One little baby *had* changed everything, especially for her.

Well, she'd had it with the McLintocks and their lies. They'd fooled her, with their poems and songs and stories and picnics. Jack must have laughed as she believed everything he told her.

Grace soothed the wailing baby and tossed clothes from the dresser onto the bed. Her bags were under the bed; she quickly filled them with clothes and managed to zip them shut. She and Mac were going to get out of here. She'd thought the boy should be with his father, but that had been another silly fantasy.

There was no such thing as the perfect family.

"HAS ANYONE SEEN GRACE?"

Jimmy-Joe shook his head. "I thought she was in the kitchen."

"No, I looked. Isabella hasn't seen her, and neither has Jason." He'd looked everywhere. She wasn't in her bedroom or at Lina's house.

"And Mac? Wherever that baby is, that's where Grace will be." Jimmy poured himself another beer from the keg packed in ice. "Hey, don't worry. She'll turn up. This is a great party."

"We had an argument," Jack said, his eyes scanning the crowd.

"Yeah?" He took a sip of the beer and frowned. "Nothing serious, I hope."

"No," Jack lied, not meeting his brother's eyes. "Nothing serious." He roamed through the crowd, shook hands with some old friends, pretended he was having a good time. He kept looking for Grace, or for someone who might have seen her, and ended up at the foot of the bandstand. He drew his finger across his neck so Jet would know to end the song, and Jet nodded.

After he announced they were taking a break, he hopped off the stage. "Hey, Jack, what's wrong?"

Jack tried to sound casual. "I can't find Grace or Mac anywhere. Thought you might have a better vantage point from the stage."

Jet tilted his hat off his face. "Shoot, Jack, you look like hell. They're probably over at Lina's trying to get the baby to sleep."

"I checked. I've checked everywhere."

His younger brother's eyes narrowed. "You two have a fight?"

"Yeah."

"Why?"

Jack hesitated. He didn't want to spoil a good party, but his heart was in his throat and he felt like he could punch something. If he didn't find Grace soon, then he was going to go out of his mind with worry. "J.T. was here."

Jet's mouth dropped open. "I thought the old man was dead."

"He's very much alive. Unfortunately."

"What's this got to do with Grace?" He lifted the guitar strap over his head and set the instrument in its case.

"She overheard some things she shouldn't have."

"What the hell are you talking about?" And then, before Jack could answer, realization lit Jet's eyes. "Mac."

"Yeah."

Jet continued to look shocked. "J.T. doesn't *want* him, does he?"

"Hell, no. He blackmailed me into giving him some money in exchange for leaving Mac alone."

"You gave him money? How much money?"

"Look, I'll explain later. After I talk to Grace."

Jet whistled. "You should have told us. We could have helped you out. We all will—"

"I can't talk about this now, Jet."

"Have you looked for her car?"

"There's no way she could get out of here. There's no way any of us can. Have you seen how many cars are parked in front of the shed?" Even as he said the words, he knew that if Grace wanted to leave she would have figured out how to do it. Jack looked at the barn.

"You can't ride a horse to Dallas," Jet pointed out, reading his mind.

"No," Jack said, looking toward the outhouse. "But I can take a bus."

"No, Jack. It won't—"

"Yes, it will." If that woman thought she could leave him without a word, she had another think coming. He'd waited to say what he wanted to say long enough. When a McLintock made up his mind, the world better watch out. Besides, he was tired of waiting for his life to begin.

"DON'T FALL IN LOVE with a cowgirl," she told the sleepy baby. "She'll break your heart, just like the cowboys do."

Mac blinked and yawned.

"Your mama was a wise woman, except she should have picked someone else to make sure you had a daddy." Grace gripped the steering wheel and eased her foot off the gas. Anger was making her drive three miles an hour over the speed limit. "I sure haven't done a very good job of it."

She'd had her heart broken by a cowboy, just as Lucy had warned. She'd climbed into bed with the handsomest cowhand in Texas and what had happened?

"Disaster," she answered out loud. "Nothing but disaster from start to finish."

Mac closed his eyes, seemingly comforted by the motion of the car and the sound of her voice.

"What am I going to do with you now?" She would get a fancy lawyer and she would petition the court for custody. She would do everything in her power to adopt Mac. She'd tried giving him to his family, but they'd pretended he wasn't theirs. Their lives would be simpler if he didn't exist.

And he wouldn't exist. He would become Mac Daniels and live with his new mommy in Dallas. Maybe she would buy a house with a nice yard, and trees for a swing and a tree house. No, maybe not a tree house. She didn't know how kids kept from falling out of those things.

She heard honking behind her, but she paid no attention. The road was clear. Anyone could pass.

Anyway, it would be the two of them, forever. Or at least until Mac got married. She would see that he grew up to be the kind of man who would never, ever lie to a woman. She would make sure he married someone very nice and deserving of him.

Honk, honk. Grace looked in the rearview mirror. A blue bus was driving too close to her and honking like there was no tomorrow. "Go around, dummy," she muttered, returning her gaze to the stretch of highway ahead of her. "You're going to wake my baby."

Honk, honk, honk.

She looked in the rearview mirror again. It was a blue bus with the hand of a woman painted over the driver's side of the window. Her rings were blue and green, and Grace knew that on the side of the bus that painted woman would be naked, except for a strategically placed set of drums.

"Oh, no." She shook her head, hoping whoever was driving would get the message. She flipped her mirror up and gripped the steering wheel. He couldn't make her pull over.

Of course he could, she realized in less than ten minutes. He could stay behind her and honk that horn until she wanted to pull over into a rest area and get out of the car just so she could scream at him to stop. Which is what she did.

"Just what do you think you're doing, terrorizing someone on the highway?" She put her hands on her hips and glared as Jack hopped out of the bus. "And why are you driving that crazy bus? Does Jet know you stole it?"

"It was about time you stopped," Jack said, approaching her. His boots made crunching noises in the gravel. "I didn't know how much gas was left in this thing. Just where the hell did you think you were going?"

"Back home. Where I belong."

He got within two feet of her and stopped, crossing his arms across his chest. "And taking my son with you? No way."

"He's not your son."

"Who says? I believe the birth certificate says 'J. McLintock.'"

"You and I both know you're not that McLintock. You've been lying since the first time I met you."

"Not exactly. I thought one of the boys was Mac's father, but after that didn't work out, I had some investigating done."

"And you found out who Mac's father really was."

He nodded. "That's right."

"You're *proud* of it?" She couldn't believe him. Jack stood there calmly, as if they were discussing the price of beef.

"Well, I'm not proud of having J.T. for a father, that's for sure. But do you think I would let him have Mac? No way."

"He wanted Mac? What are you talking about?"

He took a step toward her and Grace backed up. A woman walking her tiny dog eyed them curiously.

"You okay over there?" she called.

"I'm fine, thank you," Grace said, trying to smile.

"Will you stop acting like I'm some kind of violent criminal?" He shoved his hands in his pockets. "Look, Gracie, all I want is for you and that boy to be happy."

Grace felt like she was missing something. "You didn't lie so you could get the money?"

Jack winced. "There isn't a lot of money left, honey. I

gave most of it to J.T. to keep him out of our lives, and I'll pay off some of the loans with the rest. I still have to sell part of—"

Relief flooded through her. "You gave him your money to keep Mac?"

"Not 'gave,' exactly. It was more like blackmail, but yes, J.T. is richer tonight. I'm back to square one again, but it looks like beef prices are going up. We'll make out all right." He smiled that charming McLintock smile. "I don't mind if you don't."

"Why should I mind?" she whispered.

His smile disappeared. He lifted her chin with one finger and looked into her eyes. "Being married to a cowboy might not be the life you want."

"Is that a proposal?"

"It sure as hell is, sweetheart. And I've never asked a woman to marry me before, so be gentle."

"I've never been asked before, so be nice. I'm thinking."

Jack frowned. "Either you say yes or you don't."

"Not about that. About money. I can sell my apartment," she said. "That ought to buy a few more cows."

He raised his eyebrows. "You want to be a rancher?"

"You're marrying a woman with assets. I'll want to invest in our business." She decided against telling him about the savings accounts and the mutual funds. She'd save some surprises for later. "Okay?"

Jack nodded, his dark eyes twinkling. "All right, but you have to learn how to ride a horse."

"Agreed." Grace touched his face with her fingertips. "Do you think all of our babies will have your chin?"

"Only if you come home with me right now." He smiled and swept her into his arms.

Some day, Gracie, you'll meet a man who will make your little heart pound faster than a runaway train. And when that happens, honey, hang on and enjoy the ride.

Epilogue

"BLOW OUT THE CANDLES and make a wish," Grace urged him. "Go ahead, it's okay."

Mac leaned forward and puffed his cheeks. He released the air, and the four candles flickered and went out. Everyone clapped, and Jack, poised across the table, clicked the camera shutter. Mac scrambled down from the chair and hurried over to his father. "Show me," he said, and then, remembering his manners, added, "Please."

"This isn't that kind of camera, Mac. Sorry."

Mac sighed. "Okay," he said, and ran back to his seat. "I want cake, too," he reminded his mother. "Please."

Grace cut thick wedges of cake for everyone and passed them around the table. They were all here for the party, though it was calving season, too. The boys came home each March, not so much because Jack needed the help, but because they all liked to work together once a year.

"Tell us about New York," Bella said, turning to Jason. "Are they treating you well at that fancy school?"

"Yes, Bella. You'll come to see me get my degree, won't you? Anne's hoping everyone will come."

Jimmy stuck him with a fork. "Don't expect us to start calling you *Dr.* McLintock."

Jet stole Jimmy's cake while he wasn't looking. "Hey, we'll all be there. I've got a tour starting next month, but I made sure we'd be on the East Coast the first weekend of May."

"I love the new song, Jet. I hear it on the radio all the

time." Grace cut another piece of cake and slid it in front of Jimmy. He looked too thin, but he was tanned and as handsome as ever. "What about you? Can you get away from those fancy starlets long enough to fly to New York?"

"Yeah, no problem. Anyone catch the show last week? I got to kiss Heather Locklear."

Jack chuckled. "We saw. You looked like you were enjoying yourself."

"She looks like a real babe," Jet agreed. "But can she sing?"

Everyone laughed while Jimmy shook his head. "I can't help it if I date actresses. Everybody in L.A. is an actor."

"I saw your picture in one of the supermarket tabloids again. You took somebody famous to the Academy Awards." Grace struggled to sit down in her chair. The next McLintock was due to make an appearance in two weeks, which couldn't happen soon enough as far as she was concerned. Her back ached miserably, and she'd gotten so she was jealous of every cow that dropped her calf. She smiled at the worried expression on her husband's face. "I'm fine. Stop looking like that."

"Nah, they had it wrong," Jimmy-Joe was saying. "I took a very nice lady to a very nice party to *watch* the Oscars."

"I'm sure you did," Bella said, patting his hand. Lina and her daughters laughed at the face he made at them.

"Mommy! Presents!" Mac patted a pile of brightly wrapped gifts. "They mine?"

"Go ahead," Grace said, trying to get comfortable on the chair so she could see every smile that crossed her son's face. He ripped apart paper and boxes to reveal Matchbox cars, a toddler-proof tape player with a thick plastic microphone, a set of storybooks with extra-strong pages and a bright bucket of oversized connecting blocks.

Mac clapped his hands and screamed with joy as each

gift emerged from its wrapping. "T'ank you, t'ank you," he cried, with kisses for everyone.

"One more," Grace told him. "Jet, behind you is a big blue box. Can you reach it for me?" He leaned over and placed the box in front of Mac. "Go on, open it," Grace said. "It's from someone very special."

Jack shot her a questioning look and leaned closer. "What's going on?"

"I found it with Lucy's things when we emptied her apartment. I know she meant it for Mac."

"Very nice," Jack said, nodding his approval. "You think up the damnedest things."

"Ooh, a horse like Daddy's!" Mac held up a stuffed brown horse whose mane and tail were made of thick black yarn. He sported a black vinyl saddle, miniature stirrups and plastic reins. "I a cowboy," the child announced.

His uncle Jet winked at him. "The ladies love cowboys, Mac, my boy."

"Don't tell him that," Grace laughed, and then felt a strange sensation wash over her. "Oh, no."

Jack was on his feet in an instant. "What's wrong?"

"I think my water broke."

His arm was around her, his face close to hers. "Oh, hell, Gracie. Now what do we do?"

She couldn't help smiling as a feeling of calm swept over her. Everything would always turn out fine as long as Jack was with her. She turned to the sea of worried faces, her family, and announced, "I guess we're about to have another McLintock."

Isabella clapped her hands with glee. Jason smiled. Jimmy-Joe turned white, and Jet shook his head. "Leave it to a rancher to have a baby during calving season."

Hearts mend, Gracie. And life goes on, just the way it was meant to.

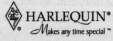